"... comparable to the best by the subgenre's masters."—*Booklist* (starred review)

BAEN

1920: AMERICA'S GREAT WAR

$7.99 U.S.
$9.99 CAN.

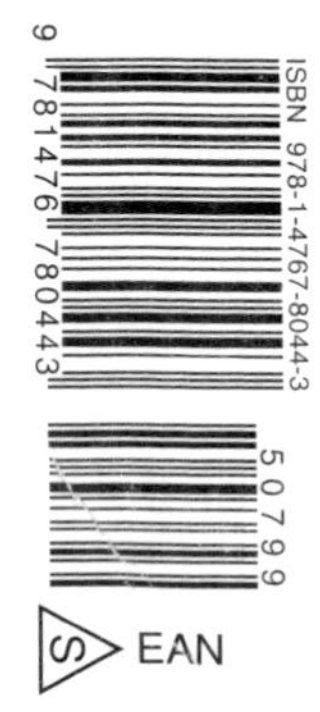

BAEN BOOKS
by
ROBERT CONROY

Himmler's War

Rising Sun

1920: America's Great War

Liberty: 1784

1882: Custer in Chains

Germanica (forthcoming)

NOT-SO-QUIET ON THE SOUTHERN FRONT

Now on his hands and knees, gasping and vomiting dirty water, Martel reached the north bank and crawled through the sand and mud. He didn't consider himself safe, not yet. Along with their ridiculous but deadly pig stickers, the Uhlans carried carbines. Would they fire across the border? Well, there wasn't much he could do about that except gather himself and continue to run like hell.

"Where you goin', boy?"

Martel looked up. Several rough-looking white men with rifles, mounted on scraggly but tough-looking horses, had emerged from the brush that had hidden them and were staring hard at him.

"I'm an American," he managed to gasp.

"That's what they all say," said a lean and wiry man in his thirties who appeared to be their leader. "Now tell me just why the fucking Germans were chasing you."

"I'm an officer in the United States Army, and the fucking Germans didn't like me snooping around them and their camps. Now who the hell are you?"

That seemed to amuse the man in charge who grinned amiably before spitting on the ground. "I'm a Texas Ranger just like all these fine young gentlemen who are accompanying me, and anybody who's being shot at by the fucking Germans can't be all bad. So we are now going to take you to our post and let you prove your tale. Then you can try to answer a question for me?"

Martel relaxed. "I'll try."

"Then tell me young soldier, just what in the hell are the Germans doing along the Rio Grande and the boundary of the state of Texas this spring of 1920?"

1920

★ ★ ★ ★ ★ ★ ★ ★ ★ ★ ★ ★ ★ ★ ★

AMERICA'S GREAT WAR

ROBERT CONROY

1920: AMERICA'S GREAT WAR

A Baen Book

Baen Publishing Enterprises
P.O. Box 1403
Riverdale, NY 10471
www.baen.com

ISBN: 978-1-4767-8044-3

Cover art by Kurt Miller

First Baen paperback printing, April 2015
Second Baen paperback printing, July 2015

Library of Congress Control Number: 2013032739

Distributed by Simon & Schuster
1230 Avenue of the Americas
New York, NY 10020

Pages by Joy Freeman (www.pagesbyjoy.com)
Printed in the United States of America

Getting a novel published will never grow old.
It was a dream come true from the first,
and remains so today.
I can only thank everyone at Baen and Spectrum
who had a hand in the development of
1920: America's Great War.
Life is good.

To Quinn and Brennan:
Ask your parents.

The Genesis of *1920*

IN THE SUMMER OF 1914, KAISER WILHELM II'S IMPERIAL German Army invaded Belgium and France. He planned a quick and brutal war that would result in a decisive victory over France and England; thus ensuring dominance in the world. At the end, national boundaries would be redrawn with provinces gained and lost as had been done in the past. Losing governments would fall and, after a few months of carnage, the world would go on.

Germany also found herself at war with Russia, but felt she could defeat France before dealing with a ponderous and slow-mobilizing Tsarist Russia.

It didn't happen as planned and the horrors and convulsions of the next hundred years and more are directly attributable to the mistakes made by both sides in the summer and fall of 1914.

In the early weeks of what came to be called the Great War and later, World War I, France and Germany fought a titanic battle near Paris along the Marne River. Because of a combination of French luck and bravery, along with German mistakes and miscalculations, the French prevailed, Paris was saved, and the world was doomed.

The ironic and unintended consequences of the unexpected and somewhat undeserved French victory condemned the world to four years of horrific trench warfare which resulted in scores of millions dead and maimed.

The Germans lost the Battle of the Marne and it took four long and bloody years for Germany to be fully defeated.

The four years of World War I resulted in the destruction of empires. The collapse of Imperial Germany led to the horrors of Hitler's Germany and World War II. Russia fell to the communists and precipitated the equally horrific years of Stalin and the Cold War. The Ottoman Empire ruled from Istanbul disappeared, which ultimately led to the present chaos in the Moslem world. The disintegration of the Habsburg Austro-Hungarian Empire resulted in nationalistic violence in the Balkans.

But what if France hadn't won at the Marne?

In this revised scenario, the Germans won the battle, took Paris, and drove the combined French and English armies south in a retreat that turned into a rout. This resulted in the taking of hundreds of thousands of French and British prisoners. Germany became the world's one remaining Great Power. England and France were humbled.

The only remaining potential threat to the ambitions of Imperial Germany would have been the United States. America, under the stubbornly idealistic and unrealistically pacifist Woodrow Wilson, would discount any possible threat from the kaiser. As a man who had stated he would go to virtually any length to avoid fighting a war, Wilson likely would have allowed imperialistic Germany more expansionary latitude than any other president since Abraham Lincoln when he had been forced to ignore France's invasion of Mexico during our Civil War. The toothless Monroe Doctrine would have been ignored.

Understanding both Wilson's frail health and his devotion to peace at any price, Germany would have made preparations to eliminate the United States as a future threat. The United States already was an economic titan. Her population was far greater than Germany's and was growing at an uncatchable rate. It is very likely that the kaiser would have wanted the U.S. eliminated as a power before she reached her full potential.

The Germans had contempt for the United States in general and Woodrow Wilson in particular. An aggressive and extremely ambitious Germany, led by the ultraimperialist Kaiser Wilhelm II, would have found it difficult to resist the temptation to eliminate the United States as a real or future threat.

This novel's point of departure from real history is that late summer and early fall of 1914 during which the First Battle of the Marne was fought. Therefore, anything that happens after that is up for conjecture and subject to my vivid and sometimes warped imagination. In some cases, I've decided to have a little fun. For instance, I have the drive to make Prohibition an amendment to the Constitution defeated. There is some logic to this, as America's bloody involvement in World War I was at least partial impetus for the silly law's approval in the first place.

Similarly, the great flu epidemic of 1918 would not have occurred in the same time period since American troops weren't training in cramped, unsanitary camps, and weren't being sent to Europe at that time. I've chosen to have it occur in early 1921. Further, sources such as the *New England Journal of Medicine* now believe it originated in the USA and not in Europe or Asia as previous epidemics and plagues did.

If the idea of Woodrow Wilson, a victim of multiple strokes and virtually bedridden in 1920, running for a third term is implausible, think again. In his lucid moments he desperately wanted a third term to vindicate his legacy and try once more to have the U.S. join the League of Nations. He would not step aside, which, in the real history of 1920 sent the Democratic Party into a state of disarray. What helped him, of course, was that his wife kept the seriousness of his condition from the rest of the world.

Strange though this position may seem, when the Democratic convention opened that summer of 1920, New York bookies had Wilson as an odds-on favorite to be the Democratic nominee.

Many historians consider World War I to have been the most significant event in the last hundred years and the Battle of the Marne the most important single incident in the war. The tragedies of the last century can all be traced to the fall of 1914.

In my novel, the world following 1914 would have been very different. But would it have been better?

—Robert Conroy

1920

★ ★ ★ ★ ★ ★ ★ ★ ★ ★ ★ ★ ★ ★ ★

AMERICA'S GREAT WAR

★ PROLOGUE ★

HOW COULD THIS HAVE COME TO PASS? REGGIE CARville wondered. He was a captain in the British Army and was about to become a prisoner of the German Army and its demented leader, Kaiser Wilhelm II. Instead of victory, he and many tens of thousands of British soldiers would be guests of the Hun until they were repatriated back to England.

What a humiliation. What a terrible, horrible way to end this dismal year of 1914. He and thousands of others were squatting in the damp and clammy mud of southern France, waiting their turn to give up. It seemed so strange to be able to look across a field and see the German soldiers they'd been trying to kill just the day before standing in plain sight. He could almost hear their laughter and his humiliation ate at him. The British Expeditionary Force, the BEF, would soon cease to exist.

Of course, Carville thought, *it was far worse for the French*. At least the British force had remained intact.

Not like the French Army; it had utterly disintegrated after its defeat on the Marne and the subsequent capture of Paris by the Germans.

And who could blame the poor French soldiers who'd finally thrown away their weapons and run like rabbits? Poorly led and poorly trained, they'd been directed to charge into the rain of bullets coming from the German machine guns. They'd been told that *Elan*, the spirit of the warrior, would carry the day. Machine guns would be as nothing in the face of Gallic courage. Instead, they died in bloody heaps, their bodies broken and the *elan* of the survivors evaporated. Hell, Carville thought, they were still wearing their traditional red and blue uniforms, which made such splendid targets. The British wore khaki and the Germans a field gray, both of which served as far better camouflage.

Ironically, the Germans hadn't been much smarter in the early days of the war. They too had marched across bloody fields in mass formations. But they quickly learned the error of their ways.

In a curious twist of linguistic irony, Field Marshal Sir John French commanded the British forces operating in France. He was widely considered to be overtimid and did not get along well with either his own officers or his allies. Carville wondered if a more aggressive leader might have avoided this debacle. Perhaps not, he concluded. There'd been too many Germans and too few British, although three hundred thousand Brits hardly counted as a trifle. They and their French so-called allies had confronted more than two million Germans.

Carville was attached to Field Marshal French's

headquarters as a junior aide and could have avoided any contact with the fighting, but his upbringing and training demanded otherwise. On several occasions he'd gone to the front and watched as highly-trained British soldiers fired their Enfield rifles with a speed and accuracy that made the Germans think they had many more machine guns than existed. In front of the British, it had been the Germans who'd died in heaps. Too bad there were only a few hundred thousand British soldiers in the entire army and too bad they were all going to have to surrender. What, he wondered, would happen to poor England without an army? At least the Royal Navy was largely intact and could probably defend the nation from a German invasion.

Being part of the headquarters' staff, Carville knew things that others didn't. He knew that, months earlier, their French allies had been informed that the German Army on the Marne had split and that a counterattack on the German westernmost flank would stop them in their tracks.

But no, the old-fashioned French generals rejected the notion because they didn't quite trust the sources. Much of the information had come from pilots who'd seen the German mistake, but they simply hadn't been believed. People who fly planes are all mad, don't y'know. The commander at Paris, General Joseph Gallieni, had begged for permission to attack the exposed German flank, but had been denied. Sit tight and wait, he'd been told. When the Germans were defeated at the Marne he could attack their retreating forces. Carville's own leader, Marshal French, had also been reluctant to authorize a risky breakout.

Of course, the British and the French had been

defeated at the Marne and Paris taken after a short but bloody siege that saw many landmarks, like the Eiffel Tower and Notre Dame, in ruins. The British and French armies had retreated south, hoping to reach the Mediterranean and rescue. Instead, they had gotten no further than the city of Clermont. The French army had disintegrated while the British stayed intact and continuously bloodied the noses of the Germans.

Carville felt pity for the French soldier, the *poilu*, and contempt for his leaders. Of course, he wasn't all that fond of the English leaders who'd led him to this surrender field. In his opinion, Field Marshal Sir John French was a horse's ass.

Carville also knew that the Germans were exhausted and at the end of their tether. Their armies were in disarray and their supply lines had been unable to keep up with their army's needs. The German Army was in rags and almost out of food and ammunition. One good push and they'd either be stopped or defeated.

One problem—the French army no longer existed and the British Army was in even worse shape than the Germans. Victory, Carville concluded, would go to the side that was least exhausted. Wellington had prevailed in battle and called it a near-run thing. Well, this campaign had been a close one, but the result had been defeat, not victory.

Carville saw Sergeant Smith—the sergeant pronounced it "Smeeth"—staring at him. "Well, Sergeant, are you ready?"

"Oy, but I'll fookin' hate it."

Carville grinned. Smith sometimes affected an outrageous accent when he felt like it. He and the diminutive, wiry and outspoken Smith went back several years. Smith was a consummate professional soldier of the King. "I can't think that anyone's looking forward to a German prison camp," Carville said. "Can't imagine it'll be for too bloody long, though."

Smith nodded glumly. "Oy don't give a shit how long it be. Oy've lost too minny mates to take kindly to Germans. Hate the bastards, I do. Next time I hope their lordships in London gives us at least a fookin' fighting chance to kill the Kraut fookers."

Carville clapped him on the shoulder. The little man had killed more than a dozen Germans with his Enfield. As a sniper, he was almost a legend. In fact, the only better shot Reggie Carville knew of was Reggie Carville.

Whistles blew and men formed up. Carville nodded at Smith and returned to headquarters. They would march out, turn in their weapons, and be returned to their encampment. Officers would be paroled to live in local hotels, and the enlisted men would be kept at the camp until arrangements were made. Carville didn't think they would take long. The Germans didn't want to have to house and feed three hundred thousand Brits any longer than they had to.

What really concerned Carville was the thought of the world with Germany as its only preeminent power. England had been defeated. France and Russia had been crushed. There was no one left to be a real rival to Imperial Germany and the ambitions of the half-mad and half-crippled kaiser. The United States was a possibility, but they seemed more than content to hide behind their ocean moats and listen to their president, Woodrow Wilson, proclaim how terrible war was and how important it was that the United States stay out of it.

Carville sighed at such naiveté. What was one do when the town bully attacks you? Someday, America and Woodrow Wilson were in for a rude awakening.

Later, as he marched through the German lines, he saw how fatigued and dispirited they were. They looked at their late enemies with dull, dispirited eyes. Their faces were gaunt, their uniforms filthy and torn. *Damn it,* Carville thought. *We could have had them.*

★ CHAPTER 1 ★

HIS HORSE WAS NEAR COLLAPSE AND THE SIX ARMED men chasing him were gaining steadily. The old and scrawny mare's chest was heaving and her whole body was covered with sweat and foam. It hadn't been such a great horse in the first place, and was thoroughly outclassed by the well-bred cavalry mounts pounding behind him and gaining with every stride.

Luke Martel would soon be helpless on the ground, confronted by a half-dozen German lancers—Uhlans—who would like nothing better than to spit him like a rodent on one of their spear points. The Uhlans' uniforms and weapons were archaic, but archaic or not, their lances could impale human flesh with ease.

Since he was pretending to be a civilian, Martel was armed with a Colt revolver and not his more powerful .45 automatic service weapon. Even though he thought lancers were an anachronism in twentieth-century warfare, the revolver he carried was an inaccurate weapon and carried such a light round that it might not stop a horse, much less a human being. That assumed he could hit either if forced to fire at a gallop from his staggering nag.

The river and safety were to his right, maybe a quarter of a mile away. But first he had to reach the river and, second, he had to cross it without getting captured or killed.

He looked behind him. His pursuers were momentarily hidden from view. A curve in the dirt track that passed for a road gave him an opportunity. Another curve was just in front of him. He slipped from his horse and slapped it hard on its flank. Freed of its unwelcome burden and motivated by the slap, the mare lurched forward and behind the curve where it disappeared from view.

Just make it a little farther, Martel begged his horse. He clambered up and behind some rocks to his left and away from the river. When the Germans realized he was on foot, he hoped they would logically assume that he'd headed directly for the river and salvation. He counted on their logic. If nothing else, Germans were so bloody damned logical.

He began to backtrack in the direction of his approaching enemy. Again, he hoped their orderly minds wouldn't expect him to do anything other than run like hell from them and their damned lances, which any reasonably sane human being would do. Of course, a reasonably sane person wouldn't have gotten himself in this mess in the first place.

Martel could hear the pursuing horses clearly now and, seconds later, they thundered past as he hid behind a rock. The lancers' faces and their gaudy uniforms were covered with dust and grime, but the Germans were grinning, laughing, and riding easily, their lances canted slightly forward. The well-conditioned German horses seemed to be enjoying themselves as well. They were hunters after the ultimate prey.

And then they were gone. But they would be back. A moment later, he heard a gunshot. He presumed they'd found his exhausted horse and put it out of its misery. Too bad, he thought. The beast had served him well.

Now the Germans were confused. They returned to a point where he could see them again, and broke up into three pairs. They began to comb the ground between the road and the river. From his perch on the rocks and behind some thin bushes, Martel could see them searching along the riverbank that was a lot closer than he'd thought. It was maybe only a couple of hundred yards away. Of course, it might as well be a hundred miles with the Germans patrolling between him and it.

After maybe an hour, the Germans formed up and returned back down the road. Had they truly given up, or were they going back for more men to conduct a more comprehensive search? If the latter was the case, someone with a brain might figure out that maybe he hadn't run directly for the river, but was waiting for an opportunity to make a move.

Martel decided it was time to get the hell out of there.

He clambered down from the rocks and, after looking as far down the road as he could, ran across. The ground was sandy and open and he felt like he was totally exposed and could be seen for miles.

He ran hard. The river was in front of him. It didn't

look deep, and he knew that it oftentimes wasn't. Maybe he could dash across without having to swim.

He heard a shout from behind him. The bastard Germans had spotted him. They weren't as dumb as he'd hoped. They'd circled back along the riverbank and not the road. And now one of them was less than a hundred yards away and coming hard.

Martel ran as fast as he'd ever run in his life. Almost immediately, he was in the river, splashing in water that was knee deep and getting deeper. He could hear the sound of the German's horse breathing behind him and he could almost feel the lance going into his back and coming out his chest.

He threw himself into the water as a Uhlan roared past him, jabbing down. Martel rolled away, lunged upward, grabbed the cavalryman's boot and jerked hard, causing the German's horse to stumble and the rider to fall into the water. The Uhlan dropped his lance and tried to stand up, but fell back to his hands and knees.

Martel kicked the German in the head and pushed himself onward. He thought about grabbing the German's horse, but the animal was already trotting back to the riverbank.

At some point, he'd be in the middle of the river and safe. At least that's the way it worked in theory. The international boundary was the middle of the river. Maybe, though, the Krauts wouldn't be too concerned about such niceties as international boundaries with countries for which they had utter contempt. They might also be enraged that one of their own had been humiliated, another reason to disregard vague boundaries.

Two more mounted Germans had entered the water and were plowing towards him. The German he'd kicked was standing unsteadily, dazed but apparently not seriously hurt.

Martel could hardly breathe as he pushed himself onward. The water that had been up to his waist was growing shallower and he looked up. The rocky north bank of the river was just before him. He turned around and saw that the mounted Germans had picked up their comrade and were withdrawing to the south bank. One turned and glared furiously at him and made an obscene gesture. What the hell had just happened? Maybe he would live long enough to see his thirtieth birthday.

Now on his hands and knees, gasping and vomiting dirty water, Martel reached the north bank and crawled through the sand and mud. He didn't consider himself safe, not yet. Along with their ridiculous but deadly pig stickers, the Uhlans carried carbines. Would they fire across the border? Well, there wasn't much he could do about that except gather himself and continue to run like hell.

"Where you goin', boy?"

Martel looked up. Several rough-looking white men with rifles, mounted on scraggly but tough-looking horses, had emerged from the brush that had hidden them and were staring hard at him.

"I'm an American," he managed to gasp.

"That's what they all say," said a lean and wiry man in his thirties who appeared to be their leader. "Now tell me just why the fucking Germans chased you all the away across the Rio Grande and into Texas."

Martel stood up and tried to regain his dignity.

"Because I'm an officer in the United States Army, and the fucking Germans didn't like me snooping around them and their camps in Mexico this spring of 1920. Now who the hell are you?"

That seemed to amuse the man in charge who grinned amiably before spitting on the ground. "First off, my name is Marcus Tovey and I'm a Texas Ranger just like all these fine young gentlemen who are accompanying me, and anybody who's being shot at by the fucking Germans can't be all bad."

Luke Martel noted that the cowboy was carrying a Winchester 30-06 carbine and that he was wearing a badge. "That's an old weapon," Luke said.

"It'll still kill," Tovey said. "So we are now going to take you to our post and let you prove your tale. Then you can try to answer a question for me?"

Martel relaxed. "I'll try."

"Then tell me, young soldier, just what the hell are the Germans doing along the Rio Grande and the boundary of the state of Texas this spring of 1920?"

★ CHAPTER 2 ★

BRIGADIER GENERAL FOX CONNOR, RECENTLY returned from commanding the United States forces in Panama, was delighted to be back in California. The military complex was called the Presidio and was in San Francisco. It had a fine view of the Golden Gate and was a far better place to be than the steamy, corrupt, and sometimes violent squalor of Central America.

Fourteen years after the devastating earthquake of 1906, San Francisco was well on its way to once again becoming a place of sophistication and prominence. In fact, one had to know where to look to find evidence of the earthquake's damage; the city's half-million people were willing to forget it ever happened. Some of the chamber of commerce types insisted that it never had, that the damage was the result of the fire and that there had been no earthquake. After all, acknowledging that an earthquake had occurred might lower property values.

Some thought the short, stocky general looked like an angry bulldog and not someone a junior officer could confide in. Not true. Connor liked nothing more than having intelligent young officers gathered around him so they could all freely exchange ideas. Connor considered it his duty and pleasure to develop the minds of those he considered to have great potential, or those he simply just liked.

This afternoon in early October, 1920, three young men sat with him. Two had potential—George Patton and Dwight Eisenhower while the third, Luke Martel, was respected and, in some ways, admired even though it was highly unlikely he would ever rise more than a couple of notches higher than his current rank, second lieutenant.

Patton, in particular, liked to tease Martel. "If the general uses words you don't understand, Luke, I'll explain them all to you later. If you're nice, maybe I'll even spell them for you."

Martel rolled his eyes and grinned while Connor pretended not to hear the banter. Martel was used to the gibes and, besides, he and Patton were friends of a sort. Martel was an anomaly. He had gotten his commission the hard way, on the battlefield. Several years earlier, he'd been a sergeant in Pershing's punitive force that had been sent into Mexico to fight the bandits who'd ravaged Texas. While on patrol, his platoon had been ambushed. His lieutenant was killed and he'd found himself in command of thirty desperate men surrounded by more than a hundred Mexicans who smelled blood and an easy victory.

Martel had rallied his men, defended their position, and then led a savage counterattack that chased the Mexicans away, leaving more than fifty of them dead or wounded after brutal hand-to-hand fighting.

Martel had killed five Mexicans himself and been badly wounded. A scar running from his forehead down his cheek was a visible reminder of that encounter with death. For that he'd been awarded the Medal of Honor and the rank of second lieutenant by a grateful Pershing, who'd seen both a bloody defeat and a public-relations disaster averted.

Pershing had also understood that Martel was a fighter, a commodity sometimes missing in many regular Army officers, especially in times of extended peace. The Army hadn't fought a war in almost two decades, a small but nasty one in the Philippines and a shorter one in Cuba. In a regular army that prided itself on the quality of its West Point graduates, Martel hadn't even completed high school. Even though intelligent, well read and self-taught, he was not one of the elite West Point Club and knew it. His latest enlistment would run out the coming spring and he had a decision to make. Hanging on as a supply officer somewhere until retirement was not something he wanted to do. Not for the first time did he wonder whether the promotion to lieutenant was more of a burden than a blessing.

General Connor thought it was a shame that no one had nominated Martel for the Academy. Since the government would have paid for it, money was not a prerequisite, and he thought Martel would have done well. Patton came from wealth, but Eisenhower's family had been poor farmers. On the other hand, maybe it was better that Martel had come up through the ranks, where he'd gained invaluable real-world experience.

There was some jealousy on the part of other officers, Patton included, of Martel's combat experience and his more recent intelligence-gathering forays into German-occupied Mexico. The latest one, where he'd nearly been killed by a number of Uhlans that grew with each telling, was quickly becoming the stuff of legend.

Even though Martel's promotion to lieutenant had first been considered temporary, the army had let him keep his rank and it was quietly understood that someday he might be promoted to captain and later retired to live off a pittance of a pension. Nobody gave him too much grief, especially since he was physically strong at nearly six feet tall and one hundred and eighty pounds. He was potentially lethal, sinister-looking thanks to the scar, and, more important, was a favorite of Pershing. That generals Hunter Liggett and Fox Connor liked him didn't hurt either.

Connor shook his head. "George, if you are through harassing our resident hero, why don't we start talking things through."

The three officers laughed. "Excellent," said Connor. "Now let's review. Patton, how would you describe the situation the United States is in?"

"Totally fucked up," said the irrepressible Patton.

Connor sighed. "Thank you, George. That's correct and concise, but I was looking for something more analytical. Now, in just about three weeks the United States will hold a presidential election. Who will win? Ike?"

Eisenhower answered quickly. "Wilson will be reelected for an unprecedented third term. It'll be close, but he's the man who ended the war in Europe and gave us eternal peace as a result of the Treaty of Princeton. Or at least that's what a lot of people believe. Like him or not, and I don't know many military men who do, he's the people's choice and will be re-elected. Warren Harding doesn't stand a chance after all the news about his private life came out."

"Hell," Patton said, "Wilson might even be dead by the time of the election or before the inauguration. We know he's exhausted and they say he has a cold, maybe even the flu, but nobody's seen him in a couple of weeks. I've heard rumors he's had a stroke. Some president we're gonna have."

Connor stood up and walked to where a map of the Southwestern Division of the United States and another one of Mexico were pinned.

"Gentlemen, militarily, who is responsible for the mess we are in? Is it Germany for starting the war of 1914–1915?"

Martel sometimes felt inadequate in these discussions, but, hell, he was among friends. "No sir, I blame the French."

Connor grinned. "Go on."

"Sir, the French had every opportunity to stop the Germans at the Marne. We now know that they'd been informed that the German armies had lost touch with each other. Reports from pilots proved that. The French commander in Paris, Gallieni, knew that the German flank was hanging and begged permission to attack it, and that might have stopped the Germans in their tracks. But the French commander, Joffre, didn't believe the intelligence. He was too traditional and fossilized to believe he'd been handed such an opportunity."

The rest, they all knew, was history. The French had been crushed at the Marne, and then retreated south in what quickly became a rout. Paris fell and the French soon capitulated. The British Army, some three hundred thousand strong, was caught by an overwhelming German force while trying to reach a Mediterranean port where the Royal Navy could evacuate them. Almost to a man, the British Army had surrendered.

The war of 1914 had ended just before Christmas in an overwhelming German victory and a catastrophic defeat for France, England, and, to a lesser extent, Imperial Russia. Some fighting in peripheral areas lingered into 1915, but the war was effectively over. Woodrow Wilson had gained further fame as a peacemaker by brokering the Treaty of Princeton which was signed a year later in Princeton, New Jersey.

"And if the French had won at the Marne, what would have happened?" Ike posed to the group. "It probably would have resulted in a bloody and drawn-out stalemate."

Martel agreed. "Still better for the French and British than a catastrophic defeat."

"Hell, they would have dug in and the two sides might still be fighting," Patton said.

Connor smiled. "Would we have been dragged in?"

Ike answered. "Not with Wilson in the White House. He's the same person who said it wasn't important when the Germans, following the peace, basically took over Mexico. He said it wasn't important enough for us to fight over." He turned to Martel and grinned. "And that is why Luke keeps visiting Mexico. Remind me, what did you find the last time?"

Martel flushed slightly. It had been six months since the last time and the wild escape that finished it. "I located six German divisions within fifty miles of the border, and evidence of another eight more in the area by reading unit insignias on officers in Mexico City."

Martel had spent several weeks posing as a fertilizer salesman from Canada before the Germans became suspicious and chased him across the Rio Grande. Patton and Ike had both joked that selling bullshit was something Luke handled very well.

They glanced at the map of Mexico which sported a number of colored pins. The green ones showed the last known locations of German units, and the red ones, the Mexican Army. The information had changed little in the last few months. Word had come from Washington that no more forays like Martel's would be tolerated. Too provocative to the Mexicans, Liggett and Connor were told. Thus, the only information they got was from Mexican refugees fleeing from their latest civil war. When interrogated, they generally knew little.

The clock on the wall chimed three. "Damn," said Connor. "We'll have to break this up and go back to duty. I have a meeting with Liggett. Just a reminder, Lieutenant Martel is carrying dispatches to Washington and will be gone for several weeks. If you have anything you want him to take, see him now."

Both Ike and Patton grinned at Martel. Connor had thrown Luke a bone. He was actually going to Washington to attend a cousin's wedding, but, since he was being used as a courier, didn't have to use any of his accumulated leave time, and the government would pay for the trip. It was characteristically thoughtful of Connor.

Patton jabbed Martel on the shoulder and grinned

wickedly. "Just try and stay out of trouble. Don't want to hear anything about Germans chasing your ass across the Potomac."

Kirsten Biel liked to ride in the early mornings. It was relatively clear and cool and southern California could get very warm; especially that part located close to the Mexico, and her home was only twenty miles north of the border.

Mornings also let her think without interference from her cousins who still didn't believe she was capable of running the ranch she'd inherited from her late husband. Ridiculous. She'd been raised on a ranch in Texas and under far harsher circumstances before being swept off her feet by Richard Biel. She admitted that the rough and hilly ground was marginal at best, but so far she'd been able to make a go of it. The land had been cheap for a good reason, yet was able to support a number of cattle that were sold for a decent profit. So far. She just hoped the troubles in nearby Mexico stayed in Mexico.

She shook her head sadly as she let the horse lead the way. Poor Richard, she thought, so suddenly dead of an infection that developed from a bruise on his leg. That was two years ago and now, at twenty-five, Kirsten found herself running an operation that included hundreds of head of cattle, hundreds of acres of land, and a half-dozen full-time employees.

She wondered what she and her cousins would argue about today. Fred and Ella Biel were decent people, but it was clear that they resented the fact that she, an outsider, was in charge of the ranch and their collective futures. They thought it would be nice if Kirsten remarried, moved out, and sold the ranch to them, at an extremely reasonable price of course.

Remarriage was not on her agenda. Although Kirsten considered herself attractive enough, she knew she did not conform to classic definitions of feminine beauty. Despite long blonde hair and green eyes, at five-eight she was a little too tall for many men's tastes, and at one hundred and forty pounds, just a little too sturdy and athletic for the average male. She'd long decided that the average male was very insecure, and her intelligence, education, and outspokenness had turned away a number of potential suitors.

She was especially outspoken when it came to political matters.

Attitudes regarding women were changing nationally. Women could now vote throughout the country even though women in California had been able to vote since 1911. Not too many people looked askance at her when she went riding while wearing a pair of Levi's denim jeans instead of something more demure. Of course, very few people, other than family and hired hands, actually saw her on horseback. She also liked it that hemlines were rising and that women going swimming could actually wear bathing suits that didn't endanger them by being so bulky they dragged the swimmer under water.

With all that was happening south of the border, she'd been told it was dangerous to ride alone. She agreed to a point and carried a model 1899 Krag carbine that had belonged to her father, and a Colt revolver she'd bought for herself in San Diego a few months ago. She was an excellent shot. She was not so familiar with the Bowie knife strapped to the outside of her boot. She jokingly said she mainly used it to clean her nails, while her cousin Ella once quietly accused her of using it to castrate suitors. Kirsten had the feeling that Ella was a fragile creature who was having a difficult time dealing with the harshness of ranch life.

Motion in the sky caught her eye. For an instant, she thought it might have been an airplane. She'd only seen a couple of them and they fascinated her as they did just about everyone. Even though they'd been invented more than fifteen years ago, they were still so rare that the very sight of one resulted in gasps of wonderment. Someday she would like to go up in one. Maybe she could use some of her precious savings to buy a ride from one of those pilots people were calling barnstormers.

But no, it was just a vulture. Then she saw a couple more. Something had disturbed them and caused them to take off from the ground. They were a mile or so away and she wondered what they were feeding on. Was it one of her cattle, perhaps a calf that had wandered off? Or was it something else?

Kirsten pulled the rifle from its sheath and checked to see that it was loaded. It always was but she always checked. She urged the horse into a trot and hoped it was only a calf.

It wasn't. Kirsten fought down the bile in her throat at the sight of the two dead men lying face down on the ground. They were Mexicans and had been shot in the back, executed, hands tied behind them. She did not dismount and examine them more closely. No point, she decided. Their wounds were just too massive.

That was about as much as she could tell after the vultures had been working on them. Their clothes were in rags and they were barefoot. More casualties from the long and bloody civil war being fought in Mexico, she thought, but these two had been chased or followed into California. They were likely soldiers of defeated General Alvaro Obregon, murdered by the victorious forces of Mexico's current president, Venustiano Carranza. If the newspapers were to be believed, Carranza had essentially proclaimed himself a dictator, thanks to the backing of Imperial Germany.

That Mexicans were killing Mexicans was nothing unusual. They'd been doing it for decades. But now they'd begun taking their fighting and their vengeance killings into the United States. The presence of the two dead men meant that they'd passed close by her ranch in order to get where she had found them, and that was very unsettling. She didn't want her ranch to become the front lines in a Mexican civil war.

What to do now, she wondered? First, she decided, she would send a detail out to bury the two men and, second, notify the sheriff. The sheriff would be powerless to do anything but take down a report and forward it to the state capital at Sacramento where they would also do nothing.

Kirsten wiped her brow with a neck kerchief. Her cousins, however well meaning, would use this as further ammunition in their argument that she should sell and move on. Maybe they were right.

She rode home and gave the instructions for the burial detail, ignoring Ella's look of concern. She went to her room, poured several buckets of water into the cast iron tub, stripped, and settled in. The water was comfortably lukewarm. She wondered what her late husband would have done about the situation she'd discovered.

Kirsten laughed quietly. She knew what Richard would have done. He would have climbed into the tub with her, washed the riding dirt from her body, and then thrown her down on the bed where they would have romped like naked bunnies. Damn, she missed him. It wasn't fair, she thought as she closed her eyes and envisioned him. It just wasn't fair.

•

"Good morning, Mister Vice President."

Secretary of State Robert Lansing was startled. Then he grinned at his secretary, the gray-haired and middle-aged spinster, Hedda Tuttle.

"Not yet, Mrs. Tuttle, and maybe never. There's still an election to be won and votes to be counted."

Robert Lansing was fifty-six years old, a distinguished-looking lawyer from New York, and had been secretary of state since June, 1915, following the resignation of William Jennings Bryan. He liked to brag that he was the only secretary of state to have a state capital named after him—Lansing, Michigan. It was a joke. The capital of Michigan had not been named after him or his family.

He had opposed Woodrow Wilson on a number of issues, which made him wonder why Wilson had chosen him to be his running mate instead of the very pliable and not overly bright Thomas Marshall, who had already served two terms as Wilson's vice president. Lansing had a nagging feeling he knew why, but was unwilling to face it just yet.

Hedda Tuttle waved her hand dismissively. The election had been the day before, and the returns were already coming in showing a substantial plurality for the ticket of Woodrow Wilson and Robert Lansing, as well as a decisive lead in the even more important Electoral College. Warren Harding had been a viable alternative until his many sexual romps with women other than his wife became public knowledge.

"Mr. Wilson will win and so will you," Mrs. Tuttle said with serene confidence. "There's no doubt about it, sir."

"Thank you for your support," Lansing said sincerely. He just hoped he would be up to the task. He wondered just what the devil was going on in the White House where a nearly invisible Woodrow Wilson allegedly resided. Nobody had seen the man for weeks.

But for now he was still the secretary of state and third in the succession to the presidency of the United States. There'd been talk of changing the Constitution so that the speaker of the house, an elected office, would be number three, but nothing had come of it.

Of more immediate concern was the bombshell that had been handed to him by the ambassador from Great Britain. It said that the Germans were up to their old tricks, were coveting more territory, and that covetousness directly involved the United States of America. He had to get to see President Wilson, no matter what Wilson's harpy of a wife said. Edith Bolling Galt, now Edith Wilson, was Woodrow Wilson's second wife. His first wife had died in 1914.

Edith Wilson was extremely protective of Woodrow Wilson, and, as his health deteriorated, had blocked almost all access to him, allowing only written notes and questions that were responded to in her hand.

Edith Wilson, some suspected, had promoted herself to the position of acting President of the United States. Lansing shook his head. Even if they could prove it, what would happen? The constitution was vague on the matter of a president being incapacitated.

Regardless, Robert Lansing had to see the president, no matter how difficult it might prove. The information provided by the British was so devastatingly important. The country had to be prepared for what might come.

"Mrs. Tuttle, is that nice young cousin still visiting you?"

She beamed. "Lieutenant Martel will be here for a couple more days. Did you know I raised him when his parents died?"

Lansing did, of course. She'd mentioned it at least a dozen times. Mrs. Tuttle was a spinster and raising the boy was the high point of her life. After he had grown, she'd moved to Washington and gotten the job as his secretary through the simple expedient of answering an ad.

"Tell you what, Mrs. Tuttle. I would like to come over and meet him. Why don't I drop by about eight?"

Hedda Tuttle was quite surprised and flustered. "That would be such an honor."

"And I might just bring another friend with me. Please tell the lieutenant to be in civilian clothes, and I know I can trust your discretion not to tell anyone of this, ah, little tryst."

A thoroughly puzzled Luke Martel sat in Hedda Tuttle's pleasantly cluttered living room. Until his arrival from out west, he'd never seen the place. She lived in a little cottage about a mile from the State

Department office where she worked. She walked to work every day, regardless of the weather.

Hedda hadn't begun her government work until after Luke had run off and enlisted. Her early letters had deplored his actions, but then, after he'd been promoted to sergeant and later awarded the Medal of Honor as well as promotion to lieutenant, her tone had changed. She was proud of him.

Luke knew he'd disappointed her by enlisting, but it seemed like the only thing to do at that time. She and he were dirt poor and he was a financial burden to her. He was deeply fond of her and wondered just what the hell was going on this evening. Sit still and wait, were her instructions.

Like most people, Cousin Hedda had no phone. Instructions had come by courier and caught him just as he'd returned from a pleasant day of sightseeing at the Smithsonian. Two important but unnamed people were going to visit him. He was to wear civilian clothes. He was to greet them warmly and neither stand at attention nor salute where anyone could see him. He was to do nothing that would draw the attention of nosy neighbors to their guests. If anybody was watching, their arrival just after nightfall was to look like the reunion of old friends.

Okay, he laughed. Washington was a city of plots and secrets, so why should he be surprised at anything?

At eight in the evening, a car pulled up and two men got out with the driver remaining behind the wheel. Martel went to the door and, despite instructions, had to fight the urge to snap to attention. Instead, he calmly gestured them to come in and closed the door behind them.

"Mr. Vice President or do you prefer Mr. Secretary?" he looked to Lansing and then, "Sir," to Lieutenant General Peyton March, the commanding general of the United States Army.

Lansing took the lead. "Even though the election is formally over and I am now the vice president elect, I will continue to be the secretary of state until my inauguration in March. Just call me sir, it's easier." He handed Martel a sheet of paper. "Read this, Lieutenant."

It was only a few paragraphs, and Luke read it quickly. His eyes widened and he swallowed. The contents were dynamite, but were they true? "With respect, General, do you have the message in the original German?"

March smiled slightly and handed over another sheet of paper while Lansing raised his eyebrows in mild surprise. Luke handed it back a moment later. "Thank you, sir."

"And what do both documents say, Lieutenant?" Lansing asked.

"Sir, they are a message from the German Foreign Minister, Arthur Zimmerman, to their ambassador to Mexico, Heinrich von Eckhardt. It says that the German Army in Mexico is directed to attack and invade California on November 18 of this year."

"Very good," said Lansing with only a hint of sarcasm. "And, just out of curiosity, where did you learn to read German?"

"Sir, a long time ago I thought things would go bad with the kaiser, so I taught myself. And I was helped along by a couple of guys I served with who were German immigrants themselves. I don't think I speak the cultured High German, but I can make myself understood and I can read it quite well."

Lansing actually smiled. "And what other languages do you have?"

"Well, Spanish of course, sir. I learned that on the border and with Pershing in Mexico."

March interjected. "Which is where the lieutenant was wounded, won the Medal, and where he got a battlefield commission."

"Excellent," said Lansing, visibly impressed. "Any other languages?"

"I can get by in French, sir."

"And where, pray tell, did you find time to learn that?" asked Lansing.

Now it was Luke's turn to grin. "I learned it from a girl in San Francisco, sir."

Lansing laughed like it felt good to laugh, and even the normally formal General March chuckled. "Mr. Secretary," Luke said, "the Zimmerman message is damning, but is it true?"

"A good question indeed," said Lansing with an audible sigh. "And, yes, we believe the message is true. We have been able to verify it through a number of sources, including British intelligence and a drunken German diplomat who apparently didn't give a care what we thought. Tomorrow, you will carry this news as quickly as possible to General Liggett in California so he can do whatever can be done to stop the Germans."

Luke turned to General March who shook his head and added. "Yes, Lieutenant, telephone or telegram would be much, much faster, but we have no way of sending it in code and any message sent in the clear would cause a panic if it was overheard or seen by an operator. You are to deliver the information by hand to General Liggett and he will also be informed that it is to be kept extremely confidential while we try to make plans to either forestall the attack or, in General Liggett's case, try to defend against it."

"Sir, it'll still take me a week to get to San Francisco, even by the fastest train."

Lansing chuckled, "Hardly. In the guise of a test of the reliability of airplane travel, General March has been setting up a series of airplanes for you. If all goes well, you'll leave at dawn and be at the Presidio with General Liggett in a couple of days at the most."

Martel gulped. If all didn't go well, he might be part of a failed experiment. He had never been in an airplane and hadn't counted on taking a crash course on their capabilities, no pun intended.

March smiled slightly. "You are packed, aren't you?"

"Yes sir, I am, and I was traveling light anyhow. May I ask why you've chosen me for this assignment?"

Lansing smiled. "Because you're here and because Mrs. Tuttle vouches for you."

March continued, "That and the fact that General Liggett also knows you and trusts you. You understand the situation, and you've seen the German Army rather up close if I recall correctly."

Martel relaxed. "I think I'm honored, General, Mr. Vice President. However, may I suggest we forewarn General Liggett by an innocuous telephone call or an equally innocuous telegram from, say, me, to a third party, like Captain Eisenhower or Patton? It could for instance, say something suggesting an 'imminent storm coming from the South?'"

Even though long-distance phone calls from Washington to California had been established in 1915, the quality was inconsistent and there were always wires going down. And there was always the possibility of operators listening in on a conversation from the White House. The use of a pair of third parties to give at least a broad warning to Liggett was intriguing and Lansing concurred with Martel's suggestion. That way, General Liggett wouldn't be totally ambushed.

Lansing patted him on the shoulder. "Get your bags. Mrs. Tuttle knows you're leaving with us. We have one other thing for you to see so General Liggett will understand what we're up against." Lansing smiled grimly. "Lieutenant, we're going to the White House to see the president."

It was almost ten by the time they arrived at the darkened White House and it took a few more minutes to get through the uniformed Secret Service guards, even though their boss, the secretary of the treasury, had briefed them on their pending arrival. The Secret Service had only begun protecting the president after the assassination of President McKinley in 1901, and were very serious about the job. The White House's chief usher, Ike Hoover, was not present.

Two other men met them. One was Supreme Court Chief Justice Edward Douglas White, an old and frail Louisianian who'd been appointed by President Taft in 1910, two years before Wilson's first term.

The second was the president's personal physician, Dr. Cary Grayson. He was also a navy admiral. To Martel's astonishment, Grayson quietly and reluctantly admitted that he hadn't seen Wilson in a couple of weeks either.

They went upstairs to the second level, the private quarters of the president. They informed a Negro servant that they'd arrived, and that it was imperative that they see President Wilson immediately.

A few moments later, an unkempt woman in a long robe emerged and glared at them. "You may not see my husband. How dare you come here unannounced at this time of night? The president is ill and needs all the rest he can get."

Lansing handed Edith Wilson a copy of the German message. "Please read it."

She scanned it quickly and returned it. "Rubbish. All lies and filth designed to upset my husband and to disparage his achievements. The Germans have signed a peace treaty and they will live up to it."

"Madame," said General March firmly, "the Germans have a history of aggression and we must prepare for it. We may be at war with Kaiser Wilhelm in a very short while. The president must know of this so we can begin to plan."

Edith Wilson would have none of it. "My husband kept us out of the war of 1914 and he negotiated the peace treaty that guarantees peace, perhaps forever. He won the Nobel Prize for his efforts, and you have the audacity to bring these lies to disturb him?" She turned and backed away. "No, you will leave."

Lansing winced. Woodrow Wilson had been co-winner of the Nobel along with the humanitarian Herbert Hoover. Hoover had won because of his efforts to feed the starving in Europe during and following the war. Rumor had it that Wilson had been furious at having to share the honor with a man he considered a rude engineer.

"No we will not leave," said Justice White as he pulled a document out of his jacket. "This order requires you to admit us to his presence or you will be found in contempt of court. It also authorizes us to use whatever force is necessary to see the president and that the Secret Service is to assist us. There is considerable doubt that the president is up to fulfilling his constitutional duties, in which case, something must be done to protect the nation."

Martel stood behind the group. It was difficult for him to breathe. What the hell had he gotten himself into? Was this a coup? Now the idea of couple of days in a small plane seemed rather pleasant.

Mrs. Wilson seemed shaken. She began to wring her hands. "I don't know what to do."

She began to sob as Lansing gently pushed her aside. He opened the door and stepped into the president's bedroom. Stale air and the stink of medicine wafted out, along with the unmistakable stench of body waste. The men went in. Luke took a deep breath and followed.

Woodrow Wilson, age sixty-four and the twenty-eighth President of the United States, lay on his back on a large bed. A cot was beside it and that was where Mrs. Wilson apparently slept. Jars of medicines were arrayed on a table. Luke felt embarrassed at invading the Wilsons' privacy. Blankets covered Woodrow Wilson's body up to his chin. His eyes were closed, his jaw was slack, and his face was drawn and gray. There was dried spittle on his chin. Martel thought the man in the bed looked worse than awful, but said nothing. Nobody spoke. Everyone was shocked by the president's condition. Luke stared at the blankets. Were they even moving? Was he breathing?

Mrs. Wilson gathered her strength. "All right, you've seen him. You can also see that he isn't up to visitors. He must rest and you must leave. Perhaps you can talk to him another day."

Doctor Grayson reached a hand out to his Commander in Chief. "Don't touch him!" Mrs. Wilson shrieked and grabbed for his arm.

Grayson ignored her and pulled the blanket down to the middle of the president's chest. He gently placed his hand on the president's wrist and then his neck. He stood up slowly. His face was pale as he turned to the others.

"Gentlemen, this man is dead."

Robert Lansing thought that the only thing worse than finding that Woodrow Wilson was a corpse was the fact that Thomas R. Marshall was next in line to be the President of the United States, and would be so for the next five critical months. Marshall was perhaps the most incompetent vice president in the history of the United States, which, he thought ruefully, was saying a lot. He'd been despised by Wilson, who totally ignored him for two terms. Marshall was shy and insecure, and the only quote ever attributed to him was his deathless comment that "what this country needs is a good five-cent cigar."

What the country really needed, Lansing thought bitterly, was a vice president qualified to fill the shoes of the president in the case of disaster. And now disaster was looming. No, he thought sadly, it was present.

General March and Lieutenant Martel departed, leaving Lansing alone. General March had been dropped off at the War Department and Martel was on his way to a local airstrip. Lansing had his driver take him to the residence of the vice president.

A moment later, the chief justice arrived and they exchanged grim nods. *Lord,* thought Lansing as he went up the walk to Marshall's house, *what a strange world we live in.*

To Lansing's surprise, Vice President Marshall answered it himself and invited them in. Except for the driver who waited patiently in the car, Lansing and Justice White were alone.

Vice President Marshall looked at the two men in puzzlement as they entered his office. "To what do I owe the honor?"

"Wilson is dead," Lansing snapped. "You are now the President of the United States."

Marshall staggered back as if struck. "No, no. It can't be."

Let's get this over with quickly, Lansing thought. The delivery of the message had been intentionally cruel and blunt. Marshall might be a political clown and buffoon but he had a role to play and what was now a farce could not degenerate into tragedy.

"Which can't be, Wilson's death or your being president?" Lansing asked. "The chief justice is here to administer the oath so you can begin immediately administering the affairs of state and leading the nation through the coming war with Germany."

Marshall looked wild-eyed with shock and looked like he was about to cry. "War? What in God's name are you talking about? I know absolutely nothing about war or any crisis and don't want to. And I most certainly don't want to be president."

"You're the next in line," Justice White said sternly, as if talking to a schoolchild. "If you don't want to be president, you must formally step aside."

Marshall took a deep breath, gathered himself, and sat down. "Gentlemen, you have surprised me. No, you have stunned me. I may not be the smartest man in the world, but I do consider myself a fairly honest one and a keen judge of my own character. I know myself and I know that I am utterly unqualified to become president of this wonderful country. If the crisis you speak of is so dire, then I should not even be an interim president until the inauguration next March. At that point you will become president, won't you, Mr. Lansing?"

Douglas answered. "He will. With the elected president dead, the vice president elect will become the president and will be sworn in for a four-year term, but not until March. Whoever he appoints as secretary of state will be the next in succession as there is no constitutional provision to appoint or elect a new vice president. Marshall, your term of office will be extremely brief, only five months. Then you can retire with honor back to Indiana."

Marshall shook his head. "If the country still exists, that is. Why are the Germans going to go to war with *us*?"

Lansing sighed. As secretary of state he had researched the contradictory and sometimes bizarre behavior of the kaiser. Experts said that the kaiser had been born with an arm that was withered because it had become entangled in his umbilical cord. This gave him feelings of inferiority. How could he be a warrior king with a withered arm? The arm even made it difficult for him to ride a horse, a task he had ultimately mastered through force of will. Other experts said that the kaiser had also been born with the umbilical tube around his neck, and this had caused a lack of oxygen to his brain, damaging him.

The result was that the kaiser, now sixty-one, saw that he only had a few more years to ensure his legacy as a conqueror. He'd defeated France, England, and Russia, and only the United States remained.

Lansing was exhausted and exasperated. "They are going to war with us because they are Germans and that's what they do. Also because they are the strongest nation on the planet and they wish to expand their strength and their empire, and because they despise us for thwarting their ambitions in Europe and in the Pacific. The kaiser and his government feel Wilson's intervention ended the war in Europe too soon. And also because the kaiser is a megalomaniac with delusions of grandeur. I might also add that the world's growing need for oil is frightening the kaiser. His warships require it and Germany has none. However, there is sufficient oil in California to fuel the German fleet's needs for quite some time."

Lansing felt sorry for the vice president.

"And if I decline to take the oath?"

"Simply declining would precipitate a constitutional crisis," Chief Justice White said. "You would have to formally step aside, at which time the current secretary of state, Mr. Lansing, will become president until he is sworn in for a four-year term in March by virtue of the fact that he is also the vice president elect."

"And Congress will not object?" Marshall inquired.

"I do not believe they will," Lansing said. "The Constitution says that Congress has to appoint a president in the event that neither the president nor the vice president are able to serve. The most recent legislation has identified the secretary of state as the third in line."

Marshall was not a stupid man and now understood the true meaning of their visit. He smiled at Lansing. "And you believe you are a better and more qualified man than I am?"

"In all honesty, Mr. Marshall, I do," said Lansing.

Marshall shook his head sadly. "And in all honesty, so do I." He took a piece of paper from a credenza and began to write. "I assume, Mr. Chief Justice, that you are here to ensure that all is honest and aboveboard?"

"Indeed."

Marshall finished and handed the paper to Justice White. "I presume this is satisfactory."

White glanced at it. "It is." He signed his name as witness.

Marshall nodded sadly, "So much for my ambitions. Every little boy says he wants to grow up and be president of the United States, and if I do what you want, I will go down as the first and doubtless only man in our history who passed on the honor."

Marshall laughed harshly. "And the dove was quite cunning, wasn't he? Wilson probably knew he wouldn't live out his next term, so he selected someone far more qualified than me to be the next in line. The only thing he didn't count on was dying before the inauguration in March. Wilson was a stubborn, willful, hateful man who despised me and now he has given me this last insult to endure. Well, damn him, I will not play his game, dead or not."

Lansing put his hand on Marshall's shoulder. "By resigning you will be honored in history as an example of an honest and virtuous man."

Marshall smiled appreciatively. "And you will go down as the man who finagled himself into the most miserable job in the world while I go and smoke a good five-cent cigar."

★ CHAPTER 3 ★

A FEW DAYS LATER, LUKE MARTEL WAS SO EXHAUSTED he could hardly stand as General Hunter Liggett read the messages from Washington. They included endorsement letters from Lansing and March along with the actual translated message stating that the Germans were going to invade. A copy of the original German text was included in case anyone on Liggett's staff wished to question the interpretation.

Liggett was sixty-three, hugely fat and slow moving, which some mistook for mental slowness, or even stupidity. They were wrong. Liggett was a man of great dignity, and a solid general with a keen and lively intellect.

He was also a man of some compassion. "For God's sake, Lieutenant, sit down."

"I may fall asleep if I do, sir."

"I'll wake you if I need to."

Two days and two sleepless nights in a series of frail and open biplanes, either rented from civilians or owned by the Signal Corps, had left Martel physically and emotionally drained. Nor had he had a moment to freshen up. He'd been met at the little airstrip outside San Francisco by a corporal driving, of all things, a motorcycle with a side car. *More wind in my face*, he thought, *but this time with the added joy of bugs in my teeth*.

A telegram from March to Liggett had directed the general to see to it that Martel be picked up and delivered to him as soon as possible. So, after thousands of miles in an open cockpit in air that was bone-chillingly cold, he had finally arrived in San Francisco and the office of Major General Hunter Liggett.

He was somewhat gratified to find that his innocuous telegram and phone call to Ike and Patton warning them of a sudden storm from the south had been passed on to Uncle Fox and Uncle Hunter as he'd requested.

"I presume you have read this?"

"Yes, sir."

"Is that vomit on your uniform?"

"It is, sir. Two days in an airplane with utterly insane pilots will do that and I didn't always make it over the side when we hit an air pocket or a storm. However, sir, there are parts of several states that have been thoroughly decorated by me, or desecrated if you prefer. The secretary of state and General March said it was urgent and that the full text could not be entrusted to the telegraph."

Liggett set the messages on his desk. "They were, of course, correct. Are you aware that Lansing is now the president?" Martel was not. It had all transpired while he was in the air.

Liggett lifted his bulk from his chair. "Martel, I want you to go to your quarters, clean up, and get some sleep. After that, you will report here for assignment as God knows what. I have a feeling events are going to begin moving very quickly and we will all need clear heads."

"Thank you, sir."

"But I do envy you, Martel. I would dearly love to go up in an airplane, but I very much doubt there's one strong enough to hold me. Now get the hell out of here and come back in a more useful state. And by the way, Uncle Fox and Uncle Hunter commend you on a job well done."

The Germans were not the sort of ally Mexican President Venustiano Carranza would have chosen, but then, beggars could not be choosers. He had needed help in the long and bloody civil war fighting the forces of his rival, Alvaro Obregon, and, in return for some small favors, Germany was more than pleased to comply. The Germans arrived, routed Obregon's forces and imposed a peace of sorts.

Now there were hundreds of thousands of German soldiers, engineers, and businessmen in Mexico, and her ports were choked with German warships and transports. Vera Cruz on the east coast and Mazatlan on the west now played host to powerful German Navy squadrons. Mountains of supplies had been moving westward. German efficiency was both incredible and frightening. The border with the United States was essentially frozen, and foreign travelers, especially Americans, were only allowed access to certain areas of Mexico.

The despised Monroe Doctrine of the equally despised United States was just so much historical rubbish. He had contempt for the arrogance of the U.S. in thinking they could dictate the foreign policy of Mexico and other nations. In his opinion, the Americans felt that way because they were filled with brown-skinned people instead of white.

Carranza's enemies and some of his friends thought he had made a pact with the devil, and perhaps he had. But Mexico was now united and would be a powerful nation once her lost provinces were returned. He was going to take a tremendous risk, but the rewards would be worth it. Texas, New Mexico, and Arizona would again be part of Mexico. California would belong to Germany and that was an annoyance, but Carranza was pragmatic. At age sixty-one, he was mature enough to know he could not have everything.

A positive side effect would be Carranza's armies finally crushing the tens of thousands of armed Mexican refugees now in the United States. These were the remnants of Obregon's forces, and they had to be destroyed in order to ensure Carranza's view of Mexico's future. This would be bloody but necessary.

Carranza had just completed a conference with the long-serving ambassador from Berlin, Heinrich von Eckhardt, and the details were finalized. The Mexican Army would thrust north towards San Antonio after first taking Laredo. They'd both laughed at the idea of the Alamo falling again, although Carranza had laughed without humor. The damned Texans considered the Alamo a holy place. He would crush its every stone into dust when it was recaptured.

A second, smaller, attack would take Brownsville,

while other Mexican units moved into Arizona and New Mexico. The Germans would attack with overwhelming force into California and move as far north as they wished.

Some of the bushy-bearded Carranza's advisors warned him that Mexico was vulnerable to counterattacks by the Yanquis since Texas was much closer and easier to reach than California. Von Eckhardt had soothed Carranza. The Americans would be far more concerned about California. He said there was enmity between Texas and the rest of the United States. Once the American military was crushed in the Pacific, a peace treaty would be signed that would guaranty Mexican sovereignty over her reacquired territories.

And Venustiano Carranza would a hero to all of Mexico, indeed, all of Central and Latin America.

Meetings of the farmers, ranchers, and townspeople were often a bore. But this one had taken on an air of urgency. The two dead men discovered by Kirsten Biel hadn't been the only bodies discovered. Ten others had been found the same day and it was supposed that still more lay rotting somewhere out in the barren land.

The small settlement named Raleigh was located ten miles north of the Mexican border and proudly called itself a town. With feet firmly planted in two centuries, Raleigh had one gas station, two blacksmith shops, and a stable. It also had a city hall, a bank, a small hotel, a couple of stores, and two churches—one Lutheran and one Methodist. A Catholic church that catered mainly to those of Mexican descent was a couple of miles out of town, where the Lutherans and

Methodists said it belonged. A railroad line heading north originated in the town, and there was a loading platform, although it had been months since anyone had seen a train.

The name of Raleigh had been chosen by a real estate developer who thought he could get rich attracting Americans to the southern edge of California. The developer had gone broke, but Raleigh remained.

The telephone hadn't yet reached Raleigh, although there were a couple of ham radio operators. Interior plumbing was considered far more important than the telephone, and even that was in short supply.

Kirsten let her cousin drive the Model T. She could drive better than he, but she knew it would irk him if she insisted. This day she dressed more demurely in a long blue dress. Hemlines were coming up, but why shock the very conservative people of Raleigh? She did tell Leonard that she intended to speak her mind at the meeting if she thought it appropriate. Leonard laughed and wondered aloud just how on earth he could stop her. Ella stayed behind to mind the ranch. Functions like this didn't interest her, and she didn't think they should interest Kirsten. Kirsten thought she was afraid of them.

Roy Olson chaired the meeting. As the largest landowner in the area and the unofficial mayor of Raleigh, he felt it was his right and no one disagreed with him. A big man in his late forties, he stood and called for silence.

"Folks, I don't think anybody's gonna argue when I say we have a problem that's getting out of control. The Mexican civil war has spilled over the border and now involves us. We've sent letters and telegrams to the federal government in San Francisco and to Governor Stephens in Sacramento, but they all say they can do nothing about it. Therefore, it's up to us to do something ourselves before the Carranza forces start attacking us instead of just the refugees. I think it's only a matter of time before that happens."

There were nods of agreement. Opinion held that Carranza was a bloodthirsty dictator who'd stop at nothing. "What are you proposing?" he was asked.

"Armed patrols," Olson said.

Kirsten stood. "And what will they do, Roy? Will they fight Carranza's army or will they fight the refugees and send them back? And what if Carranza's Germans decide to help him out?"

Olson flushed. He was used to making pronouncements, not having discussions. "The purpose of the patrols would be to protect our property and our lives, and not to go about fighting anybody unless, of course, attacked. And I don't think there's any chance of the Germans coming across the border."

"How would you organize these patrols?" Kirsten persisted. She didn't like Olson. With his wealth came arrogance and, worse, he'd tried to make a pass at her at a town social a while ago. The man was single, so there was nothing wrong with him being interested, but he'd grabbed her bottom and squeezed and that offended her. Only her late husband had been permitted that privilege.

"Roy," Kirsten added, "the patrols would have to be large enough to deter anybody and numerous enough to cover all the ground in the area, and we don't have the numbers to do that. If we used all our people, we'd never be able to work our farms and ranches."

Olson grudgingly acknowledged the truth. "I only suggest that we do what we can. I also suggest that we turn our homes into places that can more easily be defended in case the Mexicans get nasty and start raiding. I also would like us to establish means of communication so we can assemble for the common defense. Oh yes, I suggest everyone be packed and prepared to run quickly if things get out of hand."

Fair enough, thought Kirsten. But how would there be instant communications without telephones or wireless radio? Even if they'd had phone lines, which they didn't, they could easily be cut. And how long could fortified homes hold out, or where would they run to? There were too many questions and not enough answers.

Further discussion went long into the night. Nothing concrete was resolved and a highly perturbed and frustrated Olson finally adjourned the meeting with the thought that they could convene in a week's time and hopefully have some alternate and workable suggestions for their mutual defense and safety.

Kirsten and Leonard drove home in silence. It was obvious that their peaceful existence could come unraveled at any time. Perhaps peace was only ever an illusion. Two of the older men at the meeting had fought in the American Civil War and looked distraught at the thought of violence catching up to them again.

She also wondered about Roy Olson. What had he expected them to do? A handful of armed adults could not begin to defend the area around Raleigh as well as their homes. He must have known that. Or did he have some kind of plan that would work to his own advantage? She thought it likely.

Kirsten looked up at the clear, starry sky in which

seemingly millions of lights twinkled and danced. Was it an illusion too?

Ike Eisenhower grinned as he handed Luke a sheet of paper. "Congratulations and very long overdue."

Now it was Luke's turn to grin. Not only had he been promoted to first lieutenant, but there was a letter of commendation from General March, endorsed by Connor and Liggett, regarding his last intelligence-gathering mission to Mexico. That was a surprise. He'd heard that Connor and Liggett had gotten chastised for his adventure. President Wilson was afraid that such intelligence-gathering efforts would offend the Mexicans and the Germans. He knew he'd been in the clear. After all, he'd just been following orders, but he'd thought the event would just be forgotten and filed away.

"Now that we have a new president," Ike said, "it looks like we can start doing the things we should have been doing five years ago. And by the way, Patton and I have both been promoted to major so you'll still have to be nice to us."

Martel understood. Not only had the other two men been promoted, but they now held field-grade ranks, which were at least a world away from a first lieutenant. The three of them could definitely be friendly, but never friends. At least not until Martel caught up, which was profoundly unlikely.

Ike continued. "Any idea what your next assignment will be? Are you getting any kind of command?"

"Nah, who'd want me?" Luke grinned. "I'm going to be attached to Colonel Nolan."

"Best place for you. You'll be right on top of what the Germans and Mexicans are up to."

Lieutenant Colonel Dennis Nolan, West Point '96, was Hunter Liggett's chief intelligence officer, and Luke considered working with him a plum assignment. He hoped it would allow him freedom to ferret out enemy intentions.

"And yourself?" Martel asked Ike.

"Plans, with Connor. Patton has managed himself a billet with the Seventh Cavalry outside of San Diego."

"I hope this doesn't mean an end to our seminars with General Connor," Martel said.

"I hope not, either," said Ike, "but it just might be that we'll all be very busy soon when that storm from the south blows in."

Robert Lansing wore two hats and neither of them fit very well. Along with being the newly sworn in President of the United States, he was still secretary of state and had to make a decision. In the absence of a true vice president, the person Lansing appointed to replace himself at State would now become next in line to the presidency; therefore, it behooved him to choose well on two accounts.

So who would be the next secretary of state, he pondered as he paced the Oval Office? He immediately ruled out his predecessor, William Jennings Bryan. The man had not done a good job during peacetime and seemed totally dedicated to peace at any cost. How would he behave when thrust into an unwanted war? Lansing did not want to find out. Even though he was only sixty, Bryan was old beyond his years.

Some had suggested Colonel Edward House, the shadowy éminence grise behind Wilson. The title of "colonel" was strictly honorary but he was skilled in foreign policy. Too skilled, Lansing thought. The man's ego was monumental and he'd be difficult to control.

Other major figures came to mind. Warren Harding of Onio, Wilson's opponent in the last election, was an obvious choice. Also obvious were his sexual peccadillos that had achieved Olympian levels and cost him the election. The genial Harding would try to screw every woman in every country he went to as secretary of state. Harding was out.

Harding's running mate in the recent election, Calvin Coolidge, might make an excellent president but he was too taciturn and shy to be an effective dealer with other countries. General Leonard Wood wanted the presidency, but he was truculent and belligerent, excellent qualities for a general, perhaps even for a president, but not for a secretary of state. Lansing decided he needed his experienced generals in military service at this time.

In his opinion, that left two choices. First was the former Republican candidate for president and former Chief Justice of the Supreme Court, Charles Evans Hughes. Hughes had run against Wilson in 1916. Even though Lansing had run on the Democratic ticket, he thought he could get a Republican of Hughes' stature approved by the senate.

Hughes had been a favorite for the most recent Republican nomination until the death of his beloved daughter in early 1920. She'd died of tuberculosis at the young age of twenty-eight, and Hughes had withdrawn from consideration as a candidate. His personal grief was too deep to permit him to campaign. But would he be able and willing to be secretary of state in this time of crises?

Lansing's second choice was current Chief Justice Edward Douglas White, the man who had performed so well in getting Vice President Marshall to step down. However, White was seventy-four, in ill health, and, even though he had once been a Democrat, that was decades ago. It would not be White.

What other choices did that leave? He did not like the idea of tapping someone from Congress or a professional diplomat. Congressmen all seemed to be planning for the next election, and diplomats, in his opinion, had a difficult time making hard choices. More important, the more powerful men in Congress had let it be known that they weren't much interested in what they perceived as a demotion.

He made his decision. It would be Charles Evans Hughes and damn the torpedoes. He would talk to the man and appeal to his patriotism. Now he could get on with the business at hand, preparing the defense of the United States against the likely German onslaught.

That is, if it could be defended.

The door to the Oval Office was closed. Only the participants, a small, select group, were inside. There were no secretaries or clerks present and no aides. Lansing wanted no notes taken for a posterity that might consider them fools. He instructed the staff that there should be no interruptions.

Even though Washington was a city of spilled secrets, not even rumors of the pending German incursion had leaked out. Everyone in the nation's capital was abuzz with talk about Wilson's death, Marshall's abdication, and the new and totally unexpected elevation to the presidency of Robert Lansing. As far as the nation was concerned there were no problems with Imperial Germany and the kaiser. Both Germany and even Mexico were far, far away.

Along with Secretary of War Newton Baker and General Payton March were Naval Secretary Josephus Daniels, and Admiral Robert Coontz, the chief of naval operations.

Lansing called the meeting to order. "I'll get directly to the point, gentlemen. How do we stop the Germans?"

Daniels looked at him sternly. "You presume they are coming. You have only the word of the British and we all know how they would love to drag us into the next conflict with Germany. And, unless my memory fails me, don't governments like to begin war during the spring or summer, not in the late fall?"

"Agreed," said Lansing. It was common knowledge that the British and the French were planning revenge against the kaiser and desperately wanted the United States as an ally.

"And it is that last shred of doubt that has stopped me from announcing it to the world," Lansing continued, "along with the fact that such an announcement would precipitate panic and possibly even violence. If we accuse the kaiser and nothing happens, we look like fools for crying wolf. But let us assume that Zimmerman's message is true, what can we do? What are our strengths?" He turned to Secretary Baker and then to General March, who shook his head sadly.

"First," March said, "Mr. Daniels' concern about campaigning in winter is misplaced. The fighting, if it comes, will take place in southern Texas and southern California. The weather will not be an issue. If anything, campaigning during the winter in southern California will be advantageous." Daniels nodded, understanding.

"As to the army, it is in terrible shape," March said. "We have a little more than fifty thousand men on active duty, which is down significantly since the crisis of 1914. Please recall that President Wilson said there would be no more wars; therefore, why have an army? We had a devil of a time fighting the Mexicans in 1916 when Pershing went in after Pancho Villa and his bandits and nothing has changed since then. About half the reserves called to fight in Mexico never even showed up.

"I will add that the fifty thousand we do have are scattered all about the country, the Philippines, Hawaii, and elsewhere. Also, the National Guard and reserves total fewer than a hundred thousand, and they are poorly trained and even more poorly armed."

Lansing nodded sadly. "And what will the Germans throw at us?"

March glanced at his figures. "Last estimate is fourteen divisions of infantry plus a number of regiments of cavalry, some armored car units and large numbers of artillery, and all will be under the overall command of Crown Prince Wilhelm. Of course, that doesn't count an equal number of Carranza's Mexican Army, which is just lusting to cross the border. Against them, General Liggett has three regiments in California. In Texas we have skeleton garrisons at Bliss and Sam Houston."

Baker injected. "We will begin immediately to strengthen Liggett's position by adding one regiment from Nevada and another from Oregon. They will go to California under the guise of maneuvers. Still, they will be but a drop in the bucket."

"Assuming the Germans do invade," Lansing persisted, "I anticipate large numbers of people volunteering; can they be of assistance?"

March shrugged. "We have almost a million '03 Springfield rifles and millions of rounds of ammunition stockpiled at the Springfield Armory in Massachusetts, which is nowhere near California or Texas, and getting them to the fronts will be another problem. Nor do we have the artillery or the machine guns, and what we do have is largely obsolescent. I propose that we send a hundred thousand of those rifles to California immediately, along with whatever ammunition is appropriate. Similarly, we should send another hundred thousand to a warehouse in Texas. As to machine guns and cannon, we must strip National Guard units in the east and send what weapons they have to the danger points."

"Do it," Lansing said. "And do it sooner than immediately."

March made a quick note. "Nor will the volunteers be trained, which means they will be slaughtered by the Germans, and perhaps even by the Mexicans. Yes, we will have numbers of men under arms, but to use them without a number of months proper training would be to court catastrophe. And dare I add that we won't have the officers and sergeants to lead them?"

There was a knock on the door. The newly transferred Mrs. Tuttle and two smiling and well-meaning secretaries entered with coffee, tea, and little cakes. They seemed oblivious to the seriousness of the meeting they'd interrupted and Lansing's astonished glare. So much for requesting no interruptions, he thought. For a moment he considered strangling her, but, as usual, he realized that she meant well. He looked out the doorway and saw a number of curious faces staring in.

The new president stepped to the doorway and grabbed a couple of Secret Service agents. He told them in no uncertain terms that no one else was to be allowed in and that office workers were to leave the adjacent area. He had no idea if people outside the office could hear their conversations and did not wish to find out.

He returned to his desk, the same one used by Teddy Roosevelt and built from a British warship of the past century. He managed a wan smile. "Shall we have tea and cakes while we discuss war?"

Navy Secretary Daniels made a rare small joke. "At least there's no alcohol involved." Josephus Daniels had raised a storm of controversy by banning alcoholic beverages from the Navy's ships.

Daniels continued. "I must add a piece of information that only now makes sense. About two months ago, a very large German naval squadron left Wilhelmshaven in Germany, and steamed to their base in Cam Ranh Bay, in Indo-Chinese waters recently acquired from France as war booty. Assuming that the German Army does attack, I believe this powerful fleet might just appear off the California coast to assist it. If the kaiser's army is to invade on a particular date, the German naval force could easily plan to arrive off our cities on that same date."

Lansing took a deep breath, "How large a fleet?"

"At least ten modern capital ships and a dozen or so cruisers and destroyers."

"And our forces are much weaker," said Admiral Coontz, "and not just in the Pacific."

A reluctant Coontz had been in charge of enforcing the peace economies mandated by Woodrow Wilson. A number of warships had been decommissioned and were awaiting sale as scrap, and several naval bases had been closed. March added that a number of coastal forts run by the Army's Coast Artillery Corps were in bad shape. These had been designed to protect major ports but were now mere skeletons. Part of the rationale for closing them was the fact that they were very vulnerable to attack by airplanes. Intelligence said that the Germans had a large but unknown number of fighters and bombers in Mexico, while the U.S. had perhaps a dozen obsolescent British warplanes in California.

Statistically, the United States had the third largest navy in the world, but Germany was far ahead of her in second place. Great Britain's Royal Navy was alone in first place, but a number of her ships were crewless and rusting in port as a result of peace treaty obligations.

"As of this moment," Coontz continued, "our entire battle force consists of seven modern battleships and eight older ones. However, only three modern capital ships are at Mare Island on the west coast: the *Nevada*, *Arizona*, and *Pennsylvania*, and only the *Arizona* is ready for sea. The other two only have skeleton crews and will be obvious targets of the German fleet. The three older ships, the *Kansas*, *Minnesota*, and *Michigan* are already at less than half strength and would be useless in a battle with modern ships should the Germans attack Mare Island. I propose moving them to our base in Puget Sound. The base is far into the narrow waters of the Sound which should protect them. Also, the Sound is jointly held by us and Great Britain, which might deter a German attack."

Lansing rubbed his eyes. "Then for God's sake get the *Arizona* out of harm's way immediately and get the others underway as quickly as possible along with anything else that can float. Yes, send them north to Puget Sound as soon as you can. I believe we can send ships out to sea without frightening anyone."

The president stood. Every muscle in his body was tensing and he needed to stretch. "Admiral Coontz, what about the Marine Corps?"

"Approximately fourteen thousand men are scattered all over the world. Some are guarding embassies, some are maintaining discipline on what ships are now active, and others are in a variety of posts. We could likely organize a couple of regiments out of troops currently stateside. I will direct General Lejeune to commence immediately."

"Jesus wept," Lansing said. "Is there any good news at all?"

"Yes," said Baker, smiling grimly, "these little cakes are really quite good."

German tourists and travelers were not unusual along the railroad lines that ran east from California. This group of six men had arrived in San Francisco by ship the week before and had arranged train passage to St. Louis and then on to Cincinnati. When asked, they assured the curious that they had families in those cities large German communities and were going to join them.

When asked why they hadn't landed in New York, they'd explained that they'd been working as civilians at the German naval base in China. Questions were few. Frankly, nobody much cared.

Klaus Wulfram was their leader and a captain in the Imperial German Army. He was an engineer. His specialty was blowing things up, and his hobby was mountain climbing. The others were good climbers and excellent demolitions men as well. After getting his group organized, they proceeded to make a number of purchases: Cold weather clothing, rifles and pistols, ammunition, dynamite and detonator caps, electric wiring, and plungers to set off the dynamite. They purchased these in small amounts and aroused no suspicions.

Away from the coast, they changed their story. Now they were mining engineers headed into the mountains to find leftover traces of gold and other minerals for investors out east. Again, nobody noticed or cared, because it wasn't at all unusual. People were always looking for unfound remnants of the Gold Rush of 1849, or perhaps even a new mother lode. Local Californians shrugged and smiled at the new treasure hunters, wished them luck, and privately thought they were insane.

One storeowner allowed that there had been a number of young German men coming into California recently. He'd been told that they were students researching the history of Spanish missions. Wulfram had smiled in what he hoped was an engaging manner. He said that California was such a lovely state and had such potential that there might soon be many more Germans entering the area. He did not add that they would be part of the German Army.

After adding horses and mules to their party, the Germans headed east. The weapons they carried excited no curiosity. After all, they were going into the rugged mountains where bad people and the shattered remnants of the Indian community still roamed and wouldn't hesitate to steal or even kill if they saw weakness.

The Sierra Nevada range was the first they saw. It was impressive but the Rockies beyond awed them with their immensity and their grandeur. Wulfram had seen and climbed the Alps and considered the Rockies to be even more impressive. He ached for the chance to climb these new challenges. The soldier in him recognized the obvious—given the right circumstances, the mountain ranges could be a virtually impregnable barrier to an army advancing from the east. It was his job to begin that process.

Wulfram found it tempting to dwell on the mountains' majesty, but he had his duty. Where others saw beauty, he saw trestles, bridges, and vulnerability. Only a half-dozen rail lines connected California with the rest of the United States and they all ran through the mountain passes that were already filling with snow. His task, and that of the other teams he knew to be searching the other passes, was to destroy those trestles and bridges and sever the connection between California and the rest of the United States.

Whatever they destroyed could be rebuilt but, with the weather turning bad, Wulfram knew that reconstruction would not even begin for a number of months. By that time it would be too late.

As Wulfram and his men headed east through the mountains, they blew up trestles and bridges with cold efficiency. The first was a small bridge that let them test their skills. The explosion was loud and the bridge crumpled and dropped into a creek, a total ruin, as Wulfram's men cheered. Better, they had used their limited supply of dynamite sparingly and skillfully. Wulfram was not a murderer, so he left a warning in plain sight that the bridge was out. As they continued their work, he continued to leave signs. He hoped the American engineers driving the trains would get the message. He also hoped no train would come from the east without first seeing that something was terribly wrong.

They trekked eastward, destroying bridges and cutting telegraph and telephone lines. The weather was getting steadily worse. Large wet flakes of snow covered the ground, and collected on their hats and coats. Walking was becoming difficult, and the horses were struggling through the deep slop. They were running out of time. Soon they would have to concern themselves with their own survival, and not about any rail lines.

Wulfram was a man with a sense of duty. He needed to make sure he'd done his part in isolating California from the rest of the United States. Before the inevitable happened and they had to give in to the weather, he hoped for a target that would really cripple this particular line through the mountains.

And there it was. He gazed in wonder at a cut made in the side of a mountain to accommodate the tracks and realized the potential for long-term destruction. Where a bridge could be rebuilt, a mountain could not. A new cut would have to be made, carved like this one into the living rock. Certainly not impossible, since the Americans had done it, but definitely an awesome project that would take a considerable amount of time and resources. If the cut was destroyed, it would be a long time before trains came through this section of the mountains.

He placed a good deal of his remaining supply of dynamite into holes drilled below the tracks and into the mountainside. They connected the wiring and retreated to the other side of the steep valley. This would be their last demolition. They would head east and out of the mountains, hopefully to warmer places. His men deserved a respite and so did he.

Wulfram pushed the plunger and a number of explosions erupted in a line along the cut. For a second, nothing seemed to happen; then the entire side of the mountain slide down into the valley. Two hundred yards of track and earth had simply disappeared into the valley below.

He and his men were congratulating themselves when they heard the whistle of a train coming from the east. They stared at each other in surprise and dismay. For safety's sake they were a couple of hundred yards away from the demolished cut and the intervening terrain was extremely rugged. There was no way they could get to the other side and warn the oncoming train.

The train's whistle sounded again and this time dramatically closer. Wulfram prayed that it was a freight train, which would lessen the number of innocent lives lost if the engineer couldn't stop.

It wasn't. As it rounded the last bend, he saw four passenger cars connected to the coal burning engine and coal car. He was close enough to see people looking out the windows and he swore they were staring at him, damning and accusing him as if they already knew their fate. At nearly the last instant, the engineer saw the danger and slammed on the brakes which let out an obscene screech.

The train shuddered and slowed, and the Germans held their breath, hoping it would stop in time. It almost did. But, slowly, horribly, it reached the break and fell with majestic slowness down into the valley, with the cars tumbling over and over like toys thrown by a demonic child. The sound of the cars crashing and disintegrating was covered by the roar of the of the engine's boiler exploding. Clouds of white steam and brown clouds of dust surged skyward. Moments later, flames began to flicker from the now silent wreckage.

Wulfram and his men ran down into the valley to rescue as many of the passengers as they could. What they found, however, was a valley strewn with wreckage and mangled corpses. Only a literal handful had survived, and two of those were small children. Wulfram wept as did several of his men.

He gave orders to tap into the telegraph lines and report the "accidental train wreck," but the lines to the West Coast had already been severed by his men. They sent the message eastward and got a response. Rescuers were on the way, but it would be a long while.

Wulfram made a decision. They would stay with the wreck and the badly injured survivors until rescuers came close enough, then they would head south and try to escape. He didn't think it would take the Americans very long at all to realize that this was all part of a plan, a pattern.

Wulfram recalled reading that war was hell. He looked at one of the children who stared vacantly at the sky as her life ebbed away. Hell was not the proper word.

★ CHAPTER 4 ★

CHARLEY AND FRED HAD WORKED TOGETHER AS customs agents for several years on the border between California and Mexico. Their customs station was slightly east of Tijuana and was lightly used. It was just too easy to bypass. Sometimes, not even the tourists coming back from wild forays into the sin centers of Mexico bothered to stop.

Still, this night had proven even quieter than others. It was as if a curtain had been drawn down, covering Mexico. Nothing unusual in that, they thought. The presence of German soldiers and the simmering fighting south of the border meant that nothing was normal anymore.

Regardless, Charley and Fred didn't mind the quiet. Although decent guys, they were nearing retirement and weren't too interested in working hard and generally spent the night reading magazines or playing checkers. Occasionally, one or both would walk outside of their small, kerosene-lamplit shack. Nor was it unknown for them to bring in a bucket of beer to make the night more congenial, as they had this time.

Charley nodded to his friend and stepped outside. As a matter of decency, he strode several yards away from the shack to relieve himself, which he did hugely and with a contented sigh.

He was buttoning up when the night sky was split by the insane chatter. Charley quickly recognized it from his days in the National Guard as machine-gun fire. He watched in horror as scores of bullets ripped through the thin wooden walls of the guard shack. What the hell was going on? he wondered. Had Villa's raiders moved to California? Jesus, and what about poor Fred? A widower, he had recently remarried and had a wife and two kids.

Another burst of gunfire hit the shack, sending splinters of wood flying into the starry sky. The kerosene lamp had tipped over and the wooden building was burning. Charley dropped to the ground and began to crawl towards where his friend was trapped and likely badly hurt.

The sound of horses' hooves froze him and, a moment later, a long column of horsemen came into view. He recognized them as German Uhlans from the pictures he'd seen. They trooped past the shack in a column of fours, trotting insolently past and into California.

"No," Charley yelled.

Fred had staggered out of the shack. His clothing was smoldering. He was heading with agonizing slowness towards the riders. Two of the Germans broke out of the column and looked down on Fred, who had raised a bloody arm in supplication.

Charley watched in horror as the two Uhlans ran their lances through Fred's body. They shook him off like a rag and left him lying by the road. Charley groaned. It didn't take a genius to realize that his friend and coworker was dead.

More cavalry trotted by, and they were soon followed by quickly marching infantry. Charley wiped tears from his eyes as he wondered what to do. The glow of the fire was protecting him from being seen by the Germans. He took a deep breath and decided he would move a mile or so farther east and then north. He had to find a working telephone or maybe a radio. Somebody must be told what was happening and somebody must know what to do.

The ringing of firebells had been the decided-upon method of warning all the ranchers and farmers, although everyone acknowledged the method's shortcomings. So what if the bells do ring, they'd argued, where the hell do we go? If smoke was visible or gunfire could be heard, the answer was easier, but there still had to be a place for everybody to gather, especially if a ranch was under attack. Showing up piecemeal was a recipe for disaster.

They decided on Kirsten's place since it was roughly in the middle of the Raleigh area. Kirsten reluctantly agreed. She thought it would be nice to know what the problem was and where they might be going before congregating, but she had to admit that it might be expecting too much.

She recalled reading something that the term "firebells in the night" might have been written by Thomas Jefferson and was something about a slave uprising. Of course, they didn't have slaves in California, although some of the landowners treated their Mexican and occasional Indian workers as little more than slaves, which was the landowners' loss. She'd found that people—and Mexicans and Indians were people—worked harder, smarter, and better if you treated them with respect and didn't destroy their pride.

The firebells rang at three in the morning. Kirsten jumped out of bed and looked out her window. Flickering lights glowed off in the distance and she thought she heard thunder. And all of it was coming from the south, the direction of Raleigh and Mexico.

More bells added to the distant din. She dressed quickly, this time in her functional jeans, got her rifle, and went outside to wait. She'd been wearing her late husband's pajamas, which had scandalized her cousins the first time she'd done it. Not only were they more comfortable than the traditional nightgown, but they reminded her of her husband. Sometimes, she felt she could still sense a hint of the smell of his body, and it then awakened longings.

Her cousin Ella had awakened and said she'd make coffee. Might as well do something, Kirsten thought. Too bad Leonard was spending the night in town. He'd said it was a card game with friends, but she thought it was because he'd had a fight with Ella and Leonard just wanted to get drunk. She didn't think he'd gone there to get laid. There were no hookers that she knew of and there were precious few women in town who weren't married or who might be interested in Leonard.

In a surprisingly short while, riders began showing up. All eyes were on the south. The thundering seemed to have stopped, but the flickering lights continued. Fire, was the consensus, and it was in Raleigh.

With about a dozen men gathered, Roy Olson took the lead and they headed out. They'd gone only a mile or two in the growing light when they saw a Model T racing towards them and being steered erratically. Leonard, Kirsten thought, and she was right. Her cousin braked the car sharply and nearly fell out.

"The town's being bombed," he managed to gasp. He could hardly stand. His eyes were wild and crazy.

Olson glared at him. "You're drunk. What the hell do you mean? Ain't no planes bombing anything."

Leonard returned the glare. "Damn right I'm drunk and maybe the bombing's coming from cannon and not planes, but Raleigh's being destroyed. Buildings are being blown up and people are being killed. That and I think I saw soldiers coming up from the border."

"Mexicans?" asked Olson, slightly abashed. Leonard was indeed drunk but who could deny that something terrible was happening to the town?

"You just wish," Leonard said. "Naw, I saw those lances and funny headgear silhouetted by the fire. They weren't greasers, they were Germans."

Martel stared at the information on the notes before him. Once was an incident. Twice could be a coincidence. But three times was a pattern and he was looking at a developing pattern. He walked to the base's telegraph station, made a few inquiries, and confirmed his suspicions. He picked up his notes and went to Colonel Nolan's office only to be told that the colonel was in conference with General Liggett. Might as well kill two birds with one stone, Luke thought.

An astonished civilian clerk tried to stop him, but Luke ignored him and knocked firmly on the general's closed door. He entered, closing the door behind him. Let the damn clerk wonder, he thought. He'd find out soon enough. Nolan and Liggett looked up at him in mild surprise.

"You have a good reason for this, I presume," Nolan said, not ungently.

"General, Colonel, I think it's beginning."

Liggett gestured him to sit. "Go on."

"Sir, there's a pattern developing. Telegraph and telephone lines are down between here and the east. Also, there are reports that railroad bridges are down on at least three of the tracks connecting us to the rest of the country. My bet is the rest will report they're out before the day is finished."

"Conclusion, Luke," ordered Nolan.

"Sir, I'm sadly confident that German saboteurs are striking as we talk and that they are isolating us from the rest of the United States by destroying the rail lines running eastward. They are also severing communications by cutting telegraph and phone lines. It's a logical immediate precursor to an actual invasion."

"Are you certain telegraph lines are down?" Liggett asked.

"Sir, before coming here I checked with our telegraph office and they said they can't get through to the east. Of course, they said it has happened before and could be the result of the weather, but, coupled with the rail problems, makes me believe the Germans are finally on the move."

They looked at the map of California that was pinned on the wall. Only six rail lines connected California to the east and two were so close together that they might as well be one. In the south, there was a line running from Yuma, Arizona, but it was so close to the border with Mexico that it would never be of use and would be quickly overrun if the Germans crossed the border.

Farther north, lines ran from Albuquerque and Salt Lake City to San Francisco, and other lines ran from Salt Lake City and Spokane and over to Portland and Seattle.

There was silence. Liggett finally spoke. "I agree, Lieutenant. It is now time to notify Governor Stephens that his state of California is in terrible jeopardy and that he should call out the Guard."

"General, will you be informing the naval stations and coastal batteries?" Luke asked.

Liggett chuckled bitterly. "It may be a little too late, Luke. What we were discussing before you barged in was reports that saboteurs have already struck at the Army's coastal batteries and done a marvelous job of destroying them. Quite a welcoming for Admiral Sims, I dare say."

Rear Admiral William S. Sims had arrived only the last week as the newly appointed commander of the United States Pacific Fleet, replacing Admiral Hugh Rodman. The sixty-two-year-old Sims was considered by many to be a genius for his part in developing an electronic range finder that had vastly improved the accuracy of American gunnery. Prior to its development, accuracy had been a joke in the Navy. Ninety-eight percent of shots fired in the Spanish-American War missed their targets entirely. It was even more humiliating when it was realized that the Spanish ships in the Battle of Manila Bay had been anchored. The electronic range finder had greatly resolved the issue. Some people were beginning to call the calculating device a "computer."

It was also rumored that Sims had angered his superiors for making disparaging comments about draconian cost cutting and the future of battleships, and had been sent away from Washington as a form of penance. It was also understood that this would be Sims' last posting before his retirement.

"Yes, I will do that as a matter of courtesy. Of course, Sims doesn't report to me nor I to him, so we'll see what good that does. But you are right again, Lieutenant, if the German Army is out, one can only wonder what the German Navy is up to."

The *USS Fox* was a very new destroyer, launched only a year earlier in 1919. At just under twelve hundred tons, she carried a crew of one hundred and twenty-two men. Swift, she could do thirty-five knots, and her main armament consisted of turretless four-inch guns on her main deck. The *Fox* was called a flush deck because of her clean, straight lines and, since she had four smokestacks, ships like her were also called four-pipers.

This morning she was doing nowhere near her top speed. Instead, she was scarcely crawling through the gentle swells off the California coast. The cold and clammy fog had her totally imprisoned and her captain was not going to risk a collision with anything larger than a seal. The waters north of San Francisco were just too busy with commercial traffic to take such a chance.

Fine by me, thought Ensign Josh Cornell as he squinted through his binoculars at a blank wall of fog.

He was standing at the very bow of the ship after getting the wild idea that being as far forward as possible would help him see better. It hadn't helped at all, and he was beginning to feel a little foolish.

Only a year out of Annapolis, Josh originally thought assignment as a junior officer to a destroyer was a setback to his career. Most of his classmates thought serving on a battleship was the fastest way to promotion, and he'd been teased when they'd learned that he was on his way to a lowly destroyer.

Cornell was rethinking his original thoughts. On a destroyer, an officer was expected to know a lot about everything instead of being a specialist, like a gunner, although firing the great guns had to be one of the most exciting things possible. He also liked the dramatic way the destroyer knifed through the seas. To him it evoked memories of reading about Viking longships.

To his astonishment, he hadn't gotten seasick, which the rest of the crew found surprising as the *Fox*'s other newcomers spent the first few days of the cruise puking their guts out and fouling the ocean. He was from Nebraska and hadn't even seen a large lake, much less an ocean, until enrolling at the Naval Academy. Even though he was slightly built, thin haired, and looked younger than twenty-three, the men had begun to accept him. He did his work without complaint and didn't pretend to know everything just because he'd gone to Annapolis. He asked questions and respected sailors who asked him about a variety of things.

Cornell was puzzled regarding the destroyer's current assignment. Something was stirring and either nobody knew what it was or nobody was talking.

The *Fox* was patrolling off San Francisco and their home base at Mare Island in the northern half of San Francisco Bay, and everyone wondered why. Since the battleship *Arizona* had almost flown out of the base the day before and the two remaining battlewagons, the *Nevada* and *Pennsylvania*, had left before dawn this morning, the rumors were rampant. Some had the U.S. in a war with Germany, which Josh thought was utterly implausible. The destroyer's skipper said they should be prepared for anything. Or maybe the whole thing was a damned surprise maneuver.

Suddenly, the lookout above screamed, "Ship, dead ahead!"

Cornell froze. He squinted as if he could will the fog to clear. He saw nothing. No, wait . . . There was a large and shapeless object in front of him and moving closer. It was another ship and it was dangerously close. Dear God, would they collide? On the bridge behind him, he could hear the captain calling for a sharp turn to port and for more speed from the engine room.

The stranger was only yards away. It was a massive vessel whose hull towered above the *Fox*. They would not collide, but it would be close and the giant stranger's powerful wake would rock them brutally. They could handle that and Cornell started breathing again.

As the stranger slid by, he saw massive turrets and guns. Jesus, it was a warship, a battleship, but which one? It had to be reinforcements from out east. As the *Fox* pulled away, guns from the battleship's secondary battery suddenly opened fire and shells ripped through the helpless and outgunned American destroyer.

"What the hell is going on?" he heard the captain yelling. "Get on the radio," he said before another shell struck the bridge, silencing him and sending mutilated bodies flying about like toys.

The *Fox* staggered like a losing prizefighter. Debris rained down on Josh. He ran back to the ruins of the bridge. Shattered bodies and limbs were everywhere and blood ran in torrents on to the deck and into the ocean. Josh knew they should be fighting back, but with what? Her four-inch guns were popguns against a battleship, and, besides, none of the crew was at their battle stations. Finally, a machine gun on the *Fox* opened fire, impotently strafing the armored hull of the battleship.

More shells struck the *Fox* and she exploded with a deafening roar. Josh found himself flying through the air like a bird. He hit the water and it knocked the wind out of him. The cold Pacific grabbed him with icy claws. Something was wrong with his left leg. Pain was shooting up from it. He gasped and tried to breathe.

Instinctively, he tried to swim. A piece of debris floated by and he grabbed on to it. A handful of other crewmen were doing the same thing. A very small handful, he realized sadly as someone grabbed him and steadied him.

Finally, the fog cleared a little and he could see a line of gigantic battleships heading for what he presumed was the Golden Gate and the base at Mare Island. He caught sight of a flag. They were German. Since when were we at war with Germany? he wondered as he fought off the pain from his leg. He caught the name of one of the ships, the *Bayern*. According to the latest *Jane*'s she was one of Germany's newest and mightiest battleships and carried fifteen-inch guns. What the hell was she doing here?

And if she was headed for San Francisco Bay and Mare Island, there was nothing he could do about it. His first and only priority was to survive. His leg was killing him and he'd swallowed salt water which was making him vomit, and he was rapidly freezing. Still, he was an officer had to lead, had to live.

He called and gathered about him the half-dozen men floating in the water. They connected their pieces of debris into something resembling a raft and climbed on. The ocean swells kept washing over them but at least they weren't in danger of drowning if they didn't fall off and if the sea remained fairly calm.

Finally the sun came out, warming them slightly, and they could see to the horizon. Josh could see nothing to the east. The coast was too far distant and the German ships had disappeared. They were far out to sea. He wondered how long they'd have to float. They had no food or water and he'd already begun shaking from shock and the cold. One of the men was praying for a miracle. Josh joined him.

It came. After a couple of hours, a fishing boat sighted the *Fox*'s survivors and hauled them on board, where they lay gasping and shaking. The crew had them strip, dried them, and gave them blankets and hot soup. They gave the injured Navy men first aid and put a splint on Josh's leg. Of course the boat had no radio. Josh knew that would have been too much to ask for.

Hours later, as they approached the Golden Gate, they saw smoke arising from the old coastal batteries at Fort Point, along the shoreline by the Presidio complex, and well to the northeast where Mare Island was situated.

A motorized Navy launch filled with men armed with rifles and submachine guns intercepted them as they turned and headed north to the Mare Island base. Josh lurched to his feet and to the boat's rail. He recognized a petty officer named Mahoney.

"What happened, Mahoney?"

Mahoney blinked and then recognized Josh. "The fucking Germans paid us a surprise visit, sir. I guess that was why those three big ships of ours had left. Three older battleships were anchored in the bay and they were sunk or badly damaged, and then the damned Germans shot up the facilities," shouted Mahoney. "Came right through the Golden Gate like they were invited to dinner. They pounded our coastal forts which didn't fire back very much at all. Scuttlebutt says they were either abandoned or sabotaged or, hell, both."

"Jesus," said Josh.

"And then they opened fire on our ships when they came in range. Thank God they didn't land any men. They might still be here if they had. Now what happened to you, sir?"

Josh explained that his ship had been ambushed by the Germans and that almost the entire crew was dead. Mahoney said that the medical facilities at Mare Island and the city of Vallejo were swamped. He suggested the fishing boat try a civilian hospital in the city and Josh concurred. So did the skipper of the fishing boat who wanted them off his vessel as soon as possible. If war had begun, he wanted no part of it. Josh didn't blame him one bit.

Many of Kirsten's neighbors left the group, understandably fearful about their own properties. Kirsten shared that feeling, but she felt a desperate need to find out what was actually going on. Surprisingly to her, Olson was one of those who left them. So much for leadership, she thought.

Thus, only four of them approached the town of Raleigh. So far they hadn't seen any German soldiers, although they had noticed planes in the air. Kirsten suggested they dismount and spread out so as to not attract attention and the men agreed, looking nervously skyward. German planes carried machine guns.

Finally, they reached the summit of a gentle hill and looked towards the town. Black smoke was billowing from a number of buildings and several others had been smashed flat. It looked like half the town was gone. Many men were moving around in the ruins. Kirsten and the others all had binoculars and there was no question. They were looking at several hundred German soldiers in the little town of Raleigh, California.

"Would somebody explain this to me?" one of the men asked.

Nobody had an answer. Their presence above the town was useless, and they decided to leave. Now it was indeed time to return to their homes, pack up, and go. However, they soon sighted German patrols between them and their destinations and it was several hours before Kirsten decided the coast was clear enough to try to reach her ranch.

As she neared her home, she thought she saw wisps of gray smoke coming from its stone walls. She fought the urge to gallop and, instead, dismounted and approached her home with the same caution she'd used to examine Raleigh.

Her home was gone. The main house and the barn had been gutted. The walls were standing but that was it. There were bodies on the ground and there was no sign of life. Or Germans, for that matter. Whoever had attacked her home had moved on.

She carried her rifle in the crook of her arm and led her horse. She walked carefully into the compound that had been her home. The first body was Leonard's. Her cousin had been shot and his body hacked at with what she assumed were sabers. His own broken rifle lay beside him, so maybe he had gotten one of the invaders. She hoped so.

Two more bodies were those of men who worked on the ranch. She would have a lot of burying to do, she realized grimly.

"Over here." It was a woman's voice and Kirsten turned in the direction it came from. Her cook, Maria, was waving to her from a shed that hadn't been destroyed. She ran over and embraced Maria. They both cried at the simple pleasure of being alive and having found each other. Maria was older, in her forties, and had come with Kirsten from Texas.

Maria looked away. "Your other cousin, Ella, is in there," she said, pointing at the shed.

Kirsten entered. She heard animal gruntings and sobs that took her a moment to realize came from a huddled figure in the corner. It was Ella and she was wrapped in a blanket. Kirsten pulled the blanket aside. Ella was naked and her body was a mass of bruises.

Maria entered and hugged Ella, rocking her telling her everything was all right. Ella screamed and pushed her away. Finally, Ella calmed a little and Maria stood up.

"The Germans came, maybe a dozen of them and all on horseback. Leonard tried to stop them so they killed him. He managed to wound one of them and that made them very angry, so angry that they shot the other men after they finished killing Leonard. Me they left alone. I guess I was too old and fat for them. Ella, they didn't. They stripped her naked in the yard so all the men could see her and laugh at her, and then took her inside and tied her to her own bed and raped her. That was where I found her, all covered in blood and shit."

Kirsten was sickened. "All of them?"

"Probably not. Maybe only six of them. After a short while they came out. They had a young officer who was the first to rape her and he ordered the men back on their horses and to continue the patrol. The officer told me to get Ella out of the house because they were going to burn it."

Maria looked down at the ground. "I did as I was told. Ella has been like this since then. I've seen other women like this in Mexico after they were gang-raped. Sometimes they change and get better. Sometimes they don't."

Kirsten felt guilty. Leonard was dead and Ella had been ravished and here she was, unharmed. Ella's mind was full of shame and pain and fear. Ella was a fragile person and had always led a protected, sheltered life, even on the ranch. Maria was right. Ella might not ever get over the shock.

If Kirsten hadn't gone to Raleigh to see what was going on, she would have been home when the Germans had attacked. Would she have made a difference or would she have been just one more rape victim?

She knew the answer. She would have suffered like Ella had.

Two more of her hired hands showed up. They'd been away in the fields and had prudently kept it that way. Kirsten had them help her search through the charred rubble for anything useful. Only the interior of the buildings had burned since the walls were made of adobe and stone.

They were not going to stay at the ranch. No, she decided they would take to the hills and make camp. At least she and Ella and Maria would. The two hands could come along if they wished. She wouldn't blame them at all if they ran for safety. If they got to the hills, they could rest and figure out what to do.

And what would that be, she wondered despairingly? Her world was destroyed. All tangible memories of Richard, like the pajamas she'd worn, were gone in the fire. Could she start over? Would the Germans and Mexicans allow her to start over? In the meantime they would go for the hills.

Major George Patton led his tiny command, a score of Americans from the 7th Cavalry, right at the unsuspecting German force. It was a brave but futile effort. There were close to two hundred German cavalry including dozens with those intimidating medieval lances. At a hundred yards, Patton ordered his men to stop, pull out their rifles, and fire several shots in the Germans' direction. He thought they'd hit a few, but couldn't be certain.

With a whoop, the Americans turned and raced away. Looking over his shoulder, Patton saw the infuriated German cavalry thundering towards him.

Bugles sounded and still more Germans joined the attack. He had half a mile to the crossroads and his lightly encumbered men easily kept their lead, even increasing it. The Germans opened fire but their shots went wild. *This is wonderful,* Patton thought jubilantly.

They passed the crossroads and continued on with the Germans in hot but ragged pursuit. When the Germans were within two hundred yards of the road, the remainder of Patton's force from the 7th Cavalry, three hundred strong, opened fire from their concealed positions.

The Germans panicked. Men and horses fell, tumbling over each other and creating ghastly mixed piles of human and horse flesh. *God damn,* Patton exulted. Didn't the Germans give a stinking crap about the possibility of an ambush, or were they so confident and arrogant they didn't care? He only wished he had a larger force, then he'd really kick some German ass. Too damn bad that the 7th Cavalry was scattered all over the place, same as all the other American units.

The Germans were withdrawing in great haste. Patton and his men mounted up and moved out cautiously. "We gonna chase them, Major?" asked a young private, his face flushed with excitement.

Patton laughed. The boy was a fighter. Good. The Army needed fighters. Too many men had gotten soft thanks to undemanding garrison duty. "Not this time. They're headed to their main force and ain't no way we can take them all on. Maybe next time."

They counted the German casualties. Thirty-one dead and another sixteen wounded had been left behind. Two Americans had been slightly wounded. Not a bad day's work, Patton thought.

A shriek from above shocked them. A German biplane was diving on them, its machine guns firing at all the foolish Americans the pilot had caught out in the open.

Now it was the turn of Patton and the rest of the Americans to panic. Bullets tore through flesh. Men and horses screamed in pain and fear. They scattered, instinctively trying to give the German pilot little to shoot at. They scattered like three hundred rabbits running in every direction. Patton drew his new 1911 Colt Automatic and fired at the plane. The .45 caliber pistol kicked like a mule but Patton's fury overcame it. He hit nothing.

The German made pass after pass, shredding Patton's command. Finally, the German flew away. Out of ammunition or low on fuel, or maybe just bored and out of targets. Patton didn't care, just so long as it left. For whatever it was worth, he'd identified it as a Fokker VII, normally a high-altitude fighter.

Patton was lucky to be alive, shaken but alive. Planes like the German fighter usually did not fly alone, but this one had. Had there been others, the American force would all now be dead. He gathered his men. He'd suffered twenty-four dead and forty seriously enough wounded to be out of action. One of the dead was the boy who wanted to chase the Germans. *What a fucking waste,* he thought. *The boy was a fighter, damn it.*

Ironically, three captured German wounded had been killed by their own plane. *Tough shit,* Patton thought angrily. At least he still had some prisoners to be grilled. He doubted they could do anything but tell the obvious—Germany had invaded California.

Patton's victory was now ashes. General Connor had ordered him to avoid fighting and only gather intelligence. Connor was going to rip his ass and, deep down, Patton knew he deserved it.

Count Johan von Bernsdorff had been Imperial Germany's ambassador to the United States for a number of years. Ordinarily, he was a genial man who seemed to attract attention and didn't care whether or not he scandalized what he considered the sometimes puritanical people of the United States. He was frequently found in the company of women of ill repute and even more frequently overindulged in alcohol. Photos of him with prostitutes had even appeared in newspapers. When the 1914 war had broken out, the British had sought to discredit him by publicizing his personal life, but Bernsdorff had confounded them all. He simply didn't care and neither did his masters in Berlin.

He was ushered into the Oval Office where the new President of the United States awaited him. He sighed. He'd dealt with Robert Lansing on matters of state in the past and this was not going to be a pleasant meeting.

Lansing directed him to a chair. It wasn't very comfortable. Bernsdorff was mildly surprised that they were alone. There was not even anyone to take notes. Interesting, he thought. Conversations between two people can always be denied, however frank and candid they might be. Well, he could play that game as well.

Lansing began. "Let me be blunt, Count. Before your despicable and dastardly attack on our helpless ships in San Francisco, I was willing to negotiate and publish a fiction that the invasion of California was nothing more than a misguided raid against Mexican rebels. However, your attack on our ships makes it abundantly clear that Germany wants war. Tell me, sir, is all-out war with the United States what Germany desires?"

Bernsdorff felt himself starting to perspire. A shame he had drunk so much champagne the night before, but he didn't think he'd be permitted to stay in the United States very much longer and wished to enjoy what time was left. One particular prostitute had been particularly creative. A shame he would never see her again.

He took a deep breath. It was time to enlighten President Lansing as to how the world now worked. "With regrets, President Lansing, immediate peace will not occur until you make it happen by acquiescing to our needs. Our goals and those of our ally, Mexico, are far more extensive than simple raids."

Lansing shoved a piece of paper across his desk. Bernsdorff took it and read it quickly. Lansing glared at him. "Then this, Count, is correct? Assuming it is, your foreign minister, Zimmerman, has countenanced the invasion of my country and the severing of California, Arizona, New Mexico, and Texas from the United States."

Bernsdorff didn't bother to look at it. "It is entirely correct. However, it is up to you whether or not you wish to minimize the damage to the rest of your country. To use your words, you are the one with the power to contain the potential tragedy, not Imperial Germany."

Lansing was taken aback. "What do you mean?"

"Simply put, sir, Germany is the mightiest nation in the world, stronger than any alliance that can be put against her. Take a look at a world map and what do you see? As a result of the 1914 war and the subsequent treaty brokered by your pathetic predecessor, Woodrow Wilson, the nations of Belgium, Holland, and Luxembourg are now essentially part of the Second Reich, and Germany now controls the channel ports of Cherbourg and Dunkirk. France has been required to discharge the bulk of her army and decommission most of her navy. Without France as an ally, England is helpless to impose her will on anyone. France is a helpless shell and England is impotent on land. Germany now has bases in Mexico, and in what used to be Indo-China. And Ireland, of course, is allied with us since we forced England to grant her full independence.

"Because it serves our interests, we permit Denmark, Switzerland, the Scandinavian countries and a handful of others to pretend they are neutral and independent. Our allies also include the inept but gigantic Austro-Hungarian Empire, the sick but cruel Ottomans, and the chaotic and farcical creation called Italy. Germany and Austria are propping up the Romanovs against revolutionary threats, which means that Russia is now beholden to Germany as well. Your United States is the only remaining power that could possibly pose a threat to future German ambitions and you are now being cut down to size. The kaiser is getting older and wishes to pass on to his son and to the people of Germany an empire like none the world has ever seen. I would suggest you face reality, Mr. President.

Pax Germanica is the order of the day, and your nation will never be more than a second-rate power."

As Lansing recoiled from Bernsdorff's words, the German smiled tightly and leaned forward. "Now it is my turn to be even more blunt. In conjunction with Mexican forces, we are seeing to it that property stolen from Mexico is returned to her. That stolen property is, of course, what you refer to as the states of Texas, Arizona, and New Mexico, which the United States ripped from Mexico about sixty years ago. California will become part of Germany. If you allow this absolutely just action by us and Mexico to occur, the remainder of the United States will be left alone. If you resist, your nation will incur the full wrath of the Kaiser's Reich."

"Your kaiser is insane."

Bernsdorff laughed. "Quite possibly, but, as you say, crazy like a fox. The kaiser is totally unlike your saintly and naive fool President Wilson. By the by, don't even think of a formal declaration of war. If you do that, the remainder of the German High Seas Fleet will leave German waters and commence the destruction of America's east coast ports, after, of course, destroying your small navy. Following that, the mighty German Army will invade your east coast at points of its choosing and crush what remains of the United States. The result will be a peace that deprives you of far more than the four states now involved. Sign a peace and you will be able to retain northern California, Oregon, Washington, and the territory of Alaska. Don't and you will lose them as well, along with God knows what else along the east coast. Perhaps we'll take Florida and New Orleans."

Lansing's face was turning red. "Bernsdorff, have you forgotten the extent to which the United States mobilized in previous wars, such as our Civil War? This is now a nation of more than a hundred million people and they will not stand to have four states taken from her."

Bernsdorff laughed. "Your people will accept reality. France has had to deal with the loss of Alsace and Lorraine and parts of the Normandy coast, and has survived, although as a bloody mess. Denmark lost Schleswig and Holstein in the last century, and other nations have lost territories as well. Such fluctuations and corrections are the way of the world. Borders are fluid and sophisticated nations, not childlike ones like yours, understand that reality. After all, didn't you enhance your borders at the expense of Mexico? You are not being asked to like it, merely accept it as reality and move on.

"And as to your population of more than a hundred million, don't forget that many of them are ethnic Germans who will not support you in a war against us and will likely rise up against you in a second civil war that will totally involve and overwhelm your disreputable little army. You will have a bloodbath within your borders as you try to defend against us. And as to the rest of your population, many of them are immigrants who don't speak English and can't even spell America. Did you know, sir, that fully three quarters of the population of New York City is foreign born? No, we are not afraid of your numbers. They are an illusion."

"Get out of here."

Bernsdorff blinked. "Sir?"

Lansing stood. His face was red with fury. "Get the hell out of here! You attacked innocent people without provocation or warning. Dastardly! You people are cowardly barbarians."

Bernsdorff stood and walked towards the door of the Oval Office. His dismissal was nothing more than what he expected. He had a message to deliver and had done it. Now he would have to leave a country he rather enjoyed and return to a rather sterile Berlin. A shame, he thought. He would really like to remain and see just what the Americans would do and how they would do it.

He turned. "I will prepare a more diplomatic memorandum than what just transpired between us in privacy. Perhaps it will provide you with some political shelter."

Lansing laughed harshly. He was breathing hard and his pulse was racing with anger. "Don't bother. Thanks to Thomas Edison's marvelous phonograph, all of what you said was recorded. Copies will be made and sent about the country while transcripts are provided to national and international news services. Your perfidy will be totally public."

Bernsdorff was shocked. "That is not gentlemanly, sir. Our conversation was between the two of us."

Lansing stood and wanted to punch the man. "Is a surprise and sneak invasion of another nation a German's definition of gentlemanly? Once again, get the hell out of my office before I have you thrown out."

"Since you have chosen this route, President Lansing, a word of warning to the people of California. We will deal fairly and honorably with military prisoners of war, but not with civilians who oppose us. Such *Franc-tireurs* are nothing but terrorists and will be executed summarily as we did in Belgium and elsewhere. Good day, sir."

★ ★ ★

Martel crawled over the crest of the hill over to where Major George Patton lay peering through binoculars.

"Don't stand at attention and don't even think of saluting," Patton muttered.

"Glad to see you too, Major."

"Drop it," Patton said, referring to rank. It was just the two of them. "How'd you get down here so quickly?"

"Another plane. I'm almost getting used to them. The pilot was some lunatic teenager named Lindbergh and I'll swear he stayed at three feet above the ground to avoid German planes."

The sound of machine-gun fire interrupted them. They both looked through their binoculars.

"Okay, George, what do you see down there?"

Patton chuckled, "Germans, Germans, and still more Germans. They are moving ever so slowly on San Diego, which they should have taken ten minutes after crossing the border. Hell, it's only sixteen miles from Mexico."

An artillery shell screamed in and landed a hundred yards in front of them. Martel winced and Patton laughed. "You afraid, Hammer?"

"Hell, yes." Patton liked to show off his knowledge of military history by occasionally calling Luke "Hammer." Charles—"the Hammer"—Martel had defeated the Moslems at Tours in the eighth century in an epic battle that had stopped the Moslem advance into Europe and possibly changed the course of history. To the best of Luke's knowledge, he was not descended from the early medieval French warrior, but that didn't stop Patton from teasing him.

Luke peered through his own binoculars. He saw

infantry and lots of it, but no cavalry, and they were all moving very slowly and carefully. He noted the presence of several armored trucks. He thought they would be far more dangerous than cavalry in a modern war. He wondered if Patton agreed with that. Patton was a horse man.

"I can't believe they're moving so slowly," Patton said.

"I can and it's all your fault."

"What?"

"One of the prisoners you took was a staff major and needed morphine to dull the pain of his wounds. Of course, I wouldn't give him any until he talked at length and then I gave him some more and he talked at even greater length."

Patton laughed, "Luke, you are a class-A shit. I am so proud of you."

Luke grinned. "Thanks, George. At any rate, he said his division had been told to expect light resistance, but to be careful not to leave their flanks hanging. Apparently, they actually understand how close their win at the Marne in 1914 truly was and don't want to make the same nearly fatal mistake again. They are more than willing to sacrifice speed to maintain the integrity of their formations. Also, it was understood it would take time to get their army across the rugged and constrained border between California and Mexico and in position to fight. Thus, they were directed to move slowly on the defenses of San Diego."

Patton snorted, "Defenses of San Diego? What defenses of San Diego are they talking about? The place is absolutely wide open."

"George, according to their thinking it is inconceivable that a major port like San Diego wouldn't be protected by major fortifications. The Kraut major said they were to move forward and locate them. He said his senior officers would be stunned when they found out about your attack on their formation since they assumed us stupid Americans would wait in our forts to be attacked and then pulverized. He said your attack proved two things: One, that there is a major American presence in the area, and, two, San Diego would be well defended. Congratulations, George, if the major is correct, you've just bought us some time."

"Jesus."

"Oh yes. Did your men actually shoot at that German pilot?"

"Hell, yes. Every swinging dick in my command shot at the son of a bitch. And who knows, maybe we even hit him."

"And what do you think he reported?"

Patton grinned wickedly. "He's a pilot and all pilots lie like rugs, even the crazy ones and they're all crazy. He probably said he'd spotted a major American force moving on German positions, and that he bravely attacked it through a hail of bullets and barely escaped with his life." He laughed. "Hell, I'm even smarter than I thought I was."

Luke rolled his eyes. "Christ, George."

Another shell crashed into the ground in front of them, close enough for them to feel the vibrations. They didn't think the Germans were shooting at them. Instead, they were firing at places where they thought American units might be hiding. It was time to leave.

★ CHAPTER 5 ★

ELISE THOMPSON FELT SHE HAD THE BEST OF BOTH worlds. At nineteen, she was two years out of high school and now a trusted assistant to famed movie producer D.W. Griffith. David Wark Griffith was a Kentuckian who was raised to be a loyal son of the lost Confederacy. Thus, he would never have hired Elise had he known she'd been born in Chicago and moved to Los Angeles when she was twelve. He hated Northerners.

Griffith had made several major motion pictures, including *Intolerance* and *Birth of a Nation*. Now he was part of a new company, United Artists, and the future looked good for United Artists and the movie industry, much of which, in the last decade, had moved to the Hollywood section of Los Angeles.

Griffith's latest epic, and one he hoped would help him recoup that portion of his reputation lost when *Intolerance* turned out to be an expensive bust, was titled *Victory at the Marne.* It was going to be

Griffith's salute to the German victory that had changed the world. To him, the Germans were white people, while the French, along with being incompetent and dirty, also were racial mongrels. He felt it was shame that the Brits had gotten caught up with such Gallic rabble, but such is life.

The fifty-five-year-old Griffith's logic said the world was a better place because of the German victory. Germany and the United States, which to him meant the Union, were natural rivals and he hoped to portray the Germans as the potential saviors of white civilization. Some had condemned *Birth of a Nation* as racist and he rejected those criticisms. The movie told the truth as he understood it and had been brought up to believe.

To portray the 1914 battle of the Marne with the realism he demanded, trenches had been dug and impressive fortifications built on land fifty miles south and east of Los Angeles. Hundreds of extras wearing German, French, and British uniforms milled around waiting for the climactic battle scenes that were about to be filmed. Dummy cannon and machine guns were everywhere. Elise still wondered just how anyone could believe southern California resembled the interior of France. However, most people were like her and had never seen the interior of France and had nothing with which to compare.

Griffith had heard rumors of fighting between German and American soldiers along the Mexican border, but decided it didn't concern him at all. Just a border incident, he thought. Whatever was going on was more than a hundred miles away and none of his business.

Elise was exhausted and happy. One other reason

she'd gotten a job with Griffith was the fact that she wasn't an aspiring actress using the clerical job to suck up to him, sometimes literally. She hated the young women who'd spread their legs or open their heavily lipsticked mouths to get a part in a movie. Thank God for real actresses like Mary Pickford and the Gish sisters who didn't need to do those things. Elise considered herself a good girl, but was not a prude and knew full well where babies came from and what made men happy. She understood it sometimes made women happy, too, but hadn't yet tried to find out, at least not all that much.

Elise worked hard to not appear pretty. She was short, thin, and not well endowed, which made it fairly easy. Her parents said she was beautiful and she loved them for it, but she knew they were biased. She'd succeeded with Griffith through her intelligence and hard work.

Griffith stood, a megaphone in his hand. "What the devil are those?"

Half a dozen large planes were flying towards them in a rough V-formation, and a score of smaller ones seemed to be escorting the larger ones. Griffith smiled. He knew a golden opportunity when he saw one.

"Get cameras on those magnificent things." He said and turned to Elise. "Maybe we can use the footage sometime, and, heck, it's all free."

The planes flew closer, then they were over the movie-set trenches. Bombs fell and explosions rocked the large movie set, knocking people down and showering them with dirt and debris. Griffith's jaw dropped as everyone panicked, running in all directions. The smaller planes swooped down and machine guns ripped into the uniformed extras who screamed and fell by the score.

When the cameraman started to bolt, Griffith yelled at him to keep his camera rolling. The man complied for a second and then ran, hurling an obscenity at Griffith. Elise took hold of the camera and aimed it in the general direction of the carnage and began to crank away.

The bombers departed, their deadly gifts given, but the escorts returned for another and equally murderous strafing run. After what seemed an eternity, they too flew away, leaving an unnatural silence that was quickly filled with screams.

Griffith looked at Elise. She had not stopped cranking the camera, although her face was pale with shock and her actions an automatic response.

Griffith grabbed the camera from her. "Get in the car."

Elise shook herself. The carnage around her was overwhelming. "We have to help these people."

"Are you a doctor?"

"No, but I do know some first aid. I can help."

He grabbed her and pushed her into the back seat. "I need you and the film you took more then those people need you putting a bandage on them. Look, they're already being taken care of."

Still numb from the horror, Elise agreed. Incredibly enough, there were far more survivors than casualties, and every injured person seemed to have at least one or two persons performing first aid on them.

Griffith dumped the camera and its precious film in the trunk and jumped in the front seat with his driver. "We are going back to Hollywood as fast as we can to get that film developed. Then we're going to run up to either San Francisco or Sacramento and see what the government thinks of this."

Only a couple of days after the invasion, Kirsten became the *de facto* leader of a small but growing group of friends, relatives, and neighbors. Several other ranchers, remembering the decision to gather at her place, had shown up with their families and there was now a small tent village in the hills near Raleigh.

The Germans had swept through the area, taking whatever they wanted. It wasn't quite looting, since they were generally disciplined enough to take only those things they needed, and high on the list was food. They'd herded away all her cattle, at least all they could find, and emptied storage sites. They'd even left receipts which would doubtless prove worthless.

The disciplined behavior of most of the Germans contrasted sharply with the ones who had burned her home and raped her cousin. The difference was simple: do not resist and you will be left alone. Resist and you will suffer terribly.

Kirsten had come to the realization that the others in her group, both men and women, were looking to her for leadership. Was it because they were on her property, or was it some other reason?

Still, the leadership role was collaborative. They discussed matters well into the night and came to collective decisions. First, they would do nothing to antagonize the Germans. That lesson had been learned. Second, they would gather enough food to keep everyone fed and try not to attract attention. There were seven men, five women, and six children to care for.

Several said they would head north as soon as they felt the situation was safe enough. Of course, nobody had any idea just when that might be.

From a position on a hill, Kirsten could make out long lines of soldiers, infantry this time, snaking north and west. Their obvious target was San Diego. San Diego was the largest city in this area of Southern California and possessed a pretty good harbor that would be useful to the Germans if they planned to stay. And it looked very much like they planned on sticking around.

She and several others were angry enough to want to strike back, but how? They wouldn't stand a chance taking on German regulars, so what were they to do?

First, they had to get the children and the women who wanted to leave to a place of safety. Then the remainder had to realize that the only place they could strike back at the Germans was their supplies. But what would the Germans do if she or anyone in her group tried to destroy supplies or damage roads? In 1914, the papers reported that the Germans had behaved hideously in Belgium and northern France. They'd blown up cities, executed hostages or shipped men off to work camps in reprisal for guerilla attacks, and in some cases, for no good reason at all. They papers had implied mass rapes and even the killing of babies by impaling them on bayonets, and Kirsten now believed it was possible. Would they do the same to Americans? Of course they would. Ella still hadn't moved or said anything. Maria had managed to get clothes on her, and food and water in her, but her eyes were still blank. She remained in her own dark world.

A deep growling sound alerted her to the fact that several German airplanes were above her. She felt naked and helpless. Where were the American planes? She remained still. Even if the enemy pilots were looking, they were unlikely to notice her if she remained motionless. She'd hunted often enough to know that movement attracted attention and, if she stayed unmoving, she could hide in plain sight.

The planes passed from view, but the columns of German soldiers continued. How many of them were there, she wondered?

And where the hell were our American soldiers?

The film flickered on the sheet that served as a movie screen. Much of it was of poor quality but all of it was utterly horrible in its content. It showed German planes dropping their deadly load on hundreds of movie extras. It showed the victims being blown to pieces and later being strafed by escorting fighters.

The viewing only took a few minutes, but it seemed like an eternity. Ensign Josh Cornell leaned on his crutches and wished he'd asked for permission to sit down. Admiral Sims would have permitted it quickly, but the man had to be asked. He had so much on his plate, it was ridiculous to think he'd recall that his newest and very junior aide had just survived the sinking of his ship, and been pulled from the ocean with an injured leg, along with multiple cuts and bruises. He looked as if he'd gone fifteen rounds with Jack Dempsey and lost every one of them.

Fortunately, the leg wasn't broken. His knee had been dislocated and the doctors said he'd be just fine in a couple of weeks or maybe a couple of months. In the meantime, sea duty was out of the question and Josh had been tapped to serve on the newly arrived

Sims' staff for the simple reason that there wasn't any other place for him.

The admiral was receiving praise for saving the bulk of the fleet from destruction by the Germans. He'd managed to save the three newer and larger battleships and most of the smaller warships. They were now more or less safely ensconced in Puget Sound, close to Seattle.

The lights were switched on and Josh caught D.W. Griffith's young female assistant looking at him. He felt like saying "boo" to see if his appearance scared her. He recalled Griffith saying she had actually taken some of the pictures when the regular cameraman quite understandably ran away. She looked quiet and plain, but on second thought, not all that plain and she was certainly intelligent looking. He smiled at her and she blinked and seemed to smile in return. At least he hoped it looked like she'd smiled.

General Liggett and Admiral Sims sized up the moment. Finally, since it was Sims' office, he spoke first. "Mr. Griffith and Miss Thompson, thank you for bringing this to our attention. We will attempt to send it on to Washington and you will be given the proper recognition for what were obviously heroic efforts. It is ironic in the extreme that the Germans apparently mistook your movie set for a defensive work and bombed it. Although, I somehow don't believe the dead and wounded think it ironic at all."

Liggett nodded agreement. "And we're particularly impressed by Miss Thompson's bravery in continuing to take pictures."

Elise flushed. "I think I was too scared to even realize what I was doing."

"Mr. Griffith," Liggett continued, "you have a reputation as a businessman, what do you want out of this?"

Griffith nodded and half bowed. "I wish the honor and privilege of continuing to film the war. When the time comes, I will make more than enough money out of those efforts."

Sims and Liggett looked quickly at each other. Griffith would surely find a way to make some money out of his films, which made his comment a little crass, but did it matter?

Liggett spoke for the two commanders, "Done. However, you must not do anything to endanger American soldiers and sailors and you must never betray anything we say without permission. Everything must be kept secret. Of course, you must also stay out of our way."

"Agreed."

Liggett rose. "Unfortunately, the films you took, while dramatic and historical, are of little strategic or tactical value. Still, they will show the world what we're up against."

"The film can be edited to look even more dramatic," Elise found herself saying. "I would especially recommend editing out those extras dressed in German uniforms. It might be difficult to explain them to viewers in New York and elsewhere."

Both Sims and Liggett chuckled. "Indeed it would, Miss Thompson," Sims said. "Not only are you brave, but you think clearly, a fairly rare commodity. Perhaps you would consider leaving Mr. Griffith for a similar position with me?"

Griffith laughed. "She would, but she has too much of a future with me."

Elise glared at him. How dare he speak for her? She was still perturbed at him for not letting her care for the injured. "I'd be honored to work for you, Admiral. When would you wish me to start?"

Sims smiled broadly. He had barely begun to gather a staff for his newly created position and needed all the qualified help he could get. "Yesterday would have been nice."

"Elise, I thought you worked for me," Griffith lamented.

"Mr. Griffith, haven't you noticed there's a war on? Frankly, I think that's far more important than taking movies."

Josh leaned against a wall. Elise? What a lovely name. And she was going to be working for the admiral. How wonderful. And now his leg didn't hurt quite as much.

When his father died, he would be crowned Kaiser Wilhelm III. For now, he was the crown prince and he wished his father a long and happy life. He also wished his army would move a lot faster. The thirty-eight-year-old general knew he'd been given command of these armies, collectively known as "Army Group Crown Prince," because of his royal heritage. Despite that implicit handicap, he'd worked hard and studied intensely to make himself a good general and a good leader, and he had largely succeeded. He was a professional and would not make mistakes.

Even though it was frustrating, he accepted that armies sometimes moved with maddening slowness, in particular over difficult terrain and when looking for an enemy that wasn't visible but might pop up at any time. The crown prince also knew von Moltke the Elder's dictum that even the most careful and well thought out plans fell apart when an attempt was made to implement them. So be it. It was sometimes referred to as the "fog of war."

The prince had divided his forces into three very unequal prongs. In the east, along the Texas border, it was virtually an all-Mexican show. They wanted Texas back and they could have it. Already swarms of less than well trained Mexican soldiers were streaming into Brownsville and Laredo. *Good*, he thought. It would keep them out of his hair. He had little respect for Mexican President Carranza and even less respect for Carranza's army. In the crown prince's opinion, Texas was a sideshow, intended to siphon off American responses while the conquest of California took center stage.

Thus, the remaining two prongs were given over to California. Planning and execution of the invasion of California were handicapped by the miserable terrain south of the American border. The Mexican border to the west was interrupted by the Sea of California and the wastelands of the Baja Peninsula; there was absolutely no good place for a large army to assemble on the Mexican side. There was plenty of land but it was barren and there were few decent roads and no railroad lines. Bringing in food and ammunition could only be done with great difficulty. He'd managed to get a brigade of two infantry regiments and one detachment of cavalry assembled at the squalid Mexican city of Tijuana, but that was all the area could support. That brigade was now moving cautiously northward towards San Diego. Too cautiously, in the prince's opinion. Despite some nibbling attacks, it was beginning to appear that the intelligence they'd garnered was incredible but correct—there was no significant American military presence in and around San Diego. German airmen had attacked what might have been a belated attempt to build some defenses near Los Angeles, but there was much that was puzzling about that incident.

Geography dictated that the main German thrust come from the south and east of the California coast. German forces were massed south of the border near the town of Mexicali. They had begun to cross the border and advance patrols had penetrated a number of miles. Better, they had connected with the railroad line from Yuma to San Diego. This would facilitate the movement of troops over the low mountains that shielded San Diego. Both the army and the navy needed a port to gather supplies, and taking San Diego was an admirable solution.

The crown prince was also thrilled to be out of Mexico. It was a stinking island of corruption in a sea of incompetence. The Mexican Army was a joke, and the Mexican government a prime example of brutal incompetence and criminality. It galled him to have to pretend to accept that packet of filth named Carranza as a head of state. The crown prince's father was a true head of state. His father was the head of a vast empire as were the others in his extended family, such as the czar of Russia and the king of England. Mexico was a joke in comparison. And when the United States was defeated, Imperial Germany would truly be the only major power in the world and perhaps Germany's Second Reich would indeed last for a thousand years, just like the First Reich.

The prince and his staff frequently wondered just why the French had tried to establish an empire in Mexico sixty years earlier and, more important, just how had the wretched little brown people managed to defeat the French? The few Mexican Army detachments he'd included in his assault on California would function as rear echelon guards and supply soldiers, providing they didn't steal too much. They would also serve as cannon fodder, he decided mirthlessly, should such situations arise. He would not waste the lives of good German soldiers. Mexicans were another matter entirely.

The German armies would advance north and west into California, after first ensuring that the army was entirely over the border, in proper position, and with sufficient supplies. While he agreed that there would be minimal defense from the Americans, he didn't feel like handing them even a small victory on a platter. The ambush of that probing cavalry force was still on his mind. If the cavalry commander hadn't been killed, he would have been court-martialed for stupidity. According to the German embassy in Mexico City, the American press was making much ado about what the crown prince thought wasn't even worthy of being called a skirmish.

There were other differences between Mexico and the United States. For instance, the signs in the United States were in English, which he could read, instead of Spanish, which he couldn't. Also, the homes and businesses were neater and more prosperous looking, and why not? As much as he disliked the citizens of the United States, they were far preferable to the dirty and illiterate people of Mexico.

He hoped he and his army would never have to return south of the border, except, perhaps, for a victory parade or a well-deserved vacation. Both he and his father knew how close Germany had come to defeat along the Marne River near Paris in September of 1914. The German Army had suffered grievously in a bloodbath of monumental proportions that was all the more terrible because it was so unexpected. The ability of modern weapons to slaughter soldiers had been horribly underestimated.

Before the 1914 war was completely over, German armies had suffered nearly six hundred thousand casualties. He shuddered. A hundred thousand casualties a month could not be sustained by any nation. Therefore, there would never again be a war on the European continent between the major nations. Modern killing was just too efficient. Such sustained losses might also result in a revolution, such as the ones that were ripping apart the Russian and the Ottoman empires.

Therefore, Germany would seek its conquests elsewhere. First had been Mexico and now California. It had taken four years of planning and action to initially bring in a small force to Mexico, have it accepted by the pliant Wilson, and then enlarge it with every ship that docked. Now the man who would be Kaiser Wilhelm III had an invasion force of a quarter of a million that, once they got organized and onto California soil, would advance inexorably and take San Francisco. It would be the final and crowning jewel in the reign of his father.

The kaiser, the prince, and his generals all vowed never again to repeat the mistakes of 1914. The prince would not divide his forces. He would not allow his generals to ignore or disobey orders. He would insist on constant communications between his units, unlike the way the kaiser's generals operated in 1914. They would use telephone, telegraph, couriers, and pigeons if necessary to maintain contact.

Nor would he take the Americans for granted. Even though it seemed that there was little in the way of organized resistance, the crown prince recalled just how desperately the French had fought before finally collapsing. The prince would also ensure that his forces had the bulk of their supplies within reach before advancing. That might mean a slower advance than the generals in Berlin, including his father, might wish, but it was the prudent way to conquer.

Finally, the army had learned its lesson. There would no longer be attacks by massed ranks of infantry. The Americans might not have the large numbers of machine guns and artillery that his Germany Army had, but what weapons they did have could prove deadly. His force was limited in size and reinforcing it would be difficult; therefore, he would not waste lives.

Artillery rumbled in the distance and the crown prince cursed. He'd told his generals to fire only at viable targets and not to just shoot an area because it looked suspicious. They could not squander precious supplies shooting at shadows.

More artillery thundered and the prince swore again.

He heard the sound of a train whistle and grinned, his good humor returned. He urged his horse over a low rise to where he could see a long train on the tracks and it was headed west. He thanked God that the United States had such a fine railroad system. Not as good as Germany's, of course, but very good indeed when the great size of the United States was considered. When he'd realized that it was nearly three thousand miles from San Francisco to Washington, he'd been aghast. But now he and his army could move over the smallish mountains and into San Diego without further delay. Some of the men on the train saw him and waved. He laughed and waved back. The world was good. And it was becoming a German world. *Pax Germanica.*

On returning to his desk at the Presidio, Luke decided to take a few moments to catch up on news and events. First, he was delighted to see that the United States had formally declared war on Imperial Germany. Apparently there was some thought that an official declaration would not be made because of possible repercussions, but transcripts and recordings of the last meeting between President Lansing and the German ambassador had been so inflammatory that anything else was impossible.

The attacks on California and Texas, coupled with the German ambassador's arrogance, had galvanized the nation. Reports said President Lansing was cheered by Congress and that the vote in both houses was unanimous. Even the diehard pacifists couldn't deny that the United States had been invaded, and that the invader, Imperial Germany, had declared its intention to siphon off four states from the Union.

A confidential report said that California wasn't quite as cut off from the rest of the world as was first feared. Trans-Atlantic cables ran from San Francisco and Seattle to points west and then around the globe where they wound up in Washington D.C. It took several hours to get there, but it was far better than several weeks, or even months. Better, the telegraph and rail lines from Seattle eastward had not been destroyed. Luke and the rest of the army's intelligence community wondered why not and concluded that a spring thaw might find a group of German saboteurs where they'd frozen to death when a sudden storm hit them. So much for German infallibility and omnipotence, he thought. Luke did not feel sympathetic to the thought of a bunch of frozen Krauts.

National Guard troops from Washington and Oregon were moving into the northern passes to rebuild the telegraph lines and protect the one open railroad from a second German try. The destroyed rail lines would not be rebuilt before spring—if the Germans let them, that is. Colonel Nolan felt the Germans would garrison the passes and glumly said that only a few men would be required to hold them against any American advance.

National Guard troops in California had been activated by the Republican Governor of California, William Dennison Stephens. It had been rumored that Stephens was going to order the poorly trained and inexperienced guard to attack the Germans, but prompt action by President Lansing had put an end to that suicidal nonsense. The California National Guard was now under the control of General Liggett.

There was fighting in Texas between Mexican Army units and Texas National Guard, but that was not Luke's immediate concern.

"Welcome home, soldier."

Luke looked up and saw the friendly grin of Major Ike Eisenhower. "Good to be back and gather my wits," Luke said, "but I'd much rather be down south gathering info than reading about it."

"Couldn't agree more," Ike said, pulling up a chair. "Here I am, supposed to be making plans and I have nothing to plan with. I even envy Patton. He gets to ride around and actually try to accomplish something, even though it might result in his getting his butt kicked every now and then."

"So what's going to happen, Major?"

"Nothing that isn't all that obvious," Ike said. "The Krauts will very shortly take San Diego, if it hasn't fallen already. Then they will move north and into the Central Valley where it'll be easier for them to march. They will then keep on north until they can turn west and fall on San Francisco. Before that, however, I'm certain one prong will continue to move along the coast and take Los Angeles, which will give them a second major port."

"San Francisco is their goal, isn't it?"

"In my opinion, yes," Ike said. "Does Colonel Nolan agree?"

"Yes, and again, it's fairly obvious."

"At least General Liggett and Admiral Sims have agreed to try to agree on strategy," said Eisenhower, "Although it would be nice to have one overall commander."

Luke laughed. "Not in this man's army and navy."

"Speaking of navies, Luke, you are aware that three of our new battleships did make it to Seattle, along with a handful of cruisers and destroyers, and maybe a few submarines, before the Germans hit Mare Island and destroyed the three older battleships. Apparently our surviving ships were chased by the German fleet, which then decided not to enter Puget Sound because so much of it is British and they don't want to antagonize the Brits, at least not yet. Since the Krauts destroyed our coastal forts in Puget Sound as well as here, there wouldn't have been much we could have done to stop them. Sims told Liggett we actually have what he called a 'fleet in being' that we can use to tie down German naval units."

"Wonderful," Luke said. "I wish we had an army in fact instead of a fleet in being."

He was about to say something further when an enormous explosion struck the building and sent both of them to the floor. Smoke and dust filled the room. They scrambled to their feet, astonished to be unhurt, and ran outside through where part of the wall had collapsed.

Another explosion rocked them as a second shell impacted near them. They hit the ground again as more debris fell on them. In the nearby city proper, people were running and screaming. Several civilians, including women and children, lay in bloody heaps, some unmoving.

Ike and Luke ran to where they could see out into the ocean. Off in the distance, silhouetted gray shapes lay just under the horizon. The German fleet had returned to San Francisco. Lights twinkled from them, almost merrily, but each twinkle was a naval gun firing and a shell being hurled on its way. The German Navy was bombarding the city.

After a few more minutes, the bombardment stopped and the Germans steamed off, headed south. There had been no return fire from the American coastal forts.

"Son of a bitch!" Luke said. "There was no reason to bombard a helpless city!"

Ike shook his head. "Just like there wasn't any reason for the Germans to bombard and burn cities in Belgium in 1914."

Horse-drawn ambulances had begun to pick up the dead and injured, and fire engines were fighting the fires that the shelling had begun. Ironically, the earthquake and fire of 1906 had resulted in San Francisco having very efficient emergency services. Luke thought this would not be the last time they were needed.

Kirsten felt very nervous riding into Raleigh. She was in a horse-drawn carriage with an equally nervous Maria at her side. Kirsten was dressed demurely in a long skirt, wore no makeup, and her clothes were intentionally baggy and worn. Of course, as a result of the Germans burning her home, her choices of clothing were few. She didn't think she'd have any difficulties with the Germans in the town, but she was not taking any chances. What happened to Ella might have been a fluke caused by Leonard shooting at the Germans, but she would take no chances.

She was in town for several important reasons. First, the group in the hills needed supplies and she hoped the local stores still had some. That and she wanted some news as to what was going on. Up in the hills it was like they were on another planet.

Raleigh was depressing. Many of the buildings were damaged or destroyed and the smell of charred wood was still in the air. Worse, there were many German and Mexican soldiers in the little town. Some of them appeared to be working, while the others just lounged. On the plus side, they didn't give them more than a glance. Two dowdy women in a carriage pulled by a miserable-looking horse were not a threat, and it did appear that there was discipline in the town.

She pulled up at the general store where she normally shopped. It was owned by an Italian couple, the Russos. Joseph Russo was behind the counter and greeted her warmly, but with a hint of nervousness. Kirsten attributed it to the fact that a couple of German soldiers were also shopping. She wondered if they would pay or just requisition what they needed.

She pulled out a list and handed it to Joseph. He blinked and took a deep breath. "Do you have authorization, Miss Biel?"

Now it was her turn to be surprised. "What do you mean?"

He was about to answer when Roy Olson appeared at her side. "What he means, Kirsten, is that things have changed in the last couple of days. The German commander in the area, a Captain Steiner, has instituted rationing since our food supplies are rather limited and likely to stay that way for a while."

Kirsten thought it made a kind of painful sense. "I see. Now, how do I get such a permit?"

Olson smiled. "Why, you get to talk to me. Steiner appointed me administrator of the area and liaison with the occupying forces." He guided her by the arm and into the back of the store where he had established an office. She noticed that the rear of the store was filled with supplies. She wondered if Olson rationed himself.

"Steiner wants to make sure that only people who

really need food get it," Roy said. "He would be much happier if everyone came down from the hills and didn't sit up there with rifles and pose a potential threat to his men. He will not tolerate any of his soldiers being shot, which would result in tragedy. Like what happened at your home."

"Are you saying we won't be allowed to defend ourselves?" she bristled.

Olson's face hardened. "That's exactly what I'm saying. Times have changed and we have to change with them. We are no longer in charge and we'd better get used to it." He gestured to a window. "See those boys out there digging?"

She hadn't really noticed them before, she realized to her chagrin. "Yes."

"Like I said, this Steiner fellow, who's really quite pleasant as long as you don't cross him, has made a rule and it's probably the same way all over German-occupied California. All able-bodied men will work two days a week helping expand the rail siding here to accommodate more trains. So, if you've got men up in the hills with you, you'd better get them down here and registered so the Germans don't think they're guerillas. They shoot guerillas, Kirsten, and they don't ask questions."

She found a chair and sat. "So you're collaborating with the Germans."

"Of necessity, yes. Steiner drafted me to be the administrator and I did not have much choice. If I hadn't taken the position, I'd be outside digging ditches myself."

She looked at him coldly. "And how vehemently did you argue?"

"Kirsten, I have always thought of you as a reasonable, intelligent woman, so let me tell you a few things. This isn't the United States of America anymore. The Germans are here and, according to what I've learned, they aren't leaving. Not today, not tomorrow, not ever. California has become a territory of Imperial Germany and will be ruled from Berlin. We no longer live in a democracy; we now live in an autocratic empire and under military rule. Kaiser Wilhelm II is our leader, not Robert Lansing. We don't have to like it, but that is our new world, and yes, I am going to collaborate. It has taken me thirty years to build up what I have and I'm not going to lose it because of any political change. The United States can't even decide who's going to be president, much less defend us. The U.S. just went through three presidents in one week. Washington's just like the Roman Empire or a debauched Papacy."

He laughed harshly. "And have you seen the American Army? Of course not. It doesn't exist. On the other hand, I've seen thousands of German soldiers come through and this isn't even the main part of their invasion. Tomorrow, a squadron of German warplanes will land here to add to their strength.

"Someday the United States may again govern here, Kirsten, but I doubt that it will be in our lifetimes or those of our great-grandchildren."

For one of the few times in her life, Kirsten was speechless. The enormity of the events and changes was overwhelming.

"So you see," Olson continued, "it is in everyone's best interest to cooperate with the Germans. Or would you rather that California be part of Carranza's Mexico? Would you want your family to be hurt any more than they have? Poor Leonard was brave but foolish and what happened to Ella was deeply regrettable. And, yes, I do know what happened to her. Steiner told me. He assured me that the soldiers in question have been disciplined."

Kirsten stood up. She very much doubted that anything had happened to the Germans who'd raped Ella, but this was not the time for such a debate.

"You've given me much food for thought, Roy. But first, how do I get food for the women and children in the hills?" she asked, intentionally leaving out the fact that men were up there as well.

He smiled. "Why I give you permits, of course." He pulled some forms out of his desk and filled them out. "Here. Give these to Joseph out front and he'll be glad to fill your orders."

He guided her out of his office, letting his hand rest on her shoulder and drop down to her waist. She shuddered but kept her feelings under control. Yes, things had changed and she would have to figure out just how much.

And what in God's name could she do about it?

Secretary of State Charles Evans Hughes looked coldly at the man before him. "I only have a few minutes," he said pointedly.

Giovanni Golitti had been premier of Italy until a corruption scandal had resulted in his ouster. He was confident he would rise again. Corruption is so quickly forgotten, especially in the riotous politics of the still very new nation of Italy.

"I had hoped to see President Lansing," he said through a very nervous translator.

Hughes remained stern. "You are a minister without portfolio from a nation that is allied with our enemy, Germany. There are those who feel I should not waste my time by talking with you at all."

Golitti matched the glare. He'd been weaned in the rough and tumble arena of Italian politics. "Then you'd be making a huge mistake. Things are not always as they seem and there are many people in my country and other countries who are concerned about Germany's preeminence in the world and who would wish to do something about it."

"Go on," Hughes said, his curiosity piqued.

"Indeed. Germany's successes have led to even greater arrogance on their part, and that has been followed by their insistence on preferences in trade and other matters that simply are not in Italy's best interests. In short, it would not bother Italy and several other nations if Germany were cut down a little bit, perhaps even more than little bit."

"How would you accomplish that?"

"Mr. Hughes, you have a wonderfully large nation with a potential for military greatness. Sadly, you lack everything needed to fulfill that potential. I—we—propose to remedy that."

Hughes smiled, "We?"

"A number of nations, including France and England obviously, have been contacted by my government and are more than willing to help you get the equipment you lack. Others include Spain, Portugal, Sweden, and, of course, my beloved Italy."

Hughes' smile widened. "May I ask if you and your associate nations have any specific plans to assist us?"

"Your crying need is for artillery, machine guns, and

ammunition. While we would not be so foolish as to send hundreds of planes, thousands of French 75mm cannon, and tens of thousands of machine guns to you and try to hide that fact from the Germans, a thought did occur to us. You are the greatest manufacturing nation in the world, so we will send you the dies and other equipment necessary to begin the immediate manufacture of those items."

"And when will that occur?"

"It has already begun, Mr. Secretary. In anticipation of your concurrence, equipment is on trains headed for Lisbon. They are crated as farm machinery—which reminds me, the British will be sending you some special farming equipment they've been working on for the last several years and which is, I understand, quite secret."

"Excellent," Hughes beamed.

Golitti continued. "Further, it is understood that you need bases for your warships if they are to go on commerce raiding cruises. Since you are so outnumbered I don't think your navy will be looking for fleet actions, at least not yet. We will look the other way if your ships use the Azores or Canary Islands as bases, just as your navy is planning to use Catalina Island off California."

Hughes blinked. How did the little Italian learn about the plans for Catalina? "And if our ships were discovered," Hughes said, "I am certain that the nation whose resources we were using would deny complicity, demand both our immediate withdrawal and an apology from us, which we would quickly and sincerely give."

Golitti laughed, "Of course."

Hughes stood and smiled broadly. "Would you like to meet President Lansing?"

★ CHAPTER 6 ★

DESPITE NOT BEING PARTICULARLY TALL, MAJOR General John J. Pershing was a totally dominating person. Dressed in a uniform that looked like it had been painted on him and without a button or a crease out of place, he seemed to epitomize what a general should look like. He was sixty and looked at least a decade younger.

Pershing was also the only American general with significant experience in leading anything resembling a large body of men. Four years earlier, he'd taken an ad hoc division into Mexico in search of bandits who'd attacked towns and ranches in Texas. He'd fought several battles against the bandits and, later, against Mexican regulars when the Mexican government finally decided it didn't like an American army marching around in their nation.

He was often referred to as "Black Jack" Pershing, because he'd commanded Negro troops against the Apaches and, later, in the attack on what became popularly known as San Juan Hill in the Spanish-American War. There he'd met and impressed a young Theodore Roosevelt. Many Southern officers disparagingly referred to him as Nigger Jack instead of Black Jack.

Pershing was a widower. His wife and two of his three children had been killed in a fire. He was not the prude his stern appearance would seem to indicate. Indeed, after the loss of his wife, he had consoled himself by having several affairs, including one with the sister of one of his favorite young officers, George Patton.

General Payton March thought Pershing was a very good general and a very flawed man. He was also the best March had. Liggett was tied up in California and, in March's mind, the only remaining choice to command the American Army was Pershing, who was still unpopular in some quarters after Roosevelt had promoted him to brigadier rank ahead of many, many others senior to him. Major General Leonard Wood, also sixty, was available, but Wood wanted desperately to be president, not just a general, and March was concerned that his political agenda might interfere with his military one.

March smiled and the two men sat down. "General Pershing, I have a very simple request to make. The Germans must be defeated. Can you do it?"

Pershing did not blink. "Of course. However, I will need the time and resources to develop an army that can win and not be slaughtered in the attempt. You know as well as I do that despite the fact that enlistments are pouring in, there are no training camps, no uniforms, no tents, no officers, no sergeants, no machine guns, and no artillery. Oh yes, don't forget planes and armored vehicles. Once those problems are resolved, we can and will expel Germany from our country."

"And how long will that take?" March asked, dreading the answer. The treatment of volunteers was a scandal. Many thousands were freezing in inadequate facilities in poorly designed camps.

"At least a year," Pershing answered without hesitation. "And I will require approximately a million men."

March blinked. Damn Woodrow Wilson and his naive belief that the United States could stay out of war by simply wishing it. Wilson could never accept the premise that some nations were predators. "Many are enlisting," March said, "but nowhere near that number."

"Then, odious as it may seem, there must be conscription."

March leaned back in his chair. A conscription act was already working its way through Congress and would be law in about a week.

"But why so many men?" March asked. "The Germans don't have anywhere near that many in California, and Texas appears to be a totally Mexican-run operation."

Pershing smiled tightly. "You are quite correct. However, the Germans have made it plain that the declaration of war would result in attacks along the Atlantic coast. That will result in pressure on President Lansing to divert forces to garrison coastal cities against attacks that might or might not ever come. That and the fact that I would wish to outnumber the Germans when we do counterattack."

"But a year? That seems excessive."

"Let me be blunt, General March: it may take even longer. The only things we have in great numbers are Springfield rifles. Sadly, they require ammunition and trained personnel. We are like Washington at Valley Forge. We must create an army out of nothing, and an army a hundred times larger than Washington's, and we don't have a von Steuben to train them."

March nodded. "We cannot afford to strip our existing units to train recruits. We will have to use retired military personnel."

Pershing shook his head vigorously. "I do not want to use our own soldiers, or even experienced retired soldiers, to train recruits. However well intended they might be, the last war they might have fought in would have been against the Spanish in Cuba, or the Moros in the Philippines, or even the Apaches, and these are hardly examples of modern warfare. No, sir, if humanly possible, I would like the trainers to be British. They may have lost to the Germans, but they did confront the Germans and often hurt them badly. They would know their weapons and their tactics. And I would not want any French instructors. Their tactics were execrable."

March was about to say it was impossible, but the germ of an idea crept in. "Perhaps," he said with a small smile.

Pershing leaned forward. "Terrible things may happen in California and we will be unable to prevent them or strike back. The president will be under tremendous pressure to do something, anything, but to act prematurely would be disastrous."

"Are you saying General Liggett must be abandoned to his fate?"

"Sadly, yes, and he is well aware of it. He knows the state of our military and how long it will take to create an army, and, for that matter, a navy." It was a reminder that so many of the Navy's fine warships were seriously undermanned. "General Liggett is a fine general and he will do as well as anyone." Pershing grinned uncharacteristically. "Perhaps the stress of combat will cause him to lose some of the incredible weight he carries."

March smiled as well. Liggett's prodigious weight was a joke and had been a source of friendly contention between the obese Liggett and the austere and trim Pershing. Liggett was sixty-three and looked older. *Christ,* he thought. *Don't we have any generals under sixty?*

Belatedly, it annoyed March that Admiral Coontz had not been invited to this meeting, but it would have been a breach of Army-Navy protocol. It was understood that Josephus Daniels and Admiral Coontz were desperately trying to get the Navy's ships manned and supplied. And damn protocol, he needed to get together with the Navy and coordinate their efforts.

"General Pershing, is there any good news you can give?"

"I think so. First, we can and will strike at the Mexicans in Texas. That should take pressure off the president and we should be able to expel them. Also, the Germans' Achilles' heel is their supply line. We may be three thousand miles from San Francisco, but they are halfway around the world from Germany. The more we can interdict their supplies, the worse off they will be. We still hold the Panama Canal, do we not?"

"We do. The Colombians tried to take it back from us, but our small garrison and the Panamanian Army defeated the effort. There were no Germans involved in the attack, although I am sure there were advisors in the background. I have directed the local American commander to blow up the locks if capture seems imminent and to inform the Germans of our intent. If we can't have the Canal, then nobody can."

Pershing nodded. Lack of access to the Canal would force German supply ships to go the long way, or unload at Vera Cruz and ship overland. Either way, it created a monumental logistics problem for them.

The meeting ended and Pershing departed. March opened the connecting door to the adjacent office. President Lansing stepped in. He was clearly unhappy at what he had overheard.

"What Pershing said is deeply saddening," Lansing said. "Unfortunately, it has the ring of truth, and I suppose that reality will be far more complex and daunting."

"Mr. President, do you wish General Pershing to be the general commanding ground operations against the Germans and Mexicans?"

"Is there another choice?"

"Leonard Wood and Liggett himself are the only two others. Wood has too many political ambitions and has never led large numbers in battle, while Liggett's presence is required in California. I propose we give General Wood command over the eastern coastal defenses and task Pershing with ultimately driving out the Germans, however long it takes. Is Pershing acceptable to you and do you agree that his first focus must be Texas?"

Lansing took a deep breath. He was in the position of Abraham Lincoln sixty-odd years earlier. Would he choose a McClellan or a Burnside or a Hooker who would lead them to disaster? Or would he be fortunate and select perhaps a Grant.

"Pershing it is."

The sound of an approaching train woke Luke. He'd been dozing in a field in the outskirts of San Diego. Incredibly, the slow-moving Germans hadn't yet taken it. The city itself was largely abandoned. Thousands of residents, now refugees, had departed on roads headed north, joining a growing mass of humanity heading out.

He'd arrived a couple of hours earlier, and again by plane. He was beginning to get used to the lunacy of being in the air with only canvas and wood keeping him up. He admitted to his extremely young pilot that it was exhilarating. The pilot had laughed and said that's why he flew.

Patton nudged him. "Hammer-man, you expecting a train? If so, it's coming from the east."

Luke shook the cobwebs from his brain. "Christ, and that's where the Germans are."

Patton swore. "Of course it is, my friend."

Patton now commanded half the 7th Cavalry, but his half of the regiment was down to fewer than two hundred effectives. Others had been siphoned off to other places to nibble at the German advance, while all too many others were dead or wounded. He had about two hundred men to hold San Diego.

The train came into sight. It consisted of one locomotive and maybe twenty freight and flat cars. They were filled with men.

"As I suspected," Patton said, "German soldiers. And the country is so defenseless they just ride up like they were on a Sunday trip to Grandma's. Damn them. At least we're as prepared as we can be, and the German fleet hasn't arrived yet."

The consensus in San Francisco was that the Germans had shelled San Francisco just to show they could, and were on their way to San Diego, which they would use as a California port once their army had taken it.

"Open fire!" Patton yelled and two hundred soldiers emptied their bolt action Springfields at the crowded Germans. Although slowing, the train was still moving and the Germans were temporarily trapped. Finally, it slowed enough for them to jump off and begin to return fire. The clatter of a machine gun joined the din.

Patton cursed. "Of course they have machine guns. They always have machine guns."

A second German machine gun opened up, then a third. Dirt from bullets kicked up uncomfortably near them. Someone screamed.

Luke grabbed Patton's arm. "It's not getting any better, George, there's another train coming."

Patton gave the order to pull back. His men gathered their wounded and their dead and piled them on horse-drawn carts. That was another thing, why didn't the American Army have trucks?

The Germans at the rail line were content to consolidate their position and didn't follow. The Americans began to head north, all the while keeping an eye out for German planes.

"Y'know Luke," Patton said thoughtfully. "There are train lines all over the place and headed in all directions. If the Krauts could hop a train and ride into San Diego virtually unopposed, what's to stop them from taking trains to Los Angeles, or, hell, San Francisco?"

"Nothing I can think of."

"Okay, you find your little plane and pilot and get your ass back to Liggett and tell him I'm going to start destroying tracks and bridges as I pull back north. And then tell him that he'd be smart to do it anywhere else he can. If he doesn't the Germans might just unexpectedly drop in at the Presidio for lunch."

Elise Thompson sat primly, her notebook on her lap. Ensign Cornell sat along the wall across from her, a crutch beside him. He winked and she tried not to smile. Admiral Sims appeared not to notice, but she thought he had. General Liggett and Colonel Nolan completed the group in the conference room adjacent to Liggett's office. The decision had been made to keep it small. Larger groups often resulted in too much posturing by people jockeying for promotion.

The admiral smiled and began. "Miss Thompson will keep notes. I will edit them later in case we say something too treasonous. General, with your permission I will begin.

"Like yourself, General, I have been promised little or nothing in the way of reinforcements. The squadron I have is bottled up in Puget Sound, where it is safe but accomplishing little except that it keeps a larger squadron of German ships occupied. However, I do believe that my small fleet can still be of use at this time."

Cornell's ears perked up. He'd heard that Sims held

views that were radical, even heretical, in a navy that worshipped battleships.

Sims had made a name for himself by revolutionizing the way navy guns were aimed and fired. Many captains had come to the horrible conclusion that their ships couldn't hit anything. The human mind couldn't do the calculations necessary to enable the guns to aim at objects moving at speed and in different directions, and then hit what they thought they'd aimed at. Sims, along with an equally brilliant Royal Navy officer, had devised an electronic range finder that did the work. That and extensive gunnery practice, of course.

"First," said Sims, "the Germans sank or badly damaged three older battleships at Mare Island. They were little more than floating targets when the Germans arrived because I had stripped them of their crews to enable the two newer ones to flee after the *Arizona*. In doing so I did the older ships and their crews a favor. Had they fought the Germans, they would have been destroyed. Had they fled, they would have been caught and sunk. The older ships had half the firepower of the German battleships that attacked them. However badly damaged they might be, those three old ships still have many of their guns. If given enough time, some of the damaged guns can be repaired. I propose that those guns that can be salvaged be removed, shipped from Mare Island to here, and mounted on either side of the Golden Gate and elsewhere to protect San Francisco."

Liggett beamed. "That can be done?"

"Indeed. They were anchored in shallow water; thus, even the ship that sank, the *Michigan*, is resting with her superstructure above the surface."

"Excellent," Liggett said, "Anything I can do to help please ask."

"General, I will require transportation. Some of the equipment can go by barges or trains, but others will require improvisation. May I call on your engineers?"

"Of course."

"I do have a small number of other, smaller warships at Seattle, and these include a handful of cruisers and, more important, some torpedo boats and six submarines. I propose to utilize them as soon as I can to interdict German supply ships. I believe the only reason the Germans didn't dally longer off San Francisco was that they are beginning to run low on fuel after a very long voyage. It isn't yet a crisis for them, but it could be. Their fuel vulnerability is something to keep track of."

It was Liggett's turn to update the group and he informed the admiral that two more regiments of regular American Army infantry were on trains and crossing the mountains via the northern route and should be in San Francisco in a week. Monumental efforts were being made to keep the tracks open and clear of snow. He reported that the snow removal efforts had unearthed a couple of dead bodies along the northernmost route. It was presumed that these were some of the German saboteurs who had failed in their assignment.

Of more importance, the additional six thousand regular army soldiers would be useful but only a drop in the bucket when compared with the German Army now estimated at a quarter of a million.

"Where will you make your stand, General?"

Liggett winced. He was going to have to admit

that most of California was indefensible. "Ultimately, San Francisco. My engineers are designing defenses that will surround San Francisco and lead east into the mountains. It is about five hundred miles from San Diego to San Francisco and I fervently hope we can delay the Germans long enough to complete our works."

With little more to discuss, the meeting broke up. Josh Cornell thought it was interesting that both the admiral and the general appeared to be getting along. Perhaps a shared crisis makes people think more clearly and less parochially. Regardless, he had more pressing things on his mind.

He smiled at Elise, "Lunch?"

She smiled briefly in return and looked at her notes. "I think I should type these as soon as possible."

"But you do have to eat. You must conserve your strength for your typing."

She was about to retort sharply when Admiral Sims' voice boomed from his office. "For God's sake, Elise, go to lunch with him or you'll never get anything done."

Colonel Marcus Tovey of the Texas National Guard hoped he had prepared his defensive position well. He had his flanks covered and his men were dug in. He wished they had something more than just their rifles. The damned Mexicans had machine guns and artillery to go along with their excellent German rifles.

What he and his men wanted more than anything was to kill Mexicans. And if there were any Germans around they'd kill them as well.

Tovey and the rest of his men still seethed over the horror of the burning of Laredo. Granted, many of the fires had likely started during the vicious house-to-house fighting that had erupted when the citizens of that border city awoke to the fact that the Mexican Army had swarmed across the Rio Grande. Just about every man in town had grabbed his rifle or pistol and started shooting Mexicans. The battle quickly disintegrated into a chaotic brawl.

The results had left many dead, including hundreds of civilians, among them women and children. Atrocities had been committed on both sides in an orgy of violence that would take a long time to forgive. Tovey knew he would never forget the sight of several small children who'd been dismembered by an artillery shell, or a woman who'd been shot in the back of the head by Mexican soldiers as she'd tried to flee. There were rumors of rapes and the thought of Mexican soldiers assaulting white women made his blood boil.

Thus, what the Mexican command thought would take only an hour or two wound up taking three long bloody days. Buildings were destroyed and homes were burned as the fighting raged from house to house and room to room. The delay enabled Guard units like Tovey's to gather and join the fight. They had been too few and too late, and the Mexicans ultimately prevailed, but only after paying a heavy price.

He recalled that American army officer who'd crawled out of the Rio Grande so long ago, and asking him just what the hell Germans were doing south of the Rio Grande? Now Tovey knew. Everyone knew. The sons of bitches had been planning a "stab in the back" attack on the United States. And they had burned Laredo. They would pay.

A Mexican officer they'd captured said that it had

been bandits led by Pancho Villa who'd set most of the fires, and that the rest were a result of intense combat. That may have been true, but it didn't matter. "Remember Laredo" was a rallying cry. Then they hanged the Mexican son of a bitch.

Tovey's men were below the crest of a low hill maybe twenty miles north of Laredo and on the way to San Antonio. Rumor had it that San Antonio and the recapture of the Alamo were the goals of the Mexicans. Rumor also had it that the federal government in Washington was powerless to help stop the invasion. More rumors even said that Texas Governor William P. Hobby, Democrat, had rejected assistance from Washington. Rumors and more God-damned rumors. Rumor had it that pigs could fly. All he knew was that he was on a hill and the Mexican Army was coming north and nobody was going to help out.

That was okay by him, he thought and spat on the ground for emphasis. Texans didn't need help from anybody, especially to deal with a bunch of fucking greasers.

A smattering of gunfire erupted to his left. Damn Mexicans were trying to get around his flank. He could see a couple of score of them and that his men had the situation in hand. The Mexicans left a few on the ground and pulled back, joining the several thousand forming up behind the low hill in front of him.

This organized fighting was new to him. As a Texas Ranger he'd fought the Apache and the Comanche, and even some Mexican bandits, but this was nothing he'd ever experienced. One of the older guys in the unit had ridden with the Rough Riders in 1898, but even he said this was a whole lot different.

"Here they come."

Tovey grinned. Let's see how they liked his little surprise. Waves of Mexican infantry emerged from behind their own low hill, marching slowly and keeping rough formation while American rifle fire slashed through them. Flags flew above the Mexicans and music was playing. Tovey grudgingly admitted that the Mexicans were brave enough, but they still had to be killed.

The Mexicans returned fire and a number of Texans fell. Tovey wished he'd told the men to dig in deeper. Something else to learn, he realized reluctantly.

At a little more than a hundred yards away, the Mexican advance halted, the men milled in puzzlement. Tovey noticed his own men's fire slackening.

"Keep shooting, God damn it!" he yelled and the firing picked up. The massed and confused Mexicans were easy targets and the battle became a slaughter. After a couple of moments, the Mexicans pulled back, leaving heaps of dead and wounded on the ground.

Tovey grinned. Two strands of barbed wire was all it took. Two strands and the surprised dumb-ass Mexicans didn't know what to do. They couldn't go around it or over it and couldn't cut it, and didn't think to crawl under it. He wondered if anyone else understood the potential of barbed wire.

He heard the sound of artillery. Seconds later, shells landed in front of him. "Damn it to hell!" he yelled.

Mexican cannon had been an unpleasant surprise in Laredo. At first he thought it impossible that ignorant greasers could shoot cannon, but that thought had been dispelled. He only wished the Texas Army's own artillery wasn't from the Spanish-American War or older. What few pieces they'd managed to find were old 75mm cannon from warehouses in Bliss and Sam Houston or from lawns in front of town halls. They were inaccurate, slow, and, oh yeah, there wasn't much ammunition.

Before he could finish his mental laments, orders came from Governor Hobby, who'd assumed command in the field, for him to pull his men back to a new defensive position. Tovey looked at the stacked-up dead Mexicans and wondered just what the hell was wrong with his current position. He wondered if the governor knew his ass from a hole in the ground about military tactics. *Damnation,* he thought. He gave the orders for his men to pull back. He also ordered men out to recover the barbed wire.

Elise and Josh had a sandwich at a little place on California Street, a block away from the boundary of the Presidio complex. It was about as far as Josh could walk with the single crutch he was now using. He planned on graduating to a cane soon, which he thought would be more dashing.

Despite agreeing to go out with him, Elise did feel pressed to finish typing up the notes and informed him that lunch would not be extended. The typing should have been easy as the admiral's office possessed several fairly new Remington typewriters. The hard part was that she was a long ways from being the world's most accurate typist and she made mistakes that had to be corrected on both the original and the carbon copies.

She found herself enjoying Josh's company and, after learning that he was a transplanted Midwesterner too, found they had a lot to talk about.

They avoided the war and his experiences on the

Fox. She'd read the report he'd written about the destruction of the destroyer, and understood he'd seen horrible things. It was easy to tell that, despite his cheerful facade, he was haunted by the fact that so many of his comrades were dead. Instead, they concentrated on more pleasant matters. He asked her if she knew any real movie stars and she admitted that she did. She said that the Gish sisters were very nice, but that Mary Pickford was a little stuck up. She said that Charlie Chaplin wasn't very funny in person, which Josh found hilarious.

Elise wanted to know all about Annapolis. She'd never been farther east than Chicago and he told her about life at the Naval Academy, and what it was like to visit nearby Washington and other cities that had played a major role in America's history. As they started to walk back to Sims' headquarters, now also located in the Presidio, she slipped her arm in his. Even though it was cold and damp outside, Josh felt comfortable indeed.

As they turned a corner, they saw and heard a commotion up ahead. Several dozen men and women were milling and shouting outside a small store. A sign above a smashed window said it was Schultz's Bakery. Two middle-aged people, obviously the Schultzes had been dragged out onto the street. Stones and trash were being thrown at them while rough-looking men and even rougher-looking women kicked and punched them, oblivious to the fact that some of the stones were hitting them as well. Two of the women grabbed Mrs. Schultz's blouse and ripped it apart, exposing her large and pendulous breasts. She shrieked and tried to both defend herself and cover herself while her attackers roared with laughter. Cries of "fucking Krauts" and "kill the Germans" came from the mob.

Josh was aghast. "I have to stop this."

"Don't even think of it," Elise said firmly and stopped him as he started to move forward. "You're only one person, you're unarmed, and you're using a crutch. You are not going to scare anybody away."

"There must be something I can do! This is so wrong. This is like when the *Fox* was attacked and I couldn't do a thing about it. What the devil did a poor baker do to deserve this?"

"They were born Germans, Josh," she said bitterly. "The world is going crazy. Things like this have happened elsewhere, and not just in San Francisco."

Whistles filled the air. The police were arriving and the mob quickly disintegrated, its members running off in all directions. Men ran out of the bakery and, a second later, a young girl about twelve emerged. She was naked and shrieking with pain and shame. There was blood on her inner thighs.

One looter ran by, laughing. Elise grabbed Josh's crutch, swung it and hit him in the mouth. He staggered and spat out blood and teeth, but continued on, his eyes now wide with fear.

"Great shot," Josh said admiringly.

"I had to do something when I saw that poor girl."

Sobbing bitterly, the Schultzes allowed themselves to be helped back into their ruined store by police and a handful of sympathetic neighbors. They'd been bloodied, shamed, hurt, and humiliated. Loaves of bread and cakes were strewn about and all were covered with broken glass. It would be a while before the bakery opened again, if ever.

"That was insanity," Josh said. He was proud of Elise for acting so decisively. Now he could see her calmly cranking the movie camera while German planes flew overhead.

Elise continued to hold his arm tightly as she steered him back to the Presidio. "Almost as insane as your thinking you could do something about it. Don't ever even think of doing anything like that again. I don't want you getting hurt. I used to play baseball with my brothers and I used your crutch like a bat, while you need it to stand up. It's bad enough you're in the Navy, but you don't have to go looking for trouble."

Josh brightened. She didn't want him getting hurt. Wonderful. "Okay, I'll be more discreet."

She smiled warmly. "And tomorrow, my brave cavalier, you can take me to lunch someplace where it's not quite so dramatic."

Roy Olson's knees were shaking. This couldn't really be happening, could it? The man tied to the post in front of the brick wall seemed to feel the same way. His name was John Dubbins and he was a local boy. His face was swollen and bloody from where he'd been beaten with fists and kicked with German boots, but he seemed to be laughing as if this was some joke, like it wasn't really happening. Maybe the fool was still too drunk to comprehend.

"What did he do?" Olson managed to ask.

"Sabotage," Captain Steiner replied quickly. "He was caught cutting a telegraph line. The penalty for sabotage is death."

"Captain, the man was drunk. Even when sober, which isn't very often, he's an idiot. I'd bet you that some of his no good friends or one of his brothers dared him to do it and he was too stupid to realize the seriousness of what he was doing."

"A shame," Steiner snapped. He was a short, thin man in his late thirties, and he wore the insignia of the German Army's quartermaster corps. "However, I will guarantee you that we will also punish his so-called friends and family if we find them."

A crowd of nearly a hundred, mostly men, had gathered. Olson was virtually certain he knew who the "friends" were. A cluster of four men were staring incredulously at the scene as if finally realizing what terrible trouble they'd gotten their buddy into. Two were Dubbins' brothers.

A squad of six German soldiers marched out the administration building. Their Mauser rifles were slung ominously over their shoulders. They stopped in front of Dubbins who stared blankly at them. It suddenly dawned on him what was going to happen and he began to scream and cry. His body shook and his bladder and bowels released.

"Coward," muttered Steiner.

"Captain," said Olson, "you've more than made your point. Can't you show a little mercy? Throw him in jail for a while, flog him, kick the shit out of him some more, but don't shoot him for being a drunken fool."

Steiner shook his head. "This is the way we do things, Olson. And this is the side you've chosen. You see those four fellows back in the crowd? I'll bet you they were in on it with this Dubbins creature. You will find out for me."

"And if I can't?"

Steiner glared at him. "I wasn't offering the comment

for discussion. I gave you an order. And as to mercy, I showed it by not executing nine others for his actions. Remember that and explain it to your people. They are now under German control, not American, and they had better adapt. Quite literally, their lives depend on it."

The firing squad raised their rifles and aimed at Dubbins who, mercifully, had passed out. A sergeant gave the order and the volley crashed. Dubbins' scrawny body shook from the bullets' impact and the crowd groaned. Several women screamed and cried out. One of Dubbins' four buddies was doubled over, vomiting. Olson thought it might have been a brother. The others saw Olson staring at them and they returned it with a look of utter animal hatred. They turned and walked away, mounted their horses and rode off rapidly.

Olson took a deep breath. Those men were now his enemies. So be it. He had his own guards and would track them down. They were free for the moment, but that was all. He'd give them a chance to run and, hopefully, they'd be far away before he organized a posse. Olson didn't think Steiner really cared if the boys were caught or not. He just wanted stability and obedience.

Steiner was right, however. Everyone was part of Germany now and the sooner resistance ceased, the sooner the world could get to a new state of normality.

Tim and Wally Randall had been as outraged as all Americans on hearing of the treacherous German attacks on Texas and California, and, since they were young and strong, they decided they had the means to do something about it. They enlisted.

Or they tried to. The army recruiting office in Camden, New Jersey, was flooded with people. Long lines of young men stretched down the street, which made it difficult to believe the rumors that enlistments alone wouldn't be enough to fill the military's needs. Even a few Negroes tried to join the line, but they were promptly told their services weren't needed.

Inside, two enlisted men who Wally and Tim thought were corporals handed out forms to everyone they could and then told the remaining multitude that they were out of the necessary documents. Wally and Tim shrugged and went home.

They were not discouraged. They came back a couple of days later and found the corporals a lot less hassled and, yes, they now did have the sacred forms to fill out. Tim and Wally handled the forms with ease, which caused the recruiters' eyebrows to rise. When asked, they said they had graduated from high school several years earlier, and were taking evening college courses. They both had plans to be engineers, however long it took. Tim was twenty-five and Wally was a year younger, and both were stocky and powerfully built.

The corporals were elated. Most young men in the area had not graduated from high school and fewer still had gone on to college, particularly in a workingman's town like Camden. Only rich kids went to college, and Wally and Tim were clearly not rich. Not too many people in southern New Jersey were.

The brothers raised their right hands and took an oath to defend their country, which was why they'd enlisted, and were told to go home. Why, they'd asked?

Corporal Scanlon gave them the bad news. "Boys,

there aren't any training camps, aren't any uniforms, no weapons, no ammunition, and nobody to train you even if everything else fell into place. So you lucky devils get to go home and wait to be called. Hopefully it won't be too long. At least you'll get to kiss your girlfriends goodby a second time."

The boys did not admit that you first had to have a girlfriend in order to get one to kiss you. Tim had been dating a young woman named Kathy Fenton, but it wasn't serious, at least not to him. Scanlon then gave them a piece of interesting news.

"You've been recommended to be trained as noncommissioned officers. Your education and your intelligence qualify you for that high honor."

Tim and Wally stifled grins. Scanlon was an NCO and seemed far from educated or intelligent. Were they being damned with faint praise?

Scanlon continued. "Of course, it's unlikely you'll be selected as real commissioned officers. Rumor has it that officer commissions are being held for actual college graduates and Ivy League graduates in particular. The nabobs in Washington seem to feel that only Ivy Leaguers have the proper leadership skills to lead us peasants. It's all bullshit if you ask me. You lads may be smarter than any of them pansy boys from Yale and Harvard who spend all day either talking philosophy or buggering each other, but it ain't gonna matter. They'll be officers and you won't."

"We don't much care," Tim said. "We enlisted to fight and we don't give a hoot just what rank we are. We'd just as soon be privates for all we care."

Scanlon shook his head. "Yes, you will care. As an NCO you'll be able to pass out orders and use what's between your ears. And I ain't as dumb as you think. I read your minds when I said what I did about NCOs being intelligent. I may look stupid, but I'm not. By the way, as I understand it, since you're going to become NCO material whether you like it or not, you'll likely get called up first. That way, when you're trained, you can help train the enlisted recruits. A helluva lot of the men signing up can't read or write, or are right off the boat and can barely speak English. They're real good with Polish or Italian, but not English. You're gonna have lots of fun."

Tim and Wally thought that was great news. "Corporal Scanlon, may I ask a favor of you?" Tim asked.

"Go ahead?"

"Would you join us for a beer?"

Scanlon beamed. "Lads, I thought you'd never ask."

Rain and wind lashed the waters of the entrance to Puget Sound. Only the bravest, hardiest, and most foolish were outside on the shore to watch the approach of the British squadron. Two modern battleships, the *Lion* and the *Queen Elizabeth*, led a covey of cruisers and destroyers. The battleships ignored the stormy seas, bulling through them with quiet dignity while their smaller sisters rolled and shook like wet dogs.

The British, with typical arrogance, simply ignored the German squadron that was trying to blockade the sound. Britannia rules the waves and all that and, even though they'd lost the last war, the Royal Navy was not to be trifled with. The only naval blockades the Royal Navy would respect would be her own, and the Royal Navy certainly had the right to make a courtesy call on her Canadian cousins. And the Royal Navy most certainly had the obligation to ensure that the aggravating German squadron stayed well away from Canadian waters.

On board the battleship *Bayern*, the fifty-two-year-old Admiral Adolf von Trotha seethed as he watched the British ships steam past. He commanded Hipper's Northern Squadron of five battleships and he was supremely confident that he could blow the arrogant British back to London.

However and unfortunately, Germany and England were no longer at war. Along with his other brother officers, he felt disappointment that the war of 1914 had ended before the German High Seas Fleet could have sunk the British Home Fleet. They routinely hoisted beer steins to that pleasant but remote possibility.

Trotha was ambitious and confrontational. Not only was he frustrated by the state of peace that existed between England and Germany, but he'd been astonished by the just-received report from his engineers telling him not to waste oil. The fleet had used more than anticipated crossing from Indo-China to California and would have to husband its resources until oil could be shipped from southern California, and that could be a while. Thus, unless he wanted his magnificent ships to become little more than large and aimlessly floating children's toys, he'd watch his Ps and Qs, that is, pints and quarts of oil.

Like everyone, Trotha's eyes were focused on the British warships. Even though he hated them, he had to admire the stately and confident way they maneuvered around his ships and into the Sound. There was no sight of any American warships; the British were the only show in town.

Sharp eyes would have been needed to see that the British squadron was well inside the invisible boundary that separated the American portion of the Sound from the Canadian. Even on a very clear day, extremely sharp eyes would have been needed to even get a hint of the small gray shapes that were leaving the sound as the British entered, and moving so slowly that they scarcely made a ripple, much less a wave. The waves of the sound and then the ocean that surged over the small vessels made them even less visible then they normally were.

And nobody on the mighty German warships noticed those small gray shapes. Later, it would be agreed that the entire maneuver was extremely well planned and marvelously well choreographed.

★ CHAPTER 7 ★

KIRSTEN WAS LIVID. HOW COULD THE DUBBINS BROTHers have run to her hideout after their brother was hanged and after they'd later gotten drunk and beaten up a German soldier? She'd always known the Dubbins brothers weren't very bright, but this was beyond absurd. What were they thinking of, endangering her and the others like they'd done?

"Well, where else were we supposed to go?" lamented the older brother, Lew. "We worked for you and you said you were our friend."

"Lew, if I look towards the south I can see a little wisp of dust in the air and that means someone's coming. My bet is that it's either a German patrol or Roy Olson has organized a posse and they've come to haul you in."

"You'll defend us, won't you?" Lew pleaded.

"With what? Two other women and me are all that's here, and Ella's hurt. The other men and their families have all gone north. There is no way on earth I am going to get in a gunfight on your side against what's coming here. However, I will let you take what you need of our food. I've got a feeling, thanks to you fools, that we're not going to be up here much longer. When you've gone we'll tell Olson or the Germans that you forced it from us and hope to God they believe us. Now take it and get out." She shuddered. If her tale wasn't believed, would she suffer like Ella had? Or, dear God, would Ella suffer again?

The two Dubbins brothers quickly grabbed some supplies and rode off. Kirsten anxiously watched as the dust cloud grew larger and became a group of five horsemen. As they drew still closer, she easily recognized the bulk of Roy Olson in the lead. She was relieved to see no Germans in the group. Ella seemed to be improving, however slightly, but God only knew how she'd take seeing people in field gray uniforms.

Roy and the others pulled up and dismounted. Kirsten noticed with perverse satisfaction that they were tired and flushed. And Roy, a large man, was taking it the worst. He was caked with dirt and sweat and his face was almost beet red.

He plunked himself down in the shade and took some deep swallows of water, "God, that felt good. Now, where the devil are the idiot Dubbins brothers?"

"They came, they robbed me, and they rode off. Now what did they do this time?"

Olson blinked. "They robbed you? But you've got weapons."

"And I've known them for years and didn't expect trouble. I also decided that it wasn't worth resisting if they wanted some food. So what did they do?"

"One brother was executed for cutting a telegraph

line, and the others are wanted for beating up a German soldier. I finally have witnesses to that little shindig, and Captain Steiner wants the matter settled. When I bring them in, they'll hang too."

"Since when did beating somebody become a hanging offense?"

Olson laughed harshly, "Since the Germans came to town. How long ago did the boys leave?"

"Maybe two hours, maybe three. You really think you can catch them? Your horses look dead."

He looked around. The others were listening. "Come with me," he said. "We need to talk."

Olson took her by the arm and led her about a hundred yards away and behind some rocks. He pushed her against the rocks and stood in front of her, towering over her.

"You're right, Kirsten, I can't catch them. But I can bring in second prize, and that's you and the other two women, and I'm going to throw all of you in jail."

Kirsten was shocked at his barely controlled rage. "Why? What for?"

Olson wiped his sweaty brow with a once-white handkerchief. "Because you aided and abetted fugitives in fleeing from justice. You claim they robbed you and, if the Germans are satisfied with your story, you'll be allowed to go free. Of course you'll have to live in a camp in Raleigh along with everybody else."

"A concentration camp?"

She nearly spat out the phrase. The British had used such camps to imprison Boer civilians in the Boer war and the Spanish had invented the term to try to put down the rebellion in Cuba. In each case the camps were filled with innocent civilians who had died by the hundreds, perhaps thousands, as the result of neglect, bad food and water, disease, and generally unsanitary conditions.

"You cannot imprison me for no good reason," she said angrily. "If, as you say, I am found innocent, then I must be able to go and live when and where I wish."

Olson sighed and again wiped his brow. "How many times do I have to tell bloody, stubborn fools like you the world has changed? I am now the civilian law in Raleigh. These men are duly deputized, and you are under arrest. Let's not make this any more difficult than we have to. What happens to you is going to largely depend on what I say. If I don't believe your fairy tale about being robbed, then you're going to spend years in a Mexican prison if the Germans don't shoot you just for the hell of it."

Roy smiled. "However, it doesn't have to be that way." He put his hand on her shoulder and dropped it to her breast. She froze in shock as he turned her back to him and slipped it inside her shirt and under her brassiere. She thought illogically that she'd just gotten the new rubber brassiere in the mail from Sears.

He squeezed her nipple and put his other hand down her jeans. "On the other hand, if you cooperate, things could be really nice for you and your cousin. If not, she'll get it a lot worse than when the Germans hurt her the first time."

Kirsten tried to twist away but he was too large and too strong. She never saw the punch. It struck her hard in the stomach, and a second one smashed against her jaw, sending her to the ground.

Olson stood over her. "And this is just a beginning. You don't want to go to a jail. You don't want Germans or Mexicans guarding you, watching everything you do, staring every time you piss or shit, and visiting you women in your cell every time they feel like getting fucked. Hell, the Mexicans might just take you and Ella on the ground outside where everyone can see and everyone can have a turn. Don't you wonder what that'll do to the rest of Ella's brain?"

Kirsten staggered to her feet and looked at Roy in disbelief. He was never much of a friend, but he was a neighbor. When did he become an enemy, such a monster? It was hard to catch her breath and she was dizzy from the punch to her head.

"Don't worry, Kirsten, I'm not going to take you now. Too many people around and I like a little privacy, but you are coming back with me. If I have to use force to do that, people are going to get hurt, and it will be you and Ella and not me."

He pulled her back to the others. Kirsten looked in dismay at the four louts Roy had brought with him. She recognized them all as being his hired hands and they were laughing at her. They would follow Roy's orders without compunction. She wanted to cry, but wouldn't give Roy the satisfaction.

"Ella can't ride," Kirsten said softly. She was beaten, both physically and emotionally. She would have to do what he wished. "We'll have to rig a sled or something."

"Fair enough," Roy smiled in triumph. "My men'll help."

When the newspapers drew maps of the German advance in California, along with bold arrows, they drew thick draw dark lines indicating to militarily unsophisticated readers that everything south of the markers was German and anything north still belonged to the United States. The implication was that the lines were absolute and impenetrable walls. Luke Martel knew better. No army would have enough men to cover everything. They simply didn't have enough men to block the entire state even if they'd wanted to, and the rough geography in some areas would have made such an endeavor difficult if not impossible.

Luke had pressed Colonel Nolan for the opportunity to slip behind the German lines and see just what the heck was happening in the southern part of the state. He knew his results would be a like a Kodak snapshot, but it would be better then what they were currently getting from the south, which was next to nothing.

Nolan agreed and suggested a patrol of at least twenty men. Luke had argued that he should travel alone. It'd be easier, he'd said, for one person to hide and slip around the Germans, while a larger group would just attract too much attention.

They compromised on adding just one other man. Corporal Joe Flowers was a Mescalero Apache, and Luke had known him and served with him in Mexico. Small, dark, and wiry, he looked older than his forty years, and Flowers' dark eyes hinted that he had a low degree of intelligence and barely controlled violence. Martel knew better. Corporal Flowers was both highly intelligent and cunning, though he could be murderously violent when needed.

Flowers was also a skilled hunter and tracker and those skills kept the two men out of sight of the several German patrols and columns they did spot when they crossed into German-held territory. One thing was clear: the German advance, however slow and ponderous, was a massive endeavor. At one time, they halted and watched what looked like the better part of an infantry division pass within a half mile of them. Along with the size of the German force, its arrogance was also on display. They moved north as if they did not have a care in the world, which, Luke admitted ruefully, was exactly the case.

Another time, they were passed by a column of armored vehicles, trucks with machine guns protected by thin armor plating. "When the hell will we get some of our own," Luke had muttered. Flowers did not respond. He had a habit of not answering dumb questions, especially from officers, even ones he liked.

Luke might have made the same comment regarding airplanes. The skies might not be filled with them, but every one they did see was a German.

They traveled through gaps in the German advance without incident and without being noticed. Wherever possible, the enemy kept to what roads there were, which meant that Martel and Flowers could move freely off-road. As far as the Germans were concerned, the two khaki-clad soldiers were invisible, as both men preferred.

They had made it most of the way south and were resting and hoped they were out of sight behind a mound of earth. Luke had come to the conclusion that they had learned very little except the obvious—the Germans were coming in great strength—and it was just about time to head back north. The Germans were slowly but inexorably advancing on Los Angeles. He hoped the defense of that town would be strong, but doubted it.

Joe heard something, paused, then crawled to the

top of the mound of earth. He gestured for Luke to stay down. "What do you see, Joe?"

Joe answered with a straight face. "Me see heap many horses and men armed with fire sticks. Me see much danger."

Luke laughed. "Stop the dumb Indian bullshit. What do you see?"

A grin split Joe's face. Sometimes he could pull that trick on the very young lieutenants, but Martel had been around just a little too long. "Okay, Lieutenant, have it your way. I see seven people on horseback and one person being pulled on a sled or travois. And they look American and not German or greaser."

Joe Flowers hated the Mexicans even more than most Indians hated white Americans. The Mexicans had abused his people more than the gringos, and had driven his people off their lands. It was because of the Mexicans that Joe Flowers had joined the American Army. He'd seen it as a great opportunity to kill them.

Luke gave Joe his binoculars. The Indian had better eyesight and Luke had no problem admitting it. "This is interesting, Lieutenant. There are five men and two women on horseback and it looks like a third woman on the travois. She's probably sick or hurt. And the other two women are prisoners. Both have their hands bound and tied to their pommels. One woman looks Mexican and the other American. All the men look like gringos."

"What color are the women's eyes?"

"Go to hell, Lieutenant."

Women prisoners was an intriguing thought, even more so if one was indeed an American. What the devil was going on, and was it worth betraying themselves and giving away their presence? If the women actually were prisoners, then whose and why? He looked at Joe, who shrugged.

The group was moving very slowly, so it was no problem for Luke and Joe to circle around them and take up positions in front and to either side. They hid their horses and lay prone in the dirt. When the group was about fifty feet away, Luke and Joe emerged, their rifles aimed on the group.

"Hands up," Luke ordered in a loud voice and the shocked riders complied. They ordered the men off their horses and quickly disarmed them. Luke might regret such high-handedness at some future time, but he felt it was far better to apologize later then to be sorry. He did not release the women. For all he knew, they were ax murderers like Lizzie Borden.

A heavyset man, obviously the leader from the way the other men looked to him, glared at Luke. His face was red with scarcely controlled rage. "Dear God," he said angrily. "You're deserters from the American Army, aren't you? The real American Army is as extinct as Darwin's dinosaurs."

Luke smiled tightly. "Sorry to disappoint you, but we're part of a column," Luke lied. "Now, who are you and why are these women tied up?"

The man looked confused. "My name is Roy Olson and I am the law, the sheriff, in this area and these two women are under arrest for a number of crimes."

Sheriff? And way behind German lines? "And who appointed you sheriff, Mr. Olson?" Luke asked quietly. He had a discomfiting feeling he knew the answer.

The white woman looked up. There was a massive bruise on her face and anger in her eyes. "The Germans gave him the job so he could abuse real Americans.

Look what he did to me. And my crime? I gave food and water to people who apparently might have beaten up one of Olson's precious German soldiers and that's a hanging crime, according to Mr. Olson."

"Comment, Mr. Olson?"

Olson glared at the woman and turned to Luke. "Part of it's true. Of course, the Germans are in charge where we live, and, yes, we have to cooperate with them, and yes, attacking a German soldier is a capital offense. I do not make the laws, ah, Lieutenant, but I do have to obey them and I have been directed to bring these people in."

The woman sneered. "And did that include beating me and trying to rape me? The Germans burned our home, hurt and abused my cousin and now he wants us to go back with him and live in a concentration camp or, if he decides I'm a criminal, be sent to a prison in Mexico City. Unless, of course, I become his mistress. He beat me up just to make his point."

"Lying bitch," Olson snarled. "She fell off her horse."

Luke made his choice. He told Joe to cut the two women free. As he did so, one of Olson's men lunged for his rifle. The knife flew from Joe's hand and buried itself in the man's throat. A second man reached for a pistol he'd hidden in his boot, and Luke shot him in the chest. He screamed and fell back into Olson, covering him with blood. Olson fell backwards with his dead companion on top of him.

Luke chambered another bullet, and Joe had his rifle aimed at Olson and his two thoroughly shocked surviving companions.

"The Germans are going to hang you for this!" Olson said as he tried to stand up. He was covered with the other man's gore. "And maybe they'll hang hostages, too, and it'll all be your Goddamn fault."

Luke laughed. "And maybe you'll hang for being a traitor when we come back. In the meantime, you're going to give us your horses, your weapons, your boots, and anything else we think might be useful. We will leave you enough water to last you a couple of days so you don't die of thirst before you can be hanged for treason. When we come back with more of our men, I strongly suggest you be nowhere near here."

They mounted and rode off, leaving a thoroughly cowed three men behind them. Luke noticed that the woman—she'd told him her name was Kirsten—was really rather pretty in a wholesome, suntanned kind of way, or would be when the swelling on her face went down.

"That was wonderful," she said. "I had just given up all hope of seeing an American Army again. So tell me, how far away is the rest of your column?"

Luke shrugged. "Maybe five hundred miles."

German warships had begun blockading all major west coast ports including Los Angeles, San Francisco, and Seattle. Admiral Sims quickly realized that, even though the Germans had a numerical advantage in ships, there simply weren't enough of them to keep a tight blockade or watch the rest of America's lengthy Pacific coastline. Of course, when Los Angeles inevitably fell, that would free up additional ships to tighten the blockade, but there still would never be enough enemy vessels to cover every cove and bay.

Before the Germans took Los Angeles, however, Sims wanted to take some positive steps. Like everyone in the military, he was sick and tired of waiting and watching. The United States should never be used as a punching bag and that, he thought, was exactly what was happening. It was time to strike back, however small that attempt might be.

Thus, Ensign Josh Cornell found himself on the deck of a squat, ugly fishing boat not unlike the one that had rescued him off San Francisco. This one, however, was registered to the U.S. Navy as a miscellaneous ship and her crew was all U.S. Navy personnel. Despite his still gimpy leg, Josh was present to observe on Sims' behalf. Lieutenant Jesse Oldendorf commanded the ship they'd facetiously renamed the *Shark*. Her armament consisted of a couple of machine guns taken from the hulks at Mare Island and she carried a cargo that needed to be delivered to the Germans.

Oldendorf was also an Annapolis man and a decade older then Josh. Oldendorf's friends called him "Oley." Since Oley was two grades higher, Josh called him "sir." Like Josh, Oldendorf was thrilled to be out at sea even though his warship was a stinking former fishing boat that the Navy hadn't even bothered to repaint, which Josh quickly realized was intentional. There had been serious discussions with Admiral Sims as to whether or not the Germans would recognize the *Shark* as a U.S. Navy ship if she was captured, and if the crew would be treated as prisoners of war under the Geneva Convention.

Sims' response had been succinct. "Don't get captured."

Oldendorf kept the *Shark* as close as possible to the beautiful but rugged shoreline as they slipped south towards San Diego, chugging along at a sedate ten knots. He had no concern about being spotted. She would be seen by many and there would be no attempt to hide her. The *Shark* looked like what she had been, an innocuous fisher, just one of hundreds still on the water. Keeping close to shore meant they could turn and ground the ship if a German did decide to take a close look since there was no way they could outrun or outfight much of anything. That way the twelve-man crew stood at least a small chance of escaping overland and the issue of whether they were covered by the Geneva Convention would be moot.

The *Shark*'s cargo was two dozen contact mines. These would be dropped in San Diego's shipping channel and anchored to the ocean bottom, leaving the mines to bob at or just below the surface. Hopefully, an unwary ship would hit one and be sunk.

They reached their destination without incident. It was dark but not very cloudy and the crew of the *Shark* felt vulnerable and naked as they slipped into San Diego Bay's narrow channel. Oldendorf muttered that he couldn't believe the Germans' inertia. He didn't even see a patrol boat. Were they that confident? He grinned wickedly. Maybe they were overconfident.

They coasted to a dead slow speed. A ramp was opened and, one by one, the mines were dropped over. The *Shark* maintained enough speed to get out of the way of the mines when they bobbed back up to the surface.

"Be a helluva note to be sunk by our own mine," muttered one of the sailors. Oldendorf laughingly agreed and slapped the sailor on the back.

In minutes it was over. Their deadly cargo was gone and they turned to go north, to San Francisco.

Finally, a searchlight popped on and a finger of light swept the area they'd just left. They all held their breath as they steadily pulled away. The searchlight went off just as suddenly as it went on and they all commenced breathing again.

Oldendorf stood beside Josh. "Well, Ensign, do you think this night's effort was worth it?"

"Frankly sir, not really."

"Oh?"

"Sir, before the peace of 1915, both the Germans and the British sowed thousands, maybe tens of thousands of these mines, and all we dropped were twenty-four. Sorry sir, but this isn't even a pinprick."

Oldendorf was about to reply when a second searchlight flashed on and this one bathed them in its glare, forcing them to shield their eyes. A machine gun opened up from the nearby shore and a cannon boomed. A geyser of water erupted in front of them and bullets stitched the *Shark*'s wooden hull, spraying splinters over her crew. Something struck Josh's shoulder and knocked him down. He pulled himself up and looked at the devastation. Several of the *Shark*'s crew were lying on the deck and moaning, and Oldendorf, while still standing, was covered in blood from a gash in his head. Something hot, wet, and sticky was running down Josh's chest.

The minelayer's machine guns opened fire in the general direction of the searchlight and, to their astonishment, it winked out. It seemed unlikely that they'd hit it, so Josh thought they'd possibly scared the operators into turning it off.

Before they could take a deep breath, a crewman sighted ships coming from San Diego Bay. "Lead ship looks like a destroyer," Oldendorf said. "We'll run as far as we can and if we can't shake her, we'll head to shore and beach the *Shark*."

Josh watched in morbid fascination as the destroyer sliced through the water, cutting the distance with every second. It was as if the *Shark* was standing still. The destroyer was almost out of the channel and there were two patrol boats trailing her. The destroyer fired one of her deck guns and another geyser erupted a few yards off the *Shark*'s bow.

"I'm getting damn sick and tired of this!" Oldendorf yelled.

Suddenly, a flash of light erupted along the hull of the destroyer and she appeared to lift out of the ocean. The force of the explosion caused her to heel over and almost capsize. For an instant before the light faded, Josh saw men tumbling overboard. When the German destroyer righted herself, it was apparent that her back was broken and she was going to sink.

There was no more pursuit. The confused German patrol boats milled about the dying destroyer and began taking off her crew. Oldendorf again stood by Josh. "You hurt bad, Josh?"

"I don't think so, sir. It hurts like hell, but everything moves okay. I'm just a little tired of getting wounded."

Oldendorf nodded. "Amazing. The Brits drop thousands of the damned things and get little in the way of results, while we drop a couple dozen and kill a destroyer."

Josh sat down. His world was beginning to spin. Shock was again setting in. Josh thought ruefully that this was the second time he'd seen a destroyer sink.

★ ★ ★

The journey to Los Angeles was helped by Corporal Joe Flowers finding and liberating a carriage from a farmhouse. One look at his angry face and the occupants declined to argue. This meant that Ella and Maria could ride in relative comfort and the party moved along with greater speed. Ella continued to show signs of physical improvement, although her eyes had not lost their blank look. Kirsten was extremely concerned. What had happened to her had clearly been too much for her mind to handle. Ella had lived in a world where women were respected and put on pedestals, not stripped in front of a crowd and then gang-raped. Poor Ella hadn't even been in favor of women voting. She'd agreed with those men who felt that women weren't psychologically up to the heavy responsibility. Kirsten's hatred of the Germans continued to increase. So did her contempt for Roy Olson.

On the positive side, she and Luke Martel had gotten to know each other fairly well. He was a lot smarter then she'd first assumed and, like her, was self-educated and well read. And the scar on his face was just that, a scar, and not part of his personality, although it would frighten small children on Halloween. She decided she would ultimately halt her journey in San Francisco. It was a decision based on the facts that Luke was stationed there and that she had no place else to go.

Thus it was with a degree of regret, if not sadness, that they parted at the railroad station in Los Angeles. Luke had managed to find Maria, Ella, and Kirsten spots on a train headed north to safety. This was easier said than done since the sprawling city of Los Angeles was evacuating itself. Thousands of people were streaming north and away from the Germans who, it was said, were just a few hours away. The evacuation had been going on for days and there were still many tens of thousands of people in the sprawling city. People were beginning to panic as the sounds of guns and the sight of distant smoke became evident and moved ever closer.

There was a stench in the air that Luke identified as burning oil. Good. Someone was taking care of denying the Germans the oil stored in L.A.

Luke was embarrassed and frustrated to admit he was a United States soldier. He saw no other uniforms in the city that had once had a population of more than half a million. Now it was becoming a ghost town. It shocked him to see Americans moving north like hordes of beggars or migrants with nothing more than suitcases or even bags of goods to call their own. Some had no more than the clothing on their backs and few had any food. *This can't be the United States of America,* he thought.

Some of the fortunate ones had cars or carriages and these were jammed to overflowing with people and their possessions. The lucky ones had horses. Cars and trucks would only go as far as their gas tanks would take them, assuming they didn't break down in the first place, while horses could still travel on an empty stomach and leave congested roads, avoiding traffic jams.

Owners of vehicles of all kinds were charging exorbitant rates to move people away from the oncoming Germans. Rumors of German atrocities abounded, and Luke recognized some of them from the early days of the 1914 war, and these included massacres, mass rapes, and the impaling of pregnant women and children on bayonets. He didn't believe the impalements, but the murders and rapes had occurred, both in Belgium and now in California. Kirsten's cousin was proof of that.

Despite the lack of an army presence, there were large numbers of armed men congregating in Los Angeles, and they all seemed to be reporting to someone named Joseph Harper, a wealthy merchant who had taken a semblance of control of the deteriorating situation. Luke decided it was time to find this man.

Luke found Joe Harper near the Hollywood section of town, where the movie industry had relocated only a few years earlier. Now the sight of sets and production buildings in the background seemed grotesque. So too was the rumble and thunder of approaching artillery. The German Army was just down the road. Several dozen armed Mexicans lounged around, resting their horses. A young man who looked like he was their leader glared at Luke as he passed by.

Joe Harper was in his fifties and seemed a friendly sort, although clearly exhausted and stressed. "Where's the rest of your army, Lieutenant?"

"I wish I could say they'd be arriving momentarily, but I can't. May I ask what your plans are, Mr. Harper?"

"I hope to defend the city. I would not think of blaming you personally, but I hope you realize that the absence of the United States Army means we have to do it ourselves."

"And is that wise? I managed to pass through several large German units on my way here, and I estimate at least fifty thousand enemy soldiers converging on Los Angeles as we speak, as is obvious from the sounds and the smoke. How many men do you have?"

Harper looked visibly shaken. He clearly hadn't thought there'd be that many Germans. "Maybe ten thousand," he said softly.

Luke shook his head. The man was going to get

a whole lot of people killed. "Ten thousand poorly armed, inadequately trained men, and led by people who mean well, but you'll be fighting against the highly professional and well-equipped German Army. With respect Mr. Harper, they will cut you to pieces. More bluntly, they will go through your army like shit through a goose. Thousands of your men will be killed or wounded and nothing will be accomplished except unnecessary bloodshed."

Harper was angry. His face reddened. "And what do you propose we do? Leave our homes and businesses to the Hun without a fight?"

"It's better than dying for nothing. How do you have your men set up?"

Harper explained that his ten thousand, if there really were that many, were scattered about in a number of positions that he called strong points. When Luke again said his men would be overrun, Harper bristled.

"Look, Lieutenant, I was an officer in the Spanish-American War and a lot of what you're saying is right. But I just can't go abandoning people's homes. We'll stand and fight, and if we get whipped, we'll pull back and fight some more."

Luke pointed to the hills to the east. "Los Angeles is a state of mind, not a city. It's sprawled all over the place. Los Angeles has been gobbling up small communities for years and there is no one central place to defend with your small force. You simply don't have the men to defend the town, and I've seen a couple of your so-called strong points. They are nothing but sandbagged houses."

"We will do what we must with what we have."

"And Los Angeles is located in a bowl, surrounded

by high ground." Luke pointed to the foothills of the overlooking San Gabriel Mountains. "Have you at least put men up there? If you don't, the Germans will and they'll pound your men to pieces with their artillery. The Germans travel with 105mm howitzers that can easily reach you from those hills."

Luke wasn't so certain about that statement. The German guns had a range of about six miles, and the foothills might be farther than that. But he did want to shake Harper, shake some sense into the man, but Harper would have none of it and angrily told Luke to leave.

As Luke did so, he saw the apparent leader of the armed Mexicans staring at him. The man walked up to Luke and introduced himself as Tomas Montoya, a rancher from outside the city of Los Angeles. He was in his thirties, a trifle overweight, and looked angry.

"I could not help overhearing your conversation with the esteemed but very ignorant Mr. Harper. He means well but he will lead his men to disaster." The sound of artillery from the south had grown much closer. "And it may have already begun."

Both men were silent as they tried to gauge what was happening down the coast road. Finally, Montoya spoke. "I offered Harper fifty men, all armed and mounted, but he said he didn't want Mexicans in his command. He said we were the cause of the whole problem."

"Curious," Luke said. "I thought the Germans had something to do with it."

"I don't blame him," muttered Joe Flowers. "I don't like Mexicans either."

Montoya glared at him. "And I don't like Apaches."

"Enough," Luke said. "Like I said, the Germans are to blame for this, not Mexicans or Apaches."

Montoya smiled tightly. "Agreed. May I ask what your plans are?"

"To watch and then head north and report to General Liggett."

"When you leave, my men and I would like to go with you. You would be in charge, of course."

Luke accepted the offer and they waited. The sound of firing got louder and closer. Messengers came and went from where Harper was trying to control events.

The first signs of disaster were the men who ran by. Some of them still had weapons, but the majority were unarmed. They had panicked and tossed their rifles away. Some were wounded and they all looked terrified. Harper tried to stop some of them but quickly gave up.

The trickle of panic-stricken men became a flood and the chatter of small-arms fire was a distinct sound. "Let's move out of here," Luke said and his new command followed to what they hoped was a safe place. "This part of town is going to draw a lot of attention very soon."

As predicted, German howitzers from the hills did have the range. They began to pound Hollywood, and the retreating survivors of the fighting ran for their lives. Luke saw Harper still trying to bring order out of the chaos when a salvo of German shells landed on his position. A second later, Harper and a couple of other men who'd been with him had become little more than red smears on the ground.

Luke smiled grimly. "If you are under my command, Mr. Montoya, here is my first order. We ride like hell out of here."

"An excellent idea," said Montoya. "But perhaps there is something you would like to see first? Are either of you fine gentlemen good at blowing things up? If so, there are some, ah, facilities in and around Los Angeles that definitely should not fall into German hands. They are called refineries. Harper did blow up the oil storage tanks, but he neglected the refineries."

Luke looked towards Joe Flowers. "The corporal is outstanding at breaking things. Shall we proceed?"

Camp Dix was located almost in the center of New Jersey, north and east of Camden. It was big, sprawling, raw, and unfinished. The barracks were made of poorly cut and treated wood and there were gaping holes in the walls, letting the wind whip through. The roofs leaked badly, even in a mist. The result was that all of the recruits were miserably cold and wet. Most caught colds, or even pneumonia, and a scandal was growing in Washington. Still, Dix wasn't any different from the dozen or so other basic training camps springing up throughout the United States.

Even worse were the sleeping and sanitary facilities. The wood slat bunks were too narrow and too short and nobody could believe that somebody had actually gone and ordered square toilet seats. The jokes about them were too numerous to count. And the toilet paper could have stripped rust from a pipe.

Wally and Tim had been called up, trucked to Dix, and jammed into barracks, where they'd waited. After two days, they were issued uniforms that didn't fit, so they traded around with others with similar problems until they were reasonably comfortable. The food was uniformly bad and the wooden bunks were covered with thin straw mattresses. They were having serious second thoughts about the wisdom of their enlisting. If this was the Army, the Germans and Mexicans were going to have no trouble marching all the way from California to Camden.

They'd spent the two weeks waiting for a call up learning all they could about Germany, Mexico, Texas, and California. They spent time listening to a friend's short-wave radio and hearing about events in Texas. California was too far away and the reports from there dire but vague. Newspapers were full of gloom and doom and the crowds at the telegraph office were glum as well. The Germans were moving up California and the Mexicans were doing the same thing in Texas, and nobody was doing much about it. To make matters worse, there were rumors of German warships off New York and elsewhere.

The night before they were shipped to Camp Dix, Tim had actually managed to get kissed. Kathy Fenton was nineteen, pretty enough, and lived down the street. She was a cashier at a Woolworth's. They'd gone out a couple of times before and he wondered if they had a future. They'd all gotten more than a little drunk on some homemade beer. Prohibition wasn't the law yet, although some said it was coming. Home brew seemed like a good way to practice for it. It had tasted like bad piss but it did contain alcohol, which gave everyone a buzz.

At any rate, Tim and Kathy had gone into a closet and made out like bandits. He'd kissed her hard and gotten his tongue in her mouth. She'd even let him touch her breast but stopped him when he tried to unbutton her blouse.

"Nothing more until we're married," she'd gasped.

Married? What the hell was she thinking of? He kissed her again and cupped her breast, outside the dress as she insisted, and she ground her pelvis against his erection. He decided it was better than nothing. Married? He liked her, but Jesus, was he ready to get married?

Later, he picked up Wally, who was staggering drunk, and they went home, confident they'd have hellacious hangovers the next morning, which they did. It made the trip to Dix even more memorable as about half the young men on the train were in the same fix. After one guy got sick, almost everyone lost yesterday's lunches, turning the train into a stinking mess.

For several days after their arrival and getting uniforms, nothing happened in Camp Dix. They ate, they slept, and they wondered. Finally they were called out to the parade ground, all two hundred of the NCOs in training. They noticed similar groups gathering in other areas of the sprawling base.

A little man in an impeccable khaki uniform stood in front of them and ordered them to sit down on the ground. He had a multitude of stripes on his sleeve. He was barely five feet tall and skinny and wrinkled. He could have been anywhere from thirty to eighty years in age.

Instinctively, Wally and Tim knew this little man was to be both respected and feared.

"Oy yam here to train you," he said. His accent was unidentifiable but he was definitely speaking something resembling English.

"Oy yam Sergeant Smith," he pronounced it "Smeeth." "And you will obey me in all things, and you will do so without hesitation or question. What I teach you might just save your fookin' lives. If you have any difficulty with my accent or the way I talk or some strange words oy might use, it is because oy am from a little ways from here."

Wally sucked in his breath and poked Tim. "I'll say he's a ways from here. He's British. Jesus, they brought in the British Army to train us."

Sergeant Smith paused. He heard the murmurings as his young trainees figured out what he'd said and not said. It was true, he thought with a happiness he dared not let them see. Americans were an intelligent lot. Smith and his companions at Dix and many other camps were ready to begin training the recruits. So what if they were still short of rifles and other tools of war. They would somehow make sure the recruits were at least as well prepared as the men he'd led at the Marne in 1914, or against the Boers years earlier. He knew he could not give these men his years of experience, but he could damn sure see to it that they were as ready as they could be when they faced down the kaiser's hordes.

He glared at them and they met his look. They showed curiosity, even respect, but no fear. "Oy hate the fookin' Germans. Hate them with a fookin' passion." He saw he had their attention.

"Men, oy will train you to the best of your abilities. I will train you to achieve things you never thought you could possibly do and then you will do some more."

He paused. "I will train you to defeat the fookin' Germans!" His voice didn't quite rise, but it did gain in strength.

"I will train you to kill the fookin' Germans, and

I will train you to drive their fookin' Kraut asses out of your country! Now get up and get started!"

There was silence, and Smith wondered if he'd gone too far, or maybe he'd scared them, or maybe they hadn't understood his thick Yorkshire accent. Then all two hundred men stood up and started applauding, and the applause turned to cheers, and the cheers to howls. *Yes,* he thought, *this is going to be most interesting, and God damn the fookin' Germans.*

★ CHAPTER 8 ★

KIRSTEN, ELLA, AND MARIA WERE JAMMED INTO SEATS on a train that moved north from Los Angeles towards San Francisco at little more than a snail's pace.

People filled every seat and the overflow sat in the aisle of the passenger car, while others were forced to stand wherever they could find a spot. There was no place to move. The air was thick with the stench of sweat, fear, and urine, and not all came from the children and infants. A couple of fools actually tried to light up cigarettes or cigars in the confined space, which had made more people sick. They had been shouted at until they put them out.

Many adults had relieved themselves where they stood or sat, and Kirsten wondered just when her turn would come as her bladder was getting uncomfortably full. She couldn't stand if she wanted to, and several people had passed out. Some were still upright, unable to even fall.

There were several other passenger cars in the

train and she assumed they were all as stuffed with humanity as this one. Nor was anyone interested in taking tickets. A man who actually had tickets complained that people were in his family's seats; he had been beaten up by squatters while his wife and two children looked on in horror, shrieking and crying.

Kirsten wished she could talk to Ella, who had vomited on herself. In a way, Kirsten envied Ella, who seemed oblivious to the world around her. Of course, she did talk to Maria who was a wonderful woman, but, like so many like her, was undereducated and had limited interests. She simply wanted to get to family in the north, while Kirsten also wanted to talk to someone about the collapse of civilization that was going on around her. Was the world really coming to an end? And what were their real chances of survival?

She also wanted to talk to someone, anyone, about bathroom facilities, drinking water, and food. She felt sweaty and dirty, but these were the least of her worries. She estimated that the train was going maybe twenty miles an hour tops and most of the time at speeds far less than that. This meant many more hours of confinement. Of course, she could always get out and walk. But all the way to San Francisco? She'd stick with the train.

She wondered what was going on in Ella's mind. Her cousin still hadn't spoken a word since her ordeal. When she got to San Francisco, Kirsten would have to find a psychiatrist for her. If Ella didn't get better, Kirsten dreaded the thought of having to care for her, although she dreaded even more the thought of putting her into an asylum. She'd visited one once and thought she'd go mad herself at the sight of the inmates. She prayed that Ella would get better.

At least Kirsten had a window. If the wind was blowing from the right, it meant fresh air. If the wind blew from the front it meant coal smoke, cinders, and people yelling at her to close the damn thing.

A pair of specks in the sky caught her attention. Were they large birds, she wondered? No, they were airplanes. She felt a shiver of fear. Only the Germans had planes. Surely they would leave a train full of refugees alone.

The two planes banked and approached the train side on. Others in the train saw them and began to scream. Gunfire rippled from the planes' machine guns. Bullets tore through the wooden walls of the railroad car, finding packed flesh. Screams changed to howls of pain and panic, but the train rumbled on as people died and blood poured from the cars.

The planes banked and came on the train from the other side. One plane veered and attacked the engine. The boiler exploded in a plume of white steam that billowed skyward. The engine rolled off the tracks with a maniacal howl, pulling the other cars with it.

Kirsten knew horror as the car she was in tilted to her left and slid down a small embankment with scores of people screaming. It stopped abruptly on its side, and the car was filled with dust and smoke, blinding her. She clawed her way upward, thankful that the train had fallen on its left side and not the right where she had been sitting looking out the window. There were people below her and she felt them pulling at her, trying in panic to climb over her. The smoke and dust choked her. She didn't want to burn to death.

The dust and smoke settled a bit and, with the help

of others, she got the window open wide enough for people to crawl out. People pushed and tried to claw their way past her. A heavyset man succeeded and kicked her in the face. She spat blood, and somehow managed to pull a hat pin from her purse. She jabbed it into his thigh, but he didn't notice.

Finally, she climbed out and stood shakily on the side of the train. People were pouring out of the train like ants from a disturbed hill. The two German planes had disappeared. Their horrible work was done. The train was destroyed and the line itself had been damaged. No more trains would be traveling from Los Angeles to San Francisco, at least not on these tracks, for some time.

Where were Ella and Maria? She helped some people out through the window that had been by her seat while others climbed out other windows. Some were injured and bloody from bullet wounds and the crash, and a few were dead. Fortunately, most only looked stunned. Finally, Maria emerged through the window, pulling the limp form of Ella.

With help from other survivors, they got her out and down onto the ground. Ella was pale and not moving and her head was tilted in a strange position. Kirsten felt for a pulse and checked if she was breathing. Nothing.

"I tried," said Maria, "but everything was crazy and she got crushed. She couldn't defend herself against the panic."

Ella was dead. Her neck was broken. Of course she couldn't defend herself. She didn't even know what world she was in. Kirsten wanted to cry but she was too angry. Nor was Ella the only fatality. Many other bodies lay limp, bloody and broken as good Samaritans pulled everyone from the cars. Many of the dead were women and children and Kirsten had a hard time fathoming what she was seeing. She could now really understand Ella's withdrawal from reality. It was so tempting to run and hide in a world where sights like this were blocked out.

Mercifully, there had been no real fires, so everyone was spared that horror. Soon everyone, living and dead, had been taken from the train.

Some farmers came by with wagons and Kirsten could see they were appalled by the extent of the carnage. They loaded the injured onto the wagons and later came back for the dead. That evening, they buried Ella by a dirt road alongside a farmer's field. Kirsten willed herself to remember the grave's location. Thankfully, the farmer placed some rocks on the grave and logged her name and the place of her grave in a notebook. Someday they'd come back and give her a proper burial. She and Ella hadn't always gotten along, far from it, but the woman deserved the decency in death she was denied at the end of her life.

Maria raised her eyes and looked at Kirsten. Now what, she was asking. Kirsten answered. "We have no choice but to go north and continue to San Francisco. The Germans aren't going to stop at Los Angeles."

It was almost four hundred miles from Los Angeles to San Francisco and they'd traveled maybe fifty of that distance before the disaster. Earlier, she had scoffed at the idea of walking to San Francisco. Now it seemed like the only viable alternative. She and Maria had a lot of walking ahead of them.

★ ★ ★

The crown prince was elated. His army had taken two major American ports, San Diego and Los Angeles, and a number of cities in between to be used as bases for future operations. He was certain his father, the emperor, would be proud of him and he was equally proud of his generals and his men.

And now the German Navy had arrived. He watched as the line of battleships and cruisers majestically entered Los Angeles harbor and anchored. A motor launch departed from the battleship *Westfalen*, the temporary flagship of the recently designated Pacific Fleet. The Pacific Fleet was the largest offshoot of the High Seas Fleet which remained in German waters and under the command of Admiral Scheer. The High Seas Fleet confronted England and the Royal Navy's Home Fleet as it had for more than six years. The Pacific Fleet was commanded by Admiral Franz von Hipper, a fifty-seven-year-old professional. Like his subordinate, von Trotha, he'd felt cheated that there'd been no major battles in the 1914 war with the British. Von Hipper normally flew his flag from the *Bayern*, but that mighty battleship was on blockade duty off Puget Sound.

The two men greeted each other with warmth and mutual salutes. The crown prince suggested they go indoors for refreshments and the admiral happily agreed. When courtesies were over, they went to Wilhelm's office in what had been Los Angeles' city hall. A picture of Woodrow Wilson stared down at them as if in disapproval.

Hipper offered Wilhelm a cigar. "It's Cuban, and most exquisite. I have to ask, your highness, just what is that acrid stench in the air?"

Wilhelm sighed. "What the Americans couldn't take with them, they destroyed. Unfortunately, what you smell are the remains of the oil industry in Los Angeles. We have taken hostages and executed a number of them in reprisal for the damage that was caused to the refineries and storage facilities."

Hipper sat upright, shock on his face. "What? How bad was the damage?"

"Quite complete, Admiral," Wilhelm said, surprised at Hipper's reaction. "The storage tanks and the refineries are very much ruined. Why?"

"Because, sir, we were counting on that oil, the diesel in particular. My ships swallow prodigious amounts of it and we had planned to refuel here at Los Angeles. After all, the Los Angeles area currently produces nearly a quarter of the world's oil! My ships' fuel tanks are almost empty after steaming from Germany to California and we were only able to take so much in the holds of accompanying tankers, and from storage depots in Indo-China."

"Good God," the crown prince said.

"Your highness, I must ask—did you receive word that every effort was to be made to take those refineries and storage tanks as intact as possible?"

Wilhelm flushed and mentally cursed himself. No, he had not been told. Berlin's bureaucracy and the eternal rivalry between the Army and the Navy had probably raised its ugly head and someone had managed to "lose" the message. Some bureaucrat probably decided it would be great good fun if the upstart Navy ran out of fuel and was embarrassed. Of course he should have known about the fleet's fuel and other logistical requirements without being told. A modern navy needed oil. Only a few years ago, the German Navy ran on coal, which was available in many places, but oil, however abundant, had to be refined before it could be used.

The prince's own army needed oil, but in the form of gasoline which was rather more available than diesel. Cars and trucks used gas and there were many small storage facilities and gas stations to use to fill the army's trucks and other vehicles. Of course the fact that the army also used tens of thousands of horses meant they had alternatives should the supply of gas dry up.

But diesel? The prince had never really given it a thought. "Admiral, I regret that I received no such information and I deeply regret not having taken the initiative myself."

"I am most concerned about the refineries. Are they really destroyed?"

Crown Prince Wilhelm was beginning to sweat. "I will arrange for your engineers and mine to survey the refineries and render a judgement. I can only say that they appeared to be totally destroyed. If that is the case, how long will it take to rebuild them and what impact will their loss, however temporary, have on your operations?"

Hipper thought for a moment. "I too will defer to my engineers, but I believe it will take months at best to make a badly damaged refinery operational. I doubt that we have either the equipment or the skilled men to do the job, which means both will have to be imported. In the meantime, I will send messages to Berlin to have additional tankers sent here as quickly as possible, but that will take at least a month to gather them, fill them, and get them here. It would shorten the journey if we'd managed to take the Panama Canal, but that didn't happen either."

Hipper continued his analysis. "As to our current operations, we will drastically curtail them until the additional fuel arrives. We will continue to blockade Puget Sound and San Francisco, but the ships will be instructed to conserve fuel and not go chasing after shadows. Unfortunately, that will include American surface raiders should they emerge. We will also take oil from the smaller ships and give them to the larger. This means that some American ships might slip out through our blockade, but so be it."

Hipper laughed without mirth. He had no choice but to curtail operations until he could arrange for fuel from other sources. The Dutch should have some in their Pacific colonies, he thought, but simply acquiring oil was not the solution. Oil existed in abundance almost everywhere, but it was useless gunk as it came out of the ground. It had to be refined, and the damned refineries had been destroyed.

"Still, it should not change things. You've got the American Army on the run and I've got the United States Navy bottled up. It doesn't matter that things aren't going perfectly, highness, they never do."

Wilhelm recovered his aplomb. "Speaking of which, are you aware that the British have sent a squadron to Puget Sound?"

Again von Hipper was surprised. "What on earth for?"

"Apparently they are concerned for the neutrality of the Sound. They sent two battleships and a number of lighter ships as a reminder that the northern half of Puget Sound is theirs and we should not intrude. I understand they are sending a similar squadron to the St. Lawrence on the Atlantic side of this damned continent."

Hipper was anxious to get back to his ships and make the appropriate arrangements to save fuel in hostile waters. Damn the fools who hadn't informed the crown prince of the fleet's needs.

The United States Army west of the Rockies and south of San Francisco was beginning to take tentative steps to move forward and away from the initial chaos. Liggett had organized disparate groups into two divisions, grandly named the First Infantry and the Second Infantry. The First was commanded by Luke's old mentor, Fox Connor, and the Second by Major General James Harbord. They consisted of four understrength regiments each, totaling about fifteen thousand men per division. While larger than their German counterparts, they were still smaller than the American Army's table of organization specifications which called for divisions of about twenty thousand men. They were poorly equipped, having little in the way of artillery, machine guns, and ammunition, but at least they existed. For the time being each division operated independently and reported directly to Liggett, a relationship that would change as the army grew.

The Seventh Cavalry Regiment was now part of the First Division and very few of the remaining soldiers still had horses. Patton was delighted to receive the fifty mounted Mexicans under Montoya and voiced thoughts about recruiting a Mexican brigade. Patton had come to the conclusion that many thousands of

Mexicans were either refugees who hated the brutal Carranza government, or Americans of Mexican descent who hated the Carranza government as well. Either way, they were a source of eager manpower.

Thus relieved of the obligation of protecting Montoya from wrathful Californians, Martel found himself in yet another biplane headed for San Francisco. Corporal Flowers informed Luke he'd rather die than go up in one of those things and took a train.

There were numerous changes to San Francisco since Luke had departed. It now had the appearance of a city under siege. The German warships had made several moves toward the city and bombarded her again. More buildings were damaged and many of the remainder were protected by piles of sandbags. Much of the civilian population had departed and the rest were packing for the inevitable day when the German Army arrived. However, refugees were streaming in from the south and had more than replaced the people who'd fled north.

As promised by Admiral Sims, many of the twelve-inch guns from the sunk or damaged ships at Mare Island had been removed and now faced out towards the Pacific or covered the entrance to the Bay. A number of six-inch and four-inch guns had been mounted on Alcatraz Island, which covered the mouth of the entrance to the bay. That giant rock was now an unsinkable battleship.

South and east of the city, work was progressing on trenches and fortifications that would both protect the city and extend into the mountains. As Harbord's and Connor's divisions slowly retreated, they did their best to nibble at the Germans and delay them. Every day that they delayed the invaders meant more fortifications constructed and more recruits trained in the camps outside Sacramento.

General Liggett and Admiral Sims had combined their headquarters and Luke found himself working alongside naval personnel who were as bemused with him as he was with them. The war was eliminating the historic rivalries between the two services.

Luke had told Kirsten where he could be found and she said she would look him up when she finally made it to San Francisco. Thus, he was stunned and sickened when it was reported that the train she'd been traveling on had been attacked by German planes. The official report said more than fifty dead and a hundred injured, many of them badly. The injured were identified and Kirsten wasn't among them, but the list of the dead was incomplete. He recognized her cousin Ella's name, but many of the dead had been unidentifiable. He prayed that Kirsten wasn't one of them, or, if she was, that her death had been painless. *That is,* he thought bitterly, *if violent death could ever be painless.*

Even though they'd only known each other for a few days, Luke had felt a sense of kinship with her. His own relations with ladies, and not just women, had been limited at best, and the young widow had fascinated him. She was bright, pretty, intelligent, and self-reliant, not a vapid shadow like so many woman were, even in this relatively enlightened age. And now maybe she was dead.

Most maddeningly, there was nothing he could do. If she was wandering her way up north, she'd arrive when she did. If she was dead, he'd never hear anything about it. *Women should not be casualties in a war,* he thought. But, of course, they had been since time immemorial.

Elise was furious as she stood at the foot of the hospital bed. "How dare you go and get yourself wounded again! Wasn't once enough to satisfy you?"

Ensign Josh Cornell lay back on the pillows and tried to grin, but the pain from his infected shoulder wouldn't let him. By the time the *Shark* had gotten back to San Francisco, the splinters that he'd thought were so trivial had become infected. Doctors at the tent hospital on the grounds of the Presidio had worked to pull the tiny pieces of wood out of his flesh and clean the wounds with iodine and alcohol. They were of the opinion that his shoulder and arm would never fully recover and he wondered what impact that would have on a Navy career.

Elise was not done scolding. "First you hurt your leg and now you hurt your arm. What is it going to be next, your thick empty skull?"

She huffed and sat down beside his bed and Josh could see tears welling in her eyes. She was so lovely and her concern so real, he thought he would melt.

"Elise, it's not like I went looking to get shot up. It just happened. I'm in the Navy and I can't just stand back when other people are out fighting the Krauts. My job is to fight them, too."

"I know," she said softly. "This may seem very bold of me to tell you, but you are a special person in my life, and I didn't want to lose you just when I've found you."

She laughed. "Close your mouth, Ensign, your jaw is dropping."

He grinned. "It's just that I'm stunned, and very, very pleased. You are special to me too."

A nurse came and glared at Elise. Women were not supposed to be in the men's ward, even though Josh was an officer and supposedly a gentleman. A word from Admiral Sims had gotten her entry but she would not abuse the privilege.

"I have to go now," she whispered and glared at the nurse, "one of the three witches from *Macbeth* has arrived and I must get back to work. When you feel better, we will talk and begin to see where this takes us."

He watched her slender figure as she departed. Like many young women she wore a skirt that came to mid calf, and what a lovely calf it was. He had no idea why some thought Elise was plain or skinny. He thought she was a lithe young goddess. And she liked him. He would concentrate on getting better.

General Nolan walked up to Luke's desk. A mountain of paperwork was stacked on it, consisting of transcripts of interrogations of refugees and the rare prisoner. They stated the obvious and didn't need an intelligence officer to analyze them.

Nolan glanced at the unread documents and smiled wickedly. "Congratulations, you've been breveted to captain for your work down south and in particular, Los Angeles. Destroying those refineries was a stroke of genius. Now you can start destroying those papers."

He handed Luke a set of captain's bars and Luke put them on. He thought he'd be eighty before he made captain. Funny what a war can do, even if it was only a temporary rank.

"I have to give Montoya credit for destroying the refineries. He knew where they were and it was his idea."

"Montoya appears to be a good man and we're glad he's on our side, even if he is a Mexican. I've got to remember that we've got Germans, like Ike Eisenhower, working for us, and that a lot of Mexicans north of the border hate the ones south of the border. Still, it was you who agreed with Montoya and you who led the raid. And already the loss of oil is playing hell with the Krauts' plans. In other words, Luke, we finally did something right. We've intercepted word that the Germans have told their warships to cut down on fuel usage, and that Admiral Hipper is requesting fuel tankers be sent from Germany or wherever the hell the kaiser can find them. Admiral Sims and Liggett are discussing plans to do something about that as well."

Luke was too tactful to remind Nolan that Dwight Eisenhower, like millions of other Americans, was of German extraction, but not German born. Newly promoted captains do not argue with newly promoted generals.

"And Luke, I'm genuinely sorry you haven't heard anything about that woman you met down there. The fact that you haven't heard anything could actually be good news."

Luke agreed but didn't want to talk about it, which Nolan understood. He'd asked those in the intelligence division to keep an eye out for survivors of the train attack, so just about everyone knew something had gone wrong with his personal life. So much for privacy, he thought.

Along with sharing working quarters, the Army and Navy shared support personnel. One of the more helpful staffers was a rather plainish young woman named Elise Thompson who, Luke understood, was seeing a young ensign who was currently in the hospital after being shot up in a raid.

She walked over, smiled slightly, handed him a folded piece of paper and winked. Nolan left and Luke read the note: Conference Room B, was all it said.

Puzzled, he turned towards Elise who smiled, flushed and looked away. All right, it was not going to be an assignation with the ensign's thin girlfriend. He got up and walked down the short hallway to Conference Room B. He knocked and entered and nearly fell over.

"Kirsten?"

Instinctively, he reached out his hands and she came into his arms. They hugged and he kissed her on the forehead. He wanted to do more, but she pulled back. She looked like hell. Her clothes, jeans, and blouse, were filthy and torn and her hair was a mess. The bruise on her face was receding but still multicolored, like summer storm clouds.

"You're beautiful," he said, meaning it.

"And you're blind, soldier," she said, laughing. "Ah, you've been promoted. Wonderful."

"How did you get here?"

They sat at the conference table and she told him that she and Maria had started walking the morning after burying Ella. The general idea was to head north since the Germans would, sooner or later, be coming from the south. After a day of that, they'd managed a ride on a truck that took them to Bakersfield where they'd jumped on a flatcar and ridden the train up to San Francisco. She said the flatcar was covered with refugees like her and there were many flatcars, all jammed with people.

"At least the engineer kept the speed down. Otherwise people would have flown off as we went around turns. I got off as close to here as I could, but it was still across the bay and I had to take a ferry. Maria's decided to stay with some relatives, so I'm now alone. My feet hurt, I'm filthy, and I need a bath. And after that, I'll need a place to live. It's just too cold and rainy to camp out in the park. I do have some money, so I'm not destitute."

Sleeping in the park was not a facetious comment. Many of the parks were filled with tents, and chaos was starting to take over. Liggett had said he was on the verge of declaring martial law, and the hell with what Sonny Jim Rolph, the mayor of San Francisco or what William Stevenson, governor of California, thought. The city was sliding towards anarchy and something had to be done. In the meantime, there were housing shortages along with concerns about food.

"Would you settle for dinner while I figure this out?"

There was a knock on the door and Elise entered. She saw they were holding hands and smiled. "Mrs. Biel, I couldn't help but wonder if you're looking for a place to live? If you are, I have an apartment available since my so-called roommates just left for the north. It's not majestic or anything, but it does have two beds and a bath."

Kirsten smiled. "Do you read minds?"

Elise laughed. "It was too obvious. Admiral Sims and General Liggett said I should take some time and get you settled. And you, Captain Martel, General

Nolan says you should get back to work on that pile of papers."

Roy Olson looked and saw yet another corpse swinging in the breeze. The Germans had stopped shooting people. It wasted ammunition. Hanging was much cheaper and leaving the body dangling was a very dramatic warning. This one was blackened by the sun and its face had been chewed to the bone by birds. It looked as if it had been there for several days. The dead man was one of the two remaining Dubbins boys. Olson's deputies had caught him and the German, Steiner, had strung him up.

Steiner came out of his office and greeted Olson outside. Olson was always amazed how German officers could keep their uniforms so immaculate. Olson was dusty from a hard ride in from his ranch. They walked to a large barbed-wire corral in which several hundred men, white men, sat and stared at them. Most of them wore civilian clothes and only a handful were dressed in any kind of uniform. Some were angry, exuding hate, and some looked blank and fearful.

"Who the hell are these guys?" Olson asked.

"Your workforce. These are prisoners taken in the Los Angeles campaign and you will use them to perform the menial duties that used to be done by the residents of the area until they all ran away. It has already been pointed out to the prisoners that they are fortunate to be alive since they were irregulars and could have been shot as terrorists."

Fortunate indeed, Olson thought. The swinging corpse was proof that the Germans played rough with anyone who opposed them. He noticed a number of

Mexican guards around the prisoners. Steiner saw him looking and smiled. "And that is your security force. One hundred Mexicans along with the twenty ignorant barbarians you call your deputies ought to be enough to keep the prisoners in line. An early execution or two might be impressive as well."

Olson agreed. Once he might have been upset at killing Americans, but those days were long gone. He'd felt a tremor of panic when that young American officer momentarily convinced him that the U.S. Army was just over the horizon, but he quickly realized the man had tricked him. Steiner said he'd been played for a fool and Steiner was right. They'd dug in and waited several days for an American attack that never came. Now he knew that the Germans were definitely here to stay and he was damn glad to be on the right side, the winning side.

Steiner smiled. "You've made a good life for yourself, Mr. Olson. You live in a large house, you're making a lot of money and you have a lovely Mexican mistress who actually believes her husband stays alive because she lets you fuck her. He is alive, isn't he?"

"He died weeks ago." Olson said. He felt no regret. The woman, Martina, was still better off with him than whoring about the countryside. When he closed his eyes, he could imagine she was Kirsten Biel. He wondered just where she'd gone to and whether she was fucking the young officer she'd rode off with. Probably, he thought.

"When this is over," Steiner continued, "you will be well rewarded in many ways. By the way, you're not Jewish are you?"

"Of course not," he said angrily.

"Good. Neither the kaiser nor his son nor anyone in a senior position can abide Jews. Of course they are a necessary evil and some will rise to a certain level of authority based on merit, especially in banking and finance, but no Jews will hold a truly senior position in the German government. Or, if I have my way, in the province of California."

Steiner laughed. "In Germany, there are some radical organizations suggesting that all the Christ-killers be deported to someplace like Africa, but that is impractical. A pleasant thought, but impractical. It is as unlikely as actually killing all of them."

Olson smiled and shrugged. He didn't give a crap about Jews, Negroes, Chinese, Malays or anyone else. He just wanted to become an important man in the German Reich and make a lot of money. And when he got tired of little Martina—and she was starting to bore him—there would be others. Maybe someday he'd find out what happened to Kirsten Biel. Hell, she still owned property in the area, maybe she'd come back. Well, if she did, he had a big treat in store for her.

For most it began with a simple cough. Hell, everyone had a cold and everyone coughed and everyone coughed on everyone else. With so many bodies jammed so tightly in the barracks of Camp Dix, it was impossible not to.

The winter weather was wet and clammy and the barracks were a disaster. With so many openings in the walls, the soldiers joked that the walls didn't really exist, that they were just white paint on the sky. Staying warm and dry was impossible.

Of course, the training took place outside in that

same wet and clammy weather. Woolen uniforms got wet and soggy and clung to already cold and tired bodies. Overcoats hadn't arrived yet. Soon, they were told, but soon might be July the way the Army ran things. Even Sergeant Smith was concerned by the whole unhealthy state of affairs, but of course, couldn't show it.

The sneezing and sniffling evolved into coughing and the coughing into great hacking coughs with gobs of phlegm hurled about. The coughs then became fevers and men began going on sick call. Their numbers were few at first, because nobody wanted to go on sick call. That was for sissies. Real men would gut it out. After all, it was only a damn cold and colds went away after a few days, didn't they? Even the really sick refused to seek medical help. They were there to train to fight and kill the enemy, and to hell with a cough. They didn't want to be left behind.

Drill sergeants like Sergeant Smith made a point of going through the barracks and ordering the truly ill to go to the infirmary. Reluctantly, they went, and soon the medical facilities at Camp Dix were overwhelmed. Worse, recruits had begun arriving already feeling sick and transfers from other bases were showing up in the same condition, sometimes even worse. One train from the Midwest arrived with several dead soldiers on it, shocking everyone.

Tim couldn't take it any longer. Wally was sick and there was no denying it. One moment he was well and a moment later he was sick. Now his face had a blue tint to it and he was having great difficulty breathing. Tim didn't feel all that well himself. He felt weak and had begun coughing, too, which scared him. There was no way he could handle his brother and get him on sick call, so he got some of his buddies to help him take Wally to the hospital.

The hospital was hell. Tim had heard that a large number of his fellow doughboys were sick, but never realized just how many were down. Every bed was taken and patients were lying on the floor, covered with a blanket and trying to sleep in their own filth. Harassed medical personnel were trying desperately to cope and some of them looked sick as well.

He finally got someone to tell him where to put Wally. Tim and the others laid him down on the floor by a cot where a man looked like he was going to die. When he did, Wally could have the cot. Their buddies made Wally as comfortable as they could and said they'd be back to check on him and Tim. The doctors wanted the extra people out. They were in the way. No problem. Tim's friends wanted nothing more than to get the hell out of this house of death. They nodded and nearly ran outside.

Tim looked down on Wally and wondered if his baby brother understood just what was going on. He doubted it. Wally's eyes looked vacant and empty and all his efforts were concentrated on drawing the next breath. Tim tried to confront the likelihood that his younger brother was going to die and couldn't deal with it.

After an eternity, a doctor stopped by and quickly checked on Wally. He shook his head and didn't look at Tim.

The horror of the scene was overwhelming. He sat on the ground beside Wally. He would stay and keep him company until he was booted out. He overheard some other doctors wonder whether the disease had originated in the U.S. or had come from Europe. Tim wanted to say he didn't give a damn. He wanted his brother cured.

Nobody noticed when he pitched forward and then rolled onto his side. He was just one more desperately ill soldier who was likely going to die.

Generals March and Pershing wanted to congratulate the solemn young man who had wrought miracles in getting so much in the way of supplies and equipment to this staging area outside Kansas City. Newly promoted Brigadier General George Catlett Marshall didn't want approbation; he wanted results and they weren't forthcoming, at least not in the manner he wished. There were those who considered Marshall a genius and cited the vast quantities of supplies he'd gathered as proof. But the supplies weren't going anyplace and that was the problem.

Marshall had coerced a reluctant Henry Ford into manufacturing a thousand army trucks and more were coming. An additional two hundred were armor plated and awaited the machine guns or small cannon that would give them a lethal mobility like the German armored vehicles had. Other, smaller, automobile companies, like General Motors, were also supplying vehicles, and Harley Davidson was providing motorcycles, some with a sidecar that could also hold a machine gun.

Warehouses in Kansas City were stuffed with uniforms and other paraphernalia, including helmets, underwear, overcoats, boots, and socks. The Springfield Arsenal in Massachusetts had supplied a quarter of a million of the rifles that bore its name along with millions of rounds of ammunition. There were assurances that machine guns and the new Browning Automatic Rifles were on the way as well as artillery, but no one had seen anything yet. The factories were still tooling up. Production would begin soon, whenever the hell soon meant. Everyone knew that when the wheels of industry began to roll, there'd be weapons and ammunition galore, just not quite yet.

Even more frustrating, so much of the precious supplies they did have were just sitting there, out in a field, and gradually being covered with snow. With only one rail line working through the mountains to the northwestern states and then south to California, the bottleneck was enormous. And now it was the middle of the winter and a series of blizzards had struck, temporarily overwhelming any efforts to keep the tracks clear.

All three generals had come to the reluctant conclusion that significant aid to California might not be possible until late spring. General Liggett and the entire Pacific Coast Command were on their own until then. They could only hope and pray that Liggett could hold onto San Francisco. Or, barring that, at least maintain a military presence south of Portland. Or at least Seattle. Experts and intelligence said the Germans had no plans to go that far north, but who knew what the Germans would decide to do if San Francisco fell.

"If we can do nothing about California at this time, then we will move on Mexico," Pershing said and March nodded. Marshall looked away. He clearly didn't care which enemy was struck at first. He just wanted the supplies used against at least one of America's enemies.

"We have to do something," Pershing added, "and also be *seen* to be doing something. The American people are utterly frustrated by our lack of response and I cannot blame them for their anger. Between the lack of supplies, the lack of transportation, and the pneumonia in our camps, the American people are outraged. If we cannot cross into California, then we will have to take on the Mexicans and relieve the Texans."

Fighting in Texas now centered on San Antonio where a state of siege existed. The Mexicans were finding the Texans a hard nut to crack and National Guard units from nearby states had already reinforced the hard-fighting but beleaguered Texans. It was felt that Mexico was vulnerable to a strong counterattack.

A soldier on a motorcycle drove up to them, dismounted, saluted, and handed General March an envelope. March read it and paled.

"What we do may not matter at all," he said. "The disease striking our training camps has been identified as a particularly virulent form of influenza. It has apparently originated in the United States and not in Europe or Asia like epidemics normally do. Surgeon General Cumming believes this is the case because the influenza has only now begun to strike Europe. He has ordered all military facilities quarantined until further notice. All training must cease and no new recruits will be admitted. He now feels that perhaps a quarter of our army will die of this influenza; therefore, all emphasis must be on the survival of those who have not yet gotten the flu."

He crumpled the note and threw it on the ground where a puff of wind took it and spun it. "If the surgeon general is correct, we could suffer hundreds of thousands of dead without firing a shot!"

Marshall looked at the mountains of supplies and the acres of parked vehicles. Was it possible that there would be no one to use them?

★ CHAPTER 9 ★

WORK OR GET OUT OF SAN FRANCISCO WAS THE GIST of the blunt directive signed jointly by General Liggett and Admiral Sims. Despite the fact that thousands of people had been evacuated from San Francisco, many tens of thousands more had arrived from the south. The already tight situation regarding food and shelter was rapidly becoming critical. Useless mouths had to be sent away. Anyone who wished to enlist in the military or get to work on the city's defenses was welcome to stay. Others had to leave unless they could prove themselves to be useful to the defense forces.

This did not go over well with some of the population. Those who'd just arrived as refugees were exhausted, often sick, and had no inclination to flee further. Like refugees everywhere, they often had little in the way of clothing, furniture, and had no idea where to stay. Those who had been living in San Francisco had survived earthquakes and fires, and didn't feel that any damned army had the right to make them leave. There were confrontations and violence. Mayor Rolph didn't like having his power usurped and let everyone know it. A couple of newspapers, in particular Hearst's *San Francisco Examiner*, printed editorials saying the military administration was illegal and called for Californians to resist what it called an unlawful and unconstitutional occupation. General Liggett solved that problem by arresting an astonished Hearst and shutting down the *Examiner*. Skulls got cracked and a couple of people were killed by the military police. Finally, people began to get the message.

Kirsten thought the phrase "work or get out" had a marvelous ring to it. Right after arriving and getting settled in Elise's small apartment, she had volunteered to work in food distribution. That it was pretty much what Roy Olson and the Germans had been forcing the people of Raleigh to live with was a bit of irony that was not lost on her.

Before going to work, however, she'd presented a handful of drafts drawn on the Bank of Italy to its San Francisco office. The bank wasn't in Italy, of course, it was in San Francisco and had been founded by a man named A.P. Giannini. It had survived the earthquake of 1906 and Kirsten had felt that made it a solid choice for her savings, which included the proceeds from her late husband's insurance policies. She'd taken out some cash which enabled her to help Elise with some furniture issues as well as buying suitable clothing for herself. Both furniture and clothing were readily available at distressed prices.

Kirsten and a number of other clerks worked at tables in San Francisco's massive Civic Center Auditorium.

It had one hundred and twenty-two thousand square feet of floor space. The vast auditorium had been the site of the Republican Convention that had nominated the disgraced Warren Harding the previous summer. She could only wonder what might have happened had Harding won the presidency.

Kirsten confronted a very long line of confused and sometimes belligerent people. The people were hungry, tired, and confused, and why not? They'd been uprooted from their homes by an invading army that threatened to imprison them at best, murder and rape them at worst. This sort of thing just didn't happen in California. Several refugees had actually told this to Kirsten, as if she could personally do something about it.

Her job was to register their names and issue appropriate ration cards. The "useless mouths" received temporary cards good for one week. At the end of that week it was hoped they'd be in another city and somebody else's problem. They would get second cards only in the case of emergencies. She'd heard that Mayor Rolph and General Liggett were not in agreement over this, but political infighting was none of her concern.

Dealing with the refugees was heartbreaking and made her realize just how small her own problems were. She had lost her cousins and her ranch, but many refugees had lost far more. The number of people looking for missing relatives was appalling, as was the number who informed her that loved ones were dead or injured. Especially heartbreaking were the people looking for small children who'd been separated from their families in the rush north. A high school nearby was being used to feed found children and she directed those families to that location. Sadly, many of them had already been there.

Kirsten reflected that she still had her life, a good deal of money, and had struck up a friendship with an interesting gentleman in Captain Luke Martel, who was supposed to take her for a walk after work. That is, if work ever stopped. It was already late in the afternoon and the lines showed no sign of shortening. Policemen would close the doors promptly at five and only those inside would be handled. Anybody else could come back tomorrow. Kirsten thought they should work around the clock in shifts, but the managers hadn't yet come to that conclusion.

There was a commotion at the adjacent table. A Chinese family looked distraught, while the relief worker behind the counter laughed. "What's the problem, Will?" she asked.

Will Baker continued to laugh. He was a short thin man with glasses. She thought he was very self-important. "Chinks think they got a right to food, that's what."

Kirsten was puzzled. "They don't?"

"Not while there's white people in line they don't."

"Don't Chinese get hungry?"

Will's smile changed to a glare. "Who cares? Look, you're the new girl here, so do as you're supposed to. Food goes to Americans, not to the Chinks."

"And not to niggers, Indians, or Mexicans," one of Will's buddies added from another table. "Not that there's a whole lot of niggers here, but you have to set rules. White people first and everybody else last."

Kirsten nodded. "Will, you're right, I am new here and I don't know the rules. Who gave that order?"

"Right from the mayor."

Ah yes, Kirsten thought. *The mayor.* Sunny Jim Rolph was a major booster for the town and, it was rumored, was one of a group of businessmen who'd once issued brochures denying that the earthquake of 1906 had ever taken place. The fire, yes; it could not be denied. But an earthquake? Heavens no. That would be bad for potential business. But would Sunny Jim Rolph order Chinese people to starve? She didn't think so. San Francisco's Chinatown, while resented by many, had been around for decades. She concluded that Will Baker was making his own rules.

She waved the Chinese family over to her table and issued temporary cards. They nodded and thanked her profusely in broken English. They departed quickly and fearfully, as if concerned that someone would try to take the precious documents.

Finally, after what seemed an eternity, the doors closed and there would be no more refugees until tomorrow when it would start all over again. She was about to stand up when she noticed Will and two others by her table.

"Look," Will said, his pinched face red with anger, "I don't know who the hell you are and what you think you're doing, but don't put me down in front of Chinks and don't give ration cards to them either."

Kirsten kept her calm. "Aren't they supposed to eat?" she said sweetly. "Or don't they bleed or get hurt? They are human, aren't they?"

"Don't get smart with me, bitch," Will snarled. The two others nodded. None of them was particularly large or intimidating, but there were three of them. "Maybe we should take you outside and give you some punishment. Uppity women like you think you own the world since you can vote now. Maybe just an old-fashioned spanking on your sweet bare ass would be a good idea and make you realize you're not welcomed here."

"Really?" she smiled.

"There's a natural order to things, Mrs. Biel, and don't forget it. White men are on top and white women are underneath them." He laughed hugely as he realized the sexual implications of what he'd said. "Yeah, that's right. White men are always on top of white women."

Will's buddies thought that was hilarious as well. "Chinks, Indians, and Mexicans come last in this world. Hell, if the Chinks get hungry, let them eat flied lice," Will said and roared at his own humor. He reached out and cupped her chin in his hand, squeezing it. "You got that young lady?"

She pushed his hand away. "Let me show you something."

Kirsten raised her skirt above her knee, exposing an expanse of calf and thigh. Will and the other two stared. "Oh look what I've found," she said sweetly.

With stunning swiftness, the stiletto strapped to her thigh appeared in her hand and she plunged it down, impaling Will's hand to the table. He looked in shock at his mangled hand and then screamed. Kirsten removed the knife and blood poured onto the table and down to the floor.

"Silly me," she said. "I just dropped my knife. I think you ought to have that little cut looked at, don't you?"

Will and the others ran out, bumping into each

other like clowns at a circus. She wiped the knife on her handkerchief and returned it to its resting spot. She had a Derringer pistol in her handbag and a large hatpin in her hair. In these tumultuous times, weapons made her feel secure.

"Remind me not to get you angry," Luke said, walking up to her. He grabbed her hand which was still shaking.

She took a deep breath and tried to get control of her emotions. "How long were you standing there?" she said softly.

"Long enough to be prepared to step in and stop them if I thought I was needed. Obviously I wasn't. All of you were so preoccupied you didn't see me. Why don't we go for that walk, find us a bite to eat, and you can tell me what that was all about. Hopefully you'll keep that knife in its most intriguing resting place."

Kirsten laughed. "A walk and a bite to eat sounds interesting. Dealing with fools like those makes one just so hungry."

The success of German U-boats in the short war of 1914 had shocked the military world. Not only had scores of civilian ships been sunk, but several supposedly invincible Royal Navy battleships had been sent to the bottom with great loss of life. Most tragically, the old Royal Navy battleships *Cressy*, *Aboukir*, and *Hogue* had been sunk by one sub, the U-9 in September, 1914. Fourteen hundred British sailors had died in the catastrophe while their ships' captains looked on in disbelief. Thoroughly confused, they had wondered just what had happened to their ships. Attack by a sub was so unlikely, they thought the first ship had struck a mine and they had stopped to help which made them sitting ducks for the U-9.

As a result, many nations took a long look at their submarine fleets and the United States was no exception. When the war with Germany began, there were eight submarines stationed at Mare Island. Five were the longer range O-class, and three the shorter range coastal defense R-class subs. All eight subs were immediately sent to Puget Sound, where it was quickly determined that they were useless at that location.

Thus, when the British squadron made its entrance to the Sound, it was the five O-class subs that slipped out unnoticed and headed south to Catalina Island, close off the coast of California. The idea was for them to interdict German shipping to either San Diego or Los Angeles. The R-class subs would remain in the sound and protect against any German attempt to force the entrance.

Catalina Island was rugged and beautiful and had not been given much thought by the Germans, despite the fact that it was so close to the California coastline. The American subs quickly found a home a few miles north of the developing resort town of Avalon, and the few fisherman who lived there cheerfully provided the crews with food. The main concern of the American sailors was using their meager supply of fuel and torpedoes efficiently. They could not afford to waste either.

Lieutenant Ron Carter commanded the O-7. Along with not being claustrophobic, the men of any submarine had to be able to handle cramped quarters and the stench of unwashed bodies, backed up toilets, and oil. Subs weren't called pig boats for nothing, and the food tasted like crap as well. On the other hand, Carter mused, she was a warship and she was on a cruise with him in command.

Each of the five subs had four torpedo tubes in the bow and each carried a total of eight torpedoes. The boats also had one three-inch deck gun and a couple of machine guns, and carried a crew of thirty. They could do fourteen knots surfaced and half that submerged. Contrary to popular belief, submarines spent most of their time on the surface, saving their energy-guzzling ability to submerge for emergencies or special occasions, as when silent stalking was needed. Like now.

Carter peered through the periscope at the approaching ship. A freighter, but what nationality? He couldn't make out her name and her flag was hanging limp. He couldn't just go and sink anything he saw. After all, there were still a number of U.S. ships on the ocean, many of whose skippers didn't know that Los Angeles and San Diego had fallen or, for that matter, were blissfully unaware that the U.S. was at war with Germany. Hell, many merchantmen still didn't have radios.

Thus, he would surface, then hail and halt the big fat slow-moving freighter. He hoped and prayed it would be a German, although an Austrian would do just as well. Austria-Hungary had declared war on the U.S. in knee-jerk support of Germany, but there had been no attacks from that strange and polyglot empire. It didn't have much of a navy or merchant fleet to begin with. Despite that, Commander Nimitz ordered his men to consider them the enemy as well. Carter and his crew didn't need much convincing. They had all lost friends during the German sneak attack on Mare Island.

A quarter of a mile away from the freighter, he ordered the sub to surface. Carter figured seeing the sub so close would be worth some shock value. It was. As his men scrambled to man the three-inch deck gun, he could see crewmen on the freighter running like chickens with their heads cut off. Carter grinned as he identified her. She flew the German flag, and her name was the *Gudrun* out of Bremen. He watched in disbelief as a couple of the ship's crewmen waved at the sub. Did they think she was one of their U-boats?

"Gunner, take out her radio and her antenna."

The gunner smiled and fired immediately. He'd been aiming since he took up position behind the deck gun. The shell hit the structure below the antenna, sending pieces of wood and metal into the air. A second shell completed the job. The freighter struck her flag.

I will not be a butcher, Carter thought. *I will not be like the Germans and slaughter the crew.* He positioned the sub close to the freighter and was about to hail her when a fusillade of bullets struck the sub, sending men into the sea.

"Open fire," he ordered and both the deck gun and the machine guns opened up, raking the *Gudrun*. Carter pulled the sub back a couple of hundred yards and the deck gun began pumping shells into her, just below the freighter's water line.

More white flags flew and somebody tried to yell something. Too bad he couldn't hear it. The German crew began to abandon ship as smoke and flames billowed up through a hatch. Something exploded and the ship shuddered, starting to settle. The explosion must have blown out her guts.

Another ship was approaching. *What the hell?*

Carter thought. Had this part of the ocean suddenly become a damn highway? At any rate, the first ship they'd hit was beyond help.

"We gonna submerge, sir?" asked Chief Ryan, a man with nearly twenty years' experience.

"Is it a warship?"

"No sir. Looks like another big ass freighter."

Carter grunted. He wondered if the first ship had gotten off any kind of message. If it had, the message would likely have been a simple SOS, and nothing saying she was under attack. The new ship doubtless thought the O-7 was on an errand of mercy to save the *Gudrun*. If the new ship was also a German, he could also sink her without wasting a precious torpedo.

"All the men back on board?" He was told that the men who'd jumped when the bullets started to fly were wet but safe. A few bruises, but no real injuries, except to their pride.

He positioned the O-7 so that the dying German hid him from the new target. At a mile out he showed himself. The new ship also flew a German flag and her hull proudly announced that she was from Hamburg.

Burned once by the surprise of small-arms fire, Carter ordered the guns to fire immediately. Although smaller than the *Gudrun*, the new ship was more stubborn. It took a dozen solid hits before her crew began to abandon her and flames started eating at her.

Carter smiled. It was a good day. "Any more customers, Chief?"

"I see a couple, but they've turned and are running. We could chase them, but it'd take forever and we'd be out of fuel if we didn't run into the German Navy first."

Ah yes, Carter thought, *the German Navy*. The twin plumes of smoke from the sinking ships billowed high into an otherwise clear sky. Four lifeboats clustered on the water, the German crews wondering if they were going to be machine gunned or left to the mercies of a sometimes merciless sea. He would not gun them down. The Germans did that, not Americans. Let God provide.

But there was a problem and he could see it clearly. The sub base at Catalina had only five submarines. The plan was for two subs to be on patrol at all times, while the others either refueled or made it back and forth to their assigned areas. The O-7 had sunk two ships but missed the opportunity to sink at least two more. There had to be a better, more effective way of sinking enemy ships, he thought. Also, these had sailed without escort. Carter had the sinking feeling, pun intended, that German destroyers and light cruisers would soon be convoying the freighters and transports. As he thought this, the second ship exploded, sending shock waves over the O-7. Thankfully, the debris fell short of his sub.

The chief grinned. "I think she was carrying at least some ammunition."

Carter checked his fuel supply. It was time to head for the little port near Avalon, on Catalina Island. Carter's commanding officer at Catalina, Chester Nimitz, had a first-rate mind if there ever was one. Maybe Commander Nimitz would have a thought on how to catch the whole covey and not just a quail or two.

Tim Randall recovered, but with agonizing slowness. He didn't know why he'd been chosen to survive the influenza when so many others had died. He was weak as a baby and nobody wanted to be near him even though the doctors said he was no longer contagious. Fair enough. He wouldn't want to be near him either. The doctors said the epidemic had almost run its course and the young soldiers were all safe.

Nobody believed them.

No training was taking place at Camp Dix. Nobody came in and nobody left, except maybe in a box. If the doctors were right and the flu was over, that situation would change and new recruits would soon arrive.

When he felt strong enough, Tim managed to get himself to the mound of earth under which Wally's body lay. He had died while Tim was unconscious. His last memory was of laying his brother's frail body on the now empty cot, hoping that a miracle would cure him. Wally had died moments later, but Tim had been unconscious and near death himself.

Wally'd been buried in a mass grave with fifty others. Crosses lined the mound and Wally's name was duly inscribed on one, but Tim wondered if his brother's body actually lay anywhere near the spot.

He wanted to cry but it hurt too much. He and Wally had joined to fight the Germans. If that meant being killed or wounded in battle, so be it. War was tragic but heroic, and that was what they'd signed on for. Maybe they didn't totally understand the implications of warfare, but to be felled by an invisible little Goddamned germ was too much.

Nor did it help a whole lot when a deeply sympathetic Sergeant Smith told him that this was the way of war. Since time immemorial, Smith said, more warriors had been killed by disease than by the enemy. Tim found it hard to believe and checked it out with the medics. Smith had exaggerated only slightly. Modern medicine had reduced the numbers killed by illness, but not eliminated it. Even a conflict as recent as the Spanish-American War saw many more American soldiers killed by Yellow Fever than by Spanish bullets.

Tim decided he didn't give a shit. Wally was dead and who cared about numbers.

Smith tapped him on the shoulder, "Orders, Sergeant Randall."

"Sergeant?"

"You're surprised?" Smith said. "You were in training to be an NCO and you were doing very well. Now with all the casualties from the flu, the army is accelerating training for those who are left. You are one of the best who made it through the flu, so you get to be a sergeant. Not only that but you are a damn fine shot. Not as good as me, nobody is, but damned good nonetheless. You are to go to Kansas City as quickly as possible. If you are just a little creative with your travel plans, you might spend a day or two in Camden with your family."

Family? It would be nice to see them, even though he'd heard that the flu was ravaging east coast cities. And the word "sergeant" did have a nice ring to it. Regardless, it was better to move on and leave this place of mass death and the memory of his brother's dying.

Tim noticed that "Smeeth's" crazy accent had disappeared. Did he put that on just for show? He held out his hand. "Thanks Sergeant Smith."

"You're welcome, Sergeant Randall. Now get the hell out of here. New recruits are going to be coming in soon, which means I've got fresh meat to cure."

★ ★ ★

The President of the United States was appalled. According to the report in his hand, the surgeon general was now predicting that as many as forty thousand young men would die in the training camps as a result of the influenza that had originated somewhere in the American Midwest. While somewhat lower than the original estimates, it was a catastrophe nonetheless. He put his head in his hands. He wanted to weep.

However, the numbers would not go away. Three quarters of a million young men had been in the training camps when the disease erupted with a sudden and lethal fury. A third of that total had gotten ill and forty thousand would soon be dead. Many thousands more would die elsewhere, and still more thousands had yet to catch it.

Worse, the numbers of those with the flu had been so great that ill soldiers had been transferred to civilian hospitals; thus causing the hideous disease to spread throughout the civilian population. The country was staggering from this additional blow. Trucks and carts collected corpses from houses in Philadelphia, in a horrific replay of the plague in the Middle Ages.

The only good news came from the surgeon general who announced that a vaccine had been developed and that the flu seemed to be running its course. For the dead and the dying this was scant comfort. And as to the war? Dear God, Lansing thought, how would we ever be able to fight the Germans?

"Other than the surgeon general's guarded optimism, is there any actual good news?" Lansing asked.

"At least in the Navy the flu is contained," said Navy Secretary Daniels. "In those instances where it has appeared, the ships have been quarantined and that has proven effective. And the same holds true for the Marine Corps. The need to increase the number of Marines was not as great as the Army's need to increase the number of soldiers."

Secretary of War Baker could barely hide his shame. The rush to enlarge the Army was his responsibility and on his head rested the blame for the inadequate facilities and equipment. Now it was easy to say that increases in the Army's size should have been incremental and not headlong, but the nation wanted quick action, not slow growth. People would be court-martialed, and civilian contractors put on trial for their shoddy work, and perhaps some of them might even see the inside of a jail. But that would not bring back tens of thousands of young men.

More soldiers had just died of the flu than on both sides at the battle of Gettysburg. Baker had offered his resignation, but the president had declined it.

Lansing took a deep breath and sat up straight. "We cannot dwell on the past. We must look to the future and do what we can. General March, is reinforcing Liggett in California still out of the question?"

"It is," March replied. "Not only is the weather our enemy, but there have been further acts of sabotage, and the Germans have sent units of the Mexican Army to take and hold the passes. That is, all except the northernmost one which we still hold. Liggett is sending men to expel the enemy from the other passes, but he doesn't have enough to spread around."

"And Texas?" Lansing asked.

March again responded. It looked like Secretary Baker didn't want to say much of anything. "The army known as the Texas Volunteers is still holding on to

San Antonio, but for how much longer I don't know. Governor Hobby has finally asked for our help and we are going to send it to him. With Secretary Daniels' permission, a brigade of two regiments of Marines has departed with General Lejeune in command. Another two army divisions are forming and will follow. The overall command will be Pershing's."

"Will they be in time to save San Antonio?" Lansing asked. He was under intense pressure from Congress and the nation's newspapers to do something, anything. The loss of another major city like San Antonio with its legendary Alamo would be devastating.

It had been almost two months since the sneak attack by Germany and Mexico, and the American response had been virtually nothing. There seemed to be a clear understanding that California was isolated by sabotage and the weather, but Texas was another matter. The fact that the Texans had been stubborn in their confidence that they could defeat any Mexican Army with one arm tied behind them had hindered any thoughts of sending reinforcements. Until now, that is.

There was still the issue of weapons. While the ammunition supply was not critical, there was not enough, and artillery was virtually nonexistent. Soon that would change as factories were beginning to use the new foreign dies to produce weapons, but it would be a while before large quantities of anything were available.

At least the Navy was doing fairly well. Submarines off the California coast had sunk a number of freighters bringing supplies to the Germans. Light cruisers functioning as surface raiders and additional submarines were in the Atlantic and heading for Caribbean waters. German ships carrying supplies and reinforcements had to either make port at Vera Cruz or go around the world to California.

Ireland's pro-German government in Dublin had requested that German ships stop using her as a base and instead had proclaimed her neutrality. There was confusion in Ireland as so many of her sons and daughters now resided in the United States. The consensus was that the Germans would honor Ireland's request and that it wouldn't much matter. If necessary, the Germans would use the Canary Islands or the Azores. Any American plans to use those islands as bases had been abandoned.

Lansing nodded. "Then supplies are their Achilles' heel just as they are ours?"

"In the long run," said General March. "While it isn't quite a scorched earth policy, we are destroying everything of use while we retreat up California to San Francisco. In particular, we are tearing up the railroads. This means the Germans have to haul supplies by wagon or by truck, and, with the shortage of oil and fuel, this is proving difficult for them."

"I assume it also means their ships and planes are still on a short leash," Lansing said. There was agreement with his comment. "Time, then, is on our side. Would you say that, General March?"

March sighed. "No, sir, I would not say that. If they succeed in taking San Francisco, they can simply dig in and we will have to try and root them out. That, sir, would not be easy. Indeed, it might not even be possible. If San Francisco falls, most of California might have to be written off."

Lansing stood. "Then they cannot be permitted to take San Francisco."

March looked away. *Just how the hell do we accomplish that,* he wondered.

Admiral Sims returned the salute of Colonel William Mitchell, commonly called "Billy" by his friends and by the newspaper reporters who enjoyed the controversy he generally stirred up. Mitchell was not shy about stating his sometimes radical views, and that annoyed his generally very conservative superiors.

It was still unusual for the Army and the Navy to be working together and it was even more unusual for Sims to be hosting a man who'd made public declarations that airplanes could sink any of the Navy's capital ships.

Most in the Navy's hierarchy had thought that Mitchell's ideas were rubbish at best and, at worst, a heresy not to be spoken. Sims, however, had the nagging feeling that Mitchell might be on to something and wanted to know more about it, no matter how unpleasant the truth might be. In a way it reminded him of the resistance he'd confronted when he'd suggested that ships' gunners practice under realistic long-range modern conditions, and not replicate the close-in gun duels as in the War of 1812, which had proven so irrelevant in modern warfare.

Someday in the future bombs might sink capital ships. But not this day, or even this decade, Sims had concluded. The tests he'd quietly authorized Mitchell to perform had proven it. Still, he'd let the intense colonel have his say.

To his credit, Mitchell did not sugarcoat. "Things did not work out as I expected, Admiral. In sum, I was bitterly disappointed."

Sims sighed and leaned back. The German fleet would doubtless try to force San Francisco's growing but still fragile defenses and he'd hoped against hope for another weapon to use against them.

"So tell me what happened," the admiral persisted.

"Sir, our planes are too small and too slow, and the bombs they carry are just not large enough or powerful enough to be effective against heavily armored ships, assuming they could hit them in the first place. My planes flew at high altitude and dropped bags of flour at moving ships in the British side of Puget Sound and managed to hit nothing. Not a one. Dropped from significant height, the bombs landed where the ships had been and if the bomber attempted to lead a ship, he either missed outright or the ship had time to dodge. All we did was create a flour soup in the Sound, which must have mightily puzzled the fish.

"Attempts to bomb from lower and then extremely low altitudes were a little more successful, but we had to use very small planes and small bombs. We concluded that our bombs would have caused some minor damage and some casualties, but would never have sunk a heavily armored capital ship."

"I admit I'm disappointed, Colonel. Even though I love our Navy's great ships, I was hoping for a way of neutralizing the German fleet's advantages."

Mitchell nodded solemnly. "Above all else I too want to defeat the Germans. However, while the idea of dropping explosive bombs on ships appears to be an idea whose time hasn't come, I do have another thought that is just in the planning stage. It is brutal and might be against the rules of war; therefore, I'm loath to discuss it at this time."

Sims was intrigued. "Indulge me, Colonel."

Mitchell spoke for only a moment. Sims paled. He was horrified, in part because he was a sailor and what Mitchell was proposing was a sailor's worst nightmare scenario. What Mitchell was thinking was an abomination that might even be against the Geneva Convention and the rules of war. But what good were rules in time of war? The enemy possessed flamethrowers, poison gas, and had brutally invaded his country and terrorized American citizens. Rules of war? To hell with the rules of war.

"And what will you call this monstrosity?"

"Operation Firefly."

Sims pursed his lips thoughtfully. "Please work on it."

★ CHAPTER 10 ★

MARCUS TOVEY SURVEYED HIS EMPIRE. IT WASN'T much, just flat, scarred land and a handful of ruined buildings. Nothing much he could build a strong defensive position on, but somehow he had. Several Mexican attacks had been beaten off, as attested to by the bloated and stinking corpses frying in the Texas sun. But now the Mexican's dander was up and they were massing to his front. His scouts said it was a full division, more than enough to overwhelm him.

The fifteen hundred men in his command called him "general," even though nobody had actually authorized his promotion. It had just happened and he thought it amusing. Other senior officers had either gotten themselves killed or had proven themselves inadequate under the circumstances. Those had either run off or been chased away by their own men. As a result, Tovey accumulated men who'd survived other battles and inferior commanders. They seemed to welcome his commonsense approach to fighting.

His approach was quite simple—all Marcus Tovey did was kill Mexicans. Well, not all Mexicans. Even he'd had to agree that there were good Mexicans and his command now included two companies of them. Some of his Mexicans were refugees who rightly thought that the current Mexican government wanted to murder them, and some were "Tejuanos," which meant they'd been born in Texas of Mexican parents. It also meant they were American citizens. Tovey had never given a thought to their loyalties and now realized that most of them considered themselves as American as he. To his surprise, he'd even developed friendships with some of them.

After one particularly nasty skirmish, Governor Hobby had stopped by to congratulate Tovey and his men on their gallant stand. Tovey'd smiled and accepted the accolades, but thought that the governor was an utter idiot. It had been a gallant stand, but it had resulted in yet another retreat. A few more gallant stands and Mexico will have taken back all of Texas. *Fuck Hobby,* he thought and spat on the ground. And fuck the Texas government's attitude that they didn't need help from the federal government in Washington. Hell, Tovey thought with a laugh, if he'd take help from tame Mexicans, he'd take help from Washington. He'd heard rumors that things were changing in this regard, but rumors didn't put more soldiers in the trenches.

The really bad news about being a general meant he couldn't be in the front lines with his men where the fighting was. He understood and accepted the logic. He had to command and, in order to command, he had to know what was going on in all parts of his command. Anyone in the front lines of a fight sometimes didn't know what was happening ten feet away. Just as significant, generals in the front lines had a nasty habit of getting killed and leaving their armies leaderless at a critical time.

Tovey was in a secondary trench line, a quarter of a mile behind the primary one. He had telephone and telegraph contact with his other units in front of him, but wires had a bad habit of breaking or being cut. He prayed that one particular wire stayed intact for the duration of the day. He'd buried it deep enough so that—please God—it would be safe.

For dependable communications, he would depend on runners, flags, and flares. If he'd had pigeons or trained dogs, he'd have used them as well.

Six thousand Mexicans opposed his fifteen hundred men. A mile behind him lay the ruins of the Alamo. The Goddamned Mexicans had spite-shelled the sacred place and now it was a small pile of rubble. He wanted to cry. Better, he wanted to kill more Mexicans.

Trumpets blared to his front, and six thousand Mexicans surged out of their trenches, screaming as they ran towards the Texan trenches. Covey's fifteen hundred opened fire with their rifles, and the couple of Gatling guns they'd acquired spat rapid-fire death as well. The Gatlings had been ancient a generation ago, and there was very little ammunition. Covey's two cannons opened fire. They had been taken from an armory and were pre-Spanish-American-War vintage. Again, there was very little ammunition, so the gunners fired slowly and carefully. A homemade mortar dropped shells on the advancing Mexicans, but quickly ran out of ammo.

Mexicans fell by the score, by the hundreds, but still came on. As before, he had to give them credit for bravery. They were closing in on his first trench line. They would overwhelm it. They reached the barbed wire and paused. The wire was much thicker and deeper than before, but this time the Mexicans had learned. They used cutters and were delayed only momentarily. As the cutters eliminated the wire, other Mexicans lay down withering covering fire. Damned Mexicans had learned a lot, he thought. But so too had his men. They were well dug in and firing slits were well sited. The slow, the dumb, and the unlucky on both sides were long dead. What was left was as mean as a rattlesnake with the clap.

"Pull them back," he ordered. In a moment, his men left their trenches and retreated in good order, bringing their equipment and their wounded and even some of their dead. *Good,* he thought.

With a wild cheer, the Mexicans poured into the abandoned American emplacements. Tovey spat on the ground. They would not attack again, at least not for a while. They had expected a much tougher fight for Tovey's trenches, and Tovey had bet there were no plans for a further advance. The Mexicans would stay put for a while and get themselves organized for the next push. At least that was what a Tejuano informer had said, and so far, the man was right.

More Mexicans entered the trenches, which were now filled with humanity. The Mexican flag was planted and the enemy cheered it loudly. They thought they'd won the day. *Like hell.*

Tovey turned to his officers. He hoped that one line buried so deep was still intact. If it wasn't, he was going to look like a total asshole.

"Do it," he ordered.

A sergeant turned a handle and pushed it down. For a second that lasted an eternity, nothing happened. Then explosions rippled down the line of the trenches now jammed with Mexican soldiers, detonating the dynamite so lovingly placed there the day before. Explosions became eruptions as smoke and debris, much of it human, filled the sky. Then there was silence, followed by the sounds of screams. Waves of surviving Mexicans ran away, retreating in panic to their old positions, while wounded men started to crawl back.

Tovey grinned. He estimated he'd just killed at least a thousand of the Mexicans in front of him and wounded a helluva lot more. That was one Mexican division that wouldn't be doing much fighting for a while.

A courier from Governor Hobby's staff stood behind him, white-faced with shock. "What the hell'd you expect?" Tovey snarled, "A fucking beauty pageant?" He had little use for Hobby's staffers. Most were a bunch of pale-faced young pussies back from college out east.

The courier gulped. "No sir, just some news. Governor Hobby is relinquishing command to General Pershing."

Pershing for Hobby? Now that was good news indeed, Tovey thought. That was as good a trade as Ty Cobb for a used jock, except that Hobby wasn't as good as a used jock. Tovey had ridden with Pershing against Villa. He thought that Pershing was a pompous little bastard, but a damned good general. Hell, that news was almost as good as killing a thousand Mexicans.

★ ★ ★

Elise carefully fed Josh his Campbell's Chicken Noodle soup as he sat on the couch. He was totally relaxed and happy as a clam. His boots were off and his uniform jacket was draped across a chair.

They both knew he could feed himself fairly well now, but she wanted to pamper him and he rather liked the idea. The wound in his shoulder had left his arm weak, but the doctors assured him that much of his strength would return in time and he could return to active duty. Elise wanted him to get stronger, but active duty? No more, especially if it meant going out to sea to fight the Germans. Two Purple Hearts were more than enough. If his wounds kept him land bound that would be fine. She thought of him as more of a thinker than a fighter anyhow.

He had left the hospital and returned to junior officers' quarters at the Presidio. There was no privacy there, of course, so Elise had taken him to the apartment she shared with Kirsten. If any of the other women in the building thought his presence was immoral or scandalous, they kept to themselves. After all, Josh walked with a crutch and one arm was in a sling. The two Purple Hearts were pinned on his chest. If Elise wanted to bring him home for lunch, the resident busybodies probably thought he was too helpless to take advantage of frail little Elise.

Little Elise, however, did not think of herself as frail. She thought that others would be surprised at how strong she was, both mentally and physically. Perhaps she'd never be able to stab somebody in the hand like Kirsten had done, but who knew?

She took the soup away. She didn't offer him any more. He'd had three bowls. "I'd say getting away from hospital food is good for you," she said with mocking primness.

"As a term, hospital food is an oxymoron. You are spoiling me, you know."

"Do you mind?"

"Not for a moment," he said and took her hand. The crutch was on the floor and the sling was on top of it. He tried not to bother with them anymore, but Elise had suggested the crutch to impress her neighbors.

"You know I am going back to work tomorrow," he said. "Once more I'll be a very junior member of the admiral's staff." *And I'll be able to see you every day,* he thought.

"Nothing wrong with that, and don't forget to wear your medals. It'll remind them that you've done your duty." Admiral Sims was insistent on that matter. Medals, especially combat related, would be worn.

Elise sat on the couch beside him. He was very much aware of her clean and fresh scent and the warmth of her presence. She wore a stylish dress that would have been considered shockingly short back where he came from. Here in San Francisco, it was normal and he liked it.

"Josh Cornell, it has occurred to me that life has become intense, violent, and potentially short. Therefore, I would like to ask you a very blunt question."

"Go ahead," he answered, puzzled.

"Do you like me? And not as a friend, of course, but as a woman."

"Absolutely and both. I think you are a remarkable and lovely woman, and I've wondered if you truly like me, or if you are caring for me out of compassion."

"Don't worry about that," she said and slid across his lap. "I'm not hurting you, am I?"

"Not at all," he answered. It did hurt, but only a little and he'd be damned if he'd admit it. She might move away if he did and he loved the feel of her against him.

"I won't break if you kiss me."

He grinned, "You certain?"

They kissed tenderly and gently. She pulled away and looked at him, a small smile on her lips.

"Josh, I'm old-fashioned, but not totally so. Right now I am a virgin and will still be so when you leave this room. Do you understand that?"

He nodded. It was suddenly hard to speak. She unbuttoned his shirt and removed it. His undershirt followed. His chest was pale and her fingers lingered over the scars on his shoulder. She kissed where the stitches had left their mark. She couldn't help tears from falling onto his chest. Damn Germans.

With shaking hands, he removed her jacket and blouse, then slid her undergarments down to her waist. Her breasts were small but lovely and he cupped them, caressing her nipples with his fingers and then his lips. She smiled and bit her lip. Farm boys weren't all that innocent, she thought.

"Remember, we're not going all the way," she said in a whisper.

"I understand."

"But if you're a very good boy, I'll make sure we both have a wonderful afternoon."

He laughed, "Promise?"

"Absolutely," she said as she let her tongue explore his ear.

Deep down, he wondered what would happen if Kirsten Biel chose to come home. He decided he didn't care. He also thought he heard thunder. Or was it his heart beating?

Luke returned the salute of an enlisted man and walked over to where Kirsten stood. They were outside the Civic Center where civilians continued to be processed for ration cards.

Kirsten was taking a break. As supervisor of the group of clerks, she now rarely dealt directly with their customers. Her job was to resolve problems, and she generally did that by issuing a temporary card. Err on the side of mercy was her motto and nobody argued with her, although some of her coworkers cheekily made comments about making a stab at solving their problems.

A heavily bandaged Will and his two companions had departed north on the first train the military could get them on. Luke had wanted to draft them into the Army, but decided against it. He thought it might be detrimental to the Army's morale to associate with dumb shits like them. Will and his chums had managed to become the laughing stock of San Francisco. Their replacements in refugee work had all been women, which had brought an element of compassion to the office. She had to admit the work wasn't all that hard and helping people was indeed rewarding.

For once the sun was shining brightly and there were few clouds in the sky. It was easy to forget there was a war on, and that the Germans were approaching San Luis Obispo, opposed by only two small American infantry divisions.

There'd been another major change as a result of her confrontation with Will. The entire area was now under martial law. General Liggett had said the abuse of refugees was the final straw. Admiral Sims had concurred. Mayor Rolph had fumed and raged, some said he'd literally stomped his feet, but to no avail. Liggett was too tired of bureaucratic incompetence to much care what Rolph thought.

It should have happened long ago, Luke thought as he approached Kirsten. She was smiling. "And what makes you so happy today?" he asked.

"Among other things, a blue sky and a handsome man to share it with. That and the fact that the number of refugees seems to be dwindling, which makes my work so much easier. Of course, the general will likely put us all on trains when the last refugee departs."

"I hope not. I would miss you terribly."

Although a part of his mind said he was being selfish for wanting her near, she would be far safer up north and out of the way of the approach of the kaiser's legions. But then he recalled how catastrophically her last journey had turned out and wondered just what was the right thing to do.

"I am also wondering just what is going on right now in the apartment," she said and briefly explained that Elise had brought Josh over for "lunch."

Luke chuckled and thought of the quiet young couple. "Still waters do run deep, don't they? Want to just happen to drop in on them?"

She punched him on the arm. "We'll do no such thing. Let the young lovers have their moments."

"And when will we have ours?"

She took his hand, "Soon. Maybe someday very soon. Just don't push. I'm very fond of you and you are the only reason I'm staying here, but I don't want to rush into anything."

Luke understood and was somewhat satisfied. He would take things one step at a time. He heard thunder and looked up. It couldn't be raining, could it?

The flight of fifty Gotha V bombers was escorted by a score of Albatros fighters. The bombers came in at a height of ten thousand feet. They were unopposed. No American planes flew to meet them and no antiaircraft guns could reach them. A few machine-gun batteries did open up, but were quickly silenced by their commanders. They were wasting ammunition shooting at targets that high and they weren't accurate in the first place. Worse, the shells had to come down and, like the proverbial arrow, who knew on what and where. Shooting at the Gothas was an exercise in futility.

As Luke and Kirsten watched, the bombs started to fall, like dropping fruit, straight down and into the heart of the city to the bay side of the Presidio. They instinctively ducked as the explosions began even though no bombs had yet fallen anywhere near them. Ironically, it was the part of the city burned by the fire of 1906 that was being bombed.

Several bombers separated from the main force and dropped their loads on coastal batteries.

Kirsten grabbed his arm. "Look."

A handful of American planes had begun to attack the bomber formation. It was a futile gesture. They were swarmed over by the escorting Albatros fighters. A couple of American planes spiraled downward, smoke trailing behind them, while the survivors raced for safety.

But, out of luck or skill, one of the bombers was

hit and began to smoke and lose altitude. People on the street cheered the sight and both Luke and Kirsten joined in. The crippled plane was angling for a landing in the bay. Luke quickly realized that the military had to get to the wreckage first.

The remaining bombers and fighters were departing. It had taken but a few seconds for them to deposit their loads. Luke left Kirsten and ran to the waterfront. A Navy launch was just arriving. He hailed it and was soon on his way.

The wreckage was a couple of miles offshore and sinking slowly when they arrived. A couple of private boats were already there. *Damn,* he thought.

"Private boats get back," he called out. "This is military property."

A grizzled seaman looked at him. "Kiss off, soldier. I found it and I'm keeping whatever I want. Salvage, it's called."

Luke borrowed a revolver from the launch's locker and a grinning bosun took another. "And I call it martial law and military property. If you don't want your ass shot off, back off."

The scavenger's face fell when he saw the guns. "All yours," he said, "but I'm keeping the pilot. We're gonna hang his ass for bombing the city."

Christ, Luke thought, *how many enemies do we have besides the Germans?* By now they were alongside the wreck and the scavenger's little boat. An ashen-faced man lay in the bilge. He was bloody, but apparently alive.

Luke kept the gun in sight. "Maybe we can let you have him after we're through questioning him, but we need his information."

"Oh?"

"Yes. Information like where did he come from, and how many more are there?"

"Makes sense," the scavenger said grudgingly. He helped transfer the wounded German to the launch. "The other two are dead. You want them too?"

The mangled bodies were still in the plane, wrapped in the wreckage. As they watched, the bomber slipped beneath the waves. "Guess not," Luke said.

★ CHAPTER 11 ★

"IT WAS A TERROR ATTACK, NOTHING MORE," SAID a clearly agitated General Liggett. Sims nodded agreement. "They made no attempt to hit anything of military value. No bombs fell on our defenses and none on the Presidio, and they had to know this was our headquarters. Nor were any Navy ships attacked. They bombed the heart of the city just to prove they could do it."

"What are the casualties?" a slightly calmer Admiral Sims asked.

Nolan sadly gave the numbers. "Just over three hundred dead with at least twice that many injured, almost all civilians. Women and children are included in the total. Certainly some of the injured will die and other dead will be found in the rubble. Overall, however, the actual damage to San Francisco was slight. The fires have been contained and crews are already clearing up the rubble. More people are homeless, though, which is a problem."

"Which we will minimize by shipping still more civilians out of the city," Liggett snarled, "and Mayor Rolph be damned. Nolan, in your opinion, will they attack again and what can we do about it?"

"Absolutely they will come again, and there is precious little we can do to stop them. We can elevate machine guns and our few cannon to shoot skyward, but hitting a moving airplane at ten thousand feet is virtually impossible. If one of their planes should deign to fly low, we stand a chance, but not against high-flying bombers. Until and if we have enough airplanes of our own to intercept the bombers, we are helpless. I believe the only practical and useful thing we can do is dig trenches for people to take shelter in."

Nolan allowed a moment for that unpleasant truth to sink in. "Could we use civilian airplanes as interceptors?" Liggett asked. "I understand there may be several hundred in the area."

Sims decided to interrupt. "I've had conversations on that score and civilian planes are small, slow, and frail. They would be slaughtered by the German fighters and many couldn't attain the altitude necessary to fight the Gothas in the first place."

"But what concerns me more," Nolan said, "is just where did they come from? The Gotha V bomber has a range of just over five hundred miles, which means it can only be based about two hundred and fifty miles away for them to get here and back. To the best of our knowledge the Germans have still not taken San Luis Obispo, which is about two hundred miles south, and I can't imagine they'd put a bomber base too close to the front lines."

"A hidden base?" Sims asked.

At that moment, Luke entered the room and quietly took a seat behind Nolan. Liggett spotted him immediately. "Captain, you interrogated the German prisoner. Did he talk? And please tell me that you didn't threaten to cut off his testicles or anything like that."

"Wasn't necessary, sir," Luke grinned. "It seems the man is an enlisted gunner, not a pilot or an officer. He was conscripted into the German Army a few years ago and wants out of it. His name is Schmidt and he is pathetically eager to please. He also informed me he has family in Milwaukee and, in return for his cooperation, he would like to be released to them. I told him we'd consider it."

Liggett stifled a smile. "Tell us what you've found."

"First, sir, the Germans have sixty of the Gothas and a hundred fighters. Ten of the bombers didn't go on the attack because of mechanical problems. Schmidt said his officers told him the attack was designed to bring us to the negotiating table by emphasizing how helpless we are against their bomber attacks. Again, sir, it was terror, plain and simple, and designed to get us to negotiate."

"They do have a point," Liggett muttered. "Tomorrow, I'm going to have to endure a meeting with local merchants who will doubtless want San Francisco either surrendered without a fight or be declared an open city. I will, of course, tell them exactly where they can put their precious business interests. Now, how the devil did the Germans accomplish the attack? Where are they based?"

Luke continued. "Sir, they are based just south of their lines at Obispo. They managed to cover the additional distance by reducing their bomb load and by carrying additional fuel in cans. Schmidt's job was to take cans of gas and pour the gas down a funnel into the gas tanks as they flew along. By those means, they greatly extended their planes' range. It's almost like warships carrying extra barrels of oil or, in days past, bags of coal."

Sims chuckled. "It's a trick that works, but I cannot imagine sitting in a plane, ten thousand or more feet in the air, and pouring gasoline down a funnel. Instant immolation would have been only seconds away at any time."

Luke smiled, "Schmidt felt that way as well, which is another reason for him to want to change sides. He says he cannot imagine American generals being so reckless with human life."

"I can think of a few," Liggett said, drawing laughter. "But did he give you a precise position where the bombers are based?"

"He did, sir," Luke said. He caught Eisenhower smiling at him. "And I think we can come up with a way of disrupting their operations."

"But will it be in time to forestall another attack?" Sims inquired.

"Probably not, Admiral. Schmidt said they want to hit us again fast so we don't get the idea they're short on fuel. And by the way, sir, they *are* short on fuel. There's scuttlebutt in the German camps that tanker ships full of oil are only days away which will at least partially solve their problem."

Sims leaned forward eagerly. "Did your man say where the tankers were headed, San Diego, Los Angeles, or elsewhere?"

"No sir. He didn't know."

Liggett stroked his chin. "And these plans of yours to, ah, disrupt the Germans, how soon can they be implemented."

"A week to ten days," Luke answered, looking at Eisenhower who smiled slightly. There was sadness in his eyes and the smile wavered. Ike had just gotten word that his son, David Doud Eisenhower, was deathly ill. Ike wanted to be by the boy's side, but duty called. Luke continued. "Provided we can get the equipment and other resources we need."

Liggett stood. "I will personally see to it that you get everything and then more. Anybody who fails to cooperate will be on permanent latrine duty for the remainder of their lives. Tell me, Martel, is there anything that might prove difficult?"

Luke grinned. "Well sir, I could use a couple of German uniforms."

Roy Olson had seen death many times lately, but the dead body on the ground before him bothered him greatly. It was one of his Mexican soldiers and the man's skull had been bashed in. From the look of it, someone had snuck up behind him and struck him with something like a hammer and hit him a lot of times.

"Another one?" Steiner said with a sneer.

Olson jumped. He hadn't noticed the captain come up beside him. "Yeah," he finally answered. "And it's the fourth one if you're counting."

Steiner steered Olson away from the corpse. There would be no investigation. They had a man's footprints as evidence and that was all, and that told them absolutely nothing.

"And what will you do this time besides send out search parties, Mr. Olson?"

"Captain, if you've got a better idea, I'd love to hear it. You want me to hang a prisoner or two to make a point, I'll do it, but the prisoners are surly enough now. I don't think they'll take to having some of them being strung up, especially in payment for a dead Mexican that they couldn't possibly have hurt."

Steiner's response was silence. The American prisoners of war worked slowly at best, and neither man felt that a retaliatory execution would be a motivator. They needed the Yanks, however slowly they worked, to keep supplies flowing north to a hungry and thirsty German Army. The American prisoners had gotten over their shock of defeat and imprisonment and now their eyes were filled with hate. They seemed on the verge of bloody insurrection. No, it was better they work a little than not at all.

"I'm almost a hundred percent certain it's Lew Dubbins," Olson said. "He's the last of the brothers alive and the only one with half a brain."

"Maybe more than half by the way he's eluded your men."

"Maybe," Olson admitted. "Dubbins was raised here, so he knows every place to hide. He could be fifty feet from here, laughing at us while we send patrols into the mountains that come back with squat."

"So where is he?" Steiner asked.

"Probably in a hole in the ground, preferably in the shade. He's likely got a full canteen and his head is covered with a dusty brown blanket. We could walk within ten feet of him and not see him. And the son of a bitch is definitely taunting us. He could have killed the four Mexicans he murdered earlier with a rifle, but he's chosen to do it with clubs or knives."

Olson shuddered. The first two'd had their throats slit, while the third, like the latest, had his skull turned to red and gray pulp.

Steiner disagreed. "If he'd used a rifle, it'd give us a direction and distance so we'd stand a chance of tracking and chasing him. No, by killing like he does, this Dubbins creature gives away nothing. Strange, but I did not visualize any of those unwashed Dubbins cretins as being great American patriots."

Now Olson was on firmer ground. "They aren't, Captain. Lew Dubbins is out for revenge for his brothers, nothing more than that. He'll keep killing until he's caught, or until you and I are both dead. Killing the Mexicans are just ways of keeping us on our toes and up all night."

Olson mentioned that he'd found a scrawled and misspelled note on the latest victim saying that he and Steiner would be killed, too.

To Olson's delight, Steiner looked nervous and glanced around. "Send out your patrols, Olson. The fool could not have gone too far."

He hadn't. Lew Dubbins was in a storeroom in the back of one of Roy Olson's warehouses. Through a crack in the wall, he could see the two men conversing and they looked pissed. Good.

He heard a key turn in the door and he grabbed his rifle. He would go down fighting.

It was Martina Flores, Roy Olson's mistress. She laughed at him. "Put down your weapon."

Dubbins grinned at her. She'd brought food and

water. Better, she'd brought him something else. She pushed him over on his back and unbuttoned his pants. She hiked up her skirts and put one of Roy Olson's expensive condoms on Lew's erection, then straddled his manhood. She smiled down at him. It felt good to betray Roy Olson by fucking this ignorant savage.

Martina had known for some time that her husband was dead and that Olson was using her. Maybe Dubbins would kill Olson, just like he bragged he would. In the meantime, she would reward him for each enemy soldier, Mexican or German, that he killed.

She had first seen Dubbins when his brother was executed. She had seen the rage in his face and knew that he would help her. She had made contact through one of the women in the village, an older woman who understood her situation and felt sorry for her.

Dubbins wasn't much of a lover. After pawing her breasts and thighs a few times, he grunted and relaxed. "God, that was good," he said.

Martina smiled warmly. To her, his exertions were far less than average. But it was a good reward for Dubbins. Someday, when the time was right, she'd get him to kill Olson for her and maybe even Steiner. In the meantime, he could stay in the storeroom for a couple of days until the patrols came back from their fruitless endeavors. Then she would smuggle him out of the camp and he could rest and wait for his next target of opportunity.

Winter in the mountains was unpleasant at best, even to an expert like Klaus Wulfram. He was cold, miserable, and alone. He felt numbness in his fingers that presaged frostbite. The last of his men had abandoned him. He still had some dynamite on his pack horse, though, and planned to use it.

After blowing the bridges he'd been assigned, Wulfram and his crew had hidden in an abandoned barn for a few days. Then they had simply taken an eastbound train to St. Louis, this time as Swedish businessmen. Fortunately, Wulfram's ID was good, his Swedish language skills passable, and his cartoonish Swedish accent good enough to be accepted. He harbored some wild thought that he could destroy the bridges across the Mississippi, but quickly ascertained that the now aroused United States was watching them like a hawk. Also, there were more bridges than he could handle, but in the north where the great river wasn't quite so wide.

In St. Louis he received a coded telegram saying that the bridges in the northern pass had not been sufficiently damaged, if they had been damaged at all. He was saddened by the obvious fact that a team of men he knew quite well had simply disappeared. His new orders said that he would try to rectify the situation.

A simple look around St. Louis showed how necessary destruction of the northern rail line was. Military supplies were beginning to pile up by the hundreds of tons, and there were literally thousands of men in uniform. They would not be anywhere near as good as a German soldier, but there were so many that they could possibly overwhelm a German force or, worse yet, successfully defend against the German advance on San Francisco. The northern pass must not reopen until after San Francisco fell and the American Army in California was destroyed, at which time it would be a moot point.

Money talked and ten dollars got him on a train to Spokane. There he changed to a train headed towards Seattle, where the railway was blocked by snow. The conductor told him the delay was temporary and that crews were shoveling as they talked. When no one was looking, he got off and began hiking into the woods. This time he was nowhere near as well equipped or armed as before and the tracks were being guarded.

He wished the others were with him, but he'd given them the choice of volunteering to stay with him or try to make their way south to the German or Mexican lines as best they could. They'd all said no to staying with him. They'd had enough. He was disappointed, but didn't blame them.

Still, American guards could not be everywhere. Wulfram rented two horses, one for him and one for his supplies, and trekked into the snowy passes.

He managed a wan grin when he saw how deep the drifts were and how America's Pacific Northwest was cut off from the rest of the world until the tracks could be dug out. But, deep as they were, that wasn't good enough. His orders were to extend the problem for an additional several months.

He rode his horse through the waist-deep snow and wondered how far he could go before he had to admit failure and turn back. Then, just as he was about to give up, he found a bridge. A beautiful bridge, and it was over a wide and fast running branch of the Columbia River. It would more than do. The tracks on it were the only remaining link between the United States and California.

Wulfram was nearly at the limits of his endurance. He could understand how the men in the party that had disappeared could have been overwhelmed by the forces of nature. The wind whipped through his clothing and his feet were wet, almost numb. It was like walking on stumps. He thought his testicles were frozen. Whatever he was going to do would happen right now. Tomorrow, he might not be alive.

The bridge was guarded, but the guards were not in sight. Instead, tendrils of smoke blew from shacks at each end of the bridge. After all, who would be crazy enough to attack the bridge during the middle of winter? He imagined the foolish Americans playing cards, smoking, and drinking. In a way, he envied them. Warmth, food, and a chance to sleep were all he wanted.

Wulfram crawled out onto the ice and to the first of the trusses, remembering that he wanted to do more than just drop the bridge; he wanted to destroy it. A dropped bridge could be repaired, even in the winter. A destroyed one meant starting over.

Painfully, he attached the dynamite and the detonator cord to each truss. It seemed to take forever. His watch said it only took a couple of hours. Finally, he was on the southern side with the detonator. Now to attach the cord.

"Hey!"

Wulfram spun around. One of the guards had emerged from his shack and was less than a hundred yards away. Worse, he carried a rifle.

Wulfram pulled his revolver and fired a couple of shots in the guard's direction. They went wild, but the guard ran back, screaming for help. Two more men ran out of the shack, half dressed, but also carrying rifles. They spotted him and began shooting as they ran forward. The gunfire in the snow was curiously muffled, the shots sounding more like popcorn popping.

His fingers wouldn't respond. The detonator cord wouldn't stay put. He tried again. Bullets kicked up beside him. "Stand up!" someone yelled. The Americans were getting closer. "Get away from that damn plunger!"

The devil he would. Not after all his efforts. Finally, it was done. Something slammed into his back, throwing him forward. His left arm wouldn't respond. He was on his hands and knees. The plunger was in front of him. Another bullet smashed into his leg. The pain was sudden and beyond belief. He screamed. With the last of his strength, he pushed the plunger down.

As his vision faded, he saw the bridge rise up and disappear in clouds of debris.

Fifty-seven Gotha V bombers were lined up in neat rows. There had originally been sixty. Two had been shot down and one was thought to have crashed due to engine failure or pilot error, but there were no survivors so no one would ever be certain.

It was the middle of a clear and starry night and only a handful of guards were about. The airfield had the look of a temporary facility. As soon as the stubborn city of San Luis Obispo fell, the German lines would move forward and the bombers would be stationed ever closer to San Francisco. It would not be an easy move. The rugged Albatros fighters could take off and land from any field that was fairly smooth, but the great bombers were more fragile and needed an airfield that had been specially prepared for them.

In the meantime, they were basically grounded. Two additional attacks on the city had exhausted their supply of bombs and much of their fuel. No matter. More supplies were en route. Then they could pound the city into surrender.

At least that was what Captain Helmut Krause hoped. He was in charge of maintenance and security for the planes and it galled him that his beautiful and magnificent bombers were on the ground. However, it had given him the time to have his crew perform additional maintenance on the behemoths. And they were huge. Their length was nearly forty-one feet, their wingspan almost seventy-eight. Fully loaded, they weighed in at more than four tons. Sometimes he held his breath as they tried to leave the ground and, so far, they all had succeeded in defying gravity. And the next time there would be no mechanical failures. All fifty-seven would attack or he would have somebody's head.

Even when well maintained, the Gothas had their problems. They were underpowered by Mercedes engines that were too small and, as a result, the bombers could only do a rather ordinary ninety miles an hour. Still, they were fearsome things once aloft with their deadly cargoes. It never ceased to amaze him that man had first begun to fly less than twenty years earlier when the Wright brothers had taken the pathetically small steps at Kitty Hawk that signified mankind's first controlled flight. He thought it was a shame that the first flier hadn't been a German. Perhaps the Wrights were of German descent, he thought and chuckled.

Krause was alone except for the handful of guards

on the perimeter of the base. The pilots and the mechanics, their day's work done, were a couple of miles down the road, drinking and whoring. Helmut Krause had a wife and three children at home. A drink he didn't mind, or even several, but whoring? *Nein.* So many of the whores were Mexicans, uglier than sin and a lot of them had the clap to boot. Get the bombers bombing and end the war so he could go home was his plan. He was a reservist who'd been called up for the Mexican venture. Only later had it turned into an invasion of the United States.

He caught motion to his left. A column of horsemen was coming down the dirt road towards the gate. Now what? Krause was delighted to see one of his four young and inexperienced guards actually get up and challenge the newcomers. There was hope for the boy yet. Whatever was said must have been satisfactory. The gate was unlocked and the riders entered. Krause noted that the two leaders were Germans and the others Mexicans. One of the leaders was a major, the other a sergeant. He drew himself to attention and saluted the superior officer. He was mildly puzzled by the fact that the riders were fanning out.

"How may I help you, Major?"

Luke returned the salute and responded in German. "It has been decided to give you more security. There are rumors that the Yanks might try a raid. Where are the rest of your guards? Please call them in so we can coordinate our efforts."

Krause was a good German and automatically obeyed the man with the higher rank. As his few men gathered, he tried to place the major's accent. He had obviously not gone to a good school, and Krause wondered how he'd gotten a commission. Within minutes his men stood behind him.

The major smiled. "Take their weapons."

A score of rifles were pointed at the astonished Germans. Within seconds they were all disarmed and hands bound behind their backs.

"You seem like a decent sort, Captain, so if you don't make trouble, nothing will happen to you or your men. Otherwise, we will be forced to slice your throats." He gestured to one of the Mexicans, who pulled a large knife and grinned wickedly. Krause suddenly knew overwhelming fear and tried not to wet himself. He failed.

He watched sadly as the dismounted riders raced from plane to plane, setting charges. His great beautiful beasts were going to die and there was nothing he could do about it. Worse, he would bear the brunt of the blame and rightly so.

"Major, leave me a gun so I can shoot myself." Krause spoke in English to what were obviously American raiders.

"That would be too nice," the American sergeant said with a wide and engaging smile. "You and your planes have killed more than a thousand innocent civilians, women and children, and wounded many more. You should all be hanged as the barbarians you are."

Krause's head slumped in despair. Eisenhower, the "sergeant," looked on him with contempt. Luke directed the preparations for the planes' demolition, which included removal of the several 7.92mm machine guns they carried. Ike commanded the column with Luke as his second. Luke, however, wore the rank of a German major because he spoke German fluently. Ike's German was miserable at best, which both men considered ironic considering his ancestry. Montoya led the Mexicans.

When they were done, the Americans pulled back. Ike grinned infectiously. "Care to do the honors, Luke?"

"Your show, Major."

Fuses were lit and fires snaked across the field. One by one, the bombers exploded. Their fuel tanks were almost empty, but what was in them and the accumulated vapors ensured the fiery destruction of each plane. The plywood-framed behemoths quickly became torches.

"Like the Fourth of July, only better." Joe Flowers laughed.

The nearly empty fuel storage tanks followed. The sky was lit by scores of fires, large and small, and man-made thunder rolled about them.

On the other side of the base, facing the road leading to town, Tomas Montoya and his men awaited. They had four machine guns propped up and ready, along with their own rifles.

They didn't have long to wait. Scores of men from the beer halls and whorehouses down the road came running to see what was happening to their precious planes.

At fifty yards, the machine guns and rifles poured bullets into them. The Germans fell like scythed wheat. In a moment, the massacre was over. The road was filled with the dead, the dying, and the badly wounded. Not only were the Germans without their bombers, but many of their pilots and skilled mechanics had just been slaughtered.

Payback for the people of San Francisco, Luke thought as he observed from a distance.

Montoya's men mounted their horses, took the machine guns and what ammo they could carry, and joined up with Eisenhower and Martel. "A very good night's work," said an elated Eisenhower. It was his first time in combat. He would have something to tell Mamie. Perhaps news of this victory would take her mind off their son's illness, at least for a few moments.

It had been fairly easy to get through the German lines. As before, the Germans couldn't be everywhere and gaps weren't that difficult to find. Going back, however, would be more difficult. The Germans would be thoroughly pissed as word of the destruction of their bomber force spread. The soaring flames and explosions had doubtless alerted every German within twenty miles. The fact that he and Luke had worn German uniforms would entitle them to a firing squad if they were caught.

"Captain Martel."

"Major?"

"Let's get the hell out of here."

The battleship *Arizona* led. Behind her came the *Pennsylvania* with the smaller *Nevada* bringing up the rear. Two destroyers patrolled in advance of the battleships. They did not want to blunder into the German fleet in the dark and the rain. That was not the plan.

Normally the battleship division was commanded by Rear Admiral Edward Eberle, but Admiral Sims had decided to be in on the adventure. He'd told Eberle to ignore him, which was, of course, impossible. Eberle was half amused and half frustrated, but the battleship division was his and he would lead as best he could, by God.

Pride of the squadron was the *Arizona*, BB 39. She had a crew of nearly eleven hundred, displaced more than thirty-one thousand tons, and she carried a dozen fourteen-inch guns in four turrets.

Next came the *Pennsylvania*, BB 38. She had a slightly smaller crew but displaced the same tonnage as the *Arizona*. She too carried twelve fourteen-inch guns.

The *Nevada* was the smaller and older of the three, displacing just under twenty-two thousand tons and carrying only ten fourteen-inch guns.

All three had a top speed of twenty-one knots.

Lieutenant Junior Grade Josh Cornell wished he was elsewhere, in particular he wished he was in the slender and pale arms of the beautiful Elise Thompson. Along with missing Elise he was shocked to find himself in yet another combat situation with a real possibility of getting hurt once more. The three battleships were on a mission to probe the German fleet's readiness and to act as a screen for additional endeavors.

As occurred so often, the weather was a cross between mist and rain. Visibility was poor and he was quietly freezing on the open portion of the *Arizona*'s bridge. The power of the Pacific Ocean was manifesting itself in the form of giant rollers that tossed the mighty warships like toys. Josh wondered just how the Germans on blockade duty were faring.

For Josh, being on the battleship had enabled him to renew acquaintance with Annapolis classmates. To his surprise they were impressed, even jealous, by the fact that he'd not only seen the elephant twice but had also been wounded. That he was Sims' aide hadn't hurt either, nor had the fact that he hadn't gotten seasick. He'd noticed some of his old friends looking more than a little green around the gills as the battleship rocked and pitched.

Sharp cracking noises from ahead jolted him back to reality. The lead American destroyers were shooting at something. Roaring thunder counterpointed the destroyers. The German battleships were firing back. But were the Germans moving, and in which direction? Were they distracted enough? Josh prudently stuffed cotton and wax in his ears and opened his mouth to minimize the effect of the *Arizona*'s guns which were about to respond.

Eberle gave the order and the three battleships opened fire in the general direction of the German ships. The roar and concussion of the great guns nearly knocked Josh to the deck. He managed to steady himself although it did cause his shoulder to hurt.

He looked over at Sims, who was grinning like a little kid. Sims was a gunnery expert, but also a man who'd never been in combat. During the Spanish-American War, when so many officers had made their careers, he'd been the naval attaché in Paris. His specialty back then was espionage.

The Germans returned fire, but they too were largely blind. Still, a couple of shells landed close enough for him to see immense geysers roaring skyward.

Eberle turned to Sims. "Enough?"

Sims nodded, although with reluctance. The three American ships were not going to challenge five Germans. Their job was to taunt them and distract them. The American ships turned and steamed back up Puget Sound. German shells chased them and the Germans doubtless thought they'd won a minor, albeit largely moral, victory. When all was said and done, no ships had been hit and no one had been hurt on either side. Josh was singularly delighted that he hadn't been scratched either.

Sims was pleased. Initial reports said that his distraction had worked. The three American light cruisers and five destroyers had made it out into the open sea. They would stop off at Catalina with additional fuel and torpedoes for Nimitz's submarines and then set out as commerce raiders.

Josh caught the admiral laughing at him. "I told Elise I'd bring you back in one piece and so I will. It was a good night's work, Lieutenant. The next time, though, we shall stay and sink them."

★ CHAPTER 12 ★

"BE SEATED," SAID PRESIDENT LANSING, AND THE other attendees in the Oval Office sat. "May I assume, gentlemen, that the news is a mixed bag?"

"It usually is," said General March. "However, that is much better than all the news being dolefully bad."

"Then begin with the bad. What in God's name happened in the mountains? Have our efforts been undone by one man?"

March sighed, "Pretty much. One German officer, a Captain Wulfram, managed to drop the bridge over the Columbia River into said river. It will take at least two months of concerted effort to repair it once the weather eases. Sadly, we had pretty much cleared the snow out of the passes and were going to commence sending trains through again. Hundreds of men on both sides of the mountains had been shoveling night and day."

"The man must have been exceptionally brave, or foolish," the president said. "What is his status?"

"He is very seriously wounded," March continued. "He is on his way to a hospital in Chicago. Frostbite has claimed both of his feet and he may lose a leg to wounds and infection. And this poses a question, sir. Since he was not in uniform, shall we hang him?"

Lansing paused. He had not been prepared for the question. Nor was he quite prepared to hang someone, in particular someone who was so bravely and obstinately doing his duty. "No, at least not yet. We will hold him as a possible future bargaining chip. Although," he smiled, "if we should decide to hang him we will do so from a railroad trestle."

The others laughed grimly. Nothing like a little macabre humor to brighten the day, Lansing thought.

General March interrupted. "The weapons and ammo are beginning to come off the assembly lines in quantity from Detroit and elsewhere. The original plan was to ship them by rail through the northern pass to Washington State and then down to California. With this out of the question for the foreseeable future, can we plan on using Canadian rail lines as a substitute?"

An interesting question, thought Lansing. He turned to his secretary of state, "Any thoughts, Mr. Hughes?"

"We have spoken with both the governor general and the prime minister of Canada and they are reluctant to have large quantities of supplies shipped directly through Canada. They are afraid of retaliation from the German fleet if they are found out. However, they will allow humanitarian aid, such as food, and will assist us in evacuating civilians and wounded."

"Better than nothing," Lansing muttered.

Hughes continued. "I have directed our railroads

to try to rent line space from the Canadians in the form of a detour north from the broken line, into Canada, and then south. If it is done as a private venture, without the direct collaboration of the Canadian government, we might get away with it until the bridge is rebuilt."

"Will that happen?" Lansing asked.

"Not until the Canucks and the Brits are certain we can win and they're on the right side, and right now they can't be confident of that."

Railroads were something always taken for granted. One could take a train from virtually anywhere in the United States to any other place in the large and sprawling nation. And, since the highways and roads were generally quite miserable, going by train was virtually the only viable way to travel any sort of distance. The disruption of the lines between California and the rest of the world had shocked everyone. Someday there would have to be paved highways connecting at least the major cities of the United States. Right now, most roads outside major cities were little more than the same dirt trails pioneers had traveled on in the previous century.

"And I'm sure you're aware of the success we had in destroying their bomber fleet," March said proudly. "I am recommending Major Eisenhower and Captain Martel each for a medal. It was exceedingly well done."

Lansing beamed. "It indeed was." The name Martel sounded familiar. Then he recalled the young officer who'd been with him that fateful night when he became president.

"And what of the Navy's foray?" he asked.

"Successful," said Navy Secretary Daniels. "Shots

were exchanged, and the German fleet got stirred up and aggravated. They chased our ships back to the sound while the cruiser squadron slipped out unnoticed. After resupplying our subs at Catalina, the cruisers will sail forth as independent commerce raiders, while the destroyers will work in conjunction with the submarines."

"Excellent," said Lansing, "but too slow. We need something to inspire the American people. The delivery of supplies, however critical, is too prosaic. We need something dramatic."

General March smiled. "Will you take Texas?"

"Sarge, what the hell did that sign say?"

Tim Randall yawned. He'd been sleeping soundly, something that hadn't been happening all that much lately. The rocking of the train, however, was calming and helped him forget his personal agonies.

"What the hell do you think it said?" he answered grumpily. He had to teach these children who thought they were soldiers that you just don't go around waking up sleeping sergeants. "You can read, can't you?"

"Actually, he can't read all that well, Sarge," said one of the other men. "He's from Poland. But the sign did say we'd just entered Texas, and that's where we'll be fighting, right?"

"It is," Tim said, "but don't get your knickers twisted. For those of you who've never seen a map, Texas is larger than most countries."

"Jeez, Sarge, does that mean it's larger than Camden?"

Tim stifled a grin. Every group had at least one smartass, and it looked like he had several. "Your sergeant requires sleep, so you do whatever you want. Just stay out of trouble, Private Asshole."

Tim still couldn't believe he was on a train, one of scores of them, rolling south through Texas. He had a squad of men and he was part of the Twelfth Infantry Division, which consisted of two Marine Corps regiments and two infantry regiments that had been cobbled together out of units from Pennsylvania and New Jersey. The regiments were all understrength as a result of the flu. A normal American division consisted of twenty thousand men. He'd heard that the Twelfth had fewer than fifteen thousand, all lightly trained and still lacking heavy weapons.

The flu. God, he wished he could forget about it. He'd stopped off in Camden to visit his family. He found his parents mourning the loss of their youngest son and leaving Tim with the vague feeling that they held him responsible for his brother's death. On a whim and a need to get out of a house filled with despair and blame, he'd gone to visit Kathy Fenton. She had written him a couple of times while he was in training. She'd apologized to him for being so presumptuous their last night together and blamed it on the drink. He'd written back, apologizing for getting so stinking drunk and pawing her like a pig, although he'd phrased it a good deal more tactfully.

Kathy was in mourning too. Like Tim, she'd survived a touch of the flu, although it had been late in the season and fairly mild. However, she'd lost her sister and a cousin to the disease. She had lost a lot of weight, and was pale and gray. Her eyes looked haunted. He'd sat on her couch with her head on his shoulder while she cried. Then she'd looked in his eyes, seen his pain, and put his head on her shoulder, holding him tightly, like a baby, while he wept bitterly. Later, they parted. They'd kissed each other on the cheek and hugged. Yes, they said, they would continue to write. Tim wondered just where this would ever go.

He now commanded ten men on their way to kill other people. He knew he was inexperienced but what was truly frightening was the fact that his men were even rawer than he was. Some had only fired their rifles a couple of times. He wondered if the men in charge of the Army and the country had any idea what they were getting their men into. He'd read enough about the Civil War to know that inexperienced generals often get their men slaughtered. Pershing commanded the entire Texas Front army, while some Marine named Lejeune commanded the division. That too was funny. What the hell was a Marine doing in charge of an Army division?

"Sarge, any idea where the hell we're going in this godawful big state?" Private Asshole asked.

"No," he said, "but I'll bet there'll be Mexicans around."

D.W. Griffith worked the projector. He barely glanced at Elise who smiled at being ignored. She was history. Griffith was in his element. The screen on the wall showed the German crossing of the Salinas River at San Luis Obispo.

Patton's defensive positions were well sited, but he had too few men to seriously hinder the German onslaught, and the Salinas wasn't all that much of a barrier, even with water rushing down from the nearby mountains. It was more of a nuisance than a moat. With more men and guns, the rugged terrain would have heavily favored the defense, but Patton was short of both.

Still, the Germans had paused to consolidate and bombard Patton's defenses, which gave the defenders of San Francisco a little more time to prepare.

There were muted gasps from the dozen or so in the conference room as scores of small boats pushed off from the southern shore. Each carried a dozen German soldiers.

"I think they could have waded," muttered Nolan.

"The second group did," answered Griffith. "Patton said it was terrible intelligence work on the Germans' part. Their commander's some guy named von Seekt, and I am not impressed."

Nor was anyone else, it turned out. The overcautious Germans had missed an opportunity to overwhelm the American defenders.

As they watched, American riflemen on the north shore began to shoot up the boats and the handful of Hotchkiss machine guns and Browning Automatic Rifles the Americans possessed chewed them as well. Bodies tumbled into the bottom of the boats or into the river. In one instance a boat capsized, bewildered survivors standing up to their waists in water.

Nolan nudged Martel. "If people weren't dying that would've been funny."

All humor vanished when German machine guns on the south shore began to kill Americans. Griffith shook his head sadly. "Patton said they had fifty machine guns for each one we had. With respect, General Liggett, when the devil are we going to get our own?"

Luke recalled hearing that Griffith had been pro-German before the war. Apparently his views had changed. Well, so had a lot of people's.

"We're working on it, Mr. Griffith," Liggett said quietly.

The film ended. "That's it, folks," Griffith said in a most unmilitary manner. "And with your permission, General, I would like to arrange for a copy of it to get to Washington."

Liggett yawned. He was exhausted and the heat in the closed room had nearly put him to sleep. A telegram from Brigadier General George Marshall had exhorted him to keep the rail line to the east open despite the fact that the bridge over the Columbia tributary had been destroyed. What the hell was Marshall up to now? Regardless, he'd given the orders and the construction battalion that had been withdrawn from the pass was returned.

"By all means make a copy and we'll arrange to have it sent via Canada as diplomatic mail. Let those people out east see what we're up against."

Lieutenant Ron Carter, captain of the sub O-7, was one of the few men who thought Catalina Island was beautiful. It had a rugged and dramatic quality that appealed to him.

He was halfway up a hillside and looking down into the harbor where the five submarines were anchored. It was time to take on supplies and stores, that is, as soon as they came. Since sinking those two transports, Carter's sub had sent three more German ships to the bottom and one had a full cargo of oil. It had burned furiously. He would have exulted except he had seen a lifeboat from the transport overtaken by a wall of flames and the men inside turned into human torches. He thought he could hear them scream. He couldn't, of course, but it was the stuff of nightmares.

In the course of his cruises, he'd used all his torpedoes and most of his three-inch shells; thus, his sub was virtually helpless. He was also almost out of fuel. So too were the others. Supply ships were allegedly en route, but, until they arrived, there really wasn't much to do. Chief Ryan was on the sub with a half-dozen crewmen while the rest, like Carter, relaxed.

A trumpet blared from up the hill behind him. *What the hell,* he thought sleepily. That damn thing was only to be blown if the Germans were sighted.

Oh shit.

Carter jumped to his feet and squinted seaward. A pair of sleek gray shapes was approaching fast. They'd been hidden by the morning mist. More alarms sounded and men began to run around, some aimlessly as they realized they would never get to their subs in time. He began to run down to the little cove they were using, but he saw that Chief Ryan had already cast off the lines and was heading out to sea. Good man, Carter thought. It would have been at least fifteen minutes before he made it to the sub and it was imperative that the boat get to deep water and dive.

The Germans were at extreme range, but they commenced firing anyhow. Seconds later, shells splashed around the other four subs, which were also frantically trying to get away.

A sub was hit. Crewmen began to abandon her immediately. Seconds later, an explosion ripped through a second boat. More German shells landed around the stricken vessels while the remaining American subs found water deep enough to dive in. So too had the O-7, Carter thought gratefully as she disappeared beneath the waves. He thought her hull might be scraping the bottom, but that was better than being shelled.

Deprived of their primary targets, the Germans contented themselves with bombarding any buildings and any people they saw. Carter hid himself in a fold of earth as dirt and debris fell all around him. Nimitz crawled up beside him. "I don't know about you, Carter, but we'd all better pray the bastards don't land troops. We have nothing to fight with unless you're good at throwing stones." Neither man even had a sidearm, however futile a .45 automatic might be against a destroyer.

"How'd they find out about us, sir?"

"Guess it wasn't that big a secret. That and the fact that we had to be someplace might have led them to a logical conclusion. Do you recall if they sent over any planes to spy on us?"

Carter didn't recall seeing any, but that didn't mean they hadn't done it. He thought it possible that one of the handful of fishermen living on the island might have betrayed them. These were poor people and perhaps somebody had been bribed.

"Maybe we're just too damned close to the mainland, sir," Carter said. He regretted the comment immediately. The brass in San Francisco had chosen the place and Nimitz had concurred.

There was a strained silence that was finally broken by Nimitz. "I'm afraid you're right, Carter. We're only about twenty miles from Los Angeles and I realize now that we are way, way too close. When we get ourselves organized, we'll pull out of this mess and locate elsewhere."

"Any specific thoughts?"

Nimitz shook his head, "At the moment, no."

The guns grew silent and Carter worked up the courage to peer over the dirt that was hiding him. The German destroyers were departing. One American sub had sunk in the shallow water while a second was still afloat, but burning. A couple of launches were smashed to kindling. Of the other three subs, including Carter's, there was no sign, which was good. Hopefully, probably, they'd gotten away.

Several bodies lay on the ground, American sailors who would never again attack German shipping. Nimitz stood up and shook the sand from his uniform.

"Lieutenant, I suggest we find out whose alive and who needs help. Then we get to figure out what resources we have. Y'know, if the relief ships don't show up, we could get very hungry in a very short while."

Texas General Marcus Tovey was hungry, tired, and dirty, just like the rest of his dwindling command. He hadn't changed his clothes in a week and his beard was filthy and tangled.

They'd mauled the Mexicans and still held onto much of San Antonio, including the desecrated ruins of the Alamo which were now only a hundred yards behind him, but they couldn't hold off the much larger Mexican force much longer. It was the middle of the night and maybe they wouldn't come this morning, but who could tell. He'd beaten back another attack, leaving scores of dead and wounded Mexicans in front of him, and they didn't usually attack two days in a row. They needed time to reorganize, eat and sleep, too.

He still had fifteen hundred men, but they weren't the same fifteen hundred he'd begun the siege with. Most were replacements and, as before, a whole lot weren't even from Texas. There was some gratification in the fact that men from other states were willing to come and defend Texas. Or maybe they were defending the United States and not Texas, he thought, and decided it didn't much matter.

So many had been killed or wounded that he'd lost track. Against him were two Mexican divisions, maybe twelve thousand men, and they were totally pissed. They'd hoped to be in and through San Antonio a couple of weeks ago and his defense of the city had gutted those plans. If they overran his position he doubted they'd be in any mood to take prisoners. Well, fuck'em, he thought. He didn't much feel like surrendering and becoming a prisoner. His defenses were deep and good and protected by miles of barbed wire. If the Mexicans did make it through, maybe there wouldn't be all that many of them left . . . Sure. There'd be plenty of them left. What made his situation worse was that his men were spread too thin.

Of course he wasn't the only Texan general fighting the Mexicans. It just seemed that way since almost all their attacks were at the area he commanded. He lit another of his dwindling supply of Lucky Strikes and took a deep breath. The tobacco smoke served to hide the stench of the battlefield. Both sides had stopped removing the dead and the wounded, and the ground before him was littered with bodies that had bloated and begun to rot. He never believed anything could smell that bad. One of his boys had laughed and said the stench was so bad because of all the spicy food the Mexicans ate. At least the wounded had stopped their moaning and screaming. If the Mexicans had asked for a truce to remove them he would have denied it. Niceties were down the toilet. This was a war to the death.

A rumbling noise behind him said that the trains were still running, which was good. That meant more replacements, even if they were poorly armed and barely trained farm boys or clerks from the cities. As a result, too many new guys died in the first skirmish.

He heard people moving quietly behind him, or at least they were trying to be quiet. He turned and saw a file of men coming towards him. What looked like an officer in a pie tin helmet detached himself and walked up to Tovey, staying in a crouch. Smart man. The Mexicans had snipers, too.

"You General Tovey?"

"Yeah, who wants to know?"

The officer grinned, and Tovey saw stars on his collar. "Tovey, I'm Major General John Lejeune, U.S. Marine Corps, and now commanding the Twelfth Infantry Division. If you don't mind, I've got an advance party of about four thousand Marines who'd just love to join your little party. The rest of the division, along with some other fine young men, will be along shortly after they complete an assignment I've given them."

Tovey nodded mutely. He was afraid he was going to cry. He watched as long columns of grim-faced Marines filled in the far too many open spaces in his trenches. There was soft and easy banter between his men and the newcomers, especially when the old defenders saw the machine guns and mortars the Marines had brought.

For the first time in a long time, Tovey eagerly awaited the dawn.

"I will not go with the refugees," Kirsten said firmly. "When there are no more refugees, that'll mean the battle's right around the corner and then I will volunteer for hospital work. They will need all the help they can get."

Luke and Kirsten were walking along the waterfront after taking a cable car ride just for the sheer pleasure of it. It was early evening and the sky was clear, and there was a hint of spring in the otherwise cold air. It was so nice they could even ignore the omnipresent dark spots far out in the ocean that were the blockading German warships.

Luke was perplexed by Kirsten's reluctance to even consider leaving for safer places. "Have you ever seen the blood in a battlefield hospital? Do you really think you can handle it?" He immediately realized it was the wrong thing to say as she glared at him.

"Have you ever gelded a bull?" she snapped.

"Not recently."

Kirsten laughed. "I haven't either, but I've seen it done often enough. And no, I'm not giving you a choice, I'm staying. Even if you pick me up and put me on a train, I'll find a way to get off and come back. As long as you are here, Luke Martel, then I will be too."

Luke felt a surge of pride and affection. Yeah, he wanted her to stay. He never wanted her to leave. After thinking he'd lost her in the train attack, sending her away was the last thing he wanted to do. Still, he wanted her safe and he was torn by the dilemma. Letting her make the decision wasn't just the easy way out for him. She had every right to do as she wished, not as he wished. Okay, he thought, she would stay.

"Luke, I was married at eighteen and widowed at twenty-three. I never thought I'd get over the loss. I wasn't really certain I even wanted to.

"I realize now I was quite content living my life and feeling sorry for myself. Then came the Germans who destroyed my home, my cousins, and every tangible object I had to remember my husband by, except for the wedding ring, of course. And some money," she added with a smile.

"He was very prudent and put some money aside in the form of a life-insurance policy. When he died, I collected ten thousand dollars. I used the money to pay off some debts and saved the rest. I'm not rich, but I'll get by."

"Don't worry," Luke said wryly. "I'm not after your money. I've managed to save a little myself."

"On a soldier's pay?" she said, incredulously.

"And the ability to play a really good game of poker."

Kirsten laughed. "Well, I guess there are savings plans and there are savings plans. But can you see why I'm reluctant to commit? Right now, Elise and Josh are making like almost bunnies back in the apartment. I think it's incredible that she won't let him go all the way with her when they both want it so much."

"She trying to make him marry her?"

"Why, of course."

"I guess that was a silly question. Fortunately, we're both adults and unless your marriage was a sham, neither one of us is a foolish virgin."

Kirsten blushed slightly. "We loved each other in every way imaginable."

Now it was Luke's turn to blush. "I just hope you can consider me as part of your future."

She squeezed his hand. "If I didn't think so, I would be on the next train to Seattle."

She pulled him to her and kissed him on the lips and the hell with what anybody thought. There was a war out there and living for tomorrow might be living for a fantasy. Luke returned the kiss and pressed her body against his.

She looked up and saw him laughing. "What's so funny?"

"I was just thinking we should go back to your apartment and throw those young puppies out."

The crown prince, the man who someday would be Kaiser Wilhelm III, gestured to a chair. Major General Oskar von Hutier did as directed and sat stiffly in the presence of his commanding officer and future kaiser. He thought he knew why he'd been summoned to the prince's headquarters, but would not even think of broaching the subject himself. It was far too sensitive.

But the prince smiled warmly and dove right in. "General von Seekt is being promoted to a staff position back in Berlin where I am certain his experiences as a field commander here will enable him to excel. He will leave immediately and you will take over his corps, which, of course, represents the left wing of my army."

"I am honored," said Hutier, who currently commanded a small corps in Mackensen's army. Taking over from von Seekt would give him almost an independent command.

Honored but not surprised, Hutier thought. Von Seekt, a solid and professional senior staff officer had requested a field command and been given it. He'd been in charge of the two division corps moving up the California coast and, until a few days ago, had been doing a credible job. However, he had stopped short at the Salinas River and hesitated to cross it until he'd brought up boats and heavy artillery. This delay had taken the better part of a week. The crown prince, on the other side of the mountains, had no reason to doubt the need for the halt until it was pointed out that the river was only about a hundred yards wide and could have been waded. Von Seekt quickly became the butt of numerous jokes from both the Germans and the Americans; thus, his "promotion" to Berlin.

"There are those who think I am too cautious," the prince said, "and they are at least partly right. I am seriously constrained by the fact that my army must be fed and equipped and that those supplies must come a very great distance. And we all know that a defeat on the field could be catastrophic; hence my desire to progress slowly and cautiously. Although," he shook his head and laughed, "not quite as cautiously as von Seekt."

The prince rose and stood before a map. "We are now only a hundred miles from San Francisco and what the Americans are developing into a formidable series of defenses, and those defenses must be taken. General Hutier, you have quite a reputation. It is said you are aggressive and wish to strike, like a panther. Correct?"

Hutier smiled at the compliment. "Indeed, sir."

"They say you have devised a way of infiltrating enemy lines and bypassing strongpoints, which will enable you to pierce Liggett's works."

"I am confident the tactics will succeed."

The prince was pleased. "I wish to rein in your predatory impulses until the right time, which will be when we attack San Francisco. Until that time I wish you to curb your ambitions and coordinate with the armies moving inland along the Great Valley. When the time comes, your corps may just be reinforced into an army, and become the spearpoint which we will use to kill the Americans. Until then, we must all restrain our impulses to take precipitous actions against Liggett's army, however tempting some targets may be."

"How large do you estimate that army, sir?"

"According to our intelligence experts, Liggett has approximately fifty thousand, but most of them are still poorly trained and even more poorly armed. The destruction of the last bridge to Seattle was a devastating blow and one which will cripple them. They will have some advantage by being in defensive positions, which is why you will be needed to rupture those defenses."

"I'm honored and gratified for your confidence in me, sir," Hutier said softly. He was barely able to hold back his emotions. "I will not fail you or Germany."

"Until the happy day that we can bring this campaign to its ultimate conclusion, Hutier, I must be cognizant that we are halfway around the world from Germany. In the last war, if I needed reinforcements, six divisions would be put on trains and be in the lines in a matter of days. Now it would take six or more months to get them to California and then I would be unable to feed and supply them. Therefore, I must constantly remind myself that we must fight with what we have, and not what we wish we had. Some additional forces are en route, but not in great numbers. We have three divisions in Hanoi, but they are to be used to take Hawaii and the Philippines if the Americans do not see reason."

He declined to add that the German force would not leave Indo-China until the American Navy had at least been contained. There had been too many sinkings by submarines and now by American light cruisers working as surface raiders.

The crown prince stood, and Hutier followed quickly. The meeting was coming to an end. "Good luck, von Hutier. We will need you in the coming weeks."

★ CHAPTER 13 ★

"THOSE LOOK LIKE PIE TINS," TOVEY SAID GENIALLY to a marine sergeant named Daly. The rugged Irishman grinned.

"These helmets protect my head a lot better than that bad excuse for a cowboy hat you're wearing, General."

Tovey laughed. Lejeune now had seven thousand Marines in the lines around San Antonio and, so far, the Mexicans hadn't been able to make a dent in them. Word had it that Mexican President Carranza himself had come up from Mexico City to see San Antonio fall and was extremely angry that it hadn't happened yet.

Even though they were holding out, Tovey was still worried about the ultimate outcome of the fighting. San Antonio was virtually surrounded. Carranza poured more and more men into taking the city and the Alamo.

Lejeune slid in beside Tovey. Their command trench

was only fifty yards behind the main American trenches and some would argue they were way too close to the front lines. Others would argue that there wasn't all that much to the defenses and that almost everything had become the front lines.

Mexican artillery, never very good or numerous, opened up and a number of shells landed near them. Everyone prudently kept their heads down and, as debris rained on them, Tovey began to wonder if his men shouldn't get helmets, too. Sergeant Daly read his mind.

"See what I mean, General?"

Tovey shook the dirt from his campaign hat. "Up yours, Sergeant Daly."

"Here they come," someone yelled, followed by, "Oh Jesus, look at them all!"

From everywhere they could see, great waves of humanity poured out of the Mexican lines and rushed towards them. The Mexicans yelled and screamed while officers waved swords and pistols, urging them on.

Rifle and machine-gun fire from the Americans cut huge swaths in the Mexicans, but they kept coming, filling the places of the dead. They reached the barbed wire. Men with cutters worked frantically and brave Mexican soldiers used their bodies to crush down the wire. It worked. First in a trickle and then in a flood, the Mexicans poured through, screaming hatred and shooting wildly.

Firing was almost at point-blank range. Daly glared at Lejeune. "Begging both the generals' pardon, but I don't much feel like dying in no fucking hole in the ground."

"Fucked if I do either," said Tovey as he lurched out of the trench and headed forward.

Daly leaped across the main American trench and

waved his rifle over his head. "Come on, you sons of bitches. You want to live forever?"

Marines and Texans climbed out of the trenches and, bayonets fixed, advanced slowly towards the Mexicans.

The lead Mexicans were shocked to see the thin line of Americans coming at them, their faces contorted in fury. Their slight hesitation was fatal. The Americans fired once more at point-blank range, dropping the Mexicans into more piles of dead and dying, and then took them with the bayonet.

The Mexicans were not used to bayonets, and had little training with the primitive but psychologically fearsome weapon. When confronted with a bayonet charge, most reasonable men will look for ways to get themselves elsewhere, and the Mexicans were no exception. Those in front who'd survived the withering rifle fire either hacked futilely with their own bayonets or tried to get away. However, the press of humanity pushing behind them wouldn't let them retreat. Many of the Mexicans turned on their American tormenters and fought back desperately while others tried to claw their way back to safety.

Tovey's bayonet caught in a Mexican's chest and he lost his rifle. He pulled out his Bowie knife and his revolver and began to shoot and stab. It was nothing more than a gigantic bar brawl with thousands of Mexicans and Americans literally at each other's throats. Tovey's revolver was soon empty and he used it as a club. His knife sliced flesh every time he moved it. A Mexican screamed in his face and Tovey rammed the knife through the man's throat. Tovey was knocked down and jabbed the knife upwards into a Mexican's groin. The Mexican screamed like a burning cat.

Finally, it was too much for the Mexicans. The Mexican front lines, now thoroughly fought out, managed to bull their way through the rear ranks who promptly realized that the day was over. As Tovey and Lejeune watched, exhausted and incredulous, the Mexican host pulled back. The thin American lines were much thinner and everyone was covered with blood. Lejeune was nursing a sliced shoulder and someone had shot Tovey in the leg. He could barely stand. It didn't look like an artery'd been hit, though, so he thought he might live.

Lejeune looked at the carnage. A few feet in front of him, the bodies were piled three and four deep and not all were Mexicans. Some of the Americans had started looking for survivors, or at least pulling their own dead back from the grisly field.

"We've won," Tovey said. "But I'm gonna guess we've lost half our men."

"Easily," replied Lejeune. He'd taken a rifle butt in the jaw and talking was painful but necessary. "But they won't try this again. Carranza will have his men finish surrounding us and take us from all sides. Tomorrow at the earliest."

"Then we'd all better hope that the rest of your plan shakes out. And by the way, where the hell is Daly?"

"Right here," Daly said. His uniform was almost totally covered in blood and he looked like he'd fallen into a vat of red paint. Otherwise he didn't seem hurt and was grinning widely.

"Wasn't that a helluva battle, General Lejeune, sir, and respects to you too, General Tovey. I would say we kicked the Mexicans' asses right up between their ears."

★ ★ ★

Trains, trains, and more trains. However, there was no more riding across the country in reasonably comfortable passenger cars that had seats and windows and johns.

At Corpus Christi, Tim Randall's unit had disembarked and switched over to a freight train. Twenty men and all their supplies were jammed into a freight car and the train seemed to have scores of freight cars. And it was headed west, not south.

It could have been worse, Tim reminded himself. He'd seen some flatcars with soldiers sprawled on them. At least the boxcar kept them out of most of the weather and there wasn't much danger of falling off.

His platoon leader, Second Lieutenant Alfred Taylor, was with him in the car, a mixed blessing at best. The men didn't feel they could relax with an officer so close and the lieutenant was not the type to let down his hair or get familiar with the men.

Tim thought the lieutenant was all right. Maybe twenty-two, but looking fourteen, and with a degree in philosophy from Harvard, which made him officer material as far as the Army's standards were concerned. So far he hadn't done anything stupid, nor had he done anything to endear him to his men or make them want to follow him in battle. Tim sighed. He wondered if his squad would follow him when the time came.

Tim knew his men's names, but that was about it. Sergeant Smith had given him one last piece of advice before Tim had departed from Dix. He said don't ever get too close to men you might have to send out to die. Learn their names so you can yell at them, but don't learn about their families, their sweethearts, their kids, their old widowed mothers, or their ambitions. You do that, Smith said, and it'll tear you apart when they die, or worse, you'll sit back and play God when it comes time to send men out to do something dangerous. For instance, Smith said, you might be tempted to send a bachelor out on patrol and keep the man with two kids safe.

First, Smith continued, it wasn't fair to the single guy, and, second, maybe the married guy is the best man for the job, or it's just his turn and the men will hate you for showing favoritism. Either way, keep the men's personal lives at arm's length. After losing Wally, Tim thought he understood.

Soon enough they would find out how good they were. While the Fifth and Sixth Marine Regiments, added to the original Texas garrison, held on to a perimeter in San Antonio. The rest of the division, along with two others, was racing along the rail lines to the east of San Antonio. Racing was a relative term. With so many trains lined up, speed was not possible.

But they did not go all the way to San Antonio. The trains stopped in the middle of the night and soldiers poured out, confused and lost. Officers checked all their weapons and the empty trains moved again towards the west while the men formed up and began marching south. A lucky few rode in trucks or Ford cars, but those were senior officers and the vast majority walked. A half-dozen armored trucks accompanied them. Machine guns poked reassuringly from the sides and front of the strange, sinister-looking vehicles.

Tim thought he saw Pershing in a staff car but wasn't certain. Some soldiers bitched, but Tim thought it felt good to be walking. It wasn't very hot yet and someone had used his head in planning the march. There were stations with food and water along the way. There weren't many towns, but in what little ones there were, people came out with more food and water. At the very least they waved. Some had American flags and one confused old man waved the Confederate flag and loudly thanked Jesus that Lee had finally arrived.

"Where we at?" he asked an older woman who was maybe fifty.

"You're close on to Pleasanton," she said and Tim grinned. She had no teeth.

"Sir, where and what the hell is Pleasanton?" Tim asked the lieutenant who just shrugged. He wasn't going to admit he didn't know squat either. Officers didn't admit ignorance.

In the distance and to their right, lights flickered and they could hear thunder. It was an artillery duel and the dramatic sights and sounds sobered them. They were going into battle.

Suddenly, rifle fire erupted in front of them. They all dropped to the ground until the lieutenants and sergeants told them to get their asses up and form skirmish lines.

More rifle fire, but it was sporadic and they began to feel foolish about hitting the ground until a soldier screamed and fell over, clutching his leg. He was followed by another and another. *My God,* Tim thought in disbelief, *someone's shooting at me.*

"Forward! Faster!" Lieutenant Taylor yelled and, all along the line, men began to run. The armored trucks fanned out with them and machine guns started blazing away.

There was a cluster of buildings to their front and Tim saw people running around. Christ, they were Mexican soldiers. Lieutenant Taylor ordered a halt and his men loosed a ragged volley at the enemy. Now it was the Mexicans' turn to drop and writhe and scream.

Without further orders, the Americans rushed forward, the armored trucks first and then the infantry. In seconds, they were in between the buildings and the Mexicans were running for their lives. There hadn't been very many of them in the first place, and some were trying to surrender, while others lay on the ground, dead or wounded. Tim looked at a man who had half his head blown away. He wanted to puke, but held it down. Some of his men didn't.

They pushed through to what had been a clearing. It was piled high with wooden cases and barrels. They'd just grabbed a Mexican supply dump.

"Burn everything," came the order and, like little kids, the Yanks complied until the field was an inferno with flames soaring hundreds of feet in the air. Some idiot set fire to ammo which exploded in a massive fireworks display. A couple of Americans got hurt, but not seriously.

Taylor grabbed Tim's arm. "Get your men organized. The whole company's heading north, to San Antonio."

"Just the company, Lieutenant?" Tim asked, not fully comprehending.

Taylor laughed and Tim began to think that the boy lieutenant was okay. "The company, the battalion, the regiment, the division. The whole fucking army's heading north to San Antonio."

The men nearby roared their approval and Tim wondered just when, where and why Harvard philosophy majors learned to use the word "fuck" in their philosophical conversations.

"Christ, it stinks," Tovey said. No one argued. The recent additions to the piles of dead had joined the earlier piles of bloated, maggot-filled corpses. Vast clouds of flies periodically erupted for unknown reasons and then landed to continue their obscene dinner. Crows were having a feast.

"Now somebody tell me what all that smoke is?" Tovey asked casually. Nobody answered. His men knew their general was talking to himself again. It looked like the pillars of smoke were at least five miles away and, whatever it was, the Mexicans were strangely quiet.

General Lejeune ran up, grinning. "Get your men up and moving, General Tovey. We got a linkup to make."

The survivors of the battles for San Antonio moved forward slowly and tentatively. Crossing the killing field was difficult. First they weren't certain they wouldn't be shot at, and second, there was so much human debris that it was almost impossible not to step on something soft that squished horribly when a boot landed on it. Worst were the severed limbs and disconnected skulls that stared up at them. Tovey gagged. He'd killed men before, but this was murder on a massive scale.

Gradually, the numbers of Mexican dead dwindled, the stench faded, and it became apparent that nobody was shooting at them. Only a handful of Mexicans remained, and most of them were wounded. They held up their arms pathetically and cried out that they were surrendering.

They could hear small-arms fire in the distance. They continued to move on, now even more cautiously. They could see large numbers of Mexicans approaching, but in disarray. The firing was getting closer and it dawned on them that the Mexicans were being herded north and towards them.

On seeing the Americans, the Mexican host halted. Somebody in the Mexican ranks yelled an order and they all threw down their weapons.

Lejeune slapped Tovey on the shoulder. "Let's get all these people organized. Pershing's got plans for us."

"Tell me, General."

"South to the border at Laredo, and then God only knows where."

For President Lansing and his key advisors, it was all too easy to focus on the war with Germany and Mexico and ignore what was happening in the rest of the world.

"Mr. President, there are events occurring in Russia that are of great interest," reported Secretary of State Hughes. "The Bolsheviks have announced that the Tsar has been captured, although it does seem that the rest of his family escaped and are en route to safety in Berlin. If true, it is a tragedy for the Imperial cause. However, the presence of his family in Germany will ensure that the dynasty will continue."

Lansing nodded, "And all this because Nicholas decided to lead his armies in person? Dear God that would be as foolish as if I took a direct field command. Or are you telling me this so I won't think of trying it?"

Hughes smiled. "The generals did suggest it as a subtle reminder not to; however, there are more compelling reasons for discussing it."

In 1919, the Russian peasants had finally exploded in a bloody revolution that was quickly taken over by the Communists, or Bolsheviks, under Leon Trotsky. The Romanov family and government were quickly overwhelmed and its survivors appealed to their fellow monarchs for help. Forgetting old differences and the fact that they'd been on opposite sides in the War of 1914, both Germany and Austria pledged aid. Manpower came primarily from Austria and, for a while, it seemed that the Romanov regime would be returned to power.

But the incompetently led Austrians had squandered their advantages and much of their army. They were now on the run north towards Petrograd, the old St. Petersburg. The tsar-led White Russian Army had just suffered the defeat that led to the capture of the tsar and its disorganized and panicked remnants were also streaming north. Despised and feared Russian Communists appeared to be in charge and Communism on the rise. Thus, enter Germany as the Romanovs' savior.

"Interesting," said Lansing, "even intriguing. But what does that have to do with the situation in Texas or California, or the price of tea in China?"

General March answered. "It means that the kaiser will have to send German soldiers to prop up the Romanovs and, even though Germany has a vast army, its numbers aren't unlimited. In order to send an adequate and sizeable army to Germany, the kaiser has several choices. First, he can call up reserves, which he will be extremely reluctant to do since it would send a message that his large standing army can't control events.

"Second, he can send first-rate troops to Russia by stripping the Channel ports and other garrisons of much of their strength, something that would delight the

British by lessening the threat of a possible German invasion. Either way, he will have fewer and fewer good troops to send to the United States to reinforce either the crown prince or Carranza."

"Now that is indeed interesting," Lansing admitted. "But it might not be relevant for a while, if ever. What are the final figures from Pershing?"

March glanced at a paper. "Approximately thirty thousand Mexicans were killed, wounded, or captured in the battle for San Antonio against approximately eight thousand American casualties. The largest number of Mexican casualties consists of prisoners. Carranza himself escaped and it's rumored that he's headed south of the Rio Grande and for Monterrey where he'll try to gather another army."

"Will that happen?" asked Hughes.

March laughed. "Not if Pershing has his way. Unless you tell him not to, he intends to cross the Rio Grande and move on Monterrey. That will put him on the German supply line between Vera Cruz and California. With the Mexican Army so badly mauled and with more American divisions on the way to Mexico, the Germans might have to use their own troops to try and keep supplies flowing. Either way, we win."

Lansing nodded thoughtfully, "Very good, General. Now, pray tell, what will happen to the foolish Tsar Nicholas?"

"If Trotsky and his comrades can't get him to abdicate the throne," Hughes said, "they'll doubtless cut off his head."

"A shame," said Lansing, "but the man is clearly a bloody fool."

Lansing had not met the tsar, but had dealt with

several of his relatives and diplomats in his career and found them, almost without exception, to be living in a fairy tale land of princes, privilege, and splendor while their Holy Mother Russia rotted around them. They deserved the revolution they were getting, but not all the butchery—and did the world deserve the Bolsheviks? An insane bunch, he thought. Ironically, he hoped the Germans would defeat Trotsky's bloodthirsty hordes. Perhaps a new tsar would be less of an autocratic fool, but he doubted it. Russia was a mess.

Lansing continued. "But all of this, including Pershing and Lejeune's victory over the Mexicans, will be for naught if the Germans take San Francisco. Kindly tell me you will have that problem resolved."

There was silence. Finally General March spoke. "We are working day and night and trying, almost literally, to move mountains in our efforts to get men and supplies to Liggett. The best I can say is that it will be close. Realistically, we are likely to lose San Francisco despite what happens in Monterrey or Moscow."

The top of the hill offered a splendid view of the ocean and the line of German warships approaching, which was why it had been chosen as the site for one of several command centers. Admiral Sims, General Liggett, along with a guest, British Admiral David Beatty, watched the panorama though their binoculars.

"I make it four light cruisers and two destroyers," said Sims. Beatty concurred.

Liggett deferred to their knowledge. To him all warships looked alike at that distance. "But what the devil are they doing?" he asked.

Beatty grinned. He was fifty-one, jut-jawed and

considered handsome by many, including himself. He had arrived in Puget Sound a few days earlier with two more modern battleships and two battle cruisers. Battle cruisers were large ships that were "almost" battleships, but more lightly armored to give them speed. Sims thought they'd be of dubious value in a slugfest battle with true battleships, but it did make the British force in Puget Sound a very powerful one.

"Gentlemen," Beatty said, "I firmly believe they will try to probe your shore defenses. I am quite frankly astonished that they haven't done it sooner."

"As are we," said Sims as he continued to look at the German ships, "but no one's complaining. I agree with your assessment. In a moment those ships will turn parallel to our coast and commence shooting at us. It will be an attempt to entice us to return fire and, by doing so, give away our positions and sizes of our guns. We will not comply with their wishes."

Somewhat by virtue of the fact that the twelve-inch guns came from the warships damaged or sunk at Mare Island, Sims commanded the shore batteries. Many of the gunners were from the ships.

Liggett was surprised by Sims' comment. "Please don't tell me you're going to let them just shoot at us?"

Sims grinned. "Indeed not."

As predicted, the German cruisers turned into a neat line running parallel with the shore and began firing with their six-inch guns. The shells came up short, splashing into the water, frightening the daylights out of a handful of foolish people who'd gathered to watch, as well as a horde of seagulls who rose, screeching in panic. Civilian and military police quickly herded the people away.

A few yards behind their leaders, the respective staffs waited. Luke glanced over to Josh Cornell, who shrugged. He had no idea what his admiral was up to either. Since their respective girlfriends were rooming together they'd become friends and the four of them had shared several meals. Luke considered Cornell intelligent and, for all his bookish appearance, brave enough. His medals and wounds attested to that. For his part, Cornell thought Martel was something like a Viking or Vandal from the Dark Ages and was astonished, like so many were, at the depth of Martel's knowledge and intelligence.

The German shells began crawling closer to the American shore batteries. The batteries had been painfully built of untold tons of concrete and thousands of sandbags. This particular battery had four twelve-inch guns. It was connected to the command center by telephone, telegraph, and radio, and, if necessary, by semaphore. Sims had once snarled that they'd use smoke signals or pigeons if it was necessary to maintain communications.

"Can they hit us up here?" asked Liggett.

Sims shook his head. "If we thought they could, we'd be inside the blockhouse and not on top. We're out of their range up here, but our batteries aren't and I am not going to allow the Germans to pot at them all day."

He picked up a telephone and spoke into it. "You may use one gun in response, nothing else. Aim at the lead cruiser and fire at your convenience. Oh yes, do try to do what I taught you."

Sims smiled at Beatty and Liggett. "The battery commander was a retired naval officer who became a math teacher. He rather liked my electronic range finder and has everything out there as preplotted and preplanned as shooting at a body of water can be. He has ranges already calculated."

"Are you saying he can make a first shot hit?" said Beatty incredulously. "If that's what you're promising, I'll take that bet."

"Never. He'll be close, but a first shot hit would be more due to luck instead of skill."

The gun fired and everyone cheered. Martel watched the dot that was the shell fly through the air. He'd heard you could see them, but hadn't believed it. He did now. Down it came, splashing a few yards short of the German cruiser. A miss, but close enough to spray the enemy ship with water and shell fragments. And maybe close enough for the water pressure from the exploding shell to damage the cruiser's hull.

"Well done!" enthused Beatty. "What about a second shot hit?"

Sims was too absorbed to answer. Battles between ships had to contend with multiple variables—the fact that both ships were moving, generally in different directions and at varying speeds, which was just too much for the human mind to handle. Thus, his invention of the electronic range finder which did in seconds the work that would have required hours to calculate otherwise. This time the fact that only one of the protagonists, the ships, was moving, simplified the calculations.

Again. The shell arched toward the German who was turning to port and, quite possibly, trying to get away. The first shell had been too close for comfort. The second shell landed a hundred yards long, raising another huge splash. The cruiser was clearly in trouble and attempting to pick up speed, while her comrades were scattering.

There was an agonizing pause. They all wanted a third shell. Sims would not expose his other guns by having them open up. It was all up to this one gun and a retired math teacher.

Wham! The shell again arched skyward and they held their breath until it smashed and exploded on the cruiser's stern, destroying one of her rear turrets. Seconds later, more explosions ripped through the German. She shuddered and went still in the water as fires began to consume her.

"Don't anybody cheer," said Sims with Liggett nodding. "Kindly remember that the poor bastards out there are dying," he said, paraphrasing Admiral Dewey's comment made during the Battle of Manila Bay in 1898.

"Please don't tell me the German admiral sacrificed one of his ships on purpose?" Liggett inquired.

"I very much doubt it," said Beatty. "I rather believe a mistake was made somewhere. Perhaps a capital ship or two were supposed to be there as the primary players, and not just a cruiser. No, Hipper is a hard man but he doesn't throw away lives like that."

"Glad to hear it," Liggett muttered.

The Germans on the sinking cruiser were climbing into lifeboats or jumping in the water. The other warships were departing. They would not be permitted to approach to pick up survivors. Had they been merchant ships, perhaps he would have let them, but not warships. Any survivors who could not row away to safety would be picked up by American small boats which were already en route.

Both Luke and Josh were clearly stunned by the demonstration of firepower. Nor was there cheering from the thousands of people who'd watched the duel. They all knew that what they'd just seen was nothing more than the opening salvo of the battle for San Francisco.

★ CHAPTER 14 ★

"MAY I SEE YOUR PASSPORT, SIR?" ASKED THE butler, who grinned impishly. He was a sailor from a torpedo boat and was dressed as a pirate. He looked ridiculous and was having a great time. He was also getting paid for his efforts.

Luke smiled and handed the man ten dollars. "Does this qualify, my good man?"

The sailor added the tenner to a pile and handed them each a ticket. "You both are now qualified to enter," he said with mock solemnity.

Luke laughed and took Kirsten's arm and guided her into the crowd. "Luke, what in God's name have you taken me to?"

The combined headquarters command had begun a series of Saturday night parties at the multistoried St. Francis Hotel on Powell Street. The hotel had largely survived the 1906 earthquake and fire, and had become a refugee center in the weeks after the quake. When the refugee crises abated, it quickly reverted back to its earlier glory.

The parties had started small but had grown with each passing week. Several hundred, mainly men, now attended. The rules were simple. Officers only, dress uniforms, minimal adherence to rank, and don't get so drunk as to be a slob or a disgrace. The enlisted men and NCOs had their own parties at another hotel.

The buffet table food was plentiful and good, although mostly seafood. The drinks were of a surprisingly high quality, causing some to be thankful that the Prohibition Amendment had been defeated.

Aides and other junior personnel spent a lot of time scrounging and trading to make these events successes, and neither Liggett nor Sims minded. If there was an opportunity for those who might have to place their lives on the line to have a little fun, who the devil cared?

There was little deference to rank. As an Army captain, Luke was one of a crowd of men with similar rank. Kirsten had insisted he wear his medals and, only slightly reluctantly, he'd concurred. Some of the younger men who were also his peers in rank might have thought him old and savage-looking, but they respected his awards and many staffers knew him for what they were not: a warrior.

The more senior officers moved easily with their juniors, although the lower ranking officers made certain to not carry informality too far.

These parties had been going on for several weeks, but Luke had managed to avoid them. Mingling and laughing insincerely at jokes simply wasn't him. Kirsten's presence made him think otherwise. After all she'd been through, he thought that perhaps she'd like an opportunity to let loose a little and, more important, to dress up like the beautiful woman he knew she was. It took her all of about five seconds to say yes.

Kirsten had managed to find a light blue gown that bared her shoulders and arms and showed the merest hint of delicious cleavage. Her gown came to mid calf and Luke thought her mid calves were excellent, as were her shoulders and cleavage. In short, he felt damned lucky to have her on his arm.

Despite being in deep mourning from the recent loss of her son, Mamie Eisenhower had offered to help and suggested a secondhand dress shop to Kirsten and it was where she'd found the dress. Kirsten gratefully accepted her help. She knew that doing something to help someone was one way for Mamie to cope with her terrible personal loss.

Pragmatically, Kirsten hadn't yet decided whether she would keep the dress or sell it back next week as so many women did after a big event.

They'd eaten from the bountiful buffet—grilled salmon had tempted them and they'd succumbed—and had a glass of local wine by Inglenook which was surprisingly good. They followed with a glass of Krug champagne.

A band was playing in the corner, but no one paid it much attention. Luke was intrigued by the stares they were getting. Beauty and the Beast, he decided, and he knew which one he was.

A slightly high-pitched man's voice intruded. "My dear, I have no idea who you are, but you could have chosen better blindfolded."

Luke grinned. "Kirsten, allow me to introduce you to Major, I mean Colonel," as he saw the eagles on

Patton's shoulder, "George Patton, sometimes mentor, sometimes aggravating, but always a friend."

Patton reached over, kissed Kirsten's hand, glanced down her cleavage, and said something in French. To his astonishment, she responded in kind.

"My God, Luke, where did you find this beautiful pearl beyond price?"

Kirsten squeezed Luke's arm. "I was a damsel in distress and he my knight errant. After that, it was impossible not to like him."

"You are truly meant for each other," Patton sighed.

"And when did you become a colonel, George?" Luke asked.

Patton shrugged. "About ten minutes after they took me from the 7th Cavalry and said they had something special and important for me to do. Don't ask, because I don't frankly know what it is and, if I did, probably couldn't tell you much at all. Secrets, you know. All I do know is that I'm to be in Seattle on Monday, and, trust me, I have no idea why. Some special project with the Brits is the rumor, and that may be good news. The Brits have been snuggling closer and closer to us. I don't think they're quite ready to jump in on our side, but a few months from now? Who can tell?"

He laughed. "And as to the rank, who knows. Maybe I'll become a field marshal if this war lasts long enough."

After a few more comments, Patton departed. Luke and Kirsten socialized with those they knew and found that number surprisingly large. Of course, all his acquaintances wanted to meet Kirsten, not chat with him, and he felt a twinge of jealousy. What the hell did she see in him, anyhow? He told himself to stop acting like a little kid. There were five men to every woman at the party, so of course Kirsten would be the center of attention and why shouldn't she enjoy the hell out of it. After all, wasn't that why he'd brought her, so she could get out and enjoy herself? *Luke,* he thought to himself, *sometimes you are a complete jackass.*

About eleven, Kirsten suggested they leave and Luke concurred. Things were getting just a little bit rowdy; the senior rankers had departed. As Luke turned towards the hotel entrance, she took his arm and steered him to an elevator. "Eight," she told the stone-faced operator.

Like a lamb, Luke allowed himself to be led down a hallway to a door on the eighth floor. Kirsten took a key from her purse and unlocked it. It was not a hotel room. Instead, it was a suite and it had a stunning view of the city.

"I believe in planning ahead, Luke. I hope you don't mind. The suite belongs to Mr. Griffith and Elise borrowed it from him. He believes in helping our soldiers, while the Army, of course, helps him with his movies."

"How could I possibly mind?" he said. Was this really happening?

"Help me undress." Yes it was.

He did as ordered and, when she was naked, she undressed him. They looked on each other for a second and then couldn't contain themselves. They rushed into each other's arms and barely made it to the bed. Their coupling was frantic and intense, a tangle of bare legs and arms and clawing hands.

A short while later, their second time was a good deal more sensual and sedate as they took delicious moments to explore each other.

Later, they sprawled in the overlarge tub in the ornate bathroom and sipped glasses of Beringer wine that Kirsten had arranged for. "You will marry me, won't you dear Kirsten?"

"Of course, dear Luke. I love you more than you can imagine. But I won't marry you until this damned war is over. I have no urge to be a widow a second time. Maybe I could deal with losing a lover, but never another husband."

She ran her hands over his body, pausing at the many scars. "Just how many times *have* you been wounded?"

"I'm not too sure. I suppose it depends on how you define the term."

"Well, stop it."

"I'll do my best."

She slid on her side, exposing a luscious pink nipple. He leaned over and kissed it and she giggled. "Now you tell me—do you plan on staying in the Army?"

"No. I made that decision a while after I met you. I realized that I couldn't expect you to be a wife of an officer who would never rise very far, regardless of his abilities."

"Well then, just how do you plan on supporting me?"

"Southern California is rich and lush and people are dumping prime properties at pennies on the dollar, sometimes pennies on the ten dollar. The pessimists seem to think the Germans might win. I don't, so I've been putting my savings into buying farms and," he sipped his wine and grinned, "some wineries. I don't know much about either, but I know I can learn."

She nodded thoughtfully. He was taking a chance with all his hard-earned money and his future in the military on her behalf. By leaving the Army, he was also throwing away a pension, however small.

As to their investing in wineries, the Prohibition Amendment appeared truly dead. Only thirty states had ratified the amendment and it seemed to be losing what popularity it had. Wine-making was an intriguing thought and one she'd looked into for herself. There were more than two hundred vineyards in the Sonoma Valley alone.

She smiled as she realized that she'd been idly stroking his manhood as she used to do with her husband, and it had responded magnificently. *Dear, dear,* she thought, *it has been a while for the poor man.* And for herself as well, she added.

She straddled him carefully, so as to not splash water on the floor, and guided him into her. Like the first times, she gasped with pleasure and half closed her eyes as he filled her. He thought she looked like a cat ready to pounce on a mouse and he was the mouse.

"Go slowly," she purred. "Very, very slowly."

George Catlett Marshall hated being called a genius. All he wanted to do was do his job in the best manner possible. Nature, however, was conspiring just now to make him look like a fool. He stood on the east bank of the Columbia River tributary and looked across the rapidly flowing water. His engineers were crawling all over the bridge destroyed by Klaus Wulfram, and had already determined that, yes, it could be rebuilt, but, no, it wouldn't be anytime soon. It was all he had expected, but he was supposed to solve the problem. After all, he was a genius, wasn't he?

Therefore, he had to figure a way to get the mountains of equipment accumulating on the east side across the swollen and ice-choked river. And let's not forget the tens of thousands of men freezing their tails off in tent cities all along the rail line.

Worse, when he looked across the river he could see his compatriots on the other side. Sometimes they waved to each other. So near, yet so far.

The first part of his plan was to build railheads at each side of the river and this had been done. The second part of the plan called for the westbound trains to halt at the river, unload, and have the men and material ferried across the river or, in case of soldiers, marched across via pontoon bridges. It would be slow and labor intensive, but it would work.

But the river wouldn't cooperate. Pontoon bridges were built and then swept away, killing several of the engineers, and Marshall put a halt to their construction. Too dangerous for the men involved, he'd said.

Flat-bottom barges had been brought in by train with the idea that they could be pulled back and forth by a combination of ropes and pulleys. Again, it would have worked if the river had cooperated. After losing some equipment and nearly losing more men, this idea was abandoned. The pulley combinations simply didn't generate enough strength to enable the barges to bull their way through the soft ice and maintain control in the current.

Even adding newfangled Evinrude outboard motors had only helped a little. Material could be shuffled across the river but only in very small quantities and it was considered too dangerous to send soldiers, a fact greatly appreciated by the troops.

He'd even sent key men and a tiny quantity of supplies by plane.

Marshall was of the opinion that the problem might be an engineering one. Therefore he had brought west with him the world's preeminent mining engineer, Herbert Hoover. If Marshall was considered dour, he was positively gregarious and loquacious in comparison with Hoover, a man who rarely spoke. It was hard to believe that such a silent man had been the driving force in providing food to the starving people of Belgium until the Germans decided they did have an obligation to feed their newly captive nation. Marshall could wait no longer, "Your thoughts, Mr. Hoover?"

"How many pontoon bridges can you build and how quickly can you build them if the river cooperates?"

Marshall blinked. The question was long enough to be an oration for Hoover. "If the river cooperates, I can get three or four across in eight hours. We could move men marching in two columns and trucks if we spaced them carefully. We could move an army in two weeks. Unfortunately, that army would still be at least a week away from San Francisco, which is why it is imperative that we move quickly."

Again the maddening silence from Hoover, who was obviously thinking deep thoughts. He kept turning his head left and right as he surveyed, literally, the situation.

He turned to walk away, then paused and stared at Marshall. "Get ready."

Joe Sullivan was gaunt and forever hungry. It had been this way since he'd been captured by the Germans when Los Angeles fell to them. There simply wasn't enough food provided to fill the bellies of both the soldiers and the prisoners. Their numbers dwindled as many sickened and died. There was plenty of food, but little for the prisoners. The warehouses were filled with it and the POWs could only stare at it as they loaded crates of rations onto northbound trains.

Their neglect was Roy Olson's fault and they wanted to hang him from a tree after skinning him alive. Olson was the worst of all men in their opinion. He was a traitor, a collaborator. He was rich and getting richer on the sweat, blood, and lives of American prisoners of war. Hell, if the son of a bitch only bought and sold supplies or booze to Krauts, you could argue that he was simply making a living. But no, the prisoners had to work for Olson, slave for Olson, along with helping Olson suck up to his German masters.

Joe had first thought that Martina Flores was nothing more than a cocksucking whore and a female version of Olson. She was a lot prettier than he thought a whore should be and that bothered him. But then, his knowledge of whores came from lurid stories and cheap novels. He was nineteen and a sophomore at Southern California University in Los Angeles.

She also looked haunted and that puzzled Joe. She was eating and had a good life with Olson, so why wasn't she happy? He made eye contact through the barbed wire and she smiled sadly at him. He mentioned it to Captain Rice who was senior among the prisoners and was told, sure, go ahead and try to make further contact.

One of Joe's skills was Morse code. He'd been a radio operator during the fighting. He wrote out a message along with the code on a piece of paper with an innovation on his part. Left hand was dots, while right was dashes. The uncoded message was simple—Will you help us? He tied the paper to a rock and waited for her to come by. When she did, some of the guys started a mock fight and everyone rushed to see it, even some of the Mexican guards who were as bored as everyone else. Joe lobbed the rock over the fence and watched it bounce by her. She looked surprised and then stood over the rock, covering it with her long skirt.

Lucky rock, Joe thought. What could it see if it had eyes? A moment later, she casually reached down and put it in her skirt pocket and departed.

An hour later, she returned and smiled at him. With her left and right hands alternating, she spelled out her answer: Yes.

George Patton loved intrigue as much as the next man, but this was almost too much. His arrival in Seattle had been as secretive as possible. He'd ridden alone in a mail car with some people from the Secret Service. They declined to speak with him other than to confirm that they were indeed on their way to Seattle. What the hell, he thought angrily. He already knew that.

Their arrival was timed for the dead of night. He was whisked away by car to a large warehouse that had its own rail spur. There was an office and a bunk in the corner. It was suggested that he try to get some sleep. He tried but sleep wouldn't come. Nor could he get access to the rest of the warehouse. All doors were locked and the window was papered over. What the hell was he doing here? General Connor had just told him to go and pack some warm clothing.

He was told he would meet someone and that all would become clear. He waited. About noon, a touring car arrived and a dapper, slightly plump, well-dressed man in his mid-forties got out. Patton thought he looked vaguely familiar but couldn't place him.

The man introduced himself, speaking with a slight stutter and an upper-class British accent. "My name is Winston Churchill and I am with the Admiralty."

Patton knew better. Churchill was far more important than the understated "with the Admiralty." Winston Churchill was Second Sea Lord, and considered to be a first-class snob, which was fine by Patton who considered himself a first-class snob as well. But what the devil was Royal Navy's Second Sea Lord doing meeting an American cavalry officer?

"Your European cousins have brought you a present," Churchill continued. "Come, come."

They went into the vastness of the warehouse. It was empty save for a strange-looking contraption in the corner. Several British soldiers who'd been lounging around snapped to attention and were waved away.

The contraption was a vehicle, but it was on tracks instead of wheels, much like a farm tractor. Obviously armored and ready for war, it had a 20mm cannon in a turret.

Churchill smiled grimly. "This is one of our most closely guarded secrets, the Mark D, which tells you this little wonder had predecessors from which it evolved. The crates they were first shipped in were labeled 'water tanks' to guard them from curious eyes, and we've taken to calling them by that name, tanks.

The Mark D and its predecessors were designed over the last several years to crunch through trench lines and other fortifications. It was still a designer's fantasy when we surrendered in 1915, but the military never lost track of its significance; thus, this beauty."

Patton's mind was whirling as his mind tried to absorb the machine's potential. "How fast will it go?"

"Up to fifteen miles an hour. It has either a 20mm cannon in its turret or a pair of machine guns. The turret revolves. Earlier versions had a fixed turret, which makes this a vast improvement. It can go over rough terrain or down a road and has a crew of four. It weighs twenty tons and, as I said, can go fifteen miles an hour on flat terrain with a range of one hundred miles. We do not believe the Germans have anything to send against it."

Patton saw its potential with astonishing and sudden clarity. This was the future of cavalry. For all that he loved horses, he'd seen too many of them chewed to screaming pieces by machine guns and massed rifle fire. The day of the horse, already over, would become the day of the tank. Aristocrats like him would be replaced by mechanics and tinkerers. Damn. He would have to adapt.

"Is this the only one?"

"It's one of fifty. The rest remain crated and hidden. This too will return to its box and all will be trundled down to San Francisco, again in secret. They must be a complete surprise to the Germans."

Patton could visualize scores of these metal monsters rumbling towards German soldiers who were either fleeing or being crushed under their treads. Yes, the secrecy must be maintained at all costs. He grinned devilishly. "A horrible surprise, I hope. Pity the poor Krauts. If I didn't hate them so much, I could almost feel sorry for them."

A delighted Churchill almost clapped his hands in childish glee that someone appreciated his tanks, and it occurred to Patton that this Churchill creature wasn't very mature. "I can see why Generals Liggett and Connor selected you to command these tanks. There was concern that you might be too tied to horse cavalry to see this kind of iron beast's potential."

"Time passes and everything changes. If it works, and you wouldn't have brought it all this way if it didn't, the horse will be seen only in Fourth of July parades."

Churchill continued with a smile, "Tragic thing, the Fourth of July." Both men laughed at his little joke. Churchill was half American and proud of it. "Regardless, the generals and I all see the same thing: Waves of infantry accompanied by dozens of tanks moving in tandem and overwhelming the German infantry, crushing them to bloody pulps. Isn't that a beautiful picture?"

Patton's mind was racing so quickly he thought he might grow faint. "Actually, Mister Churchill, I believe I might have an even better idea how these weapons should be deployed."

Luke always felt a little awkward standing in front of others and using a pointer for emphasis. It reminded him of the grade schools he'd attended during his shortened formal education. This time, the chart of emphasis was a reworking of the German table of organization. Crown Prince Wilhelm remained at the top, but the presence of what appeared to be an independent, or quasi-independent, command was the subject of discussion.

Luke commenced. "The replacement of General von Seekt was not surprising. He was, and is, an excellent staff officer and we believe he was given a field command as a means of completing his military education. When the German Army broke off into two unequal parts, his was by far the smaller of the two and assigned responsibility for moving up the coast with the mountains to his right and the ocean to his left. While he was doing that, of course, the bulk of the German Army was and is moving up the Central Valley."

Liggett nodded. "And this von Seekt character screwed up and has been sent packing. Correct, Captain?"

"To a point, sir. The Germans are always planning ahead and I don't think they are terribly concerned that Seekt didn't perform satisfactorily. I would not be surprised if he became Ludendorff's chief of staff during an invasion of Bolshevik Russia and performs brilliantly."

"Curious reasoning," muttered Liggett.

"Not necessarily," said Admiral Sims. "Kindly recall that one of the world's great naval theoreticians, our Admiral Alfred Thayer Mahan, was absolutely miserable as a captain of a ship."

Liggett smiled, "Point taken. Continue, Captain."

"Yes sir. The Germans replaced Seekt with General Oskar von Hutier, age sixty-three. He is actually older than Seekt, but is far more aggressive and has a reputation for being innovative. Thus, if the coastal command is a military backwater, then it is no place for a man of Hutier's drive and skills. In short, sirs, they are up to something."

It was enough talking for a captain. General Nolan

took over the pointer. "We believe that the main thrust of the Germans will be up the Central Valley. However, von Hutier has two—maybe three—divisions and an attack by his force at the other end of our lines could be very dangerous. We simply don't have enough skilled men to be everywhere and the Germans know that."

Sims interrupted. "Thanks to the efforts of your General Marshall, we now have telegraph service between here and the rest of the United States. I have just been informed by the Office of Naval Intelligence, that two of the three divisions being held in reserve by the Germans at Haiphong are now en route to California. Might one or both be intended to reinforce this von Hutier?"

Liggett was dismayed but not surprised. Two additional divisions? Just what he didn't need. "How good is your information, Admiral?"

"Very good. The ONI reports that the Germans are behaving in a beastly manner towards the occupied French and Indo-Chinese and those groups are happily giving us information. The two divisions have indeed sailed."

"And where will they land?" Liggett asked the room. "If not with Hutier, then where? Might they land to our north?"

"Not likely," said Sims. "The only possible spot north of San Francisco might be Point Reyes, but I think it's too isolated and is surrounded by mountainous terrain. A landing there could easily be contained."

Sims sighed. "Gentlemen, it's time to let you in on a major secret. Our ONI is reading much of the German's mail and has compromised a number of their codes. I do not believe they will land north of San Francisco no matter how tempting that might look on a map. The terrain is too rugged for easy maneuver, and it would leave the German force out on a limb. The Germans do not have significant amphibious capabilities and there are no major ports for them to seize. Indeed, all the ports they need they already have. Gentlemen, I believe the two divisions will reinforce the existing army and I believe it's likely that Hutier will get at least one of them."

Liggett turned to Nolan. "You said that Hutier is innovative. How so, Captain Martel?"

"Sir, he's written papers on infantry tactics and how necessary it is to reach a goal before the defender's modern firepower shreds the attackers. In a nutshell, he's said it will be necessary to swarm an enemy's defenses with elite forces he calls 'shock troops' and bypass strong points. They will be left for secondary forces to mop up."

Liggett awkwardly eased his bulk back in his chair. He'd lost nearly thirty pounds since the war commenced, but even he conceded it was a drop in the bucket.

"And now this so-called innovative and aggressive general commands several divisions on our right flank. Damn, but I do not like that."

Night was the best time for a submarine attack. Hidden by darkness, the small boats could sneak up on the surface and be fairly confident that the enemy wouldn't see them first.

Commander Nimitz's plan was to use all three of the remaining O-class subs in a crudely coordinated attack on the expected German convoy. This would not be easy; the German Navy was getting smarter. Scout planes still operating out of Catalina Island said the approaching German convoy was being escorted by a half-dozen destroyers and that more were en route from Los Angeles to meet it.

Regardless of the difficulties, the American subs would attack. The prize was too valuable—a dozen tankers loaded with refined oil. It was fuel for the energy-starved German fleet. Sending any or all of that oil to the bottom of the Pacific would put a serious crimp in the German plans.

The scout plane's pilot had given them the convoy's time, distance, and direction, and then cheerfully informed them that he'd been spotted. So what would the Germans do now? Continue on their original course? Nimitz thought they would. How else would the convoy rendezvous with the reinforcing warships?

Of course it meant that the Krauts would be doubly edgy and on guard. Carter's sub had the task of distracting the escorts. He would close, submerge, and fire a torpedo at a destroyer and then scoot like hell. Hopefully, the Germans would chase him and leave a gap in their defenses, enabling the other subs to slip in close enough to make a number of kills. Hopefully, too, Carter and the O-7 would make good their escape.

One torpedo and one tanker, was Nimitz's plan. The three subs carried a grand total of twenty-four torpedoes and there were a total of eighteen German ships, counting the escorts. Even with a whole lot of luck, that was cutting it close, very close. Firing a torpedo from a sub just wasn't that accurate. Nor was it a good idea to surface and fire on the ships with the sub's three-inch cannon. Unless all the escorts were destroyed or otherwise accounted for, the subs would be just too vulnerable to German gunfire.

Carter could see the convoy through his periscope. The ships were running without lights and were dark blobs on the horizon. The smaller blobs were the destroyers and they were running well away from the tankers. They wanted to catch a sub on the surface. Well, that was fine with Carter. He wanted a destroyer.

Christ. There was one and it was only a few hundred yards away. How the hell had it gotten so close? It was the curse of limited visibility while submerged. Range and course were confirmed and a torpedo sped on its way. Suddenly, the German destroyer started to desperately change course. It had seen the torpedo's wake. Carter ordered down periscope and began evasive action. More precious time went by and no explosion. At nearly point blank range, they had missed and, worse, a thoroughly pissed-off German destroyer was heading towards them, tracking back through what remained of the torpedo's wake.

They went deep and stayed there, immobile and silent. Overhead, they could hear destroyer's propellers slicing the water above them. Did the Krauts have depth charges? Most German ships didn't, he'd been told. He hoped this one wasn't an exception.

The men of the O-7 heard explosions in the distance and grinned. This could only mean that some German tankers had been hit by the other American subs. Their attempt to draw off the German escorts might have been the cause.

Carter couldn't wait. He ordered the sub to periscope depth and stared at the outside world. In the distance a number of ships were on fire. Great, greasy billows of flame reached for the stars. The other two subs had killed at least some of the tankers.

He was counting the dead and dying ships when he sensed motion. He swivelled the periscope and saw a German destroyer less than a hundred yards away and picking up speed as it headed toward him. It had sat unmoving and silent on the surface hoping to catch the American sub unawares. It had succeeded. Sharp eyes on the destroyer had spotted the periscope silhouetted against the burning tankers.

"Dive, dive, dive!" Carter screamed. The crew reacted desperately, but it was too late. The knife-edged prow of the German destroyer sliced through the hull and conning tower of the O-7. Carter's last thoughts were of sheer terror as he and his sub were cut in half by the larger ship. The two sections sank quickly. There were no survivors.

The captain of the German destroyer glared angrily at the debris and the handful of mangled bodies that bobbed to the surface. He had won a Pyrrhic victory. The American sub was dead, but the destroyer's hull had been badly damaged by the collision and she was taking water. Damage control parties were working desperately to shore up ruptured bulkheads. He would have a devil of a time getting his ship back to Los Angeles. Already the destroyer was down by the bow and his executive officer sadly informed him that she would probably sink. Worse, the American sub attack had destroyed perhaps half of the desperately needed tankers.

At least there were no more American submarines to contend with. Reports said there'd been three and that all three had been destroyed. But who, he wondered, had won the battle?

★ CHAPTER 15 ★

JOSH RATHER LIKED BEING DRIVEN AROUND IN A STAFF car by an enlisted driver, even though the driver was an Army private who must be wondering just what Josh had done to deserve him. At any rate, they drove in relative luxury until, about ten miles outside of town; they exchanged the car for a motorcycle and sidecar, with Josh in the sidecar. At this point, the driver turned into a lunatic who drove as fast as he could over the rutted dirt roads that rapidly deteriorated into crude paths in the dense and rugged woods.

Josh hung on for dear life as he was pitched back and forth. More than once his head hit the windscreen and he wondered if the bruises would qualify as yet another wound. When he questioned the driver, he was told that he was supposed to get Josh to the site by three. Josh thought they could have left a little earlier and driven more slowly, but such was life in the military.

A few minutes before three, they pulled up before a log gate that was guarded by a pair of grim-faced soldiers armed with Thompson submachine guns. Other guards were visible in the woods behind, and barbed-wire fencing ran as far as he could see.

The guards checked their ID and let them through. They drove down a hillside and into a valley. A tent city was at one end along with a crude airfield. Chalk outlines and rough structures that looked vaguely familiar were scattered about. Several dozen small biplanes were scattered about. From the miscellany of colors and styles, he assumed they were civilian craft, but what the devil were they doing in an army installation?

He would find out in a minute. He got out of the sidecar, checked his bruises and limbs to see that all was there and promptly snapped to attention. Colonel Billy Mitchell stood beside him.

"At ease, Lieutenant. How was your trip?"

"Sir, about as frightening as the thought of going up in one of those little planes."

Mitchell chuckled. "We will arrange a ride to complete your education."

Josh was about to say something when he realized that Mitchell was serious. "Sir, the admiral only said you were working on something to harm the German fleet and that I was to talk to you about your progress. May I ask what that is?"

Mitchell glared at him. "Certainly you are not alluding to my attempts to sink warships with bombs are you? While my attempts might have failed, I do believe such will happen and in the not to distant future."

"As in the next few weeks, sir? I would dearly love to see the German fleet destroyed," Josh asked hopefully.

"As I told your admiral, absolutely not," he said as they walked over to a two-seater biplane. Josh was suddenly filled with dread. "Get in the rear and take two of those bags of flour with you."

Josh did as the colonel ordered. A grinning mechanic handed him two bags of flour and then showed him how to use the speaker tubes to communicate with the pilot, Mitchell, if he didn't feel like screaming at the top of his lungs. Mitchell started the engine and the mechanic spun the propeller, and they started bouncing down the dirt field.

"Don't worry about freezing to death, Lieutenant; you won't be up all that long." They cleared a stand of trees by a few inches and climbed only a little. "And we won't be going so high that you won't be able to breathe. That doesn't happen until about ten thousand feet."

Josh didn't know whether to feel reassured or not. The plane banked and Josh had a marvelous view of the camp and what he presumed were targets. He'd quickly realized that the shapes were intended to be ships and the collections of poles and canvas mimicked warships' superstructures. The size of the targets told him that German battleships were what they were going to go after.

"Lieutenant, what we are going to do is very simple. I'm going to fly over the target and you're going to drop a flour bag and try to hit the damn thing anywhere you can. The bags weigh twenty-five pounds each and will be awkward to handle, so just do your best. I don't expect accuracy from you, only an understanding of what we're doing out here and what we're up against."

Mitchell banked the plane again and came straight in on the port side of a target ship. "Drop when you're ready," Mitchell said.

Good god, Josh thought, *we're only about twenty feet off the ground. Or ocean,* he corrected himself. The bag was heavy and awkward to handle, but he managed to hold it over the side.

"Some day soon would be nice," Mitchell snapped.

Josh dropped the bag and twisted to see. The plane banked and he spotted a white blob and a puff of dust on the ground about a hundred feet short of the outline of the hull.

Mitchell laughed. "Actually, that wasn't half bad for a first try by someone who'd never been on a plane. Grab another bag and we'll do it again."

They did and, this time, Josh dropped with more decisiveness and confidence. He still missed but was much closer. Mitchell landed the plane and they got out, which was just as well as Josh was starting to feel very cold. Now he understood why pilots were heavily bundled up even in warm weather.

"Not bad at all for a rookie," Mitchell said. "A few more tries and you'd be hitting the target with monotonous regularity. Now you can tell Sims how easy it is. But tell me one thing, Lieutenant."

"Sir?"

"Could you hit the target at night with fires burning all around you and with a score of assholes with machine guns trying to blow you out of the sky? And, oh yeah, your target might just be moving erratically at twenty knots an hour in an attempt to shake you off."

Josh saw the point. "I hope I would give it a helluva try, Colonel."

"Good answer. Now watch."

A group of small planes lifted over the hill and descended in an attack pattern. The flour Josh had dropped had been washed away by the ground crew and the new pilots had a clean target. Twelve bags were dropped and seven of them hit.

"Good, but they can and will do better. Thank God we don't have a shortage of gas or, for that matter, flour."

Josh looked around at the number of other pilots who'd gathered near them. He was shocked to see that some were women. Mitchell commented that, yes, a dozen or so were women, but that all were civilians.

"And if Admiral Sims is concerned about the fair sex getting into combat, tell him not to worry. I have no intention of letting women fly when we do attack."

Josh understood. Mitchell was covering his ass. When push came to shove, there would be little anyone could do to prevent a civilian woman from getting into her plane and doing whatever the hell she wished to help her country. Josh felt a surge of pride for the volunteers, male and female.

Sunlight was just starting to fade and Mitchell said that Josh would stay the night. When he protested that he really should get back to San Francisco, Mitchell laughed.

"Why I'll bet you got a girl back there, don't you? Well, I'll just bet she'd like you alive and in one piece, now wouldn't she? You saw how miserable that road was in the daytime, now think of your driver trying to navigate that dangerous trail in the dark. You crash and your body will be eaten by bears or cougars before you can say jack shit."

Bears? Cougars? All of a sudden a night with a bunch of crazy civilian pilots didn't seem like a bad idea after all.

★ ★ ★

A few dozen yards away and obscured by shadows, twenty-three-year-old Amelia Earhart watched the two men converse. She was surprised to see the lone junior officer gain access to the field. Mitchell was obsessive about security, so the young man must represent someone important. Sims, she concluded.

Amelia had managed to get fairly close to the visitor and concluded that he was fairly cute but not her type. Too bookish, she thought and laughed silently. She lived for the adventure of flying.

Amelia had been flying planes for more than a year. She'd fallen in love with the freedom of flight and had taken lessons. She'd proven an apt pupil. Her family had recently moved to Long Beach; thus, she was able to join the strange force created by General Billy Mitchell and called the "Fireflies."

She sometimes wondered if Mitchell was aware that she and several other pilots were women. The female pilots dressed like men and didn't flaunt their femininity. Maybe Mitchell was kept ignorant of the gender of some of his pilots, or maybe he was just desperate for qualified pilots.

Either way, she had a plane, a Curtiss JN4 biplane. As a warplane in the 1916 campaign in Mexico, it had been a failure. It was now only used as a trainer. Some had even been sold to civilians which is how she got hers.

Fully loaded with five hundred pounds of cargo, its ninety-horsepower in-line engine could barely get the plane off the ground. The plane was a two seater, but Amelia liked flying alone.

Amelia also thought she'd heard the colonel say something about women pilots not going into combat.

The comment made her laugh. She would do what she bloody well wished.

Sometimes the prisoners would ignore Martina Flores when she walked by the compound, except, of course, to stare at her ripe femininity. The day before she'd signaled that she wanted a distraction. She said throw stones at her.

"*Puta*! Whore! Bitch!" yelled the men as she strolled by. She made an obscene gesture. The men behind the wire hurled rocks, being careful to make sure none hit her.

Martina screamed back at them and threw her own rock over the fence. None of the guards noticed that it wasn't one that had been thrown at her, and none of them noticed it really wasn't a rock.

Joe Sullivan picked it up and tucked it in his sleeve. It was a small package. When Martina ran away, the uproar ended. As instructed, he waited a few minutes and then delivered it to Captain Rice, who took it and walked away. When Rice was in the collection of rags he called his tent, he carefully opened the package. His eyes widened. Two keys lay snug in the box. One was labeled "Main Gate," and the other said "Armory."

Well, well, Rice thought and smiled. The captive Americans had been in their prison near Raleigh for a couple of months and, by now, all had sharp objects they could use as knives. But a key to the German's armory? That meant rifles. Well, well indeed.

"General Marshall, I really think you should come and look at the river."

Marshall stood and stretched. He'd been working

on yet another response to Washington outlining the futility of it all. "Thank you, Sergeant," he said grumpily and walked the hundred yards to the ice-filled torrent.

What torrent? What river? His eyes widened as he took in the scene. Scores of soldiers were standing by the edge of the river. "Sir, it's just like someone turned off a faucet."

Indeed, it was. Marshall's mind raced. The river was placid and calm and the depth was dropping rapidly. What the hell had Hoover done? Had he actually found a faucet? But the strange man had said to get ready. So Marshall's men were ready.

"Barges and bridges," Marshall yelled. "I want barges in the water and I want them stuffed with everything we've got. And get those pontoons across now!"

Everything had been loaded and waiting for several days. Preassembled pontoons were run out and connected, followed by planking for men and vehicles. The river did not complain. It continued to drop and was now only a few feet deep and moving very slowly. Barges pushed out like a Biblical horde, delivering men and supplies to the other side and then returning for more.

In only a few hours, the first bridge was finished, and then the second. A third and fourth would follow shortly. One bridge was for vehicles, and trucks began to move carefully across the bobbing structures. Infantry started their trek across the second bridge.

Hoover materialized beside Marshall. His face was grim, but there was a satisfied glint in his eyes. "What the devil did you do, Mr. Hoover?"

"Blew up a couple of mountains and choked the gorges. That created rough dams."

"How long will they last?"

Hoover shrugged. "No idea. I would hurry, however. We are trying to ease pressure on the dams by allowing some water to run through, but the dams can't last long."

Marshall saw infantry moving slowly. "Double time, damn it," he yelled.

"No!" Hoover said softly. "Vibrations will damage the bridges. Have them walk normally."

Damn it, Marshall thought. *I knew that.* He was too anxious to get men across. Still, they could and did hurry with no gaps between the men.

Marshall had a horrible thought. He visualized a tidal wave rushing downstream when the dams gave up the ghost. "How much warning will we have and will the water rise quickly or gradually?"

"I have no idea. I do have men ready to signal if the dams collapse. Just keep your people moving."

A truck stalled on the vehicle bridge and some men started to work on it. "Push it in the river," Marshall yelled. "Nothing delays the crossing." Men heaved and the truck fell off the shaking pontoons and into the river.

"I wonder if this is like Moses crossing the Red Sea," Marshall said. "The Bible said the sea parted but never said the land was perfectly dry. Was it was something like this, with everybody running like the devil to get across in time?" He laughed harshly. "It doesn't matter. I've an army to get across and it still might not get to San Francisco in time."

Hoover didn't reply. His mind was already someplace else.

★ ★ ★

The joint Army-Navy headquarters complex at the Presidio was a madhouse of activity as armed soldiers and sailors either took up stationary positions or patrolled the extensive grounds. The command and communications system had broken down and there was fear that the headquarters was in grave danger.

Civilian employees like Elise were either shuffled out of the compound or denied entry. Inside, Luke Martel strapped on a .45 automatic and wondered just what the hell had gone wrong.

General Nolan stormed into the conference room and took charge as more senior officers deferred to him. "Gentlemen, let's review. At approximately three this morning, a boat containing eight men was spotted by one of our shore patrols as it was attempting to come ashore. The patrol and the people in the boat exchanged fire. Two of our men were killed and a couple more wounded. The occupants of the boat jumped out and ran inland. They were the survivors of the fight. We found four dead bodies and they were all German Navy Marines."

Nolan took a sip of water and continued. "Several things bother the hell out of me; first, the fact that it then took several hours for us to be notified that as many as four armed Germans were now loose in San Francisco. The fact that the officer leading the shore patrol was killed is an obvious mitigating factor, but someone dropped the ball. It took far too long for us to be informed."

There were nods all around. The timing issue was inexcusable.

"More important," Nolan went on, "is the question of why they landed in the first place. Even if they all had made it, eight Germans aren't going to cause that much harm to the war effort. They could blow up some ammunition, but we don't have a central depot. Start fires? I just don't think so. Therefore, we have come to the only remaining conclusion, and that is that the German's target is us."

"Makes sense," Liggett murmured.

Luke looked around and sucked in his breath. In the room were Liggett and Sims, Nolan, and the Army's two corps commanders, Fox Connor and James Harbord. If successful, an assassination attempt could decapitate the U.S. Army in California.

"How could they know we were all here?" a grim-faced Harbord asked.

"That's something else to be investigated," Nolan said. "Maybe they just hoped to get either Liggett or Sims, or both, and the rest would be a bonus."

"I don't wish to think of myself as anybody's bonus," Connor said to wry chuckles.

Nolan continued. "The problem is we don't have a clue as to their whereabouts. We called an alert less than an hour ago and they could be anywhere, and that includes on this base. So far, nobody's seen or heard anything unusual."

"So what do we do?" asked Sims. "We can't hide. We all have work to do and a war to run. German patrols are only fifty miles from here and we're going to need all the time we can get."

Liggett responded for the harassed Nolan. "For the next day or two, or until we find the Krauts, we have no choice but to stay here in this building under heavy guard. There are no more than four of them and if they are going to try something, it almost has to be soon. Every minute they are out there running around increases their chances of discovery."

There was a clatter down the hallway and they all jumped. They looked sheepishly at each other as they realized it came from pots and pans clanging together.

"Somebody's bringing us food," Liggett said drily, "How wonderful."

Something clicked in Luke's mind. A mess hall would be fairly easy to take over by only a handful of people. "Anybody check these people out?" he said as he drew his pistol.

"Damn it to hell," snarled Nolan. He drew his own pistol and ran into the hallway. The deafening roar of automatic weapons fire greeted him. Nolan fell over, nearly cut in half. A man dressed as a cook stood in the doorway. He had what Luke recognized as an MP18 German submachine gun and began shooting, awkwardly spraying the room. Luke dropped to his knees and shot him in the chest. The impact of the .45 bullet sent him flying backwards. Two more Germans appeared and began wildly firing their own automatic weapons. Now everybody in the room and others outside were shooting. The Germans fell and Liggett yelled cease fire. Then there was silence.

There had been four Germans. Luke had killed one and everybody had shot the two in the doorway, while the fourth had been killed in the hallway, apparently by Ike Eisenhower, who'd come running from his own office with a pistol in his hand. Inside the conference room, a distraught Liggett looked over Nolan's mangled body. General Connor had taken a bullet in the thigh and the wound was bleeding profusely.

Luke looked around. His smoking pistol was still in his hand. Liggett and Sims were unhurt except for some scratches. Harbord was bleeding from a wound in his arm that didn't appear serious.

Medics had rushed in and were frantically working to stop the bleeding from General Connor's leg. The general's face was ghastly pale. He reached up for something and Luke grabbed his hand. "You'll be all right, General," he said, knowing it was a lie. The general was dying. No one could lose that much blood and live.

Connor blinked and seemed to recognize Luke. He closed his eyes and sighed deeply. After a couple of minutes more, the medics gave up. The bullet had hit an artery and Fox Connor, a friend and mentor to many young officers, had bled to death.

"Sorry, sir," the lead medic said to General Liggett, "but his artery was shredded. We couldn't find a way to stop it."

Liggett nodded sadly. "You did your best."

They withdrew to Liggett's office while the conference room was cleaned up. There were decisions to make and most of them were Liggett's.

"We lost good friends today, but we still have to continue. We are not unlike a line outfit that just lost a couple of buddies in a skirmish with the enemy. We will not be permitted the luxury of mourning.

"Therefore, I have determined the following. First, General Nolan will be put in for a medal for his heroism in storming that door. Captain Martel, we will do something for you as well, just don't ask me what.

"Next, we must have replacements. Eisenhower will replace Nolan. For a number of reasons, not the least that you're far too junior and inexperienced, I cannot promote you, Captain Martel."

"Understood, sir." Luke actually felt relief. He didn't feel qualified to step in for Nolan.

"Good. And what the devil is that you're playing with, Luke?"

"Sir, I took it off one of the Germans. It's a German submachine gun, 9mm, Model MP18. This version came with a thirty-two-shot magazine which actually might have saved some lives. The thirty-two-shot magazine is considered very awkward to use, unlike ones with a twenty-shot magazine, which is much more stable. We may have been lucky that they used the wrong weapon."

Luke handed the weapon to Liggett who examined it briefly, muttered something, and gave it back.

"To continue, General Cameron will succeed General Connor as corps commander. Other changes will have to be made, but those can wait at least a little while. I also want Mr. Hearst to send a reporter here to view the carnage and let the world know what barbarians the Germans are, not that the Germans care. I am frankly stunned that the German Navy would stoop to murder and assassination. Yes, I know we are all soldiers and, therefore, prime targets, but it is one thing to be shot on a battlefield and quite another to be killed while gathered around a conference table. I didn't think Admiral Hipper would stoop to that."

"Perhaps he didn't," Sims said.

"Pardon?" said Liggett.

"Gentlemen," Sims said, "the Office of Naval Intelligence is getting information that neither the German Army nor the German Navy are in total lockstep with their superior officers. In the German Navy in particular, the ship captains are very frustrated that they have been relegated to boring blockade duties, while the Army gets the glory of fighting us."

"Some glory," said Harbord.

"Agreed, but the German Navy is the new and junior service, very insecure, and very testy when it comes to getting a slice of the action. Like that stupid attempt to bombard our batteries that cost the Germans a cruiser, this too may have been an independent action by some overaggressive and overzealous junior commander. Gentlemen, they either want to fight us in a glorious fleet action, or get back to Europe and try to entice the British into fighting them in a high-seas battle. The German Navy has to prove its worth to a country that never really had a navy until relatively recently. It may even be possible to use that insecurity to our advantage if we can get the German Navy to do something truly foolish.

"Gentlemen," Sims continued, "I will contact Admiral Hipper under flag of truce and tell him what his people did. I would bet money that he will issue an apology of sorts and claim that he didn't know anything about it, which is possibly the truth."

Luke left shortly after. A flag of truce to complain about shooting an enemy general? What the devil was the world coming to? Joe Flowers would have sliced throats or cut off balls, while Luke would have shot every German officer he could.

Josh Cornell ran up. "Where the hell have you been?" Luke asked.

"Sims sent me out to the country to check on something. Jesus, is it as bad as they say?"

"Define bad, Josh," Luke said grimly. "Connor and Nolan are dead, but Sims and Liggett are fine. There's still hope for the world, but damn, it hurts."

"Hey, Lieutenant, I hear we got a new division commander. Should I be concerned?"

Lieutenant Taylor yawned hugely and stretched out as far as he could in his seat in the passenger car of the slow moving train. "Normally, Sergeant Randall, I would agree that those of us so far down the ladder would have nothing to worry about, but I've heard some intriguing things about this Douglas MacArthur character."

Tim laughed and continued cleaning his Springfield. "I hear character is the really tactful word for him."

The Twelfth Division had undergone a major reorganization. Gone were the two Marine regiments and with them went General Lejeune. He now commanded a true Marine division of four regiments and was en route to the Mexican border, if he hadn't already reached it. Two additional and very inexperienced infantry regiments were added to the Twelfth and so too was a new division commander, Major General Douglas MacArthur.

The Twelfth had managed to cross the Columbia before the water rose and the pontoon bridges were swept away. A trickle of supplies still made it across on motor-powered barges, but it would be a while before large numbers of troops and supplies could cross again. The Twelfth was not the only unit to make it across, but Tim didn't know just how many other men were now on trains heading for Seattle and then south to San Francisco.

Rumors of the new commanding general had emerged only minutes before MacArthur himself had strolled down the train, speaking briefly to the men. Tim admitted he was impressed. MacArthur was taller than average, lean, and had eyes that pierced you. He was young, maybe forty, and had a deep, dramatic, and compelling voice. He wore a rumpled officer's hat and Tim guessed it was for effect. Others joked that he couldn't afford a new one.

"MacArthur's going to be interesting," said Taylor. "The man's an unquestioned genius. He broke almost all academic records at West Point and he reorganized the place as its commandant. He's also a man of unquestioned personal courage. It's rumored that he personally gunned down some Mexican bandits during the 1914 incursion at Vera Cruz."

"Nothing wrong with courage, Lieutenant."

"Not unless it's my courage he's playing with, Sergeant. Keep it under your hat, but the dark side of the rumor mill says he's a glory hound, and that means he could lead us into some reckless messes."

"Damn," said Tim.

The lieutenant's frank assessment was unusual. Most times officers banded together and presented a wall of silence instead of permitting criticism of a brother officer, but Tim and the lieutenant had been through a lot together in a short time, and an easy relationship had formed. Tim looked out the soot-covered window. Despite the dirt covering the glass, he could see massive stands of snow covered pine trees and deep valleys. Every second took them closer to the front and the likelihood that they'd be fighting first-line German soldiers who would be a lot more lethal than the disorganized and poorly-trained Mexicans they'd whipped outside San Antonio.

"Yeah," said Taylor. "All I want to do is finish this war and then get back to my daddy's Wall Street law practice where I can get rich squashing ordinary people like you and driving you further into financial ruin."

"Jeez, you're all heart, Lieutenant."

The Rio Grande. Tovey and his men cheered when the river came into view. Shallow and sandy, it had become a symbol of Texas pride and independence, as had the burned-out hulk that had once been the proud city of Laredo.

Tovey now commanded the First Texas Volunteer Brigade and served alongside the First Marine Division now commanded by General John Lejeune. After the intense fighting at San Antonio, the Marines and the men of the Texas Brigade had formed a bond, one created in blood. Undisciplined though the Texans were, the Marines recognized fighters when they saw them. For their part, the Texans stood in some awe of the thoroughly deadly and totally professional Marines.

As they approached Laredo, they could see the rear of the Mexican Army crossing back to their own country. Rank and file soldiers wondered if the Mexicans had reached sanctuary or if the army would be allowed to pursue. To a man they wanted to chase the Mexicans as far south as they could.

Carefully, soldiers and Marines entered the shattered city of Laredo, looking for booby-traps and snipers. Most buildings were charred hulks and those that hadn't been burned out were at least badly damaged. The city stank of death. A handful of emaciated dogs emerged from someplace and growled at the approaching Americans. Tovey wondered what they'd been eating. He decided he already knew. The dogs would have to die. A shame. He liked dogs.

Astonishingly, a handful of people remained in Laredo. A few old men and a handful of scraggly women emerged and looked at them with a mixture of relief and uncertainty. The men had hidden in caves and basements, while the women had worked for the Mexicans to pick up a little food by doing their cooking and laundry. Some had doubtless whored for them as well, but Tovey wasn't in the mood to be judgmental. Let them answer to their God, their neighbors, and maybe the laws of the State of Texas.

Sporadic gunfire kept the men on their toes. Mexican and American snipers sparred with each other from their respective sides of the river. Tovey sprawled behind a ruined wall and took a swallow of brackish water from his canteen. Lejeune dropped down beside him. "Tovey, what do you want to do about the bastards who destroyed this town?"

Tovey grinned wickedly. "Chase the sons of bitches back to the halls of Montezuma, General, and then maybe all the way to the fucking shores of Tripoli."

Lejeune roared. "Good one. Instead of going that far, why don't we make a little compromise? Why don't we just go as far south as Monterrey? That way maybe we can catch that butcher Carranza and cut the German supply route from Vera Cruz to the west."

Tovey sloshed his parched mouth with what remained of the contents of his canteen. He'd likely have to fill up in the Rio Grande and God only knew who'd been shitting and pissing in that river.

"Great idea," he said. "When do we go?"

Lejeune looked over the situation. Several battalions

had made it to the shallow running river and the Mexican presence across in the town of Ciudad Juarez seemed minimal.

"I'd say there's no time like the present."

"Hot damn," said Tovey. He stood and waved his rifle. "Texans, get off your asses and cross this fucking river! Now, now, now!"

Texans and Marines roared their approval and surged forward, crossing in a rush, with machine guns covering their approach. Mexican resistance, limited already, melted entirely. Within minutes, several thousand Americans were in Ciudad Juarez, Mexican territory.

Lejeune slapped Marcus on the back. "Tovey, your speech was the most inspirational and eloquent I've ever heard. You should've been a Marine."

★ CHAPTER 16 ★

DWIGHT EISENHOWER HAD ALWAYS BEEN A QUICK study, but he found himself overwhelmed by the scope of the job he'd been handed. Through hard work and a sleepless night, however, he felt he had begun to get a handle on the basics.

Ike rubbed his eyes and took a sip of coffee. He winced. It had gotten cold and he couldn't stand cold coffee. Luke got him another one.

"Luke, tell me some things I don't know."

Luke grinned. The two of them were alone in Ike's office, the one that had been Nolan's. That man's personal possessions had been taken down and a handful of Ike's put up. A photo of Mamie Eisenhower smiled proudly at Ike from across his desk, and why shouldn't she be proud? Her husband had just been promoted to the temporary rank of brigadier general.

"General, there isn't much to tell. Since the Germans are the ones doing the advancing, we haven't gotten many prisoners, and those we did capture are as ignorant of their superiors' intentions as we are, except for the obvious. They want San Francisco. There are no rumors saying they're going all the way to Canada, or anyplace else. German soldiers do not communicate with officers like ours do. Their job is to execute not to discuss strategy. It's a very totalitarian army."

Ike sipped some of his fresh coffee. "Now, this is more like it. Good, solid army coffee. How many old socks went into its preparation?"

"Just a few, General; they're being rationed."

Ike laughed. "You know, I'm really going to miss those sessions with you and Patton in Connor's office. Damn the Krauts for killing him, and, no, I haven't forgotten I'm a Kraut too." He sighed. "Everybody's got opinions, so let's hear yours, Luke. What will the Germans do when they appear on our doorstep and quit calling me 'general' when it's just the two of us. We have too much history for that."

Luke wasn't certain about that, but he went along. "Ike, I think they will continue in the meticulous manner that they've shown all throughout their advance. I think they will reach us, dig in extensively, and prepare for overwhelming assaults on selected portions of our defenses. Their trenches won't be as extensive or as deep as ours because they will be intended to keep us in, while ours are intended to keep them out. Still, I think they will take time to mass and prepare."

"But not too much time," Ike said. "They have to know that a goodly number of our men made it across the Columbia and brought a lot of equipment with them. Not enough to face them man to man and, of course, our people aren't half as well trained or as well armed as theirs, but enough to help hold our defenses."

"Which is why they will pick a point or two in our lines and attempt to overwhelm us," Luke added.

"And Hutier's shock force will be one of them, won't it?"

"Has to be, Ike. Even if it's not their main thrust, they have to know that we'd be concerned. We can't be everywhere and they will play off that simple mathematical fact."

They turned to the map of California. Arrows and pins showed the Germans approaching Monterey on the coast and to the west of Fresno.

"Ike, I keep hearing rumors of secret weapons. Anything to them?"

"I hear the same rumors, Luke. Sims and Billy Mitchell have something called Operation Firefly and I have no idea what it is. Mitchell is half crazy and half a genius, so if Sims sees something in it, it might be interesting. Then there's the question of what Patton is up to in the north. I asked and was told it had nothing to do with my gathering intelligence about the Germans."

Luke shook his head. "So we may have secrets?"

"I put no faith in secret weapons. If they were so good, why wouldn't we already have them? No, give me some well-trained men, some Lewis machine guns, some Browning Automatic Rifles and, oh yes, lots of artillery. No secrets there, just some good weapons to put in the hands of good men."

Captain Adolf Steiner looked up from his desk and smiled tightly. "Olson, you look worried. Why is that?"

"Captain, I am always worried. Show me a man

without a care in the world and I'll show you a fool. So, yes, I am worried."

Steiner sat back in his chair. It used to be Olson's. "About what?"

"Rumors are swirling that the Mexicans got themselves defeated at San Antonio and are retreating towards the Rio Grande. Our Mexican allies, in particular the men I'm using as guards, are very concerned, and that makes me worry about their loyalty."

Steiner sighed. He'd known this moment would come. "Your stalwart Mexican guards have a right to be concerned. Not only was their army in Texas defeated, it was virtually destroyed. And the American Army under someone named Pershing is not headed towards the Rio Grande; it has already crossed the Rio Grande and might be on its way to Monterrey. If that has occurred, Carranza may be on his way to becoming a footnote to history."

Olson paled. "Then Mexico is out of the war?"

"Hardly. Mexico is doing yeoman service in tying down the vast majority of the uniformed mob the United States calls its army. Every American moving south towards Monterrey is one who is not moving north and west to reinforce Liggett. In fact, every step Pershing's army takes places them farther away from doing something useful. Olson, the Mexicans were never meant to win. Their job was to die on our behalf and they are doing an admirable job of it." He laughed. "Of course, they didn't realize it at the time, although perhaps it's dawning on that fool, Carranza."

"And if the Americans take Vera Cruz and eliminate your base, or there's another government in Mexico City that is hostile to Germany, what then?"

"We no longer need Vera Cruz as a base, although we might try to hang on to it to tie up the Americans. A few divisions from Germany will stiffen Mexico's spine. Or we will simply take over whatever the Americans don't want. Or we will just abandon Mexico to its well-deserved fate at the hands of vengeful and vindictive Americans. Vera Cruz has become redundant thanks to the capture of San Diego and Los Angeles. Why in God's name would we haul supplies overland when we can send them by ship to those ports? Or haven't you noted the slackening of material coming from the east?"

Olson flushed. He had but he had put it down to a lessening need for an Atlantic base, not a total lack of a need for one.

"Look, Steiner, there will be desertions when the Mexican guards find out, and we need those people to maintain order. I'm afraid they'll change their allegiance back to Obregon the minute they sense that Carranza's done with."

Steiner glared. Olson was taking liberties. Steiner preferred to be addressed by rank. "Then you stop them, Olson. Kill a few of the guards if you have to, and if too many of our guards run, then do something about the prisoners. We can't have them rushing us and slicing our throats with the knives they've doubtless got hidden everywhere in their camp, now can we?"

Olson had a horrible thought. "What do you mean by doing something about the prisoners?"

He laughed savagely. "Why Olson, if it comes down to it, you will have to kill them."

Olson's mind reeled. Kill all the American prisoners? Dear God, had he backed the wrong dog in this fight? He forced himself to be logical. Steiner liked logic.

"I don't think the Mexicans would do it even if ordered, and I know damn well my own men won't. They'll all kill enemies in battle, but they won't slaughter helpless prisoners." Well, maybe a couple of them would, he thought.

Steiner smiled tightly. "Then you'd better learn to sleep lightly and with a gun under your pillow."

The crown prince and the admiral finished a pleasant meal of grilled salmon accompanied by a surprisingly good white wine. They were in a wealthy man's mansion south of Monterey, California, and seated on a patio overlooking the ocean. The homeowner had departed weeks earlier. The wine came from the owner's private stock. Like so many people in the area, he'd made his own.

The scenery was beyond fantastic. Great waves crashed among massive, craggy rocks. Both men admitted they could watch the waves for hours if only the war would let them. Only the two German battleships anchored offshore intruded on the area's natural beauty.

They were told that the homeowner had been a banker before the war; now the man was a refugee. The size of the estate, however, had given them a further understanding of the wealth and potential of California, a land that would soon join the Reich. It was understood that, after the war, many Americans would leave and migrate east of the Rockies, which would be the new boundary. In their place would come good, solid German immigrants to California.

The admiral and the crown prince had their own concerns about the Mexican defeat and how it would affect them. The prince waved away the servants who were hovering near them. They left the patio and gave the two men privacy. The first topic of discussion was the deteriorating situation with Mexico. They were shocked that the Mexican collapse had been so quick and so total. Obviously, Mexico had been a weak reed.

Admiral Hipper laughed. "Since I have no Mexicans among my crews, I must consider myself fortunate. Tell me, Majesty, just how much do you depend on those cretins?"

"Less and less each day. I use them as workers rather than as soldiers. The ones guarding the mountain passes are the exception. Since you were kind enough to deliver those two divisions of German soldiers from Indo-China, I will use one to buttress the Mexicans and even take over from them in the passes should it prove necessary."

Both men understood that this had not been the plan. The two divisions were intended to reinforce the drive to San Francisco, not function as guards over unruly Mexicans guarding the mountain passes. However, plans always went to hell the minute they were implemented, and one worked with the tools one had.

Wilhelm wiped his mouth with a napkin and took a sip of the homemade wine. Really quite pleasant, he thought, although just a little too sweet. "And how is your fleet? I too have heard rumors that all is not as well as it should be."

Hipper scowled. "Unfortunately, the rumors are correct. The officers are impatient and feel that they are missing out on the glory of the war by performing tedious blockade duty. They want me to storm San Francisco Bay and blow the town to pieces, after which they want to steam north and do likewise to the Americans in Puget Sound. You heard I lost a cruiser because a squadron commander got impatient? Well, I'm afraid there might be more of that if something doesn't happen soon.

"And the morale among the enlisted sailors is very low. They are living in cramped quarters in ships that were never intended to be at sea for this long. Our ships were built to rule the Baltic and the North Atlantic, returning periodically to warm, comfortable barracks, not to travel around the world like the British ships. I am afraid that illness, like the American flu, might strike. That and the fact that the lower decks are filled with radicals and communists who could cause trouble at the first chance concern me."

"Can you give your men shore leave?"

"Only at the cost of weakening the blockade, Majesty."

The prince understood the admiral's dilemma. His own army was wearing down as well, although that had been expected and even built into their plans.

The German Army was on the doorstep of San Francisco. A couple of weeks and they would be able to attack and overwhelm the Americans.

The crown prince sighed. "Do what you can for your men. I am rotating my own out of the lines as much as I can. Perhaps we shouldn't be so concerned about the Americans breaking our blockade. Kindly consider some form of shore leave to keep your men fresh. As to your bloodthirsty young officers, tell them they'll have all the fighting they can handle in a very little while."

★ ★ ★

Patton did not like to admit to uncertainty. Indecisiveness and timidity were for fools and incompetents. He now had a vision as to how his precious new tanks should be used and it was at odds with division and corps commanders who greatly outranked him.

Thus, he was now in a Come to Jesus meeting with II Corps Commander, Major General James Harbord, and the army's overall commander, Lieutenant General Hunter Liggett. Harbord was definitely against Patton's ideas, while Liggett seemed curious, possibly receptive.

Patton took a deep breath. He wasn't awed by either man. His family was wealthy and he was descended from at least one general in the American Revolution, Hugh Mercer, and many of his family had served with the Confederacy. Patton had been born in California and deeply felt the agony of the invasion. No man would ever awe him.

Patton was intrigued by the idea of reincarnation and frequently wondered if he had been a great war leader in another life, maybe Hannibal or Caesar. Whether it was true or not, Patton felt he was destined for greatness. Perhaps a future young soldier would wonder if he was a reincarnated Patton. The thought pleased him.

Harbord's idea was quite simple. The tanks were excellent ideas and would, if accompanied by infantry, be able to penetrate German defenses on a broad front. Patton agreed that it would happen. He simply did not agree that it was the best usage of the new weapon.

"Gentlemen, I see the tank as replacing heavy cavalry of old. The tank is the reincarnation of the medieval knight and neither the knights nor other heavy cavalry were dispersed across a battlefield. No, they were massed and first they destroyed enemy cavalry and then they ran amuck behind the enemy's infantry, slaughtering those poor fools as they ran in panic for safety. Better, and unlike the knights of old, we do not have to worry about the Germans having tanks of their own."

Harbord interrupted, "But what about the German armored cars and trucks?"

Patton laughed harshly. "They are toys. They don't have the guns to damage my tanks and don't have the armor to protect against the weapons of my tanks."

"But won't you be putting all your eggs in one basket if you mass them?" Liggett asked. "What if they're taken by an artillery barrage? They could all be destroyed."

"General, that's all the more reason to keep them together and moving so fast that the artillery can't range on them. And with all due respects to your infantry, General Harbord, even if accompanied by tanks, they will not be able to do any more than push the Germans back a little ways, if even that. We do not have enough infantry to do any more. We're still feeling the effects of the damned influenza along with other factors."

Patton turned to Harbord, who glowered. "General, along with insufficient numbers, your men are simply not well enough trained or experienced to attack what will be formidable German defenses. Also, the Germans will have their own artillery, particularly those damned 75s on line and my tanks cannot stand up to them, particularly since, according to your plan, the tanks will be forced to move as slowly as the infantry. When the Germans arrive in a few days, they will immediately dig in and that will present problems for infantry."

"But not for armor?" Harbord asked.

"No sir," Patton responded. "Tanks are tracked vehicles and can go across rugged terrain, and that includes bridging trenches. The Germans will dig theirs narrow to protect against our mortars and that means they can be crossed by tanks. Barbed wire won't hinder tanks at all, although they would slow down or even stop infantry."

Patton lowered his voice to a conciliatory tone. It was difficult since he knew he was right. He so much wanted to shove his version of the truth down their throats. Where the hell was Eisenhower to help him keep his emotions in check?

"I know this is radical and desperate, but these are desperate times calling for desperate measures. We have a chance to shock the hell out of the Krauts and reduce their numerical advantage. Gentlemen, this is not only our best chance, it is our only chance."

The Germans were a mile or so away and digging in. They weren't present yet in great numbers, but would soon be. The handful of them shoveling away were the first in a great host that would besiege San Francisco. In the distance Luke saw dust where the German columns were coming down the road.

"Ike, if you have some artillery, now would be a good time to use it."

Eisenhower just shook his head. "Look at them. All lined up like they were on parade. Yeah, Luke, if we had our own guns we could blow them back to Berlin."

Other German units were closing in on the American lines. Soon the city of San Francisco would be under siege. In a short while, the Germans would bring up their own heavy artillery. These would not be the truly big siege guns they'd used to smash the fortifications at Liege and Paris in 1914, but they would be large enough at 155mm.

An American artillery piece boomed and, seconds later, a cloud of dirt erupted from in front of a German trench, scattering Germans in their coal-scuttle helmets. Luke idly wondered if they were better then the pie tins some American soldiers wore. Most Americans didn't have anything more than hat and hair to protect their skulls. Guns and ammunition had priority, not helmets.

German guns quickly responded. They were the smaller caliber ones and did no real damage. Relatively speaking, the siege was opening with a whimper, not a bang.

Luke peered through his binoculars. The Germans were already back at their digging and more men had arrived. Any chance of sortieing out and smacking them before they were dug in was quickly disappearing. Liggett had forbidden it anyhow. He would not squander his troops in a meaningless attack.

"Y'know, Ike, when they get a few miles closer, their guns will be able to hit the bridge from across the bay."

"I know," Ike said.

The Dumbarton Railroad Bridge had been completed in 1910, but it crossed the southern end of the bay which would put it in range of German artillery fairly soon unless, by a miracle, the Germans were halted in their tracks. Neither man believed in miracles.

German trucks were now arriving and rolls of barbed

wire were thrown on the ground with practiced skill. "They've done this before, haven't they?" Ike asked with grim humor.

More German shells hit near their position. American soldiers cringed in terror. Sergeants had to physically restrain a couple from running in panic for the rear. The men weren't really cowards, just part of a poorly-trained garrison that hadn't seen any combat, and weren't aware that they were safer in their trenches than running around unprotected by dirt walls.

It was time to go. Martel and Eisenhower grabbed their equipment and moved back and away from the front lines. They were painfully aware of angry glares from soldiers who had to stay. Luke heard someone mutter "rear-echelon cowards." He turned angrily but everyone was looking at the sky.

Ike grabbed his arm. "Let it be, Luke. If I had to stay here while some brass headed for a warm bed, I'd be pissed too."

*

Mexican President Venustiano Carranza and his staff had commandeered a large hacienda a few miles north of Monterrey. It was located on a hill and Carranza could see for miles to the north. The Americans were coming in their thousands and he needed help to stop them. But his army, the one that had invaded Texas, no longer existed.

From his hilltop, the Mexican president sent message after message back to Mexico City calling for reinforcements. The gringos under Pershing were only a few miles away. If they took Monterrey, it would be an enormous blow to Mexican pride. Monterrey was one of the largest cities in Mexico, capital of Nueva

Leon province, and a center of Mexican industry. Loss of Monterrey would also mean that the German overland supply line running west from Vera Cruz would be threatened.

An aide ran in gasping. "Horsemen coming from the south, your excellency."

"How many?"

"Perhaps a hundred, sir."

A hundred, he thought. That's all? But maybe they were the advance guard of a much larger relief force. Yes, that must be it.

A little while later he heard the clatter of hoofs and the shouts of men. He heard a name and shuddered. Villa. Pancho Villa had arrived. Impossible. Villa was the bandit fool who'd started the 1916 war with the United States by attacking Texas towns and ranches, thus causing an American army, again led by Pershing, to invade Mexico. It had taken almost a year to get rid of the Americans and now Pershing was back with an even larger army.

Carranza had another worry. Which side was the bandit on today?

"Excellency!" Villa boomed as he entered the living room where Carranza sat. "I bring wonderful news from Mexico City."

Carranza forced a smile. He neither liked nor trusted the stocky, filthy, and heavily mustachioed Villa. But if he had good news and reinforcements, he would put up with the barbarian.

"Then don't keep me waiting, General Villa," he said with feigned warmth. "Tell me."

A servant had brought fresh cold water that Villa gulped, then wiped his mouth on his sleeve. "Mexico

City is not a happy place, but that would not surprise you. The loss of so many men, even if most were merely captured, is an enormous blow to Mexican pride. They are wondering how you will redeem it."

Carranza felt himself flushing. How dare this oafish shit talk to him like that? "If the government in Mexico City, my government, will get off their asses and give me a new army, I will not only stop the Americans before they get to Monterrey, but I will destroy them."

"Brave words," Villa said and Carranza wanted to strangle him.

"They will be more than brave when I get my army. When will the rest of it arrive? The Americans are almost here. If we lose Monterrey we will be humiliated."

Villa shrugged. Several more of his men had entered the room and taken station beside him. "Mexico City feels that the fall of Monterrey is inevitable and that the war with the United States was a huge and tragic mistake, and one that must be rectified."

"Indeed?" said Carranza. "If that is what Mexico City thinks, then they are wrong. Give me another army and we will win. And once we have won, we will negotiate a treaty from a position of strength. Anything less and I will personally be humiliated."

"Martyred," said Villa.

"What?" said Carranza, sudden desperation growing in his voice.

"You will be revered as the President of Mexico who was brave enough to give his life for his country."

Villa pulled a revolver from inside his shirt and fired three bullets that struck Carranza in the chest.

One of his men shot Carranza's aide. Villa himself administered the *coup de grace*, a bullet to the back of Carranza's head and then to the aide's. He detailed a squad to remain in the hacienda, while the remainder of the men who'd accompanied Carranza ran away from the killings.

Villa's men still had a job to do.

General Lejeune watched as Tovey's men approached the white stone hacienda at the top of the hill. Reports said there were Mexicans holed up in it. The building had to be cleared as it commanded the approach to Monterrey.

The Texans fanned out and moved cautiously up the hill. Lejeune had to admit that Tovey was a damned good general and his men fought well. And, somewhat surprisingly, there had been little in the way of discipline problems in Mexico. A few men had gotten drunk and one man was in jail accused of rape, but the drunks had their asses kicked by their sergeants, and the alleged rapist was scared to death. He'd be released later as an investigation showed that the alleged victim was a prostitute. The benefit of the doubt would go to the soldier. Still, Tovey'd decided to let the stupid kid stew in jail for a couple of days, thinking he was going to spend the rest of his miserable life in prison breaking rocks. Hopefully, he'd realize that no piece of ass was worth that much.

Gunfire erupted from the hacienda, only a few scattered shots, but enough to send Tovey's men to ground. An American machine gun opened up and, after a few long bursts, the fire from the hacienda ceased.

Tovey's men ran cautiously up to the hacienda and into it. There was no more gunfire. Lejeune swore as he saw General Tovey far too close to the action.

Moments later, Tovey emerged and waved towards Lejeune who swore again. The crazy Texan wanted him to come over and climb up that hill.

Tovey greeted the Marine general outside the hacienda. "I think we got something Washington isn't going to like."

Lejeune took a deep breath. He was fifty-three and maybe getting too old to climb mountains, although he'd be double damned if he'd ever admit it.

"Come on in here, General," Tovey said and Lejeune followed.

Two men lay on the floor. One was a young officer and the other an older man with a full beard. Lejeune recognized him from his photos. Carranza.

"Did we kill him?"

Tovey shrugged. "Not damn likely, but we'll get the blame. Carranza'll be a hero for standing up to us and dying for dear old Mexico. There'll be statues of the fat asshole all over Mexico in a few days and he'll be a rallying cry for them like the burning of Laredo was for us. No, he was shot and killed well before we got here."

"How do you know that?"

Tovey laughed. "I was a Texas Ranger, which meant I had to know a little about police work, and even I can tell you those bodies are pretty damn cold for fresh casualties, and, oh yeah, one more thing."

"What?"

"Along with gunshots to the chest, both those poor sons of bitches were shot in the back of the head."

★ CHAPTER 17 ★

PRESIDENT ROBERT LANSING LOOKED AT THE GRISLY photos. He wanted to turn away but couldn't. This too was part of his job. The gaping wound in the back of Carranza's head was clearly visible. He put them face down on his desk, and swallowed to keep his stomach from rising.

"Incredible," he said. "And now the new Mexican government has the audacity to accuse us of murdering Carranza? I knew nothing was ever straightforward in Mexican politics, but to now have the Obregon government nominating that butcher Carranza for sainthood is a little much. It's incredible after all we did to protect Obregon and his people."

Secretary of State Charles Evans Hughes chuckled mirthlessly. "It is, of course, just their little way of deflecting blame to another source. Since we took Texas and the other states from them seventy years ago, we have been their favorite monster under the bed."

"And what will come of this?" General March asked.

Hughes answered. "I believe a very pragmatic new government in Mexico City will ponder matters for a while and then sue for peace while they still have enough of a country left to run. The last thing a new Obregon government wishes is to have us gobble up more Mexican territory. Monterrey is an important city and a major railhead. I believe we can let them, well, huff and puff for a while and then begin back door peace talks."

March agreed. "They also know that Pershing is consolidating his hold on the Monterrey area and is awaiting word as to whether he should push farther south. In the meantime, his men are digging in and awaiting a Mexican counterattack, which, if we sit there long enough, will surely come."

"And what are the Germans doing in Vera Cruz?" the president asked.

March grinned. "They appear to be packing up. Vera Cruz is useless to them."

"As is Mexico," Hughes injected.

"Agreed," said Lansing. "And here is what we will do. First, we will continue to reinforce and resupply Pershing. His army must become strong enough to repel any Mexican attacks. Tell him he may probe aggressively, but I do not want the army risked farther south. He may also probe from El Paso and Brownsville. Hopefully, this will frighten Obregon into thinking that we might annex northern Mexico and motivate him to the peace table."

"And if it doesn't?" March asked.

"Then we will annex northern Mexico," Lansing said.

A few more comments and General March departed, leaving Hughes and Lansing alone. "Tell me, Charles, what are the British up to? Will they ever come in on our side?"

Hughes sighed. "I wonder. I've been in contact with Winston Churchill and he is of the opinion that the Royal Navy lusts after war with Germany, but that the British Army isn't quite ready."

"The British Army may never be ready," Lansing muttered. "It is far too small and there's no interest in enlarging it except for defensive purposes. They see Germany across the Channel and they are rightfully concerned, but worry about us and go to war for us? Never."

Lansing sighed. "A naval confrontation between Great Britain and Imperial Germany, with us aiding the British, is a marvelous vision."

"I've heard it said that the Germans have warned the British in their part of Puget Sound not to try and exit the Sound either at night or without forewarning the Germans. I understand the British are contemptuous of such requests."

"Charles, are you saying an incident might occur?"

Hughes smiled. "One can only hope so."

Even though he was only thirty-five, the younger guards had begun calling Pedro Sanchez "grandfather." Of course, most of them were so much younger than he, mere children in their mid-teens. What the hell was the Mexican Army coming to, he wondered, if it enlisted children who were barely out of diapers?

As to his position as a guard at the camp in southern California, he had only himself to blame. He had supported Carranza, supported the changes needed to be made in the way Mexicans lived, and, worse, had believed in Carranza's promises. He now realized that Carranza never had any intention of keeping those high-sounding promises.

Now he was hundreds of miles away from his home in a village that was south of Ciudad Juarez, which was just across the border from the American city of El Paso. Worse, as rumors spun out of control, he was beginning to wonder if he'd ever see it or his family again. At first, joining the army had seemed like a lark. He'd never been more than a few miles away from his home and he'd wanted to see a little of the rest of the world before he died. He'd been to Monterrey, but that was it. Now he knew he'd made a terrible mistake. Staring at a couple hundred sullen and half-starved American prisoners was nobody's idea of seeing the world.

San Diego and the ocean were only a few days' march away, but he was convinced he'd see them when he was in heaven and looking down. Even more annoying were the Germans. Their arrogance was beyond belief. Did they think he was an animal? A slave? He spat on the ground. To hell with Carranza and the Germans he'd invited in to help rule Mexico.

Because of his age and apparent maturity, Captain Torres had grandly proclaimed that Pedro was the senior sergeant in the overlarge platoon sent to help guard the Americans. Thus, the men in his platoon, his children, often came to him for advice. Rumors were spinning out of control and the men were worried. Well, so was Sergeant Pedro Sanchez.

He'd tried to ask Captain Torres, but that man was too busy either stealing German supplies or screwing a Mexican whore in Raleigh to bother. Still, Pedro had figured out that all was not well with Mexico's campaign to drive the Americans out of Texas. He thanked his lucky stars and the Virgin Mary, whichever worked best, that he was not involved in the bloody fighting in Texas.

Communications between Mexico City, Texas, and California were miserable at best and nobody thought to inform the illiterate creatures who were the enlisted men. Captain Torres was the worst. When asked, he'd caustically told Sanchez and the others to do their duty and let officers like him do the thinking.

His only source of possibly accurate information was the Mexican woman who was the mistress of the pig of an American who worked with the Germans. Sanchez despised traitors and Olson had betrayed his country.

Martina Flores had confirmed the bloody defeat of the Mexican Army in Texas and had then given him several pieces of additional bad news.

First, she said that Carranza was dead. If that was really true, and Martina's source was a good one, then who did he owe his allegiance to? Obregon? How about to himself, he was thinking.

Second, and most horribly, the Americans were in Monterrey. His family had fled to Monterrey. He didn't think they'd be molesting his wife. She was grossly overweight, bad tempered, and had few of her teeth left, all of which had influenced his decision to enlist. However, he had a daughter who was fourteen and ripening into a beauty. He became coldly angry at the thought of Americans touching her pale skin and frustrated because he was so far away that he could not protect his little angel.

The third thing Martina told him had shocked him to the depths of his soul. If the Germans pulled out, his men were supposed to kill the American prisoners. Mother of God, he could not do that. He supposed he could kill in battle, or in self-defense, or to protect his daughter's fragile virtue, but he could not massacre the Americans who had done nothing to him. Some of them had been quite pleasant, even friendly, and he'd been surprised that so many spoke his language. Murder them? But what would he do if either Torres or the German, Steiner, ordered him to? Or what would he do if the Germans began to massacre the Americans? He dimly recalled the now discredited parish priest once telling him that people who do nothing in the face of evil are sinners as guilty as those who actually commit the act. If he did nothing, he concluded, he would go to Hell.

Mother of God, he repeated, what had he done to get into this mess? Not counting his drunken ass of a captain, Pedro Sanchez had forty men looking to him for guidance and leadership and all he wanted to do was go home. Mother of God.

Pedro Sanchez worried about his future.

Luke heard the drone of distant engines and looked into the cloudless sky. He assumed it was another visit from German fighters. German Albatros D-III fighters were common as they photographed the American fortifications or occasionally strafed an exposed position. American machine guns, mounted on trucks with their barrels elevated, functioned as antiaircraft guns and their accuracy was getting better as they got more practice. Several Albatroses had been shot from the sky and others had been sent running back to German lines with smoke streaming from their engines.

But this sound was deeper, more ominous. Luke shielded his eyes and stared to the south. Bombers. The Gothas had risen from the dead. Escorted by a swarm of fighters, a dozen of the monsters flew in at heights well above the antiaircraft guns. Once again, the American Army was impotent to stop the Germans.

Still, the American gunners opened fire and Luke watched as the tracers arched skyward and then fell back to earth. An Albatros fighter peeled off from his escort position and followed the tracers down to the offending gun. Bullets shredded the truck and the gunners and the victorious German pilot flew off. Luke could only shake his head. The American gunners had forgotten a basic fact: tracers traced both ways.

How had the Gotha bombers returned? His job was Intelligence and he was supposed to know these things. Hadn't he and Ike destroyed their bomber fleet? Had they managed to ship additional planes to Los Angeles or had resourceful German mechanics been able to cannibalize the destroyed planes for enough parts to create this smaller Gotha fleet?

Since American spies had not detected the arrival of new planes, he decided it was likely the latter and reluctantly gave credit to that Captain Krause. He had been almost weeping with despondency at the loss of his planes. Now, somehow, he had gotten a number of them airborne. Luke didn't think he'd want to fly in something held together with strings and baling wire, but Krause obviously found pilots and crew.

Luke recalled that they hadn't had time to look for and destroy the ammo dump where the bombs were stored. As explosions rocked the area, he regretted that fact. The Germans were raiding again.

But for what purpose? It was a virtual given that the American defenses could not be seriously harmed by the handful of bombers. Terror? Possibly, but the risk to the handful of planes was too great for that purpose.

The planes continued overhead. In a few moments he heard more explosions to the north and realized the source. They were aiming for the Dumbarton Railroad Bridge that connected San Francisco with the rest of the world.

Luke chuckled mirthlessly. Even if the Krauts managed to hit the bridge, a highly unlikely event, the bridge could be repaired and rather quickly. And while it was being repaired, the Army would resort to using the barges and ferries that had been in use before the bridge's completion ten years earlier.

At best, therefore, the Gotha raids were nuisances. He didn't think Liggett would let Ike and him try another raid to destroy them. This time the Germans would have the airstrip well secured.

D.W. Griffith was ecstatic as he examined the packages before him. "I love you, my fair Elise."

Elise smiled tolerantly. It was not the first time she'd heard the pun between her name and "Für Elise," the elegant and delightful solo piano piece by Beethoven. She took it as the compliment it was.

The boxes contained what Griffith craved even more than publicity—film. The war was an insatiable beast and Griffith's men had been filming anything and everything and sending copies out east via Canadian rail. The rest of the country was now able to view scenes of carnage and destruction, which helped galvanize American attitudes. The films of the burning of

Los Angeles and the bombing of San Francisco had outraged the American public. So too had scenes of dead on the battlefield and the badly wounded and terribly maimed young men lying in hospitals.

Griffith had also filmed large numbers of terrified Americans trying to flee north and east. All of these served to fuel American anger.

"David, I sincerely hope you realize that these packages represent ammunition and other war material that didn't get through." It was a small lie. The Canadian government wouldn't let weapons and ammunition be shipped on their neutral railways, but film was allowed.

"I know and please tell both Liggett and Sims that I am profoundly grateful."

As well you should be, she thought. In a couple of hours she would be with Josh. At least he wasn't out in a ship or on some secret mission. Today he was involved in something to do with naval construction.

How to hide an elephant in a small room, was the question. The answer was simple. You didn't. Admiral Sims had reluctantly come to the conclusion that he'd made a mistake; ergo, he would have to own up to it. The elephant was just too big to hide.

Having his few big naval guns pointing out to the Pacific would do no good whatsoever in stopping the Germans from crashing through the Golden Gate and into San Francisco Bay where there would be no American defenses. No, most guns would have to be placed where they could fire directly at the Germans as they attacked the narrow Gate and directly on them if they made it into the bay itself. Once the German fleet was inside the bay, guns pointing out to the Pacific would be useless. A couple would be kept pointing out to the Pacific to keep the Germans honest along with a number of dummy guns, but the rest would be moved.

Even though the guns belonged to the Navy, overland engineering expertise belonged to the army. The chief Army engineer, a genial, ruddy-faced major named Scully, had taken on the obduracy of the challenge with equanimity. Everybody admitted that the easiest way would have been to lower the disassembled guns onto ships by way of cranes. However, that would have enabled to Krauts to see what was up, and might have precipitated an attack.

So that left moving them overland, and Scully happily said it reminded him of what he'd read about the Egyptians building the pyramids. While visiting, Sims overheard the comment and reminded Scully that he didn't want pyramids, just the damn guns moved. Scully didn't take Sims' anger seriously.

Detached from their firing mechanisms and supports, the gun barrels were the major problem—some weighed well over twenty tons.

"Would be nice if we had a railroad," Scully had mused, "but we don't."

The closest thing was the cable-car system and nobody thought the cars and tracks could support the weight of a twelve-inch gun barrel.

Then there were the hills. Scully said the guns could probably be manhandled up, but the thought of trying to control them on the way down was frankly terrifying. Josh concurred. He had a nightmare vision of a gun barrel rolling down Nob Hill and crushing houses, cars, and people in its path.

So that left dragging the damn things over level ground, which is what they did, dragging them down San Francisco's streets with literally hundreds of soldiers, sailors, and civilian volunteers pulling on control and guide ropes while trucks pulled in tandem.

To add to the difficulty, it all had to be done at night in order to keep German reconnaissance planes from discovering the secret and attacking. German pilots had come to respect the truck-mounted antiaircraft machine guns, but a photo plane didn't have to fly within their range.

But they did it. Over the course of two nights, eight twelve-inch guns were moved and reassembled in their new sites facing inward onto the bay. Josh had to admit that it was indeed an epic evocative of building the pyramids or, as Scully said, a place in England called Stonehenge.

Dummy guns, consisting of telephone poles painted black, were left in their place to confuse the Germans. Sims congratulated the insufferable Scully, who informed the admiral that it had been a piece of cake and that he should have called on the Army sooner to bail him out of hot water. Sims was too pleased to take offense.

Off in the channel, Josh could see Oley Oldendorf out in his trawler, the very lucky *Shark*, laying more mines. Oldendorf, now a lieutenant commander, was out sowing his crop of mines almost every day. The Germans were clearly watching but had made little move to interrupt his efforts, except to lob some shells at extreme long range. Josh hoped the threat of mines would at least slow down the Germans.

It was mid-morning when an exhausted and dirty

Josh Cornell dragged himself to Elise's apartment. He'd been given the day off by Sims to rest and cleanup as Josh had given his best pulling on the tow ropes even though his injured shoulder now hurt like the devil. He had no hopes of seeing Elise. She would be at work with Sims. What he really needed was a chance to sleep.

He was just about to use his key on her apartment door when it opened and a smiling Elise stood there, wearing a long blue robe. Her bare feet poked out from under it. He suddenly felt awake and alive.

She grabbed him by the arm. "Come in, you silly boy. You're dirty and tired and you need little Elise to take care of you."

Lew Dubbins awoke with a start. The feel of cold steel against his throat was as great a shock as could be imagined and his bladder almost released. He'd gone to sleep in what he called his spider hole, a narrow slit in the ground hidden from view by a rock overhang and made comfortable by the fact that it was in the shade most of the afternoon. He and the hole were also covered by a blanket. When he peered through the bushes, it also commanded a good view of the Raleigh area.

The pressure of the knife increased and he felt even more extreme pressure to void his bladder. "Don't talk, don't move," a man's voice hissed. "You understand me? Blink a lot if you do." Dubbins blinked like a man possessed.

The pressure eased a little. "You're Dubbins, aren't you?"

Dubbins nodded. There was no point in denying it. Who the hell else could he be? Olson and the Germans had finally caught him and he was going to hang. He could only hope that he would die bravely. "Who are you?" he managed to croak.

"My name is Joe and I'll wait to tell you my last name, 'cause you might laugh and then I'll really have to kill you. You see, I can't stand people laughing at me. I'm a scout with the U.S. Army."

Dubbins felt like crying with relief. "Jesus, I've been waiting a long time for you guys to come. They killed my brothers and they're hurting a lot of soldiers down there." The knife disappeared. "You could have killed me, you know. What if I'd jumped?"

Joe Flowers laughed mirthlessly. "I used the blunt edge, you asshole."

Dubbins turned and saw the grim face of Joe Flowers glaring at him. *This man is an Indian and very dangerous,* he thought. "You here to help the prisoners?"

"No, I'm prospecting for gold and then I'm going to plant cotton," Flowers said. "Yeah, and I hope you're gonna help me."

"Can I kill Olson and Steiner?"

"Can't make any promises," Joe said, "but I'll do everything I can to make it happen."

Dubbins had a sudden fear of the two of them taking on the Germans and the Mexicans. "You alone?"

"No."

Dubbins smiled. "Good. Then let me out of this hole so I can take a piss and I'll let you in on what's happening down there. You do know we have someone inside, don't you?"

Joe Flowers did not know that. Something more to let Montoya and the dozen Mexican-American cavalrymen he'd brought in on.

★ ★ ★

General Oskar von Hutier watched his men maneuver. The training wasn't going to be perfect given the limited amount of time he had, but he was confident it would be enough. It had to be. He was thankful that the American Army was so awful. Had it been any better, the combination of good troops and rugged terrain would have either stalled the advance or made it so costly as to be unsustainable.

As it was, climbing up and down the rugged, brush-covered foothills was exhausting his men, and using up food and supplies at an enormous rate. He was thankful also for the fact that the German Navy controlled Los Angeles, which meant a steady stream of ships bringing those badly needed supplies.

He saw one of his favorite young officers. "I trust all is going well, Captain Richter."

Captain Horst Richter saluted and grinned. "Very well indeed, General. The Yanks will get a tremendous shock when our storm troopers swarm all over them. I only wish we had started this training so much sooner."

"So do I, Richter, so do I. But we must make do with what we have. And besides, the Yanks weren't holding still for us to attack and kill them like we wished."

"Indeed, sir." Richter saluted again and the general moved away to watch some other units train themselves to ignore fire and swarm enemy defenses. It was a simple truth that modern soldiers in the defense could lay down such a withering fire that slowly approaching attackers would be cut to pieces. It was also true that attacking soldiers being fired on would very logically go to ground to protect themselves from such a deadly rain of fire.

Thus, it was necessary to move quickly and punch hard at selected points, ignoring strong ones, and rushing through the weak. If it worked, his men would be in the American rear as an unstoppable force.

That is, if it worked.

Kirsten thought that her work on a ranch had inured her to the sight of blood. As a ranch owner, she'd helped mend the cut flesh and broken bones of her ranch hands. She'd stitched them and splinted them and, while some had complained, none had died. She'd known to use basic sanitation, which was still an undiscovered art in some places.

And of course, she'd helped her husband, Richard, while his infected leg grew gangrenous and caused his death. She cursed the fact that there was no doctor in the vicinity at that time, and that poor stubborn Richard had kept his injury a secret for so long. A bruise was all he'd called it until his leg had swollen up and red lines extended from the "bruise." When she'd finally gotten him to a hospital in San Diego, the doctors there had amputated the leg, but the infection had already spread too far.

St. Ignatius College, located on the corner of Hayes and Schrader Streets, was the site of the new military hospital. Several of the Jesuits on the faculty had also volunteered and a few even had some medical experience, although informal and from the school of hard knocks.

She was stunned by the sights and smells. Even though so-called experts, including journalists, said that the fighting had barely begun, there were hundreds of casualties in St. Ignatius and elsewhere.

Kirsten's decision to volunteer had come from the fact that she was no longer needed to distribute ration cards to civilians. Most civilians had departed, leaving San Francisco a garrisoned ghost town. Those few civilians who remained were, like her, part of the war effort.

The first time she'd seen a man disemboweled she'd vomited. Doctor Rossini, the surgeon who headed her group, had congratulated her on being able to make it outdoors before puking on his floor. Since the floor was already covered with blood and dirt, she assumed he was being sarcastic. He wasn't. Rossini wanted the place clean and, after a brief and terse discussion, cleaning it up was Kirsten's new job.

Over the next few days, she slowly graduated to getting supplies for the harassed doctors and nurses. When they found that she could keep her lunch down and could both read and follow directions, she was considered an asset. Even the acid-tongued Rossini grudgingly gave her respect.

If Luke was occupied, which was usually the case, she spent her spare time talking to the wounded and comforting the dying. It was a task she hated, but if she could give comfort to someone in agony, or terrified of being a cripple, or, worse, of dying, then it was her duty. She did not quite think of volunteering as an honor, but one other volunteer did.

Rossini came over and grabbed her arm. "I need a nurse and you just volunteered. Congratulations."

He took her to a surgical table. A young man, he couldn't have been in his twenties, lay naked on his back and on the table. Another doctor was picking pieces of shrapnel and other debris out of his body.

The boy was only marginally unconscious. He groaned and tried to turn, but others held him still.

"Hold this," Rossini said and handed her a tray. She held it while the doctors dug into the boy's shattered body and plunked items into it.

Rossini laughed bitterly. "When he really wakes up, he's going to be in a sea of pain and not realize how lucky he is. He'll have a ton of sores and scars, but nothing vital was touched. All he has to do is avoid infection."

"My husband couldn't do that," she blurted. "He died of gangrene despite all I and anyone else could do."

Rossini's expression softened a little. "I didn't know, of course. Can you deal with this?"

"Now I can handle anything you want me to."

Rossini laughed again, this time with a bit of humor. "Congratulations, you are now my assistant."

★ CHAPTER 18 ★

THE EARTH ERUPTED AND DEBRIS FELL DOWN ON Luke's helmet, making a tinny, pattering sound that would have been amusing, even pleasant, under other circumstances. Today it reminded him that death was only inches away.

Luke turned to his companion in the muddy trench, the alleged British journalist, Reggie Carville. "Is this what you would call a barrage?" Luke asked.

Carville smiled tolerantly. The Englishman was about Luke's age, lean, and had the look of a greyhound about him. Certainly, he was an aristocrat and Luke tried not to let that intimidate him.

"A barrage? No, not even a whiff of one. This, my dear Martel, is just probing fire, not a barrage."

Several other shells went off in the area, but other than shaking the earth, they did no harm to anyone in the trenches. The trenches were narrow, which meant that only a direct hit would cause casualties, and the trenches zigged and zagged which, along with providing flanking and covering fire, would minimize casualties in the event of a direct hit. The shock wave would be funneled and then dissipated. Luke thought it would be minimal good news if he was directly hit.

The trenches were also dirty, muddy, and cold. Luke's toes felt clammy and he wondered if he shouldn't have worn different boots. He noticed that other soldiers didn't have better boots and wondered if this was something that needed to be corrected. Certainly a long siege would result in serious foot problems.

Carville peered through a firing slit at the German lines. Much of the brush and small trees on the hill had been cleared away to provide clear lines of fire. Unfortunately, this had the negative effect of showing the Germans exactly where the American lines were. Areas around the growing German trench lines had likewise been cleared. Through his binoculars, Luke could see German soldiers moving around. They had no serious fear of American artillery. If and when they desired, the Germans could launch a barrage, but not so the Americans, who were starved of cannon.

Carville turned and sat down in the trench. His expensive-looking civilian suit was getting dirty but the man didn't seem to care. He took a drink from his flask and from the way he grimaced, Luke deduced that it didn't contain water.

"Ah, that was good. I'd offer you some, but it may be against the rules of being an international journalist to share alcohol with combatants. Drinking might also make you lose control and want to kill someone, like those damned Germans. No, this pitiful bombardment is far from serious. German gun theory is quite simple and based on everybody else's. When the time comes, the Krauts will simply line up all the artillery they have, some hundreds of guns, and pack them wheel to wheel. Then they will fire them all at the same time and at roughly the same place; thus pulverizing it. They did it a few times in 1914 and later, and it was damnably effective. I understand it sometimes drove good men simply insane and unable to function, except their bladders and bowels which empty continuously."

"Sounds terrible, Mr. Carville. Effective, but terrible."

Carville took another swallow, changed his mind and offered the flask to Luke who took a small swallow. It was scotch. "Please call me Reggie and quit looking at me like that. A soldier might get the wrong impression."

Luke savored his drink. "I think you are more than you say."

"Nonsense, I'm a writer for the *London Times*."

"And I'm the pope. Benedict the Fifteenth to be precise."

Carville grinned. "Then hear my confession, Benedict, for I have surely sinned in thought, word, and deed. You are right, of course, I am more than I seem, but aren't we all? Even if I was, say, an English officer with experience fighting the Germans in France and with a background at Eton and Sandhurst, it would be veddy inappropriate for me to admit that. After all, England is neutral and cannot be seen by your enemies as giving advice and comfort to you. Therefore, please don't speculate as to my background and I won't ask how many Mexicans you killed under Pershing in 1916 in order to become an officer up from the ranks."

Luke laughed, "Touché."

"I will cheerfully admit to being a British officer in 1914 and to fighting the Huns in France. I will admit to being in trenches, wounded, and serving time as a prisoner before being returned to England and then becoming, ah, a reporter."

Luke was impressed. "Now, from nothing more than a reporter's perspective, what do you think of our fortifications?"

Carville took another swallow and again handed the flask to Luke. "Potentially excellent, but totally inadequate. I love the fact that you actually have three separate defensive lines mutually supporting each other. Someone paid attention during classes at West Point. Obviously, you hope that the Huns will destroy themselves trying to force their way through and, in a different world, you might be right."

"But this is not that world, is it?"

"Not hardly, as you people so ungrammatically put it. You don't have enough machine guns or artillery to hold the Germans at bay and you don't have enough ammunition for the guns you do have. And you certainly don't have enough planes to keep theirs from bombing and strafing your trenches. You can harm their planes, but you can't stop them. Also, your men are, for the most part, enthusiastic amateurs, most of whom haven't been in the army more than three months. To say their training has been inadequate would be a gross understatement. I have it from good sources that many of your men have never fired a rifle in their lives. Oh yes, and there aren't enough men to compensate for their inadequacies. You can't overwhelm the Germans by weight of numbers like the Russians tried. This can't be news to you."

"Not hardly," Luke agreed sadly.

Carville went on to say that the trenches lacked proper drainage, although the bombproof bunkers were quite strong, and that much more barbed wire was needed.

Another shell landed reasonably nearby, causing both men to duck. "However, Luke, the Hun may be doing you a favor with this very sissified shelling. Most of your men have never been under fire, and now they will have been when the big German attack comes, and they will know that it is indeed possible to survive."

The flask was empty. Luke handed it back. "Will they survive a real barrage when it comes?"

"You're the intelligence man, so you tell me. You and Eisenhower have gotten information from clandestine observers at Los Angeles; therefore, you know that the Germans have landed some very large pieces of artillery, the type that broke up the Belgium fortifications and the kind that crushed us, I mean the British, south of Paris."

My, my, Luke thought, the Brit was on the ball. Was someone in his office feeding him information? The Germans had just landed a number of 210mm howitzers and 170mm artillery pieces.

Carville read his mind. "General Liggett and Admiral Sims some time ago decided that, ah, my people and yours should share information. You should be congratulated, Luke. You, Ike, and the late General Logan have set up a first-class intelligence-gathering apparatus in an astonishingly short period of time."

"Two things astonish me, Carville."

"And what might they be?"

"One is that we share such sensitive data with reporters who are known to blab, and, second, why you brought such a bloody small flask."

Sir Edward Grey had been Great Britain's foreign secretary in 1914 and was now ambassador to the United States. He was admitted to the Oval Office by a beaming Hedda Tuttle. He had been waiting but a few moments and had charmed her to the point where she was weak-kneed and giggly. In 1914 and as foreign secretary, Grey had been the author of the comment that the "lights were going out all over Europe." They hadn't quite. After the defeat in France, England's lights were indeed dimmed.

Robert Lansing rolled his eyes at Hedda's immature behavior and bade the ambassador to take a seat. "To what do I owe the honor, Ambassador?"

The world of diplomacy is a small one, and the two men had known each other for years. While not exactly bosom friends, there was a high degree of mutual respect between the men. There was also a realization that England was supportive of the United States in its war with Imperial Germany, even though the British were understandably reluctant to provide more than advice and information. The Royal Navy was still mainly intact and superior to the kaiser's, but the British Army remained small in comparison to the hordes that Germany could unleash if she could somehow cross the Channel and invade England. Discretion, therefore, was the British policy of the moment. Action might come later.

"Mr. President, I have the honor of representing Mexico as a third-party honest and honorable peace broker. Insofar as Mexico no longer has an embassy here, they have asked me to discuss certain matters with you."

Lansing nodded thoughtfully. It was interesting that the Mexicans had asked a *de facto* American ally, England, to be its spokesman rather than another Hispanic country, such as Brasil or Argentina.

Mrs. Tuttle served tea and departed, flushed and happy. "And what matters do you wish to discuss?" Lansing asked.

"You will not be surprised to know that Mexico wants peace. They desire a return to the status quo antebellum, or at least as close as they can get to it. They feel that, with a new administration in Mexico City, bygones can be bygones and the past essentially forgotten. They wish to move on in mutual harmony to a new and bright future."

Lansing snorted. "Is that what they told you?"

Grey smiled benignly. "Yes."

"Did you tell them they had a snowball's chance in hell of it happening?"

"Of course, but they had to try. They are in a desperate situation and want out of it. Let's face it, they've lost nearly half their army of almost two hundred thousand men killed, wounded, captured, and missing, and they've lost a large part of a major province as well as the vital city of Monterrey. They feel they have suffered very badly."

"As have we, Ambassador. At last count, at least fifteen thousand American soldiers were killed or wounded fighting Mexico, and approximately three thousand civilians were killed or wounded, most in the massacre at Laredo. And may I remind you that both Laredo and San Antonio were utterly destroyed. Laredo, in particular, was treated savagely. Her people were brutalized and civilian homes were burned. Of course we will have peace, but Mexico will pay a price for us to withdraw."

Grey sighed and began to take notes. "Mexico is pathetically poor. If you want money, she doesn't have it."

"She has mineral wealth and we will have concessions to exploit those resources. I hope Señor Obregon realizes that it will also provide jobs for Mexicans."

"He will."

"Aside from consolidating our defenses at Monterrey and scouting out Mexican positions, we will not advance any farther south except in response to Mexican attacks. In return, we expect Mexico to expel the Germans from Vera Cruz."

"The Germans may be too strong for Mexico to accomplish that. Obregon might not even be able to get his army to attack the Germans."

"Then tell Obregon that Vera Cruz must at least be isolated. Further, there are approximately twenty thousand Mexican soldiers performing support duties for the Germans in California. They must be recalled to Mexico immediately."

Grey understood fully. The Mexicans were helping to guard the mountain passes as part of their support duties. "They will simply be replaced by Germans. Of course, Mr. President, that will weaken the main German force by the number they have to use to hold the passes and perform other guard duties."

"There is more, Ambassador. Obregon must announce that we did not kill Carranza. We have it on good authority that it was Pancho Villa who actually pulled the trigger and, since Villa is a bandit, he can be the villain. Blaming us for the murder has enraged people in other Central and South American countries. This has resulted in the beatings, even deaths, of American civilians."

"Obregon will be so informed. Anything else?"

Lansing smiled grimly. "Right of passage. We demand the right to send our army westward through Mexican territory as needed."

Ambassador Grey wrote quickly. *My, my,* he thought. *This is going to get very interesting.*

Kirsten dragged herself up the stairs to her apartment. She no longer shared cramped quarters with Elise. With so many civilians evacuated north, there was a surplus of living quarters for the remaining civilians. They each now had a pleasant apartment in the same building. Their landlady had also departed north, which meant they now lived rent free, as if that was important with a war raging just a few miles south. The landlady simply asked them to do their best to protect her property and then promised to pray for them.

Kirsten was exhausted. She smelled of blood, sweat, and God only knew what other odors. She generally wore a smock at the hospital, but smocks couldn't stop an eruption of blood or pus when a wound was penetrated by Dr. Rossini's scalpel.

The work was awful, but she was pleased that she was doing something useful, although useful seemed too trite a word.

That she had helped save lives was true, but it was

also true that many young men had died. Nor were all the casualties soldiers and sailors. Civilians were also hit in the now almost continuous skirmishing. German artillery had not yet targeted San Francisco proper, and there were rumors that they wouldn't hit the city intentionally because they wanted it intact for themselves. But plenty of shells had fallen on civilian areas, causing more casualties, whether on purpose or not. She wondered just what the hell civilians were doing, remaining so close to the lines? Staying in their homes because that's where they live, that's what.

Would the Germans ultimately decide to shell San Francisco if the siege dragged on? In 1914, they'd had no qualms about destroying Brussels, Louvain, and much of Paris, so why wouldn't they level San Francisco? Rumors, bloody damned rumors, said that the kaiser wanted the city spared so it could be the capital of his new province of California. Luke had laughed at that idea.

"The only reason the shells aren't falling are that they aren't yet close enough and they've got military targets closer in. Watch out if they break through and the fighting becomes street to street. They'll destroy everything and, if they win, rebuild later, except it will all look like a town in Bavaria."

Shelters and trenches had been dug around the hospital and every other occupied building in San Francisco.

She disrobed and stepped into her tub. The water was chill but it refreshed her. She couldn't help but think of a more innocent time when she'd taken baths like this at her ranch. She wanted to cry, but she was just too damn tired. She wanted Luke to come and press his hard body against hers. Like her, however, he was busy. Moments together were few and far between.

Food was served at the hospital, and she had learned to eat without listening to the cries or smelling the stench of the wounded. She hadn't grown immune to the sounds of agony, but she could block them out. And they kept telling her that this was only the beginning. Wait until the real battles began and then the casualties would pile up.

She heard noises, familiar noises, at the door to the apartment and she smiled. It had to be the dog and cat. She hadn't named them yet. She didn't even know if they'd stay or if she wanted them to. They'd attached themselves to her for the simple reason that she'd fed them some scraps and given them some water. They were an unlikely pair and must have lived together in past times. In a city emptying of humans, many animals had been left behind and could be heard howling pathetically. More casualties, she thought. If she and the two animals survived, she'd take them with her and give them proper names.

Finished bathing, Kirsten dried herself and put on a robe. Then, with a revolver in her hand, she checked the door. The two animals stared up at her as if she was God. She laughed and they trotted in happily and raced to their food dishes.

Damned British arrogance, thought Admiral von Trotha. Every few days, all or most of the British battleship squadron would emerge from Puget Sound and steam around for a day and then return. They did not stop and identify themselves, nor did they ask permission. Arrogance, he seethed. Still, they were in international waters and there was no war between Great Britain and Imperial Germany, at least not yet.

Like any German naval officer, he longed for the day when his capital ships could send the British battleships to the bottom of the Pacific. Like all German officers, he was concerned that the British were finding ways around the limitations imposed on them by the Peace of 1915. True, there had been no increase in the number of British battleships, but the treaty had large holes in it. For instance, there was no prohibition on submarines, a mistake which Trotha found appalling. He knew what damage German U-boats had done to British and French shipping in that short war. Intelligence said the Limeys were launching subs in large numbers.

It was further rumored that the British were experimenting with using ships as platforms for airplanes. Rumor said that a half-completed battlecruiser had been reworked with a landing deck so that planes could be launched and landed. Trotha didn't think the impact would be large in the short run, since only small airplanes would be able to land on such a ship and small planes carried small bombs. Still, it was something to think about as planes got larger and more deadly. The warplanes of 1920 bore little resemblance to the tiny things of 1914.

Something else to think about was the three-battleship British squadron, with attendant destroyers and cruisers, that was steaming just over the horizon. His picket ships had identified the three British ships and he would not impede their progress, however much he would like to. He would ignore them with the same contempt the British showed him.

Trotha turned to Roth, his aide. "Another pleasure cruise. I wonder if the Limeys sell tickets."

Roth smiled dutifully. At least the admiral wasn't in his usually foul mood when the British exited the Sound. "One of these days, Admiral, I pray that the pleasure will be ours."

Later that night, lookouts on the picket ships spotted the British returning. However, there was one disturbing problem. Instead of three battleships, only one was headed back to Puget Sound, with fewer escorts. Two light cruisers and a pair of destroyers also seemed to have disappeared.

Trotha received the information in silence. His stomach curdled and he tasted bile. Where the devil were the two other two British warships? Had they steamed west to Hong Kong or some other British possession? They could be on their way to India, for that matter, and he prayed to his Lutheran God that they were. But why would the British weaken their squadron in the face of the German one?

Or? His stomach erupted in acid. When he got control of himself he sent a radio message to a contact in what was, allegedly at least, neutral Canada. How many British warships remained in the Sound? How many Americans?

It took an eternity lasting only until midday for the response to come. All British warships, especially battleships, were present and accounted for. However, two American battleships, the *Arizona* and the *Pennsylvania*, were nowhere to be seen.

He sank heavily into his chair. His enemy had slipped the leash and were somewhere in the vastness of the Pacific.

★ ★ ★

If Crown Prince Wilhelm was surprised to see Foreign Minister Arthur Zimmerman, he was far too poised and imperial to show it. After a quick lunch, champagne and cigars were provided. Zimmerman relaxed slightly.

"Highness, I'm certain you've heard rumors that the Mexican alliance is going to hell."

"Of course," he snapped. Had Zimmerman come all this way to tell him that?

Zimmerman wiped his brow. He'd had a miserable trip. He'd been in Mexico City making a courtesy call on the Carranza government when the regime changed. He'd been there to try and bolster Mexico and ensure that she stayed the course as an ally of Germany. Now all that was ashes. *Damned foolish Mexicans*, he thought. They would pay for this betrayal.

As quickly as possible, he'd taken a train from Mexico City north and west, carefully avoiding possible fighting at Monterrey, and then on to San Diego, where he'd been driven north to the crown prince's headquarters.

"I wanted you to know that it appears to be the worst possible outcome," Zimmerman said. "With Carranza dead, it is only a matter of time before the Mexicans abandon us."

The prince smiled tolerantly. Did Zimmerman think he was a fool? Of course he'd been aware of the possibility that Mexico would abandon Germany and that the thousands of Mexican soldiers in his command would either become prisoners or deserters. He did not think they had the guts to become his enemies. They would become prisoners.

In short, poor Zimmerman had wasted a trip. He

should have exited Mexico via Vera Cruz and been on his way to the comforts of Berlin. Still, the foolish little man was his father's envoy.

"More champagne?" he offered and Zimmerman nodded. The servants had been sent away, so Wilhelm filled their glasses himself.

"I'm glad you came, Minister, and you can be assured that your information is greatly appreciated. I think you will be pleased to know that we have had contingency plans ready to put into effect should the ungrateful Mexicans decide to so treacherously leave us."

"I'm glad," said Zimmerman, then yawning hugely. The effects of the long trip and the champagne were beginning to tell. Zimmerman was in his late sixties and the trip would have been exhausting for a younger man. His heavily waxed handlebar mustache was beginning to droop, which Wilhelm found amusing.

"Everything will be under control thanks to your initiative," Wilhelm said soothingly.

"Wonderful, sir. However there is one other thing. I received a cable from your esteemed father just before leaving. He is concerned that this campaign is taking too long in light of emerging problems in Russia and the apparent resurgence of England and France. He wishes California secured as soon as possible."

Wilhelm nodded. He understood fully that his beloved but insecure father was vacillating once again. The kaiser was the one who had told him to move cautiously and carefully and chance nothing. Now he wanted California secured and that meant taking San Francisco as soon as possible.

Damn.

Admiral Hipper hid his anger over the incompetence of von Trotha and his captains. Complacency had reared its ugly head and there was nothing he could do about it. The two American battleships were gone and that was that. Would he be hearing from them? Of course.

Captain Wilhelm Canaris, Hipper's chief of staff, looked at him inquisitively. The admiral shook his head. There would be no recriminations. Trotha would handle the scolding and disciplining of the captains who'd failed to get close enough to the escaping ships to make sure of their identity, and Hipper would chastise Trotha for failure to control his captains. No heads would roll, if only because there were no replacement captains or admirals available. The young German Navy would hide its mistake, but Trotha would likely never see a promotion or an independent command again.

"Admiral, you are aware that the British are denying everything."

"I'm not surprised. The British would lie about the time of day if it would serve their purposes. What in particular are they saying?"

Canaris looked over the admiral's shoulder. "Sir, Admiral Beatty said that three battleships went out and three came in and if we saw only one, perhaps it was because our lookouts had been drinking schnapps while on duty. Admiral Beatty alleges to be offended by our inference that he'd aided the Americans into escaping."

"Offended, my ass," Hipper snarled.

"Sir, may I ask why all three American battleships didn't break out?"

Hipper scowled. "Because the *Nevada*, the one left

behind, is the oldest and smallest of the three and, after our victory at Mare Island, the American ships have only the ammunition they carried with them. The *Nevada* was probably stripped of ammunition which was sent to the other ships and she was left behind."

Hipper paced a few times. "Send a message to Trotha. He and his capital ships are to depart Puget Sound and steam to Los Angeles. He is to leave only a token force to watch the remaining American battleship. There is no reason to use so many ships to guard a nearly empty harbor."

The admiral pounded his desk. "Damn it, Canaris, we have convoys heading for Los Angeles. They cannot fall prey to the Yanks. They carry vitally needed ammunition and additional troops for the crown prince. Trotha's ships will be required to find the Americans. I only wish I knew whether the Americans will be hunting together or separately. Either way, it will be a daunting task to find them in the vastness of the Pacific. I can only hope they will try raiding along the routes that close in on Los Angeles."

"Not San Francisco or San Diego, sir?"

"Who the devil knows? However, we have a larger force by far blockading San Francisco, and San Diego is shrinking in importance since Los Angeles is so much closer to San Francisco."

"Does the crown prince know of this situation?"

"Not yet. He has more important things on his mind."

★ CHAPTER 19 ★

Luke hunkered down in a dug-in position about a mile behind the first line of American defenses. The first line was wreathed in smoke and was being pulverized by a massive German artillery barrage.

Beside him was Reggie Carville. "Now *this*," Carville said happily, "is a bombardment."

The earth was quivering beneath their feet. It felt as if it was turning to mud, even jelly, the same as it had seemed to those who'd lived through the San Francisco earthquake of 1906. Luke wondered just how the poor men closer to the front were enduring it. Or were they going mad from fear? Most of the men would be hiding in reinforced concrete bunkers and would not emerge until the bombardment stopped.

Thunderclaps rolled over them. Both men had placed cotton in their ears to protect their hearing. American guns were not yet dueling with the Germans. There were just too few of them. The Americans would wait. Overhead, a flight of German Albatros fighters patrolled.

Their job was to interdict reinforcements coming down the roads to the area under attack.

Reggie grabbed Luke's arm and pointed. Waves of German soldiers had emerged from their own trenches and were advancing. While they were hardly in parade ground formation, separate units were distinct. They had a good mile to cross before they encountered American barbed wire. A few moments later, American artillery finally opened fire. Explosions erupted among the Germans, sending bodies skyward. Some shells were timed as air bursts which shredded the people beneath them. What had been a pleasant green field was turning into a bloody and cratered charnel house.

Some German artillery lifted and tried to find the American guns. Carville slapped Luke on the shoulder. "Beautiful. You actually are hurting them. Liggett and Harbord do know what they're doing. Just a shame you're going to lose anyhow. Just too damn many Germans, y'know."

Overhead, a German plane's engine sputtered. It was trailing smoke and began tumbling to the ground. Luke smiled grimly. "We had some of our precious machine guns hidden along those roads, Reggie. Now their damned planes will be more careful when they attack our trucks. A little bird told us where the attack would come."

"Ah, a little bird. God bless little birds, warm puppies, and fluffy kittens. Have a drink."

Luke accepted. He and Ike had a number of little birds hidden behind German lines, risking their lives and reporting on the massive buildup of forces in this sector. The reports had come by short wave or, incredibly, by telephone. The Germans had neglected to cut all the lines. The Germans were so contemptuous of the American Army that they hadn't even made a real attempt to hide what they were doing. Yes, they would doubtless carry this defense line, but their arrogance would cost them.

"Good grief, look at that!" Reggie exclaimed. A score of armored trucks had crossed from the German trenches and were advancing, their machine guns spitting fire.

"This, Major Martel, might just be the wave of the future, the gas-driven vehicle used as a weapon."

The German bombardment stopped suddenly. The Germans were still more than a quarter of a mile away from the American trenches.

"A ruse," Luke exclaimed and Carville nodded his understanding. The Germans would wait until the bunkers had emptied of men and the trenches were full. Then they would shell the trenches, although briefly, as their men were getting very close and might be hit by their own shells.

As predicted, the Germans again opened fire. Luke and Reggie looked at each other. The men had been warned about this trick. Had they enough discipline to wait?

The Germans were at the barbed wire and their guns ceased, although American artillery and trench mortars picked up the pace. Again, Germans fell by the score, proving that Americans were alive in the trenches, but they kept on advancing. The German armored vehicles tried to push their way through the barbed wire and, in many cases, failed. Several halted, stuck in shell holes, while others hung up in thickets of wire where they were easy targets for American machine guns. Only a few made it to the trenches, where they were raked by guns. Soft spots were found and the halted trucks began to burn and blow up.

Germans infantry were within yards of the trenches and began hurling their distinctive potato masher grenades. American threw their own grenades in a brief but bloody duel.

However, nothing stopped the German infantry who cut their way through the wire and pushed on to the American trenches. Some Germans fell onto the wire so their comrades could climb across them. More Germans were shot, but still more Germans came on.

"Nobody said the fucking Huns weren't brave," Carville muttered.

The Germans clambered into the American trenches and Luke could only begin to imagine the horror of close in, hand-to-hand combat. Along with their Springfields, many Yanks had submachine guns and sawed off shotguns, ideal for killing at close quarters. The Germans had their MP18 9mm automatic weapons with their thirty-two-round magazines. They might be awkward and difficult to aim, but did it matter when you were trying to kill someone at a distance of ten feet?

American soldiers began pulling back from the trenches. Some were running for their lives, understandably, Luke thought, while whole units began to disintegrate.

"I think we should leave," Carville suggested and Luke concurred. "The Huns won't advance any farther this day. You've hurt them, but, like I said, they will prevail. They will clear out the trenches to their left and right and gather for a second attack."

Luke picked up his gear. He had a report to give to Ike and perhaps Liggett. "When?"

"A couple of days. No more than that."

Martel was filthy and disheveled, but Liggett wanted information immediately. Carville had prudently disappeared, doubtless to communicate to his British masters.

Even though the first of three fortified lines had been lost, Liggett and the other generals were somewhat pleased. Their soldiers had endured a heavy bombardment, the likes of which hadn't been seen on American soil since Gettysburg, and had prevailed. They had emerged from their bunkers and mowed down large numbers of Germans soldiers.

D.W. Griffith had provided film coverage that had transfixed them. The film canisters would be sent north to Canada as diplomatic mail and make their way to the East Coast. When properly edited, the American people who would finally see war in all its horror. Griffith's films showed the dead and the dying in graphic detail.

"How many casualties did we suffer?" Liggett asked.

"Rough estimate is five thousand," Ike responded.

"And theirs?"

"Based on what Martel and I have seen and discussed, probably close to the same."

Liggett shook his head. "Attackers are supposed to lose more than defenders."

"Perhaps it will happen that way the next time, sir," Harbord said. "Our men are becoming experienced and, even though they reacted well, the next time they will perform even better. To use a cliché from a previous war, they have seen the elephant."

Liggett reluctantly concurred. "However, we cannot get into a battle of attrition. They still outnumber us significantly, even if some of their troops are heading out to take over the defense of the passes from the Mexicans." Liggett paused. "Anything else of note?" he asked.

"One thing, sir," Luke said. "Their armored trucks were a disaster on wheels. They sent about twenty of them in the attack and lost at least half. Trucks can't traverse dug-up ground and they don't have the power to bull a path through concentrated barbed wire. You need a much bigger and stronger vehicle for that."

Luke caught Liggett and Harbord glancing at each other. What were they not telling?

Harbord leaned forward. "Yet our armored trucks performed well in Texas, did they not?"

"Yes sir, but circumstances were very different. For one thing, the terrain was fairly flat and, for another, the Mexicans were out in the open and not dug in. That also meant not much in the way of barbed wire. My counterpart in Lejeune's corps also said that a number of trucks still had difficulty. I hate to repeat myself, but today's trucks just aren't strong enough."

"Good observation, Major," said Liggett, "Very good indeed."

Major General Douglas MacArthur was livid with scarcely contained fury. Theirs was the first in a long series of troop trains and they had been stopped just outside of Seattle. The plump army major in front of MacArthur was named Small but was standing tall before MacArthur's attempts to dominate him. MacArthur wasn't all that tall himself, but he was intimidating. A few yards away, Sergeant Tim Randall and Lieutenant Taylor tried to make themselves very, very tiny. They were concerned that they had just picked a terrible spot to rest.

Major Small folded his arms across his ample stomach and glared back. "I understand your frustration, General, but I have my orders. It's more than eight hundred miles from Seattle to San Francisco. There's effectively just about one rail line going that way and a lot of it goes through some godawful terrain and, oh yes, it's still winter."

MacArthur's face had begun to turn red. "Major, I fully understand the weather and distance, but I am in the forefront of three divisions, nearly fifty thousand men, ready to assist the brave young men who are holding the lines at San Francisco. They are laying down their lives and fifty thousand good men are just sitting here. We must have trains. Or do you expect us to walk those eight hundred miles?"

Tim and the lieutenant looked at each other. Walk eight hundred miles through snow-covered mountains and forests? That would be madness. They had the nagging feeling that MacArthur might consider such an alternative.

"Three months," Taylor whispered. "It would take us at least three months and probably a lot longer to walk to San Francisco. The weather and terrain would slow us to a crawl. By then the war would be over."

They had to go by rail. Hell, Tim thought. Neither he nor Lieutenant Taylor had realized they were still that far from their destination. Like many young Americans they were learning just how large the United States was.

Small continued. "General, the dilemma is obvious. Do we send supplies down to the men who have so little, or do we send men carrying only the supplies on their back? It's a helluva choice, but General Liggett's orders are specific and he outranks you. Your men are to wait until the most needed supplies make it down there. We're sending supply trains as fast as we can, but it's still not enough. And sending men without additional supplies would exacerbate the problem."

Tim quickly did the math. At forty men to a car, and fifty cars to a train, each train could carry two thousand men. Averaging twenty miles an hour, they could begin to arrive in San Francisco in two or three days, depending on interruptions, and not three plus months by shank's mare. So near yet so far. Of course, it would take at least a day to load up each train and it would take a good twenty-five or thirty trains.

"Someday, I will have your hide, Major."

"Someday I'll be a civilian again, General."

MacArthur wheeled away and, to Tim's horror, spotted them. "You heard that, I presume?"

The two men stood and snapped to attention and Tim responded. "Couldn't much help it, sir, and if I may say so, we've got to get down to San Francisco. We are useless as tits on a boar sitting up here. To be blunt sir, I didn't enlist so I could sit on my ass in Seattle while my fellow Americans are fighting in San Francisco."

MacArthur's features showed surprise at Tim's bluntness and then softened. His men were agreeing with him and he liked that. He was about to respond when Major Small came trotting up, huffing from the exertion.

"General MacArthur, I don't know what the hell's going on but General Liggett's changed his mind. He wants your division down south as fast as you can go. I don't know what the devil's happened but he wants you yesterday. You get your men ready while I round up the trains."

MacArthur's face split into a grin. He shook both Tim and the Taylor's hands. "You men are good luck."

MacArthur strode briskly away, looking for his aides and bellowing orders. Taylor shook his head. "Tim, that little speech of yours was more bullshit than I spout in a year of lawyering. You sure you don't want to be an attorney?"

Tim grinned. "Funny thing is, sir, I meant a lot of it."

And now they were going to San Francisco.

Martina Flores stood and stared at the prisoners as she carefully hand signaled her message—tonight.

Joe Sullivan pulled on his ear lobe, the response that he understood. He got up and found Captain Rice. "Martina says tonight, sir." Rice nodded. Their long days and nights of waiting were over.

It seemed to take forever for the sun to set. The men lay down in their blankets and pretended to sleep. Rice and other key men watched as their Mexican guards took up station. It got darker. The stars came out and a coyote howled in the distance.

And then they were gone. The Mexicans had disappeared. There were no guards watching over them. Rice and his men stared at each other. Where their eyes playing tricks? Were the Mexicans truly gone or were they lying in wait?

Rice took a deep breath. It was time. "Now," he said softly.

A score of men rose up and ran with him to the

main gate. Rice fumbled with the key Martina had given. He almost dropped it but caught it and stuck it in. The lock opened.

Rice and others pushed it aside and ran to the building that housed the weapons. A few kicks and the outside door was smashed open. There was no guard inside, but a metal door barred them. Another key and it was open. Jubilant Americans began passing out rifles and ammunition. The weapons were a miscellany of Krags, Winchesters, and Springfields. They grabbed as much ammunition as they could. It would have to be sorted out later. Gunfire from outside had begun and was getting heavy. There was no time to dither.

"Who the hell do we shoot?" someone yelled.

"Germans!" Rice answered. "And anybody who shoots at us."

On the other side of the camp, Steiner's thin line of German soldiers, most of them clerks, had opened fire on the fleeing Mexicans. Men screamed and fell, and Steiner laughed. The Mexicans had tried to be silent, but he'd posted men to watch them. It was so easy and they were so obvious. One of the first Mexicans to die had been their treacherous sergeant, Sanchez.

Steiner's men might not be combat troops, but any German was better than a group of confused and disorganized Mexicans. Beside him, Olson brought up his own men. Steiner waved him off.

"Go back and watch the prisoners."

As Olson moved to comply, rifle fire opened up from outside the camp. A pair of Germans fell screaming. Steiner looked at the flashes of gunfire. Mexicans or Americans? It didn't matter. More gunfire erupted, and this time to his rear. What the devil? The prisoners must have escaped and gotten weapons. Steiner swore. He was no longer in charge and the situation was deteriorating.

With that, Steiner blew a whistle and his Germans, like trained dogs, gathered around him and began a fighting withdrawal to the railroad tracks.

Men were shouting in English. Most were yelling at others not to shoot them, while some of Olson's men were trying to surrender. Steiner could see Olson crumple and start to scream. Seeing him fall, the rest of his men disappeared into the night, leaving Olson alone on the ground. Soon, Steiner and his men were long gone.

In a few minutes, Olson was surrounded by the now heavily armed former prisoners, while some Mexicans in American uniforms watched. "Okay," he said through his pain. "You win. I'm your prisoner."

The prisoners' leader, Captain Rice, looked down on him and spat in his face. This amused the others. Olson saw Martina walk toward him and it was suddenly difficult to breathe. Martina looked like a tigress stalking prey.

Martina pulled a large knife from her belt. In Spanish, she asked for Montoya's men to hold Olson. They happily complied, and with one motion, she ripped open his stomach. He stared in disbelief at the blood pouring from his gut. The men holding him let him go, and ignored his screams. Olson curled up into a ball and groaned while he bled to death. Martina was not a good surgeon.

★ ★ ★

Josh stole a moment to get some food from the Army's mess hall at the Presidio. More meetings were going on and he was not needed. A mere lieutenant junior grade was not going to impact the war. Sometimes he had the feeling that Admiral Sims barely tolerated his presence. Perhaps it was because of Elise or maybe the admiral thought he was a good messenger. Either way, he was not involved in combat and, however Elise felt about it, it ate at Josh.

Of course, the Navy at San Francisco wasn't in a position to do much of anything except point a few shore guns at the Germans who now prudently stayed out of range, and prepare for the inevitable German ground assault. The reported escape of the *Arizona* and the *Pennsylvania* from Puget Sound had electrified everyone in San Francisco. The drawback of the escape was that the German battleships previously assigned to blockade them were now stationed off San Francisco.

Lieutenant Commander Jesse Oldendorf was seated alone at a small table in the large but half-empty dining hall stuffing food into his mouth. Despite shortages, the cooks had done their usual excellent job and the aromas were enticing.

Josh envied the man. Almost every day, he was out there on the noble former trawler, the *Shark*, laying or inspecting the minefields. And just to keep things interesting, every now and then the distant Germans would lob a shell in his direction. They'd never come close, but a lucky hit was always a possibility. Even a near miss would send water a hundred feet into the air and create pressures that would crush the *Shark*'s hull.

Oldendorf saw him and waved him over. "How are things with the gods on Mount Olympus?" he asked cheerfully. "And how are you with the beautiful Miss Elise? Still seeing her or has she come to her senses?"

Josh laughed. "The gods tell me very darn little, and Elise has not yet regained consciousness."

"Then don't let her. She's a prize."

"She doesn't want me out on any more combat missions."

"And smart, too." Oldendorf finished devouring a slightly overcooked pork chop which was just the way he liked it. "Of course, the Navy hasn't had much to do with half a dozen Kraut battleships watching us like German hawks."

The German warships patrolling Puget Sound had arrived and four had promptly departed in pairs. Obviously, their job was to try to search out the *Arizona* and the *Pennsylvania*. If the American warships stayed together, any battle with a pair of German ships would be fairly even, but the Americans could not afford to lose any ships, while the Germans could replace their losses. If the American ships split up, which Josh considered likely, then they would be outnumbered two to one if they met up with either German squadron.

Of course, it was a very big ocean, and intercepted intelligence said the German ships would return in a few days. That news was ominous. There was only one reason for them to return and that was to attack.

"At least you are doing something useful, Commander."

Oldendorf looked at him curiously. "And just what am I doing, Lieutenant?"

Josh was puzzled. "Why, you're out their laying mines for the time when the Germans try to bull their way through the Golden Gate."

"You think they'll try to do that?" he asked with a grin.

"They have to, sir. The Kraut officers want action and they won't get it sitting out there while the army takes San Francisco. No, sir, they will bull their way in and we will try to stop them with our shore guns and your mines."

Oldendorf pushed his empty plate away. "And how many mines have you seen the *Shark* lay?"

Now Josh was truly confused. "Maybe hundreds."

Oldendorf smiled sadly. "I am now going to let you in on a little secret, Josh. You haven't seen me lay a single mine. They've been rocks, Josh, rocks. You've seen the *Shark* and her loyal crew throw rocks overboard every day. Both you and the Krauts think we've been mining the entrance, which means they'll come in real slow and cautious. When they do, our shore guns will try to pound the crap out of them. If we've fooled a man as keen as you, then we've fooled them as well."

Josh felt his jaw dropping. "Rocks? And you're not kidding?"

"Nope. We only had a handful of mines when the war started, and we used them all trying to stop the Krauts from leaving San Diego. You do remember that little escapade, don't you?"

Josh shook his head, "I still can't believe that was all of them."

"Every last stinking one, young Lieutenant. Now, Josh, I've gone and told you a deep dark military secret. I want you to tell me something."

"Shoot."

"What the hell is 'Operation Firefly'?"

★ ★ ★

Captain Heinz Muller was commodore of the convoy and its escorts. It consisted of a dozen transports, freighters, and fuel tankers all traveling slowly and in formation. Neat and tidy like good little Germans, Muller liked to think. Muller had a decent sense of humor and his crew, except for the Communists and anarchists among the enlisted men, liked and respected him.

Muller had retired from active duty five years earlier and held the rank of captain in the naval reserves. At age sixty, he fully expected to finish his life in a rocking chair with a beer in his hand and a buxom young fraulein to hop off his lap and keep the glass full. He was a bachelor and the fantasy came easily to mind. But then came the war and the surprise order from the kaiser to take command of both the ancient pre-dreadnaught battleship *Preussen* and the hastily gathered convoy.

Four destroyers and the light cruiser *Pillau* accompanied him and his battleship as additional escorts.

The fourteen-thousand-ton *Preussen* was a virtual museum piece. She'd been commissioned in 1905. She was primitive in comparison with modern ships, such as the *Bayern* or, he shuddered, the American *Arizona* or *Pennsylvania*. Since the 1906 launch of the British super-ship, the *Dreadnaught*, naval architecture and warship design had been revolutionized. It was ironic that the *Dreadnaught* herself was now considered obsolete after only fifteen years of existence.

The *Preussen* carried a mere four eleven-inch guns and a number of 6.7-inch guns, none of which could stand up to the Americans who had escaped from Puget Sound. If it hadn't been for the damned

American submarines, now long dead, Muller and his ship would have been back in Germany and the transports steaming on their own. The destroyers were there to herd the civilian ships and the light cruiser's job was to watch over the destroyers. The *Pillau* could steam at twenty-seven knots, but carried only six-inch guns. Nobody had expected that they would have to look out for American battleships.

The Yank submarine menace was gone, but, even before the escape of the Americans, there was the fear of Yankee surface raiders. Not every destroyer or cruiser had been accounted for and the Americans certainly had other subs, but they were in the Atlantic. At least that's where German intelligence said they were. He harrumphed to himself. German intelligence had been far from perfect so far.

"Ship on the horizon!" a lookout yelled and Muller cursed.

"Two ships," the lookout corrected.

Scores of telescopes and binoculars were instantly trained on the distant smudges, upperworks just beginning to appear over the horizon. Muller's heart skipped a beat. They were large and their design wasn't German. *Please let a merciful God make those ships British and not American,* he thought.

God was not merciful. A few moments later and Muller's worst dreams had been realized. He had found the *Arizona* and the *Pennsylvania*. "Order the convoy to scatter and run for their lives. The destroyers and the *Pillau* will follow me."

They were two hundred miles away from Los Angeles, and, while his radio was broadcasting the alarm, he knew it was a fruitless gesture. Were there any

German warships in the vicinity? Highly unlikely, he admitted to himself.

Flashes on the American ships showed that their great fourteen-inch guns had fired. A moment passed and shells fell short of the *Preussen*. Muller fired his forward turret. His own shells fell well short. He had fired just to show the Yanks that the *Preussen* had teeth. Maybe it would delay the Americans and give his sheep a chance of escaping. The Americans fired again and this time the shells landed long. They were bracketed.

"Tell the destroyers and the *Pillau* to try to escape," Muller ordered sadly. "And keep trying to raise our fleet. They have to be out there someplace, damn it."

More shells landed, and water splashed over the German battleship. Fragments from the shells struck down on the deck. A dozen crewmen fell in screaming bloody heaps.

Suddenly, Muller was lying face down on the deck of the bridge. Bodies lay around him. The ship was rocking violently and flames were shooting out from a score of places. A human arm lay near him. It was his. He tried to get up but hands held him down and placed a tourniquet on the stump of his shattered arm.

"Status!" Muller screamed through waves of pain. The report was dismal. The forward eleven-inch turret had been destroyed and the engines were not responding. His ship was dead in the water and sinking. He sobbed and gave the order to abandon ship. The *Preussen* hadn't lasted ten minutes against the Americans.

As he was being lowered into a lifeboat he realized that the Americans were no longer firing at the helpless old battleship. A small mercy, he thought. A shell struck the *Pillau* and the five-thousand-ton cruiser broke in half. One of the American battleships was in with the transports, sinking them with her secondary battery of five-inch guns. One did not use fourteen-inch shells on a transport any more than one used a shotgun to kill a fly. It also occurred to him that perhaps the Americans didn't have an abundance of fourteen-inch shells.

A couple of transports struck their colors. Their crews began abandoning ship. There weren't enough boats for the men on the troop transport and they spilled into the water. Many would drown. God help them, Muller thought.

Two hours later, the *Preussen* still stubbornly held onto life. From where he sat in a lifeboat, Muller could see that she listed well to port and would sooner or later capsize. A brave ship, Muller thought. More ships were appearing over the horizon. The German Navy had arrived. *Finally*, Muller thought bitterly. The Americans had wrought their havoc and long since disappeared.

★ CHAPTER 20 ★

W*HY ME,* THOUGHT LUKE AS HE STOOD IN FRONT of what was thought to be an empty wood-frame house. *Because you're the only one available, that's why,* he thought as he answered his own question. He gripped his .45 automatic and waited while the rest of the detachment, six soldiers from the provost marshal's office, came up. Four took up positions by the front door and two in the rear.

The house looked as if it had survived the earthquake of 1906, but might not make it much longer. Windows were shuttered and paint was peeling.

Luke took a deep breath. He wasn't a cop but he was going to have to act like one. "We know you're in there. Come out with your hands up or you'll get shot."

There was silence and then a voice cried out. "I'm not going back!" Luke picked up on the sense of desperation in the man's voice.

A second voice added, "We've got guns and we'll

use them. Leave us alone. That's all we ask, just leave us alone."

Of course they have weapons, Luke thought. They're soldiers, or once upon a time they were. Now they're deserters and would hang if caught. A police patrol happened to see motion in what was thought to be an abandoned house and shots were fired when the cops went to investigate. Fortunately, no cops had been hit in the skirmish, but it had proven that the deserters were indeed desperate.

Even in peacetime, desertion was a problem, and now it was especially severe. After the major German attack on the trenches, Luke had seen hundreds of men running in panic towards safety in the rear. That happened all the time with inexperienced troops. Men broke and ran. Most of them came back after a while, all sheepish and shamefaced. Sometimes they were punished with extra duty and sometimes a sympathetic commander let them back in their units with little more than a scolding. Every soldier understood terror. Modern battle was a terrifying thing.

But the men in the house had not come back to duty. They'd stolen food, shot at cops, and now were a threat to Luke and his men. He couldn't just leave them there despite their entreaties.

"If you surrender and come out, I promise you a fair trial and that you won't hang if you're guilty."

Of course they're guilty, he thought. They wouldn't be in that house if they weren't. The not-hanging promise had been concurred with by Liggett. A long and hard prison sentence awaited them, with them probably breaking rocks for most of the rest of their lives. *Maybe hanging would be more merciful,* he thought. With the Germans only ten miles away from the city, no one was inclined to be merciful.

"Fuck you, soldier!" someone yelled from the house.

Luke turned to the corporal in charge of the enlisted men. "Well, that settles it. I don't think they like us. Throw in some tear gas."

The corporal grinned wickedly and he and his men lobbed tear gas grenades through the windows, smashing what remained of the glass. *The original owners of the house are going to be pissed when they come back*, Luke thought.

They could hear coughing and choking from inside. Someone fired wildly through a window and they ducked. "Stupid sons of bitches," snarled the corporal. "Should we shoot inside, sir?"

"No. Hold off for a minute." The house was frame and he was concerned that bullets would go right through and innocent people would be hit by strays. Already, a crowd of spectators had gathered and police were having a hard time keeping them out of the way.

"More gas," he ordered and a half-dozen more grenades added to the choking fumes.

A moment later, the front door opened and a man came out. He had a revolver and fired it wildly. The corporal did not need an invitation. He fired and hit the man in the chest. The deserter went down, flapping his arms.

The two others emerged, also blinded and firing wildly. Luke's men returned fire and both men fell, wounded. The corporal and another man dragged the three deserters from the doorway. The first man was dead and the others seriously wounded. With luck they would live until they were hanged. Liggett had been adamant on that further point. There would be no mercy if they didn't surrender.

One of the deserters, a boy about eighteen, was crying and not just because of the tear gas. He was hurt and he was going to die. Maybe not today, but very soon, and he was scared to death. Luke wondered if the others had led him on. Too bad. He was old enough to make his own decisions and he had made a tragically bad one.

A couple of trucks were driven up and the prisoners were dumped inside. One of the wounded screamed. Luke thought he should chide the corporal for letting that happen, but what the hell. Those men had let down their comrades and then tried to kill Luke and the other soldiers. Maybe the people who wrote the Geneva Convention wouldn't like it, but Luke didn't recall signing the damned thing.

The Dumbarton Railroad Bridge ran from the eastern shore of San Francisco Bay to the village of Menlo Park, just south of the city of San Francisco. It was essential to the existence of the city since no other railroads ran into the city. A spur line ran from the bridge north to the heart of town, but the Dumbarton Bridge stood alone.

The bridge had been completed in 1910. Prior to its existence, food, supplies, clothing, and anything else that arrived in Oakland were either ferried across the bay or driven the long way around it.

And now its existence was being challenged. German artillery had begun firing at it from long range. Granted, the shelling was inaccurate, but it was only a matter of time before the bridge was struck and the city would be back once again to its dependence on ferries.

From several miles away, Kirsten and Elise watched as shells splashed in the water and sent geysers skyward. It was morbidly beautiful.

"Today the bridge, tomorrow the city," Kirsten murmured and Elise nodded solemn agreement.

"I guess I never realized we were so vulnerable," Elise said. "With the exception of the attack on that movie production site, war was always so far away. I watched others plan, but never watched it in action. Even the bombings and shellings seemed like aberrations that would stop and go away."

"I know. When I see those poor boys in the hospital, I don't particularly think of them as having come from down the road. Perhaps from another world, but not someplace nearby."

The number of casualties had diminished, if only for a while, and exhausted medical personnel and volunteers like Kirsten had been given blessed relief from their sometimes terrible duties.

Kirsten looked up suddenly. "I just realized something. Tell me, do you see any trains crossing?"

"No."

"And you won't. The Germans don't actually have to hit the bridge to stop train traffic; all they have to do is come close."

Elise shook her head. She ached to see Josh and herself safe and out of San Francisco. "So we're cut off, aren't we?"

"Not quite. There will still be barges and other ships crossing the bay to the city proper, but a major link has indeed been severed. And that means the Germans have won another round, damn them to hell."

★ ★ ★

President Lansing and Secretary of State Hughes beamed. "Ambassador Grey, what a pleasure. Come in and please sit down."

Grey sat on a couch and Lansing sat across from him. Hughes took a chair behind Lansing. A clearly flustered Mrs. Tuttle entered with tea, coffee, and cookies. "Now, sir, to what do I owe the honor of your visit?" inquired Lansing.

Grey sighed dramatically. "I'm afraid I'm the bearer of bad tidings. His Imperial majesty, Kaiser Wilhelm, is protesting the loose manner in which both Canada and the United States are paying attention to the integrity of their respective borders."

"Oh dear, dear me," said the president.

"Indeed. The kaiser now has information that military goods are being shipped from Canada and into the United States via rail to Seattle."

"I'm shocked, devastated. Please have a cookie."

"Thank you, and my compliments to Mrs. Tuttle."

"I believe she has a crush on you."

Grey smiled. "Ah, and who can blame her. Now, as to the border, our foreign office has informed the kaiser that our border agents are checking what comes into Canada, and are not particularly interested in what goes out, in this case to the United States. The task of checking what goes into the United States belongs to the United States. We told him we sincerely doubted you Americans would voluntarily halt the flow of badly needed war materiel to your country."

"Did he take it well?"

"Actually, no. He called us duplicitous liars and closet allies of America."

"The nerve of the man, calling you duplicitous after

he's invaded France, Belgium, and the United States, among other places."

Grey continued with additional mock solemnity. "They have further informed us that they have reasons to suspect that American merchant ships are running their Puget Sound blockade by flying British flags and carrying false manifests. The Germans are aware that Admiral Beatty has told British merchant captains that, under no circumstances, may Germans board and inspect our ships and we've informed the Germans that such would constitute piracy or something like that. They are not concerned about our feelings, but they are worried by us Brits. Beatty has told them they may check manifests, but from a small boat alongside the merchant, and that is all. The Hun right now respects that because he does not wish to risk another war with Great Britain. At least, not yet."

Lansing nodded solemnly and glanced at Hughes who maintained a good poker face. It had taken too much time for someone to come up with the scheme. British-flagged ships were now loaded with war material at either Boston, New York, or, with the strange Italian Golitti's assistance, in Lisbon. They transited the Panama Canal, still solidly in American hands, and sailed insolently up the Pacific to Puget Sound and Seattle where they offloaded and returned. So far more than a score of ships had made the journey, and others were en route. If the output of America's factories could not be sent overland, they would go by sea.

The first ships had unloaded fourteen-inch shells for the *Nevada*, which was now ready to attack the smaller German ships still blockading the Sound. Other ships brought artillery, machine guns, and ammunition. If Lansing recalled correctly, half a hundred crated airplanes had also been unloaded. Their pilots had traveled the land route as Canadian citizens and simply crossed the border without incident. The planes were now being assembled under the direction of an officer named Mitchell.

Lord Grey smiled. The president's mind was easy to read. "I am concerned, Mr. Lansing, that the Germans will grow impatient and do something rash like searching a British flagged ship and then finding contraband in its hold. That would be quite embarrassing. What would we do? Would we scold the Germans for violating the sanctity of the British flag, however fraudulent its use, or would we chastise you for using our flag for immoral purposes?" Grey sighed expansively. "I just don't know what we will do. Are there any more cookies?"

Hughes passed a new tray. "I believe Mrs. Tuttle would marry you if she could."

"If only for the cookies, I might take her up on it. Family might not approve, however. Where were we?"

"Your options," said Lansing.

"Yes. Indeed. Should a ship be found carrying contraband, we would profess shock and dismay that it occurred, and tell the kaiser that we will work diligently to ensure that it doesn't happen again. We would ask for and get an apology from you for your actions."

Lansing smiled wickedly. "I will write it now if you'd like."

Twenty feet below ground in a dimly lit man-made cavern, Luke felt the earth tremble from the massive explosions. It felt as if the Germans were trying to destroy all life on the earth. He was beyond fear. He was terrified. He could die at any moment, and the thought made him want to whimper. How the hell did people endure it? Because they had to, was the only answer.

A real question might be what the devil made him volunteer to come to the front for information at just the time the Germans were launching another offensive. During the previous assault, he'd been a spectator and off to the side. This time he was right in the middle of the titanic battle.

Some of the other soldiers in the bunker looked to him for leadership. The cement roof above them vibrated and quivered. Martel saw the fear on their faces and hoped it wasn't reflected on his own. The air in the bunker was clammy and some of the men felt weak from the poor circulation, but at least it was safe. Some fools even smoked cigarettes, which further fouled air that was already ripe with the smell of urine, sweat, shit, and fear.

They might be relatively secure in the well-constructed bunker, but they would soon have to emerge to a new and frightening surface where they would confront the prospect of horrible and violent death.

Dust trickled down from the ceiling and covered them all with a light film as enemy shells hit above them. The soldiers, Luke included, were lucky; they had helmets that kept their heads reasonably clean. Small pieces of debris patted like raindrops on their helmets.

The young captain who commanded the troops in the bunker sat beside Luke on the wooden bench. His name was Ward and he was a friendly sort, even though he was harsh when it came to dealing with subordinates. He was trying to convince them that he knew what he was doing and wasn't afraid of the Germans.

The shelling had been going on for hours. It was beyond Luke's comprehension and belief. There was nothing in his experience to even remotely compare with what was going on above him. And it was all prelude, the real battle had yet to commence.

It had also been a most unpleasant surprise. Luke's intentions had been to visit the front, observe, take some notes, and leave, but the sudden and unexpected shelling had trapped him. Now he wondered if his coming to the front was going to be a tragic mistake.

Ward laughed hesitantly. "At least the bombardment keeps the Krauts away, sir. When it stops, it will mean that their damned infantry will be well on their way to our trenches. While they're trying to keep us pinned down, they'll attempt a barrage in front of their advancing troops."

At which point, the Americans would pour out of the bunker and into their own trenches, and rain small-arms fire on the attackers. Luke knew all this, but understood that Ward felt a need to talk, to prove that he knew what was happening and that neither he nor his men should be fearful.

A crack appeared in the roof of the bunker and dirt poured onto the floor. For a moment they all thought it was going to collapse, but it didn't and they began to breathe again. "It's like an earthquake," Luke said.

Ward nodded. "The ground, the solidest earth, seems to be turned into mud by the shelling. It has no substance. It must be what an earthquake is like."

"Wouldn't know," Luke said. "And I'd prefer to keep it that way." Ward laughed and a couple of soldiers within hearing distance nodded appreciatively.

Martel turned and looked at the infantrymen stare at him and Ward. They were the poor bloody bastards who were going to try and stop the Germans who would soon be assaulting from their positions.

If the bunker in which he cowered was any indication, the German artillery had been ineffective. There had been numerous direct hits on the roof of the bunker, but it had withstood them all. Even the new crack above them seemed stable. They understood that German infantry doctrine would have the cannon fire stop well before the actual assault to prevent hitting their own troops. It was a prudent measure, but the brief warning caused by the halt would enable the Americans to take their positions and begin killing Germans.

Luke tried to act relaxed. "Captain Ward, has anyone considered what might happen if a shell blocks our exit?"

"That, sir, is why we have built several exits. If all else fails, I have thirty men who will dig like fools to get ourselves out before we suffocate."

The firing seemed to diminish. Ward barked an order and two men went to the tunnel that led up to the trench. They opened the door and one of them gingerly went out and up the stairway. The second followed behind him.

Martel heard the crack of an explosion and the last soldier was thrown back into the bunker, engulfed in a cloud of smoke. A long metal splinter from a shell had been driven into his chest. He screamed once and fell silent as blood poured from the wound.

Incredibly, the first soldier returned unhurt as the shelling picked up again.

"Not clear yet, sir," the soldier reported quickly and unnecessarily.

The shelling intensified and reached a new crescendo. "This is the end of it," Ward said. Luke agreed. It was like a Fourth of July fireworks display with everything fired as the climax and finale.

There was a sudden and ominous silence. Ward took a deep breath and looked at his frightened troops. He was as scared as they, but he would never let them know it. Suddenly, Luke wanted to stay in the bunker for the rest of his life.

Incongruously, the phone rang. The buried phone lines hadn't been severed by the bombardment. Ward answered it and listened for a second before hanging up.

"Come on," he said with a calmness that impressed Luke, "let's kill some Germans."

Luke waited until the last soldier had left the bunker. They had positions to go to; he did not. As he emerged into the smoke-filled daylight, he choked, then blinked to regain his vision. Automatically, his mind began to assess the damage done by the German artillery. It was surprisingly little.

In some places, a trench had been hit and the walls collapsed, but these were infrequent. Shell craters pocked the land in front of and behind the trenches, but the trench lines themselves were basically intact. So too were the thickets of barbed wire. Some had been tossed about and rearranged, but, like the trenches, they were fundamentally undamaged. Luke made another mental note.

He took a deep breath. In place of the clammy air of the bunker was the scent of cordite and the sickly-sweet stench of burning flesh. It told Martel that the dug-in American Army had not escaped entirely unscathed, although common sense told him that much of the burning flesh was more likely horse than human.

The infantrymen had taken their places on their firing stations and were aiming their rifles down the slight slope. The Americans had one real advantage; they held the high ground. The hill wasn't much, but it enabled them to look across the valley and down to the German lines. It also meant that their trenches were fairly dry, and not filled with mud and muck.

"Krauts!" Ward hollered.

Martel squinted into the distance. The smoke caused a whitish haze, but he saw wavy rows of dots in the tall, thick grass. He looked through his binoculars and the dots became men trudging towards him. Their rifles were at the ready and they were burdened with packs. They seemed to move slowly, agonizingly slowly, even though he knew they were trotting.

As before, American artillery opened up and shells hit in and above the advancing ranks. Men dropped or were hurled aside like toys, while other shells ripped flesh to pieces. Martel felt ill at the killing. This was not fighting. It was murder on an assembly-line basis, warfare designed by Henry Ford.

The smoky haze from the artillery served to further obscure the advancing Germans from few American machine-gunners. Luke thought it ironic that the American artillery trying to kill the Germans was helping to save them.

The Germans were close enough for the riflemen to fire at. Methodically working their Springfields, their massed fire wreaked further havoc. As yet there was little return fire from the Germans. The effect was a bloody drill.

Still the Germans came on. German light artillery opened up and Martel was covered by a shower of dirt from a near miss. Someone screamed and an American soldier fell wounded in the trench beside him. Luke fought the urge to run back to the bunker. This was not like any kind of war he'd ever seen. He had an overwhelming urge to piss. For a moment he recalled the three deserters and felt he could empathize with their urge to flee.

Luke put down his binoculars. He no longer needed them to pick out the individual features of the oncoming enemy. Nor did he want to see the contorted facial expressions of men who were about to die. Bullets began to smack into trenches as some of the Germans paused to shoot at their tormentors. More Americans fell. Luke saw a young man he'd spoken to earlier in the day fall back with a bullet in his face. With only their upper bodies exposed, head wounds were common.

The first German soldiers reached the barbed wire. Some paused and tried to find their way through, while others continued to shoot at the Americans. A bullet struck near Martel and he ducked to the bottom of the trench. In some areas, the Germans were stalled by the effects of their own artillery where it had piled up the barbed wire into an impenetrable mass.

The Germans were less than a hundred yards from the American soldiers, who continued to pour fire into them. That so many of the Germans remained alive was a miracle and likely due to the tendency of soldiers to fire wildly in battle.

And then the Germans were in the trenches. Scores of screaming enemy soldiers poured over the American defenses, shooting and stabbing with bayonets and trench knives. Luke had his pistol out and shot a German in the chest. The man fell back, a look of shock on his face. Another German lunged at him with a bayonet and Luke fired quickly, hitting him in the leg.

"Get out, sir!" screamed Ward. He motioned to a communication trench that led to the rear. American soldiers were already running down it.

Luke picked up a Tommy-gun that someone had discarded. *A helluva lot better than a pistol,* he thought. He backed his way down the communications trench with Ward squeezed at his side. A pair of Germans tried to follow and Luke fired a burst. One dropped and the other ducked.

Ward gave a gurgling scream and fell. A bullet had blown off his jaw. Luke picked him up and carried him over his shoulder to the secondary trench line, a few hundred yards behind, while other soldiers covered them.

He arrived exhausted and handed over his bloody burden. A medic took Ward and laid him on the ground. "Sorry, sir, but he's dead."

Luke was about to reply, when something struck him in the chest and he collapsed to the ground, the breath knocked out of him. The medic checked him quickly. He laughed bitterly and handed Luke a piece of metal.

"Your lucky day, sir. You got hit by a spent bullet. Otherwise you'd be lying there with your buddy."

Yeah, Luke thought as he put the distorted bullet in his pocket, *my lucky day. We just lost the second of three defensive lines and I've got a piece of lead for a souvenir.*

★ CHAPTER 21 ★

A FEW HOURS LATER, LUKE STOOD BEFORE LIGGETT and Sims. The general glowered at him in mock anger. "Just once I'd like you to report to me wearing a clean uniform. Good lord, is that blood?"

"It is sir, but not mine." He told them about carrying the dying Captain Ward away from the trenches.

"That was well done; however tragic the results, but your adventure was ill-advised. Had you been killed I would have lost a valuable officer. Had you been captured, the Germans would have been given a key member of my intelligence staff. They would have interrogated you, even tortured you, in order to find what you knew. In plain English, your presence in the trenches was an act of consummate stupidity."

"Yes sir." Luke declined to comment that he'd realized that the instant the shells began to fall. He also didn't add that he'd had no plans to be taken alive. However, he did wonder if he had the courage to kill himself.

"You will promise me that you will not go near the front lines again."

"Promised, sir. I will absolutely stay away from the front lines."

Liggett's expression softened while Sims remained impassive. "Unless, of course, the front lines come to you, which could happen if the Krauts breach our third and last line of defenses. If that happens, your being captured and tortured for information will have become moot since the city will have fallen. Also, I've heard it that you killed a dozen Germans while covering the retreat. Any truth to that?"

"I killed maybe two and wounded a third."

Liggett actually smiled. "We'll let the rumors swirl. We need a hero and if a little exaggeration makes you qualify, we'll let it happen. Now, get the hell out of here and go clean up."

He was on his way to the officers' quarters when Kirsten ran up and grabbed his arm. Her eyes were red from crying.

"You are a fool, a complete idiot," she said as she first grabbed his arms, then let go and began pounding on his chest. "What on earth were you thinking of, risking your life like that? They gave you rank and responsibility so you could stay safe and use your brain, not your gun."

"I'm sorry," he said lamely. A scolding from a three-star general he could endure. Kirsten's wrath, never.

"You almost made me a widow a second time and we're not even married yet."

"Do you want to marry me?"

"Yes, but not until after this is over."

"And why aren't you at the hospital?"

"Because they don't need me right now. There's been an influx of trained personnel from up north, so now I'm back to being a clerk, cataloging the wounded and trying to notify their families. It's important, sometimes even heartbreaking, but it can wait a few hours."

She had taken his arm and was steering him away from the Presidio. "Where are we going?"

"To the apartment. You can clean up, get fed, and I'll let you play with the dog and cat."

Luke leaned against her. He was exhausted, both mentally and physically. Still, he grinned. "Can I play with their owner?"

The long line of trains from American occupied Monterrey moved slowly through northern Mexico and then into Arizona where they linked up with the rail lines heading to San Diego and Los Angeles. They moved slowly because not all Mexicans agreed with their new government's decision to allow the American Army access to their trains and railway system. Isolated pockets of Carranza's men still remained and, allied with small German units, disrupted the American advance by blowing up tracks. Some of the officers and men on the trains referred to the trains as long, slow targets. Others thought of worse names as they waited for the tracks to be repaired by the repairmen they'd brought with them.

Marcus Tovey had originally thought he'd remain in Mexico as part of the shrinking garrison that occupied Monterrey. The city was hostage to Mexican good intentions and, so far, the Obregon government had given every indication that it was going to obey the new rules.

It had been somewhat of a surprise when Lejeune had selected Tovey's force to accompany the First Marine Division on its journey to southern California. Lejeune had laughingly informed Tovey that he considered the Texas Ranger and his men to be worthwhile additions to his force. "You people are damned good fighters. Almost good enough to be U.S. Marines," he'd added.

Other caravans of trains were forming and several Army divisions under Pershing were almost ready to move west. It would be a long, slow process, however. Whatever was going to happen to San Francisco would be long over before any substantial American relief force from the south could get near the place.

The train lurched to a halt and the men spilled out, their rifles at the ready. In the distance they could hear the snap of rifle fire and the chatter of machine guns. Someone was taking a stand near where the right of way narrowed as it went though a canyon.

The Texas Brigade was on the fourth train, which meant it was a long ways from the action. A number of horses were in a car a few back. Tovey grabbed one and rode bareback towards the front. It felt good to be mounted. Hell, he was a Texas Ranger and belonged on a horse. He trotted forward past several long trains and hundreds of dismounting men. It was obvious that something serious was happening.

General Lejeune spotted Tovey. "Germans are to our front. Goddamned Krauts have taken over from the greasers and are blocking the road. Worse, it looks like a solid regiment. I've ordered an immediate attack."

The rail line ran through a notch bordered by rugged hills. The Germans were at the top. Their trenches were scars on the hillside and they were firing down at probing Marine units. Nothing was going to move down that rail line until the Germans were kicked out.

Tovey watched with growing dismay as lines of Marines moved toward the hastily dug-in Germans. He wanted to remind Lejeune that the Germans were a whole lot different from the Mexicans, but, hell, the general already knew that, didn't he? And what did Tovey know about fighting Krauts? The only ones he'd seen were along the Rio Grande and at a distance. The Marines really knew only one way to fight—attack. The time spent on the defensive outside San Antonio had irked them. They wanted to bring the fight to the enemy and now they were doing it.

The Americans advanced in orderly waves, but the orderliness didn't last very long. Bullets ripped through them and machine guns cut them down like wheat. Some men fell in neat rows. Tovey could almost hear sergeants and officers screaming for the men to advance, keep advancing. The only way to safety, they yelled, was to kill the Germans. German light artillery, their 75mm cannon and some light mortars, dropped shells into the Marines, causing more carnage.

The Marines stopped advancing and began to dig in, using anything to protect themselves from the scything fury of the German guns. Tovey glanced at Lejeune, who was pale with anger and frustration. He'd made a mistake and his Marines were paying for it.

He turned away. "We'll reinforce the men at night and attack again at dawn."

"It'll be a bloodbath," Tovey said. He wasn't afraid of speaking his mind to the Marine general. Hell, when the war was over, he'd go back to being a Texas Ranger, not a soldier. "General, you've read your history. It's like the Spartans at Thermopylae. They can hold us at bay until they run out of ammunition or we run out of men."

"We outnumber them," Lejeune said stubbornly.

"But not by that much. If that's a full regiment, and I think it is, that's maybe three thousand men and not three hundred like the Spartans had. We've got about twelve thousand, and not the half million the Persians had. I'll bet we lost five hundred men in today's attack and the Krauts not one tenth of that."

"How the hell do you know so much about ancient history?"

Tovey grinned. "I may be a dumb-ass Texan but I'm a dumb-ass Texan who knows how to read."

Several of Lejeune's aides had moved away, waiting for the general to explode. It didn't happen. "What do you suggest?" Lejeune asked softly.

"The Persians found a way around the Spartans and slaughtered them. That's what we have to do. Keep their heads down by shooting at them and pretending to attack and find a way around this mess."

"All right, Tovey, you've got all night to find me a way. But I still attack tomorrow. We can't stay here until the Krauts decide to let us pass."

The woman entered Tovey's tent accompanied by a lieutenant who was waved out. She was light olive-skinned and petite. There was anger in her eyes. He decided she looked more Spanish than Mexican. If it wasn't for the anger, she might be very pretty.

"Who are you?"

"My name is Martina Flores and I want to help you."

"Why?"

"To hurt the Germans who caused all this. My husband was killed by Carranza's men and I was held captive by the Germans and some American collaborators. They first took my husband and then took my pride. They kept me prisoner and their slave until I escaped and helped free some American prisoners. Then I returned here."

Tovey nodded. American collaborators? Well, he supposed it was inevitable. Someone would always kiss the ass of the new playground bully. When they were caught they would hang, but first they had to be caught. And what did she mean by taking her pride? He thought he knew and decided not to ask. And what about free American prisoners?

She looked at him eagerly. "I grew up around here and know the area. I had family on both sides of the border. I can find you a path around the Germans."

"And how do I know it isn't a trap?"

She shrugged. "I will have to go with you to show the path to you. If it's a trap, you can shoot me."

"Fair enough," Tovey said and went off to find Lejeune.

Two hours later, the column of Texans snaked its way south of the now stalled fighting and around the German lines. Dressed in men's clothing, Martina guided them along a path that was barely fit for goats. Tovey now had no doubts as to the truth of her tale.

Slowly and carefully, they marched through the night. A couple of men were injured falling down the almost mountainous terrain. Martina was exhausted but didn't complain. Once, she stumbled and he grabbed her arm to steady her and she ripped it from his grasp.

She glared at him and then softened. "I'm sorry.

You meant well. It's just that I'm not used to kindness yet."

Dawn found them approaching a compound of several dozen tents. It was a supply depot for the troops defending the hill. Wagons and trucks were parked nearby and there were some more of their damned cannon. The men in the compound were facing the hills and didn't notice the Texans approaching from the wrong direction.

On the other side of the hill, American and German artillery were dueling and they could hear rifle fire. Lejeune said he'd attack at dawn whether Tovey made it or not. Son of a bitch, Tovey thought, it was time to get moving. He noticed that Martina's eyes glowed with a near-maniacal fury.

Tovey ordered his men forward at a steady run. The Germans continued looking ahead and not behind. They didn't turn and see them until the Texans were almost on them. Screaming and howling, the Texans tore through the camp, shooting and killing as they went. Scores of Germans surrendered, while others ran in all direction.

"Up the hill," Tovey ordered. Now they would take the main German lines in the rear.

They didn't have to. Within minutes, German soldiers began to withdraw from their trenches and pour over the crest. They'd heard the fighting behind them and could see that their camp had fallen. The American Army was both in front and behind them and it was time to get the hell out of this place.

The Texans took up firing positions and now it was the Germans' turn to die. Out in the open, Tovey's men cut them down by the scores and then by the hundreds. Advancing Marines appeared over the crest line and joined in the slaughter. German soldiers began throwing down their weapons and holding their arms up high.

Tovey walked over and looked at the vaunted German soldiers. It was the first he'd seen them up close. Their field gray uniforms looked like they were good camouflage and their coal scuttle helmets looked like good protection. They appeared to be good soldiers, but not superhuman like people said they were. They bled and died like ordinary men. The ones who were trying to surrender looked terrified and some were crying, although a number looked furious. Their generals had betrayed them.

Lejeune found him. "Well done, Marcus. This is one Kraut regiment that won't pester us again." Then he shook his head sadly. "I just wish it hadn't cost us six hundred men to do it."

He found Martina staring at the carnage. The fury was gone from her eyes, now replaced by deep sadness. At first she'd wanted to accompany him on the attack and he'd threatened to use force to stop her. She'd relented and stayed behind, just not too far behind. He wanted to comfort her, but remembered how she'd recoiled from his inadvertent touch before.

"Enough killing," she said softly. She turned and put her head on his shoulder. He put his arm around her and held her as she shuddered. "Where are you going now?" she asked.

"On to southern California. We'll visit San Diego and maybe Los Angeles."

"Then I will go with you, at least part of the way. I need to see some people and make sure they're okay."

Lejeune said, "We'll be heading that way, but we'll be walking."

Tovey looked down the line. The tracks had been ripped up as far as he could see.

Was there anything more majestic than a German battleship? thought the crown prince. Given his birthright as the kaiser's heir, he'd been on a number of them, but this was his first trip to a glorious monster like the *Bayern*, the flagship of the mighty German Pacific Fleet.

The *Bayern* was truly imposing. She displaced thirty-two thousand tons and her main armament was eight fifteen-inch guns in four turrets. They were larger than anything the Americans had and only equaled by the Royal Navy's Queen Elizabeth class battleships.

Her secondary battery consisted of sixteen 5.9-inch guns and a multitude of smaller guns and a handful of torpedo turrets. She could steam eight thousand nautical miles without refueling and do so at twenty-two knots. Many cars, he thought, could not achieve that speed. She and her three sister ships, the *Baden*, *Sachsen*, and *Wurttemberg*, were the mightiest ships in the German Navy. Only the *Bayern* was off California. The others remained in Germany.

The prince carefully climbed the stairway to the deck. A stumble would not do for the imperial dignity and, despite calm seas, the massive ship was moving slightly. He was greeted by Admiral Hipper and Admiral Trotha. The ubiquitous Captain Canaris stood behind Hipper. The prince reviewed the immaculately uniformed crew and then the men retreated to Hipper's quarters for lunch, brandy, and cigars. The prince found himself wistfully thinking that it would be wonderful to have such a movable fort on land. He mentioned it to the two admirals who chuckled.

"We could build it," Hipper said cheerfully, "but how in God's name would we ever move it?"

Hipper gave an almost invisible signal and Trotha departed, leaving him alone with the prince. "Sir, I am honored that you came."

"And I am honored by the invitation. Your ship is truly marvelous."

"Indeed, sir, but neither she nor her sisters have yet accomplished a thing. I know that blockade work is essential, but it is anticlimactic, boring, and does nothing for the reputation of Germany's newest weapon, her mighty fleet."

The prince sighed. He had expected this. "I assume you wish to share in the final assault."

"Sir, our honor demands it. I have brought four minesweepers to clear the channel. All I need from you is the date and time of your attack and my fleet will blast its way into San Francisco Bay. When the Americans realize they are being assaulted by land and sea, they will panic and resistance will crumble."

"You will lose some of your ships," Wilhelm said quietly.

"As you will lose men, sir."

The prince frowned. The German Army had suffered another ten thousand casualties storming the American's second line. Intelligence said that the Yank third line was the most formidable and was where what machine guns and artillery they had were massed. He was confident he could carry it, but at what price? Anything the Navy could do to make his job less bloody would be welcomed.

There were other factors, political factors, affecting the admiral's request to be included in the fighting. Germany's reputation was that of a land power and the proud German Navy was a new and basically untried force. Worse, it hadn't accomplished much in the 1914 war and very little in this fight. Modern ships were exorbitantly expensive and the money men in Berlin were questioning the new navy's usefulness in a modern war. Hipper and the other admirals feared that their navy might be relegated to a secondary force, and they had good reason to worry. No new capital ships had been launched in three years. Wait and see was Berlin's attitude, while the generals sat back and smirked. A joint victory by the German Army and Navy would ensure that more warships joined the navy.

"And what of the American battleships, Admiral? The *Nevada* is doubtless joining her sisters, thus constituting a serious fleet in being."

To the German command's dismay, the *Nevada* had somehow been refueled and rearmed. It was presumed from smuggled supplies and another useless protest would be lodged with the British.

The *Nevada* had emerged from the night and bulled her way past the destroyers and light cruisers loosely blockading Puget Sound. One destroyer had been sunk and a cruiser damaged with no apparent harm to the *Nevada*.

"The Americans have three battleships at sea," said Hipper, "whilst we have ten. I am not concerned about them. In fact, let them come and do battle instead of attacking convoys. They are wretched cowards," he sniffed.

Hipper exuded confidence, but he couldn't quite hide his lingering doubts. Even though the American force would be smaller in numbers, it would still be quite formidable. The *Bayern* was the only German battleship with fifteen-inch guns. The others had twelve-inch batteries, with the exception of the *Nassau* and *Posen,* which only had eleven-inch main guns. The three American battleships all had fourteen-inch weapons. The *Bayern* could sink any one of them, but what if she was attacked by two or by all three?

Hipper had decided that he would keep his battleships together so the smaller American force could be overwhelmed. And why the devil hadn't the kaiser permitted at least one other of the *Bayern*'s sisters to accompany her, or even some of the lighter battlecruisers that had cost so much and accomplished so little? The majority of the German High Seas Fleet had stayed at home, left to stare at the Royal Navy.

Prudently, Hipper had ordered all convoys to remain in Cam Ranh Bay until the Americans had been destroyed.

Hipper continued. "As I understand it, sir, your attack will be with a degree of urgency. Haven't the Americans broken through in the south?"

The prince sighed. "They have, but not in great numbers and they are five hundred miles away. I made a mistake, Admiral. I assigned an inexperienced general and an inexperienced regiment to guard the southern approach as replacements for the duplicitous Mexicans. Their commander was ordered to avoid a full battle. He was told to nibble at them as they had nibbled at us in our advance northward. He was to keep between them and their target, whether it was

San Diego or the Central Valley. But no, the fool decided to make a heroic stand against a much larger American force. He lost half his men and, fortunately for him, his life. Thank God the senior surviving officer, a major named Rommel, had the presence of mind to continue destroying the railroad tracks as he and the remnants of the regiment fled north. The Yanks will be delayed for some time."

"A shame, but mistakes do happen," Hipper said. "Trotha is still cursing himself for letting the Americans escape from Puget Sound."

"War is imperfect," the prince said. "After we take San Francisco, I will detach a corps and send it south to squash the Americans before they can bring additional troops. Yes, you may join in the attack on the city. It will occur in only a few days and, yes, the idea of your ships rampaging in San Francisco Bay is intoxicating. I almost wish I could be on the bridge of the *Bayern* when you blast the Americans."

Hipper laughed. "Consider yourself invited, sir."

The prince smiled. "But understand that you may be fog bound when we do attack. You must not take unnecessary risks with the fleet."

"Trust me, sir. I will be brave, but discreet. If we cannot see the Golden Gate, we will not move. I have absolutely no intention of going down in history as the German admiral who rammed his fleet onto the California coast."

"When and where?" Ike wondered and Luke had no answer. The American lines ran about fifty miles across from just south of Santa Cruz on the Pacific coast to south of Modesto where they veered north and petered out in the foothills. Each side scouted the other to prevent an end around, but the Germans didn't seem interested in trying such a maneuver and the Americans lacked the capability to pull it off.

The German works paralleled the American's and were, on average, a mere mile away from them. There was sniping and patrolling all along the lines. Casualties were light, but this was scant comfort to those who were killed and wounded in the skirmishes. Each side was waiting. The Germans were gathering their strength and the waiting would be over very shortly.

A knock on the door to his office and a burly sergeant stuck his head in. "Got a prisoner for you, sir. General Eisenhower thinks you should talk to him."

Luke smiled and stood up. "What the general wants, the general gets."

The prisoner was under guard in a converted conference room. A pair of thuggish goons from the provost marshal's office glared down at him. They had billy-clubs in their hands and twirled them menacingly. A slight, wiry youth, scarcely out of his teens, his eyes darted around the room and at the angry Americans who looked like they wanted to kill him, which was the impression that Luke wanted them to give.

Luke sized up the situation and ordered the others out. Now he would be the good-guy interrogator. He offered the young man water and food. The boy brightened considerably.

"What's your name, son?"

"Hans, sir, Hans Kessler."

"And where are you from?"

"Sir, I was born and raised in Innsbruck."

Luke stiffened. Innsbruck was in Austria and, even

though the Austrians had declared war on the United States as dutiful allies of Imperial Germany, the act hadn't meant much. Austria was a long ways away. Or was it? Had the young Austro-Hungarian emperor, Karl I, been talked into a more active role by the belligerent and domineering kaiser?

A roast beef sandwich arrived along with a couple of cookies and a glass of Coca Cola. Kessler proceeded to devour them as if he was starving. Of course, a healthy young man like him could be desperately hungry in a matter of hours.

"What did you do before you joined the army, Hans?"

"I worked on the mountains with my father and brothers. Sometimes we taught tourists how to ski and sometimes we had to rescue the fools when they got hurt or lost." He grinned. "Sometimes the women were very grateful."

Luke laughed along with the prisoner and thought that maybe he wasn't as young or innocent as he first thought. "Along with skiing, did you do any real mountain climbing?"

Kessler rolled his eyes. "A lot, sir, and that's why I'm here. I got drafted into the Alpine Corps and then my regiment was sent here. They say we volunteered for it, but I don't remember volunteering for anything." He shrugged. "Of course, nobody in any army ever volunteers for anything."

Ike had found the prisoner's information intriguing enough to ask for an audience with the two senior military commanders.

Luke summarized the prisoner's testimony. "In short, he's a member of an elite Austrian Alpine regiment that's now in California and listed as volunteers. Their job is to probe the hills and mountains around San Francisco and gather information as well as find weak points in our defenses."

Liggett leaned forward. "And these so-called volunteers are assigned to General Hutier?"

"Yes sir, at least this man's regiment is. He didn't know of any other Austrian units in California and I believe him."

Sims was puzzled. "Why is his attachment to Hutier of such a concern?"

Liggett answered. "Hutier is an innovator. He may be a genius or a fool, depending, of course on whether or not he succeeds. He may have read of the Union General Emory Upton in the later stages of our Civil War, since his own theories mimic Upton's. In short, Hutier believes in brief, intense bombardments followed by sharp, limited attacks at weak points that have been identified by people such as those in an Alpine regiment. Perhaps they will even use poison gas. The attackers swarm through in limited fronts, bypassing strongpoints, leaving them for followup forces to destroy."

"Then Hutier's corps is going to carry out the main attack?" Sims asked.

"Not likely," Liggett answered. "There are too many logistical and geographic problems. Hutier's corps is separated by bad terrain from the rest of the Germans, which limits the forces that can be used against the city. I am confident that the main German attack will come along the east side of the bay and try to sweep north of a monumentally outnumbered and outgunned American army in San Francisco, which must then either surrender or be pounded to pieces.

"Hutier's attack, however, could be devastating if he manages to punch through to the city proper. It's a digression without much cost. We must defend against it. If it succeeds, they will have won an inexpensive victory. In theory, Hutier's tactics will work for a while, but his troops will sustain heavy casualties and run out of energy when dealing with a defense in depth. Unfortunately, the Germans are already through two of our three levels of fortification; thus, we do not really possess a defense in depth. If we are distracted by a massive assault elsewhere, Hutier may try to punch his way into the city and he may succeed."

"We need to reinforce the city, sir," said Ike.

"Easier said than done," answered Liggett. "We'd have to strip lines where we think the main attack will come. In the meantime, I am creating a floating reserve by stripping badly needed men and guns from our trenches and placing them in a position where they can reinforce the point of attack."

"Excellent," said Sims.

"Possibly," said Liggett. "The Germans will have doubtless anticipated this and will use their aerial superiority to interdict any attempt to reinforce the main army. We will use every plane we have to protect those troops moving up."

Sims nodded. *Not every plane, though,* he thought. "General Eisenhower, do you have a good idea where the attack will come?"

"Yes, Admiral," He walked to the map and pointed to an area ten miles east of the bay in the middle of General von Mackensen's army. Like Hutier, Mackensen was an exponent of sharp, limited attacks. Although seventy years old, the general was still a very competent field commander. "Our spies and the few flyovers we've managed to make indicate a major buildup in this area."

Sims was puzzled. "Far be it for me to question army tactics, General, but why not reinforce the threatened area now? Why wait until the attack begins when it is reasonably obvious that's where it will fall?"

Liggett mulled it over. Part of him hated being told his job by a damned admiral, no matter how close they'd become. But did Sims have a better idea than his? Damn. He remembered the dictum that he who defends everything winds up defending nothing. If he kept his army where it was, it would be too weak to repel a major assault. If he immediately reinforced the likely area of attack, he would strip other areas of what men and weapons they had. But then, they would be defeated anyhow. If he reinforced the area now and didn't wait for the attack, he wouldn't have to worry that much about German planes.

"We'll do it," he decided. "However, we do have men coming down by train from Seattle. When they arrive, they will immediately be sent to San Francisco. These are the men who made it across the Columbia River. It's maddening that it's taking so long for them to get here, but there is only one railroad line and virtually no other roads through the north that are useable this time of year."

"I pray they will be in time," said Sims. "But in the name of God, what about poison gas? Could the Germans be barbaric enough to introduce it?"

Poison gas had not been used by either side in the 1914 War, but the Germans had used it in Russia against the Reds. The horrific results had stunned the world and further cast the kaiser in the role of Attila the Hun.

Liggett glared. "When you consider their other atrocities, why not?"

"With respect, sirs," Luke injected, "I think it's highly unlikely they'll introduce gas. The prevailing winds are from the west-northwest, which means they'd likely blow the gas back over the German lines."

"What a pleasant thought, Luke. Are you a hundred percent certain of that?" Liggett asked.

"No sir, I'm not. There could always be exceptions. Also, I have no idea how many German casualties the kaiser's oldest son is willing to accept in order to achieve victory. Having gone this far, however, I think the Germans would be willing to accept enormous casualties to achieve their goals."

★ CHAPTER 22 ★

THE FINAL BOMBARDMENT BEGAN AT FIRST LIGHT. The shells landed on the area where Luke and Ike had predicted. Now they could only hope it wasn't a well-orchestrated feint. There was no corresponding shelling of American positions on von Hutier's front.

This time, Luke was prudently far back. Still, as before, the ground shuddered and shook. He recalled the feeling of terror he'd had just a few days earlier when the shells rained down on the bunker. Kirsten was already at the hospital and this time she would be helping with the growing influx of wounded. Letter writing and bookkeeping could come later.

"Poor bloody infantry," said a familiar voice.

"Hello Reggie, and are you supposed to be here?"

"Dashing young correspondents can dash about wherever they wish," Carville said as he dumped down a suitcase. "And I have a chit from Liggett that says so, and another one from the kaiser himself if I should happen to be picked up by those nice people from Berlin. Just don't ask how I happened to come by it."

Overhead, scores of German planes dipped and swooped like gulls skimming the sea. Only they were strafing the trenches and not looking for fish. Or were they, Luke thought. Maybe they were looking for human fish. Gotha bombers dropped their loads from height and succeeded in hitting not much at all. The explosions, however, were impressive, and must have added to the primal fear of the men underneath them.

Reggie laughed. "High-level bombing is very much a work in process."

"Thank God."

"Ah, and here comes the infantry, entering stage left."

As before, waves of Germans flowed out of their trenches and around their own barbed wire. They hadn't gone far before the American barrage opened up on them, this time with much more intensity than before. There was no longer reason to save shells or hide guns. The American front had been strengthened by troops from other areas. Luke could only hope that neither the crown prince nor General Mackensen realized that the rest of the American line was virtually defenseless.

This time concentrated machine-gun fire came from the Americans and not the Germans, and Luke exulted. Men were dying in great bloody piles, but they were Germans, not Americans.

But the Germans were coming on. More left their trenches and began the inexorable move to reinforce the first wave. Behind them, Luke made out a third wave forming and a fourth. Mackensen had done the same thing Liggett had. All of the German Army was in front of him. He felt the sickening reality that the German weight of numbers and firepower would still prevail. He got up.

"Where to now?" Reggie asked.

"Back to headquarters. Liggett will want to know about this firsthand. What are you going to do?"

Carville smiled, and Luke noticed that his eyes were cold. "Why, I believe I'll just sit here until the Germans arrive and see if any of them want to be interviewed."

Admiral Hipper received word of the main infantry attack. He angrily paced the bridge of the *Bayern*. He was frustrated. The moment of glory was at hand and all he could see was fog, damned bloody fog. He couldn't see more than a few feet in front of him. He heard one of the junior officers joking that he had just made an obscene gesture to himself and couldn't see it. He felt like strangling the little snot.

The German fleet was approximately ten miles off the coast of California and, if his navigators were any good, directly in front of the Golden Gate, the entrance to San Francisco Bay.

But he couldn't do anything. Not only because of the promise he'd made to the crown prince, but because moving towards the coast would be foolhardy, not brave. And if he managed to ground one or more of his battleships, or God help him, the whole fleet, he and the German Navy would be disgraced for all eternity.

However, he had to do something. The ship moved forward at dead slow, barely moving. The other behemoth battleships crawled slowly as well in response to his orders. They were in line abreast, which meant there was little or no danger of a rear end collision. When—if?—the damned fog lifted, they'd be in position to move quickly. That is, if the minesweepers could clear the channel in enough time.

"Oh," someone said and the ship was suddenly bathed in wonderful, miraculous sunshine. And straight in front of them was the Golden Gate. Hipper exultantly pounded his fist into the palm of his hand while others clapped and cheered. Not only had the fog lifted, but, thanks to superb navigation, he'd managed to creep close to the American shore without being seen. He laughed. Perhaps fog wasn't a bad thing after all.

"Send in the minesweepers."

Hipper gave the order and it was relayed to the small, M-class minesweepers that had all been built in the previous couple of years. The need for them hadn't existed until the Royal Navy had sown thousands of mines in the waters off Germany in the 1914 War.

The task of the sixteen-knot, 360-ton craft was doubly dangerous. First was their primary purpose—finding and removing mines so the fleet could charge through the channel to the bay. Second, they had to do this while enduring the American shore batteries at nearly point-blank range. Hipper thought all the crews of fifty men on each ship deserved medals.

"They're doomed," said Trotha from his position behind him.

Hipper didn't want to look through his binoculars at what likely to be their destruction. He simply nodded. In a few moments, the American shore batteries opened fire. Near miss shells lifted enormous amounts of water much higher than the puny sweepers as they pushed forward.

Suddenly, one of them disappeared as a shell struck it, causing it to disintegrate in a cloud of splinters and human flesh. Hipper winced and Trotha cursed. Still, the brave little ships attempted to do their duty. They were inside the channel and taking fire from two directions. Now gunfire came from a third direction, as the guns from Alcatraz Island joined in. A second minesweeper was hit, and then a third was turned into a flaming ruin. All the batteries focused on the remaining one. A message blinked from a signal light. *Her radio must be gone,* Hipper thought. A shell struck her and she too began to sink. The American guns ceased fire. All four brave ships were destroyed, but had they succeeded?

He translated the Morse code from the last mine sweeper—No mines. "Damn them to hell," Hipper raged. No mines. He had sacrificed four ships and two hundred men for nothing.

But had he? They now knew exactly where the American guns were located and how big they were. This would help immeasurably when he sent in his battleships.

Trotha was reading his mind, "When, Admiral?"

It was nearly noon. Hipper made up his mind quickly. "Now."

Luke found Patton and his huge metal creatures a few miles from where the Germans were attacking. They were in a large grove of trees and hidden from sight. The thunder of battle, however, was loud and clear. With others around, he kept it formal and saluted.

"Change of plans, General."

Patton poked his head out from the turret of his command tank. He was grease-covered and filthy, a long way from the officer who was so punctilious about his uniform.

"What the hell are you talking about, Acting Major Martel? I'm ready to launch a counterattack in a matter of moments, and it's all based on the fact that the intelligence you and Ike gave me is proving accurate. You have noticed the firing off to the west, haven't you?"

"I have indeed, Acting General Patton, and that's the concern."

"The hell with anybody's concerns," Patton snapped. "When the Germans are tied up in our trenches I'm going to hit their flank and roll them up. We're gonna go through them like shit through a goose."

Luke shook his head. "Harbord wants your tanks behind our lines as a means of blunting their attack."

Patton turned red. "Bullshit. Not only is that bad tactics but it's damned near impossible as well. Using tanks like that would be a waste of their potential. They'd get ground up in a fight and destroyed. No, we use them as planned."

Luke glanced around and whispered. "Harbord's given orders, George."

"Look about and what do you see?"

Luke did as told. "George, I see scores of tanks and what look like armored trucks hidden under tarps and covered with branches. I also don't seem them being attacked by any German planes. Good job, George."

"Damned straight it's a good job. I've assembled all fifty tanks and more than a hundred lightly armored trucks with machine guns to follow up the tanks when we attack. It's taken me more than a week to bring them here without anybody noticing and camouflage them from the German planes, which, if you and General Harbord haven't noticed, rule the skies. If I even attempt to move them where Harbord wants them, every German plane they have will attack them. At least most of the tanks should make it through a strafing, but the trucks will be slaughtered. Their side armor isn't that thick and they have nothing on top. In short, nearly half my force won't make it to where Harbord thinks he wants them.

"And one other thing, Major Martel, even if the tanks did make it, it won't be today. I just can't pick them up and change their direction like that. They aren't fucking chess pieces and Harbord knows that."

Luke was of the opinion that Patton was trying to blow smoke up his ass regarding the time necessary to move his outfit—that was typical Patton. But the man did have good points. Tanks were radical new weapons and certainly not designed to slug it out in the trenches. Striking the German flank and rear, like cavalry of old, did seem like the logical way of using them. He decided to change the subject a little.

"George, what are those things draped on the tanks?"

Patton grinned happily, "Another one of my brilliant ideas. Those are heavy rope cables and I got them in Seattle. It occurred to me that the wheels and tracks of the tanks and trucks were the most vulnerable, so I've draped woven ropes where they're most needed. The ropes are lightweight and bulletproof."

Luke wondered just what the hell else was going on in Patton's fertile mind. "George, when are you attacking?"

"In an hour or so."

Luke rolled his eyes and looked skyward. No German planes were in sight. He made his decision. "I suggest you make it sooner, George, and I never found you."

★ ★ ★

Once upon a time, Tim Randall thought trees were beautiful and loved to spend as much time as he could in a park or in the country. Not now. Everywhere he looked in Washington, Oregon, and northern California there were trees. The Pacific coast states were nothing but one long pine forest, and a snow-covered pine forest at that.

What he'd naively proclaimed would take only a couple of days had taken more than a week and they still hadn't arrived at their destination. Everyone grudgingly admitted that they were closing in on San Francisco, but you couldn't tell it by looking out a window. The troops saw nothing but snow-covered trees.

Nor had the trip been totally safe. Stuffed as they were in boxcars, many soldiers came down with colds that devolved into pneumonia. Always present was the fear that influenza would again rear its ugly head. Their company commander was in a hospital a couple of hundred miles to their north, which meant that Lieutenant Taylor was now the CO and Sergeant Tim Randall now ran the platoon. Christ, Tim thought, next thing, they'd make him an officer. Would that be such a bad thing? His family would be proud, sort of. The latest letters he'd received still bitterly held him responsible for Wally's death. He'd pretty well decided he wasn't going back to Camden. He couldn't bring himself to hate his parents, but he'd be damned if he would let their bitterness dominate his life. He hadn't put a gun to Wally's head and forced him to enlist. No, Wally had been an adult and had volunteered. Wally had been as insistent as Tim that they join the Army. Who the hell knew a bug would kill him?

At least the letters he continued to get from Kathy

Fenton were uplifting. After a rocky beginning, the two of them were getting to know each other pretty well as a result of their correspondence. He'd told her he wasn't returning to Camden and implied that she should join him wherever he landed and she'd seemed intrigued. First, of course, there was the little matter of the war.

He yawned. General MacArthur had done a great job of getting them headed south. Tim was actually on the first train. Scores of other trains were coming along behind him, sooner or later. More than fifty thousand men were en route to San Francisco, which, according to MacArthur's frequent bulletins and announcements, desperately needed them.

One of his men looked out the cracked door of the boxcar. They were fairly warm and out of the wind as long as it was closed, and by now they were used to sleeping on either the hard ground or the hard wooden floor of the boxcar. At least it wasn't snowing inside. He seemed to recall reading that California was sunny and bright, but obviously the author of that epistle had been terribly misinformed.

The train began to slow. Damn, another stop. They'd get out, stretch their legs, piss, and wait to get started up again. At least pissing while standing on the ground was better than aiming a stream through one of the many cracks in the floor while the train was moving. Like little kids, some of the guys had made a contest of it.

"Everybody out and take all your shit!"

They didn't know who said it, but they all complied. They wondered what the hell was happening now. They formed up and walked forward and past the engine. They paused and stared. A large body of water lay before them and a couple of miles beyond that was a city. South of the city, greasy black smoke rose skyward and now they could just hear the sounds of artillery.

They had reached San Francisco, or, more precisely, Oakland, California. Oakland had once been the western terminus of the Transcontinental Railroad. Originally, ferries were used to ship railroad cars across to San Francisco, but now it was the hub from which other lines led, including the Dumbarton Railroad Bridge at the southern end of the bay. However, the Dumbarton Bridge, which ran into the southern part of the peninsula, had been damaged by German shelling. Realization that the fighting they'd seen in Texas would be as nothing in comparison with the hell the Germans were serving up was beginning to sink in.

Lieutenant Taylor came up. "Well, weren't you anxious to get to California? Now what do you think?"

"I remember an old phrase, sir—be careful what you wish for, it might come true."

General Lejeune was angry. His face was flush with barely restrained fury. "Tell me again, young lady, precisely what has happened in this little town, Raleigh."

Martina Flores was not intimidated by the general's glare. She repeated what she knew. Maybe two hundred Americans had been held prisoner in Raleigh. They had been starved, beaten, tortured, and, in a couple of cases, executed by a German named Steiner and aided by an American collaborator named Olson. No, she corrected herself, the Americans had not been executed, they'd been murdered. She added that

American civilians had also died at the hands of the Germans and American collaborators.

When she'd fled from the fighting that had liberated the prisoners and after killing Olson, she'd found a horse and ridden wildly away from the scene. It had been an act of mindless relief and terror and, when she'd finally stopped running, she'd then wondered how and if she could bring help to the prisoners. Granted, they'd been freed by Dubbins and Montoya and the Apache with the ridiculous name, but how long could they remain at large and safe in a land dominated by Germany? For all she knew, Steiner was hunting them down like animals.

Thus, when she'd given it some thought, she'd decided to head east and try to find the Americans who were heading towards California.

"I cannot believe an American like this Olson character would do anything so base and vile," Lejeune snarled. "The bastard is up there with Benedict Arnold and John Wilkes Booth."

Oh, she thought, *you have no idea how base and vile Olson was.* She thought of the humiliation she'd endured while kneeling between his thighs and servicing him. Or the times he lay upon her, his bulk crushing her, while he forced himself into her while she tried not to cry out in pain and shame. And all the time she knew that he hated her because she was Mexican, or that she wasn't some American woman who'd scorned him.

"And what happened to this Olson?" Lejeune asked.

"Last time I saw him, he was lying on the ground and probably bleeding to death."

"And why was that?" Lejeune asked.

"Because I stabbed him in the gut," she answered calmly.

Marcus Tovey kept his face expressionless. Last night, she had told him the story of her abuse at Olson's hands. She had shaken and sobbed almost hysterically as she'd purged herself of the terrible memories. He'd held her until her quivering subsided and she'd fallen asleep against his shoulder. When she awoke, she'd begged forgiveness for what she called her sins and he told her he didn't see any sin on her part. She'd been forced to do what she did, and the true sinners were Steiner and Olson. The American collaborator had paid a terrible and just price for his sins, while Steiner remained at large.

Martina trusted him and he liked that. There were only a few Mexicans he thought highly of, and she was on the list. He reminded himself never to piss her off in the future, if they ever had a future.

"General, I do have an idea," said Tovey.

"You always do, but do I have to remind you that we are moving very slowly because some German officer has gathered up the remnants of that regiment and they are fighting a masterful retreat."

The name of the German leader, Erwin Rommel, had come from a prisoner. This Rommel had organized several hundred men into a unit and, while some tore up the tracks, others harassed the Americans and slowed their advance. As a result of constant skirmishing, Rommel now likely had fewer than a hundred men, but he was still doing damage and moving just fast enough to keep the rest of his men out of their way.

Tovey began to pace. "General, if the objective is Raleigh and the freed prisoners, give me a cavalry unit and we'll bypass the tracks and the Krauts. From what other prisoners have said, there's nobody between us and Raleigh or even San Diego."

"How many of my Marines do you want?"

Tovey laughed. "Not a damn one, unless they're really good horsemen, and I kind of doubt any are."

Lejeune agreed reluctantly. "Most of my Marines don't know which end of a horse goes first."

"General, give me all the horses we have and I'll mount up as many of my Texans as we have horses, and we'll go to Raleigh."

Lejeune nodded. "All of my horses? That means I'll have to give you my personal horse and that beast has carried my butt for several years."

Martina smiled. "I'll ride him and take good care of him."

"You're going too?" Lejeune asked. He was not surprised.

She shrugged. "Like here, it's my territory. I can take Marcus where we need to go."

Lejeune smiled to himself. "Very well, but as to my horse, you will not ride him and or take good care of him."

Martina was puzzled, "Why not?"

Lejeune grinned wickedly. "Because Daisy's not a him."

The shells were indiscriminate. Even though the hospital was clearly marked with red crosses, mistakes were made. Kirsten hoped they were mistakes. She had a hard time believing that the kaiser's army would be so base and cruel as to intentionally shell medical facilities. Luke didn't share her beliefs. He felt that the

Germans were capable of almost anything. He'd read of their atrocities in Belgium and northern France in 1914–15, and in Africa a decade earlier. Luke had told her that the cousin of one of the German admirals, von Trotha, had been instrumental in the massacre of thousands of helpless Herero tribesmen. If monsters like the von Trothas were to be victorious, she thought, God help the people of California.

The German fleet was probing the Golden Gate, the channel to San Francisco Bay, and both sides were lobbing shells at each other. One struck the hospital, sending scores of already badly mangled young men to an even more badly mangled death. Kirsten helped pick up the bodies, and the pieces of bodies. This, she realized, is what it must be like at the heart of the battle now raging a few miles to the south and east.

She felt worse when someone told her the shell that struck the hospital had come from an American battery on the north side of the channel. Doctor Rossini had simply shrugged and told her things like that happen. "You shoot an arrow in the air and who knows where it comes down. The same thing applies to rifle and cannon fire."

The wounded were coming in droves. The battle for the third line of defense was intense. It looked, however, that the American lines were holding, at least for a while. *Good,* she thought, *make the German bastards pay.*

To take her mind off the horrors around her, she tried to think of her home and the town of Raleigh. Would she ever go back there? Likely not, she decided. If she and Luke survived this, and if the United States prevailed, she and he would make their homes closer to San Francisco and either farm or grow vines and make wine.

Then she thought ruefully that she'd spoken two very big ifs.

"Mr. Griffith, just how many cameramen do you have available?" Elise asked coolly.

"At the moment four, my dear young lady. Why, do you have uses for them?"

"Where do you have them?"

"One is in the trenches where the attacks are taking place. I am so proud of our American boys who are holding up the Germans."

So far, she thought.

"And I was instructed to have another with a young officer named Patton, while two others are watching the German fleet."

"Mr. Griffith, I am about to let you in on at least one military secret. The German fleet is going to force the channel and wind up in San Francisco Bay. Therefore I would suggest you have at least one of your men on the Oakland side to watch what is going to happen when they begin to duel with our other guns."

"And what will happen, Elise?"

She smiled grimly. "Admiral Sims wishes to destroy them all. It is something called Firefly."

Captain Horst Richter urged his men forward, "Hurry, you ugly sons of bitches! Move or they'll kill you."

The Alpine troops, the Austrian "volunteers," had done a marvelous job of picking a path through the American wire and other defenses. Now it was time for the shock troops, the spearpoint of Hutier's attack on San Francisco, to make their move.

According to plan, the artillery barrage had been short and intense, just enough to keep the Americans' heads down. When it lifted, the first line of his shock troops were within a hundred yards of the American trenches and through the wire that had been cut the night before by the Austrians. Up and over, the Germans went, screaming like wild men, shooting and stabbing at anything that moved. In the face of such ferocity, American resistance wavered and soldiers fell back. Some gathered themselves and tried to retake ground seized by the Germans. The fighting was bloody and intense.

Richter shot an American defender in the face with his Luger. "Forward!" he screamed. "Keep moving forward. Leave them for the follow-up troops."

In the heat of battle, most of his exhortations were lost and he had to physically grab men, sending them out of this trench and onward to others. The breach made was small, and others would widen it. A German fell dead beside him. The Americans were recovering and fighting back. *Too late,* he exulted. He waved his men forward.

Richter and a score of his fighters emerged from the American trenches. Some astonished rear-echelon soldiers either ran or tried to surrender. Richter ignored them. His little band pressed forward. He looked behind and saw more coal-scuttle helmets and soldiers in field gray. He laughed. They were through. Hutier's tactics were working.

He paused and looked forward. In the distance he could not yet see downtown San Francisco, but buildings and houses were in plain view. More important, there was no sign of any further American defenses. They were through and before him lay the city of San Francisco. Richter knew he had to wait, if only a little while. Twenty men would not take the city. Nor could a few hundred. Others were joining him as the breach was widened, but it would be a while before he had an attack force. He laughed as he saw that Hutier was joining them. The old general was out of shape and breathing heavily. His once immaculate uniform was filthy, but he was grinning happily.

"Excellent work, Richter. You will be promoted and given a medal."

"Thank you, sir, but it was all your idea. The men really executed it."

"No modesty, please. Now, let us gather a force and head to San Francisco. Great God, we have waited so long for this. With a little bit of luck, we will have supper in the officers' club at their Presidio. Perhaps General Liggett will join us, eh?"

Richter grinned impishly. "Perhaps we can serve him humble pie."

★ CHAPTER 23 ★

ADMIRAL HIPPER WAS NOT A COWARD, SO IT GALLED him to place his flagship, the mighty *Bayern*, fifth in the line of ships steaming towards the Golden Gate and the confines of San Francisco Bay. It galled him, but it was necessary. The American shore batteries would be strong and deadly as the ships passed through the narrow confines of the curiously named Golden Gate.

The *Nassau* and *Posen* would lead. They were older and had smaller guns than the other ships. They would be the sacrificial lambs or "forlorn hopes" whose job was to duel with the shore batteries and destroy them. If they were sunk or damaged, so be it. It would be a bitter price, but far less than losing the *Bayern*. All ten German battleships were present, but Hipper had to keep in mind the fact that there were three American battleships loose in the Pacific. He would need the *Bayern*'s fifteen-inch guns if they should show up.

Equally perturbing was the fact that the British squadron under Beatty had also left Puget Sound. It was presumed that they were en route to their base at Hong Kong, but then came the word that a second large British detachment had sailed from Hong Kong and was on its way God only knew where. A rendezvous with Beatty? If so, why?

The remaining German ships off Puget Sound had gotten a measure of revenge. With all the capital ships gone and her forts without guns, a handful of cruisers and destroyers had entered the sound and bombarded Seattle's waterfront, causing extensive damage and large fires. Explosions were noted by the German captains and they could only have been ammunition stored for shipment south to the Americans in San Francisco.

Gunfire brought his attention back to reality. The *Posen* and *Nassau* had begun dueling with the Yank guns as they advanced. Splashes near the warships lifted water high and the Germans were able to estimate their weight. Twelve-inch and eight-inch guns were the largest and there were more of the sixes, especially firing down from Alcatraz Island.

The spacing between ships was greater than he would have liked, but he was acutely aware that his lead ships might be hit and disabled, and a ship dead in the water was a collision danger. His ships needed room to maneuver.

The *Nassau* was already burning. He swore and pounded his fist on the railing of the bridge. "It cannot be helped, sir," Canaris said. Hipper was not comforted. Those were good German sailors dying on the battleship.

Still, she was steaming forward, although at a much

slower speed and the *Posen* was already almost through the channel. Now the other, larger ships, including the *Bayern*, entered the fray. The thunder of the other ships' great guns shook the *Bayern* even though she was a mile away. The American batteries continued to fire, but there were fewer guns and their rate of fire was much slower.

It was suggested that everyone don earplugs and the men complied. A moment later and the *Bayern*'s guns joined the others. Despite the earplugs, the sound was deafening. The shock wave almost knocked them over. The firing from the shore ceased. Hipper exulted. In moments they would be in the bay.

A shell struck the hull of the *Bayern*, just beneath the bridge. Hipper and others were thrown to the deck, and there were screams from the wounded. Not *all* the American guns had been silenced, Hipper thought bitterly.

The damage report came quickly. The damage was negligible. The *Bayern*'s armor was almost fourteen inches thick. The Americans had nothing on shore that could penetrate it.

As they entered the bay and began to circle, the American guns facing the inner bay opened up. Again, no surprise. Spies in the city had reported on their position and the German warships quickly pulverized them.

Canaris grabbed his arm. "Sir," he said and gestured. The *Nassau* was burning from stem to stern and the *Posen* was listing to port and sinking. Hipper cursed the Americans and he silently cursed the kaiser who had sent him only one of the four mighty fifteen-gun ships. Why hadn't he sent at least one of the *Bayern*'s sisters and left the old ships like the *Nassau* and *Posen* back in Germany?

The German Navy had paid a heavy price, but they were in San Francisco Bay. The city's waterfront was burning. Could surrender be far behind? If the army had accomplished half what it had intended to do, the Americans would come crawling as they realized that their position in San Francisco was utterly untenable.

Better, the future of the German Navy would be golden.

Josh Cornell and the rest of the joint Army-Navy headquarters staff could only stare helplessly as the German warships bulled their way through the channel and into San Francisco Bay.

So much for our well-laid plans, he thought bitterly. All the digging of fortifications and the dragging of guns through the city had been for naught. The German warships had pounded the American works to dust. Yes, they had badly damaged, perhaps sunk, at least two of the enemy ships, and others had been hurt to varying degrees, but the remainder were now safely ensconced in the bay.

"Will we surrender?"

The question came from a Hearst reporter who had managed to attach himself to the group. Both Liggett and Sims glared at him. "Hell no," Sims said. "I have not yet begun to fight."

Liggett shook his head sadly, "Not very original but my sentiments exactly." He spotted Cornell. "Is Firefly ready to commence?"

Josh looked at the sky. It was cloudy and gloomy. Twilight would arrive fairly soon. "In a short while, sir."

A very young Army private ran up. He was filthy and out of breath. He looked at both Sims and Liggett in confusion. He'd doubtless never seen an admiral or a general and now he had both to contend with.

"Report to me, son," Liggett said gently.

The private took a deep breath. "General Bullard's respects, sir, but the Krauts have broken through and are only a couple of miles away."

Joe Flowers and Tomas Montoya had taken the freed American prisoners under their wing. They now had another hundred and fifty mouths to feed and shelter. Fortunately, the Germans had squirreled away enough foodstuffs to solve that problem for the foreseeable future. The Germans had also left enough clothing to cover the raggedy prisoners although a few grumbled at having to wear portions of German uniforms. When asked if they preferred going naked, they stopped complaining, although they took steps to ensure they didn't look too much like German soldiers.

They had rifles and ammunition enough, again thanks to the German stockpiles, but what they didn't have was real numbers or a destination. With potentially angry Mexicans to the south and definitely angry Germans to the north, there was no safe place to go. The decision was made to stay put and hope for a rescue, while evading German patrols.

That the Germans were interested in what was going on in Raleigh was obvious. Small patrols from San Diego scouted the area routinely, but were kept away with only minor skirmishing. Dubbins had been killed in one such fight. Nobody mourned him. Without vengeance as a motive, he'd taken to stealing things from the other Americans.

No major German force had yet shown up, but they felt it was only a matter of time. To forestall this, they had taken to the hills. It meant sleeping in tents or out of doors, but it might ensure safety. Captain Barnes and his men moved about a mile away and out of sight.

Flowers and Montoya had chosen what they felt was a good defensive position facing west toward German-occupied San Diego. They were on a hill and in the distance they could see the abandoned prison camp. They both were shocked and angry when they suddenly realized that a large force of mounted men had just been spotted approaching from the east. Although too distant to make out specifics, it was clearly a military outfit, but whose? They didn't ride in a crisp formation like the Germans. They were more like a gaggle of geese, like the Mexicans. Only, they didn't seem to be Mexicans. At least Flowers and Montoya were out of sight. With some irony, they were in the rabbit holes made by the late and unlamented Dubbins when he was spying on the camp.

"I think we've been outflanked, Joe." Montoya said with dismay in his voice. Only his men and a handful of others were mounted. The freed prisoners were half-trained infantry at best, and men who had not yet regained their full physical strength. If they had to run for it, they'd be caught in a short while and slaughtered.

"Maybe," Flowers said, "and maybe not."

"Please make sense," Montoya snapped. Even though

the two men still had feelings of ethnic enmity, they'd established a working truce. It was either that or chaos.

They were joined in the hole by Barnes. Below them, the mounted men fanned out and moved easily through the ruins of Raleigh and what had been the American's prison. They stopped in the center of town where a naked flagpole stood. They watched intently as two men attached a flag and ran it up. The wind snapped it.

"Jesus Christ," gasped Flowers. His eyes were better and he had the binoculars.

"What?" chorused Rice and Montoya.

"It's the stars and stripes. They're ours."

A few minutes later, the two groups had united with much cheering and backslapping. As the ranking officer, Tovey took charge and the others were happy to let him do it. He quickly sent a patrol west to make sure nothing was coming from that direction. As he did, a thought was forming.

Barnes again pumped his hand. "I gotta ask, General, how did you know we were here?"

"Thank her," he said, pointing to where Martina Flores sat on her horse. She took off her wide brimmed hat and waved shyly.

"Holy hell," yelled Barnes, "Tina came back. Now's she's saved us twice!"

With that, dozens of cheering former prisoners surrounded Martina and lifted her off her equally startled horse. Sitting her on Barnes' shoulders, they began parading her around while chanting "Tee-nah! Tee-nah!"

At first confused, she broke into a wide smile

and then happily waved her arms as tears began to stream down her cheeks. Tovey watched in satisfaction as more of her tormented past was purged. After a few moments they put her on the ground where she hugged and kissed a number of them, especially a young man named Sullivan who, Tovey was told, had been her contact with the prisoners.

Finally, she stood beside Tovey and discreetly took his hand, establishing ground rules that very much pleased Tovey.

"Gentlemen and lady," Tovey announced. "I have it on good authority that a full U.S. division is about a half day behind us under a nasty Marine general named Lejeune, and that other units are right on his tail. He has wiped out some Krauts who were delaying him and now is riding the rails and making good speed. Therefore, I have a proposal. How many of you want to stay here and wait for him?"

"What's your other choice?" asked Montoya.

"Simple. I don't think there's much of anything between us and San Diego but hills. You men can do as you see fit, but I've always wanted to see San Diego."

Tim Randall was part of a confused mass of armed humanity trying to push and shove its way onto ferries. "Tickets, please," someone yelled in a mock falsetto and the response was a chorus of obscenities.

Tim, Lieutenant Taylor, and the rest of the company were in the bow of the large, stubby ship. It had been designed to carry railroad cars, not men, and it had no accommodations for them. This was a mixed blessing as they were exposed to the weather, which was calm and clear for the moment, but did give them a view of what they were about to do. The lack of cover also meant that any German plane could see what they were up to and possibly strafe them. Tim hoped that all the German planes were occupied supporting their army.

Packed elbow to elbow with soldiers, the ferry cast off and slowly churned the water of San Francisco Bay. "I get seasick," said the same voice that cried out for tickets. "I'm going to puke." It was followed by more obscenities.

"My God," said Taylor, "look where we are again."

Douglas MacArthur was in the small cabin, standing behind the captain, and only about fifteen feet away.

"Maybe we really are his lucky charm," Tim said.

But just how lucky were they, he wondered. They could hear explosions in all directions. Most disconcerting was the fact that there was fighting in the Golden Gate channel. Tim envisioned German warships pouring through while the totally unarmed ferry was still in the bay.

Taylor had heard a messenger explain that MacArthur's division was to go directly to the city as an unexpectedly heavy attack on it had been launched by some German general named "Hooter."

The remaining two divisions that were coming behind them would fill in the trenches to the east of the city and where a major attack by the whole German Army was taking place. MacArthur had commented that the decision to send his men over was the right one. If the city fell to General von Hutier, as MacArthur corrected the pronunciation, then there was no point in continuing the fighting elsewhere.

About halfway across the bay, Tim saw in horror that a German battleship was emerging through the channel. It was burning and the men cheered. A moment later, they stopped as one of the guns in her secondary battery opened fire on the flotilla of ferries. More guns fired from the burning ship and shells began to land around them. The captain of the ferry announced that he was turning back.

"The hell you are," snarled MacArthur, "keep on towards shore. Forget about Fisherman's Wharf. It's too dangerous."

"So's going on ahead," whined the captain. "I'm turning back before you get us all killed. I'm captain of this goddamn ship and what I say goes."

MacArthur pulled his .45 automatic, cocked it, and placed it against the ferryman's head. "If you don't go on, I will shoot and kill you and your ship will have a dead captain. I've killed before and shooting one more sniveling coward won't matter. If you go on, you at least have a chance at living."

Another shell landed near them, showering them all with water. The captain moaned but the ferry kept on.

An explosion rocked and shook them. A shell had struck another ferry a hundred yards to their right. Men and parts of men were flying through the air while hundreds of soldiers fell into the water. Others jumped in order to flee the sinking craft.

An aide stared in horror. "General, do we stop and save them?"

MacArthur's face showed intense emotional pain. "No. Our duty is to land these men. Then our brave captain here can retrieve the survivors on his way back."

A few moments later the first of the remaining

ferries hit the docks. Ropes quickly anchored them and officers yelled for the men to get off. They needed no urging. A second German warship had emerged and, although this one too was damaged, it still had working guns.

Men fell into the water and were helped out by comrades. There was chaos as several thousand soldiers disembarked from ferries that landed wherever they could. Units were mixed and any sense of cohesion was lost. Tim saw an officer pushing his way through the throng towards MacArthur.

"General," Luke said as he saluted. He had just arrived from Oakland on an earlier ship and reported to Liggett. "I'm Major Martel from General Liggett's staff. Your men are needed urgently. The Krauts have broken through and are advancing past the Laguna de la Merced and will be crossing Ocean Avenue. After that they've got a straight shot to the Presidio."

MacArthur glared at him. "Martel, I have absolutely no idea where the devil those places are. May I assume you can lead us to where General Liggett wants us?"

"Yes sir. You are needed in great haste."

"Then lead on. We will follow you." To the men around him, he ordered, "Everybody after me! Don't even think of trying to find your units. Just come."

The army surged from the waterfront. When MacArthur felt the men had all cleared the docks, he turned and hollered, "Double time, men, double time. We have Germans to kill."

Both the crown prince and General Mackensen were frustrated. Two waves of infantry had moved along a narrow front designed to punch their way through the American lines. It hadn't yet happened. Twenty thousand men were hung up in the American lines and fighting the Yanks tooth and nail. It was clear that American intelligence had divined exactly where the attack would fall and that the Americans had reinforced that area.

It was also evident that more American defenders were coming down the rail line from Seattle and were beginning to enter the fighting. German planes attempted to strafe them, but American machine guns and the handful of fighters they owned had disrupted this. Gothas had tried to bomb the railway and only confirmed again that it was difficult for them to hit a small target with any degree of accuracy.

This day would be critical. There had been word that Hutier's men might have broken through, in which case the city would fall to Germany without a need to defeat the Americans in front of them. Word had also reached them that the fleet was in the bay. Victory was almost theirs.

Almost, however, was not quite success. The tide could turn against Germany in a hurry. They had to win here as well as in the city to ensure victory. Nothing could be left to chance.

To further complicate matters, word had been received that a large American force had emerged far in their rear and was threatening San Diego. Even though San Diego was hundreds of miles away, it was a solemn reminder that the United States could field a large army if given enough time. The stubborn defense of San Francisco was also a case in point. Time was running out for the German invasion force. Although the danger was far from immediate, the Americans were getting stronger. He had to finish off the defenders of San Francisco and then send a sufficient force south towards San Diego to defeat the new threat.

"San Francisco must fall today," the prince said.

"Our men are exhausted," said Mackensen. "They have marched and fought their way up California almost without letup. Granted, the American defenders were less than splendid, but the army is almost worn out."

"Almost, General, but they still have one good fight in them, perhaps more. Still, I am not going to squander our limited resources in a meatgrinder operation. No, the two other waves ready to attack will do so immediately, but not into the current arena of fighting. They will swing to our right and attack just to the east of the current fighting. The American lines are denuded of manpower there and will crumble. The American defenders are frozen into place and your two waves will roll through them and catch them in a giant claw."

Mackensen was clearly unhappy. "If we attack as you suggest, there will be confusion as units get mixed up."

The prince stood stiffly. "I did not make a suggestion, General Mackensen. It was an order and yes, I do understand that problems will ensue. However, they cannot be any larger than losing more men and the attack bogging down where we are."

Mackensen came to attention. "Yes, Majesty."

The old general would do his utmost, although he was wondering just why he'd agreed to come out of a well-deserved retirement. He was going to ask the prince if he knew anything about the strange goings-on in the area of the new attack, but decided against further aggravating a clearly frustrated crown prince.

Besides, when the attack succeeded as it would, he would find out firsthand what the Yanks were up to.

George Patton stared in disbelief. It looked as if the entire German Army was coming out of its trenches and awkwardly turning in his direction, their neat formations disintegrating into what resembled a horde. What the hell were they doing? Had they all decided to attack him? That was a crazy thought. They had no idea his force was in front of them. He laughed. No, they had just handed him a grand opportunity.

Patton turned and faced the dozen officers and men who were watching him expectantly. Rank in a mechanized outfit had a way of becoming blurred as men became filthy with dirt and grease. It annoyed the normally immaculate Patton that he again looked like a bum.

He raised a riding crop and yelled, "To your steeds, men. The U.S. Army's first armored mechanized regiment, or whatever the hell they're going to call us, is going to roll! Mount up."

Moments later, fifty formerly British tanks emerged and crossed the American trenches. On their hulls was proudly painted the letters "U.S.A." and in red, white, and blue respectively. Behind the tanks came close to a hundred armored trucks, each with four light machine guns. Armored trucks had performed poorly for the Germans, but Patton thought they might do better in support of the larger armored vehicles.

A smart-boy engineer had concluded that bullets were more likely to bounce off the trucks' thin metal plating if the armor was slanted, and damned if tests hadn't proven the young man right. Of course, tests and combat were hugely different stories. Somebody else had determined that both truck tires and tank treads could be protected a little by hanging woven cables alongside the vehicles. *Now we'll see how it works in the real world,* he thought.

Patton was jammed into a modified tank that served as his command vehicle. No way was he going to miss out on the first great attack by tanks in warfare. He only hoped it wouldn't be the last. His real concerns, however, were the propensity of the beasts to break down and the real difficulty of directing the operation once fighting began. The vehicles would be buttoned up so crews wouldn't be killed by shrapnel or bullets, which meant that commanders and drivers couldn't communicate. Wireless radios had been suggested, but they were too cumbersome and fragile for today's battle. It was something to think about for the future.

The host of German infantry was directly in front of them and only a few hundred yards off. The Germans halted as the metal apparitions lumbered closer. The noise of the tanks' engines drowned out all but the sound of bullets hitting like small hailstones pattering harmlessly off the tanks' hulls.

As one, the American guns returned fire, with hundreds, then thousands, of bullets ripping through the massed German ranks. Dead and wounded fell in rows as the tanks moved forward at a sedate ten miles an hour. They could go faster, but why strain the engines or take a chance on bad terrain damaging them? The armored trucks drew alongside the tanks and their guns added to the slaughter.

As they neared the Germans, individual faces, their mouths wide with shock, anger, and terror grew plain.

Peering through a firing slit, Patton exulted. "You bastards are going to die. How do you like war now, you Kraut sons of bitches?"

When the tanks were less than a hundred yards away, the Germans began to pull back. Their sergeants and officers tried to maintain discipline, but it didn't help, as they were cut down with the rest. The American machine guns indiscriminately killed everything in front of them.

The slow retreat disintegrated, becoming first a fast walk, and then a run as the proud German Army fell back in utter disarray. Confused and terrified, soldiers threw away their rifles and packs, and then their helmets. Patton had never seen such a glorious sight. The armored advance continued and he felt the sickening crunch of tank treads grinding over the bodies of the dead and dying. The tank's engine was not always loud enough to drown out the screams of those being squashed.

Some brave Germans tried to jump on the tanks and fight their way in. A grenade exploding inside a tank would have been catastrophic. This was when the trucks earned their pay. Their light Browning Automatic Rifles swept enemy soldiers from the tanks' hulls before the Germans could open the hatches and drop in a potato masher grenade. Finally, there were no Germans standing, although a number were crawling and limping away.

Patton paused and opened the hatch. Signalling wildly, he finally got the attention of most of his commanders. He counted noses. Thirty-eight of his mighty beasts remained. He presumed most of the missing had mechanical problems. Better, almost all of the trucks were still with him. The ropes and the slanted armor appeared to have worked.

What to do now? he pondered. The German attack was broken, but there were still many other Germans attacking the American trenches. He could turn to the right and his tanks could attack the German rear and get them between the proverbial rock and the hard place.

Or they could go left and slice into the main German Army's rear and continue pushing the Krauts backward. A German artillery shell landed nearby and reminded him that one thing he couldn't do was stay where he was.

Right or left, that was the question. Patton was confident that the fighting to his right would break up. American reinforcements were arriving and he intuitively felt that the German high-water mark had been reached. He could already see men leaving the German forward positions and running back across the corpse-littered field.

"Left," he ordered, and then because it seemed so appropriate, "Charge!"

Not since the days of antiquity could a general see the entire battlefield. Neither the crown prince nor General Mackensen saw anything other than what was directly in front of them. Their position had been predicated on observing the massive, four-division attack on the American trenches and the decision to switch the focus of the fighting left them with nothing in view.

The two divisions that made up their reserves had marched out, veered right, and disappeared. The sounds of fighting came from both the front and the right. The prince and the general could do nothing but worry while maintaining a facade of aloof indifference. No thought was given to moving the headquarters. That would have taken too much time. The telephone and telegraph lines ended here.

An operator took a call. He turned to the two men, shock on his face. "Sir," he said to the prince, "there is a report that our men are being attacked by metal monsters that are impervious to bullets and shells."

"Rubbish," snapped Mackensen. "Call other units and find out what the devil is going on." He laughed nervously. "Has someone gotten drunk in the middle of a battle? Monsters? What next?"

The operator did as directed. Moments later, he clarified his report. "Sir, armored vehicles of a strange type along with armored trucks have struck the troops advancing on our right. Our men are suffering heavy casualties and are falling back in great disorder."

Now it was time to move. Both men left the bunker and climbed to higher ground where they could see at least a good portion of the battlefield. They didn't like what they saw.

Mackensen and Crown Prince Wilhelm watched in horror as the army was destroyed by a few dozen metal monsters. The pride of the German Army was fleeing in panic. While the actual numbers of dead and wounded would ultimately only amount to a couple of thousand at most, the wounds to the German Army's morale and pride would be immense and long lasting. After all the time spent campaigning up California, victory was being denied them. His army was confused, defeated and half a world away from home.

And now the beasts were turning in Wilhelm's direction. What to do? His army was in full flight.

"General Mackensen, I suggest we find a safer place to conduct the war."

Mackensen was shocked, "A retreat?"

The prince sighed. "Yes, it certainly looks like that, doesn't it? We shall pull back and regroup. Those iron beasts are mortal and should run out of gas sooner or later and need to be refueled. Perhaps they will even break down. Meanwhile, we will figure out how to defeat them. If necessary, we will retreat down the coast to Santa Cruz or even Monterey where Hipper's fleet can protect us until we are reinforced and resupplied."

Assuming, he thought bitterly, his army stopped running before it reached Los Angeles.

Then another horrible thought intruded. Admiral Hipper was in San Francisco Bay. The admiral's grand attack had succeeded, but now the game had changed. The prince needed to ensure that the fleet was intact, or at least strong enough to fend off the American warships now prowling the Pacific. Hipper must remain strong to protect the army and ensure reinforcements and supplies made it safely.

The prince turned to an aide. "Send a message to Admiral Hipper and inform him of our, ah, tactical withdrawal. Tell him he must sortie out of San Francisco Bay as soon as possible lest his ships become trapped."

A most disconsolate Mackensen looked at him, "And what about Hutier?"

The prince sat down heavily as aides packed up their infernal papers. The American land monsters were coming closer with every minute. He could see someone standing with his head and shoulders out of a turret, giving directions. Why didn't someone shoot him? But no, the insane fool led a charmed life.

It was time to go, time to retreat and time to fight another day. But what if Hutier did succeed? Then San Francisco would be theirs and the hell with the metal monsters chewing up the German Army. There was still a chance. If San Francisco was truly taken, there was no need for this days' defeat by the metal monsters to be fatal.

"We will pray for Hutier's success."

★ CHAPTER 24 ★

Barricades had been thrown up across the streets leading south towards where the Germans had penetrated. The barricades were made up of cars, trucks, and wagons that had been tilted on their sides. Furniture had been added and stuffed in to make a wall maybe ten feet high. Where possible, soldiers had taken up flanking positions. The ad hoc defenses had been skillfully laid. The only problems were the lack of manpower and firepower. The headquarters had been stripped of all army and navy personnel and a number of civilians and retreating soldiers had joined the force. General Liggett estimated that he had perhaps a thousand men.

The main German force was coming up 40th Avenue, a straight road that led directly to the U.S. Military Preserve and the Golden Gate Cemetery. Before that, however, was the Golden Gate Park, and it was at the southern end of the park that the barricades were put up.

Liggett had taken direct command and decided they would try to funnel the German advance down the streets, rather than giving them a chance to fan out in the park and use their firepower and numbers to advantage. So far, it had worked, but because only a relatively few Germans had made it that far. Several Germans had been killed or wounded by the initial burst of fire. The wounded had been picked up by German soldiers under flag of truce. Now all the American defenders could do was wait for the Germans to get organized and launch a real assault.

A forward scout scrambled back from his position a few blocks in advance of the barricades. "They're forming up, General, and it looks like at least a full regiment, maybe more. They'll be coming down this street in a few minutes."

At which point we'll all be dead or prisoners, Liggett thought, and he saw the same thought on Admiral Sims' face. Sims and the other naval personnel looked incongruous in their blue uniforms carrying rifles. Many looked like they'd never seen a rifle before. At least the sailors weren't wearing white. That would have made them ideal targets.

Liggett nodded and the scout began to return to his position down the street. Suddenly, he wheeled and ran back.

"Oh shit, sir, here they come."

Waves of soldiers in field gray uniforms were advancing up 40th Avenue, a close-packed mass of humanity in metal helmets. So far they were walking, but they would charge when they got close enough and overwhelm the barricade by sheer weight of numbers. Through his binoculars, Liggett recognized a German general—von Hutier? Well, he thought, the man at least had the courage of his convictions.

"Where do you want my men, General?"

Liggett wheeled and smiled. He'd been so engrossed that he hadn't noticed the sounds of boots pounding on the pavement behind him, many boots.

"Douglas, it's so good to see you. Luke, what the devil took you so long?"

Before either could reply, Liggett continued, "General MacArthur, place your men as you see fit, but please do so in a hurry."

MacArthur looked down the street and gasped. "Fill in everywhere, men, just fill in!" He saw Randall and Taylor. "You two stay with me."

"Oh Jesus," Tim muttered, "just what we need."

The newly arrived Americans had no artillery, but they did have machine guns, both BARs and Hotchkiss guns, along with some Browning weapons. Liggett could only stare and smile. What he would have given for those machine guns when the Germans were advancing up the valley.

"Now!"

At MacArthur's command, hell broke loose from the Americans. Tim ran along behind his men and urged them to keep aiming low, just like they'd been taught. Tim stopped and aimed at a German. He squeezed off a shot just the way he'd done in camp and saw the man fall. He fired a second time and another German grasped his leg and tumbled. *Look at that,* he thought, *the Germans can die just like anybody else.* All around him, men were firing and Germans were falling.

It wasn't one sided. Germans paused and fired their Mausers coolly and steadily and with deadly effect.

Lieutenant Taylor screamed and fell back, clutching his shoulder. Tim started to reach for him when MacArthur snarled at him to keep shooting and let the medics care for his friend. As an aside, MacArthur told Tim he was now in charge of Taylor's company.

The Germans stopped advancing. MacArthur sensed that this was the moment of truth. He leaped to the top of the barricade, firing his pistol at the Germans. Bullets whipped by him but none hit. MacArthur had a coldly maniacal look on his face, as if he knew it was not his destiny to die this day.

"Fix bayonets!" he ordered and thousands of men complied.

Again MacArthur fired his pistol in the direction of the Germans. "Now charge!" he yelled and jumped down to the other side, running forward, confronting the Germans.

Aw shit! Tim thought as he landed beside MacArthur and began to move forward.

Admiral Hipper was disconcerted and confused. The garbled radio message from the prince seemed to say that he should depart the bay, which was what he'd already decided. A fleet should never be landlocked any longer than necessary. The German Navy had proven its mettle by crashing through into San Francisco Bay. The American defenses had been destroyed and there was no reason to remain. A few barges or ferries carrying troops had managed to cross the bay, but others had been destroyed with great loss of life. Bodies of dead Americans floated everywhere. It was a great victory.

The loss of the *Nassau* and *Posen* would prove that

a blood price had been paid and that German naval courage could not ever be doubted.

The survivors from the two battleships had been picked up and the wounded were being cared for. In a short while it would indeed be prudent to seek the open ocean, but what was the rush? From the sounds of it, there was fighting in San Francisco proper and it was inconceivable that the main attack had failed. Yet, that was what the miserable and static-filled radio communication seemed to indicate. Technology was so wonderful except when it didn't work.

He'd launched a floatplane to fly over the battlefield but some fool on one side or the other had shot it down.

Twilight was coming and he didn't want to rush through unfamiliar waters in darkness. It was either leave now or wait until morning.

A confirmation was radioed in. Something had gone horribly wrong with the main attack and Mackensen's army was pulling back, *presumably to try again tomorrow,* Hipper thought. Leaving now, therefore, was the right thing to do. If they remained, they would be at the mercy of American field artillery which, while more annoying than anything else, might still present a danger to his precious ships. As to what was happening in San Francisco, it was clearly not any of his immediate concern.

He gave the order to Canaris, who began to relay the proper commands to the other ships. Eight great capital ships were at anchor and it would take a few minutes haul them up and begin their way out. No matter. With the Yank shore batteries silenced, the German fleet could return tomorrow if needed. If not, then honor had been satisfied.

"What the devil?"

A burst of fire erupted from the deck of the battleship *Kaiserin* and billowed skyward. In the light of the flames, he could see dots, like moths, flitting about. They were planes, he realized with horror, American planes.

Amelia Earhart flew low, extremely low, over the ground and then over the blue water of San Francisco Bay. A German cruiser was in front of her and she had to gain altitude to clear it. As it was, she saw shocked faces beneath her. She thought about waving.

Scores of other little airplanes had commenced departing their secret airfield. The total number of Fireflies would be close to two hundred. She was to drop her load and return to the airfield for another and, God willing, another and another.

Today's cargo consisted of one female pilot and a number of containers rigged to drop from the plane when she pulled the appropriate handle. The containers were filled with gasoline and had a crude detonator for each. Even though the gasoline made takeoffs extremely dangerous, she had convinced a couple of mechanics to go along with her plans. Without a second person in the plane, it meant she could carry that much more gasoline.

Something exploded to her right and she saw a ship on fire. Good, the Germans were beginning to pay. Oops, bad. Now they would be alert. As she thought that, glowing fingers of tracer bullets leaped from the German ships but didn't touch her.

"Look at that," she said to herself.

A truly massive ship was coming up fast. She gauged the distance and pulled a switch. Two of the containers dropped. She banked the plane to see and yelled with delight as the ship's rearmost turret began to burn. Gas was thinner than water. The gasoline would find cracks and crevices that would stop the thicker liquid. The gas didn't even have to ignite immediately. Sooner or later, it would likely come in contact with something hot or burning and flare up. She visualized gallons of flaming gasoline going down hatches and into the interior of the huge ship, coming in contact with red hot shells.

Her plane shuddered. *Oh, Christ,* she thought. Her left wing was damaged and the rudder wasn't responding. Nor were her legs, she realized. Blood was running down them and into her boots. She'd been shot and didn't know when.

The plane began to cartwheel and Amelia Earhart knew she was going to die. She whimpered as the sea drew closer. Her last thought as the plane struck the water and exploded was the fervent hope that at least some of her body would be found so her parents could give her a proper funeral.

MacArthur's detractors in the small American Army, Luke included, might have considered him arrogant or pompous, but he wasn't a coward. His actions at Vera Cruz a few years earlier had proven that. Yelling and screaming, he charged into the Germans. Luke fired into the chest of a German only a few feet away, wheeled and stuck another in the gut with his bayonet. He tried to pull it out and it stuck. The German howled and tried to grab the rifle.

Luke fired, killing the Kraut and freeing the bayonet. He slid in a fresh clip and continued firing. More Americans had joined what was now a brawl. Suddenly, the rifle was knocked from his hands. He pulled his pistol and looked for someone to shoot.

A middle-aged man was staggering in front of him. The man looked confused and disoriented. He also looked important. Luke grabbed him by the lapel and jabbed the pistol under his chin. "Surrender or I'll blow your fucking head off," he said and then repeated it in German.

The man looked startled. His eyes were glazed. He raised his hands. "*Bitte*, *bitte*," he said, please, please. As he did, other Germans began to do the same thing.

A younger German officer approached tentatively, his hands open. "My name is von Richter. It's over. Let me help my general."

Luke's mind whirled. General? What the hell had he just gone and done? "Great, but who is this guy?"

Von Richter smiled wanly as the sounds of battle faded into unnatural silence. "Please let me present General Oskar von Hutier."

Hipper was outraged and frustrated. A tiny plane had dropped something on the *Bayern*'s rearmost turret and now the damn thing was burning furiously. Damage-control parties were working hard to contain the blaze lest the flames reach the ammunition in the turret or, God forbid, an ammunition magazine and cause a catastrophic explosion. His beautiful ship, the *Bayern*, was damaged and one quarter of her weapons were out of action.

Little planes, like little bugs, swarmed around the ships, sometimes flying so low they couldn't be seen and sometimes flying between ships so guns couldn't be fired for fear of hitting another German ship.

The little planes, gnats he thought, were wreaking havoc. If it wasn't so tragic, it would be funny.

Everyone knew that planes couldn't bomb warships and do much damage, but everyone had assumed the bombs would be explosive, not flammable. How wrong could they have been?

Many of the little gnats had been blown from the sky, swatted like the bugs they were. Perhaps dozens had fallen, but there were still so many that the ships' guns couldn't kill them all. In a corner of his mind, Hipper made the mental note that future warships would have to have many, many more antiaircraft guns as everyone would soon know of this despicable trick pulled by the Americans. Also, seals around turrets and hatches would have to be tighter. He wondered if he would live long enough to transmit this information.

Two other of his battleships, the *Koenig* and the *Thuringen*, were burning badly. As he watched, the front turret of the *Koenig* exploded, sending wreckage into the air. The turret itself lifted off the ship and fell into the ocean with a mighty splash. The *Thuringen* ceased moving and men began throwing themselves off the burning wreck and into the relative safety of the bay. Some of the German sailors were themselves on fire and Hipper allowed himself a moment of pity before he realized what he had to do.

"Sortie!" Hipper screamed. "All ships sortie!"

To hell with formation and to hell with dignity, he thought. He had to get the remainder of his fleet out of this death trap. He'd entered with ten battleships and was now down to six, and the remainder all damaged to some extent. The *Koenig* and the *Thuringen* might not even make it to sea. The German Navy had won its honor but had just been defeated by a most unlikely and improbable enemy.

"Full speed," he ordered. The *Bayern* raced through the channel and out into the ocean.

His great ship shuddered. Something was erupting in the stern where the fire raged. He was afraid to look. The ship shook again and a shock wave passed over and through the *Bayern*. D-turret had exploded.

Kirsten ran to where she could see what was happening in the bay. Earlier, she'd watched in dismay as the mighty German fleet hammered its way in. She wondered if this was the end of it. Would San Francisco fall to Germany despite all their efforts to defend it?

Curiously, the flow of wounded to the hospital had slowed to less than a trickle. There was a great battle raging to the east, but those wounded were cut off from her hospital facilities because the bay was now controlled by the Germans. There was fighting to the direct south and that concerned her deeply, as it did Elise who was with her. Both Luke and Josh were down to the south, and the fighting was close enough for them to discern the sound of small-arms fire.

But the chaos in San Francisco Bay was beyond belief. Elise had told her what the Fireflies were, and what they were going to attempt to do. Kirsten had thought it a hopeless endeavor and one that would result in many needless deaths.

But now she'd changed her mind. Not only were the damned Hun ships withdrawing, but the little Fireflies had caused significant damage. Two German ships were burning furiously and dead in the water. They would never leave the bay.

All of the German ships were hurt and burning to some extent. Fire was the great fear of men on ships and she'd been told that firefighting was practiced constantly. Once out of the bay and out of the range of the Fireflies, the flames would be brought under control and the German ships saved.

However, the flames on the largest ship, the *Bayern*, were not yet under control. It looked like the metal stern of the ship was so hot it was glowing, perhaps melting. As she was thinking that, the *Bayern*'s rearmost turret exploded, sending debris high into the air. People in the crowd around her gasped as shock waves shook the battleship like it was a toy.

The German fleet, now down to six battleships, moved out to sea. The handful of cruisers that had also made it into the bay made their own escape, largely ignored by the Fireflies and the few shore batteries.

Splashes suddenly appeared around the German ships. Geysers lifted higher than the superstructures themselves. What was going on? Kirsten and the other spectators had been so transfixed by the German ships that they'd ignored the horizon. Three grey silhouettes were moving and circling slowly and firing their guns. The *Arizona*, *Pennsylvania*, and *Nevada* had arrived.

Elise smiled. She had been privy to the great secret. "Admiral Sims had them hiding only fifty miles north of here. They were already on their way when the Fireflies attacked."

Sims had taken a great chance. If the Firefly attack had failed, the American ships would have had to run for their lives. Again.

It was difficult to follow, but it seemed like the *Arizona* was focusing on the damaged *Bayern*, while the other two American battleships attacked other foes.

Yes, Kirsten concluded, the *Arizona* and *Bayern*

were dueling. The two great ships moved closer to each other until it seemed like they were fighting a battle from the War of 1812. The *Bayern* had lost one turret, but her six remaining fifteen-inch guns were larger than her opponent's, and she inflicted damage on the *Arizona,* which itself began to burn.

After a while, both ships were torches and Kirsten couldn't begin to imagine the horrors going on inside them. Then both ships ceased firing and began to move slowly towards the shore.

"What are they doing?"

Admiral Sims appeared beside her. He was filthy and bleeding. She told him she should get him to a hospital, but he waved her off. This, the culmination of all his plans, was something he had to see.

"There are others far worse than me, young lady. As to the ships, they are beaching themselves so they don't sink. Look, the *Nevada* is attempting the same thing."

The *Nevada* didn't make it. A few hundred yards from shore, she rolled over and disappeared. The crowd groaned and Kirsten felt tears on her cheeks. "So many brave men," she sobbed. Elise grasped her arm and was also crying.

Two other German battleships beached themselves. Their crews filled lifeboats and rowed out to the surviving German ships. The remaining German ships were damaged, but seemed under control. They would get away. The *Pennsylvania*, dark smoke billowing from her many wounds, was withdrawing slowly and would not, could not, interfere.

"And now there are only three," Sims said. "The Germans have suffered a huge defeat. Sadly, we're in no position to celebrate. We've got only one ship left and she's badly damaged. We could bring more from the Atlantic, but so too could the Germans. It's a stalemate."

Motion from behind caught her eye. Long lines of men in field gray uniforms had begun moving past. She exulted. They were prisoners. German prisoners. She caught Luke walking alongside a youthful-looking American general. Both were limping and holding each other up.

Kirsten ran and took Luke's arm. "Kirsten, meet General Douglas MacArthur. He just saved our asses with a wild charge through the German Army."

MacArthur was in pain. "A pleasure," he grimaced.

Tim Randall took the general's arm and relieved Luke. MacArthur looked around in confusion. "Where's my other lucky charm?"

"Wounded, sir, but I think he'll be okay." Tim found it difficult to talk. MacArthur was heavy and Tim was exhausted.

Elise screamed and Kirsten and Luke saw her run down the street towards Josh. Elise had informed Kirsten that she would go wherever Josh was sent by the Navy. She hadn't informed Josh as yet. She threw her arms around him and decided that now was the time. She whispered in his ear. He nodded and hugged her tightly.

Kirsten tore her eyes away from Elise and Josh. "Do you need to go to the hospital, Luke?"

"No."

"Wonderful," she said and kissed him on the cheek. "Go do what you have to and I'll find you at the apartment. We can talk about setting a date to get married. Tomorrow would be nice."

"You sure?"

"Of course I'm sure, you ninny. I think I'm pregnant."

General Mackensen had spent most of the day and the night trying to round up his shattered army. Panic had ensued and his men had fled from the field of battle in great disarray. It was both shocking and disappointing. He'd thought that the Imperial German Army was made of sterner stuff, but the day's work had proven his soldiers to be mere mortals.

The Americans had not attacked. Their armored vehicles had withdrawn behind their own lines with nearly half of them damaged, disabled, or simply broken down. American trucks had gone out onto the field and hauled them back where they would be repaired.

Damn them, Mackensen thought. "How could the Yanks have come up with such a devastating weapon so fast?" he muttered.

"They didn't," said the crown prince. "We've had word that the British were working on something similar for the last couple of years. We've never given it much credence, nor did we think it would be such a devastating weapon."

"Now what, sir?"

Wilhelm grimaced. "Distasteful as it might be, a withdrawal is the wisest course. We will wait for resupply and reinforcements. Our army must rest and regain its collective courage. I doubt very much if God himself could make our men charge the American defenses again, especially as they are being reinforced as we speak. Who knows," he laughed harshly, "the emperor might just decide to call off this entire endeavor."

Mackensen was about to ask just what future plans

the prince had when a look of surprise appeared for just an instant on the prince's face before the front of his skull exploded, sending bone and bloody matter into the air. Some of it landed on Mackensen who, along with others, dropped to the ground.

"Sniper!" someone screamed. Of course it was a sniper, Mackensen thought. He reached for the hand of his prince and moaned. The prince's skull was a vacant mess. The heir to Kaiser Wilhelm II was well and truly dead.

A few hundred yards away, Reggie Carville hummed softly as he wrapped his beloved and disassembled rifle in what he hoped was a waterproof tarpaulin and buried it in the ground. He'd already wiped off his fingerprints, not that anybody would think of using that still fairly new crime-fighting technology on a battlefield. With a little bit of luck he'd be able to retrieve it in a few days when the Germans had evacuated the area. The rifle was a German Gehwehr 88, called by some a Mauser but was really more of a Mannlicher. Regardless, it was a German weapon and, if found, would confuse the finders.

Carville had owned it for several years and had it modified into a highly accurate sporting rifle with a telescopic sight. He had brought it, disassembled, in his suitcase.

The German headquarters was a beehive of panicked activity. No one seemed much in control and patrols were going in all directions searching for the sniper.

When he had the chance, he would tell his good friend, Sergeant "Smeeth," about his good shooting. "Smeeth" would be so jealous.

Reggie stood and brushed the dirt from his clothing. A German major ran up to him, his Luger in his hand. Reggie was unarmed and in civilian clothing. He smiled and held his hands out to show he was harmless.

"What are you doing here?" the German asked.

"I am a reporter and here are my credentials," Reggie said firmly. "And kindly note they've been signed by the kaiser himself." And outstanding forgeries they were, he thought. "Has something happened to the crown prince?"

"The late crown prince," the German said angrily. "A sniper killed him."

"Good God!"

"So, did you see any suspicious activity? As in someone running away and carrying a rifle?"

"I don't meant to sound sarcastic, Major, but I've seen a great many men running with rifles. Although, I do seem to recall a man in a German uniform running north, rather than south and west along with the rest of the army."

The major sagged and Reggie could read his mind. Could the murderer have been a German soldier? A communist or anarchist, or just someone who thought the California venture was a bloody waste of lives?

The major departed to continue his fruitless search. Reggie found a comfortable place to sit and wait for the Germans to leave and the Americans to arrive.

Ah, Reggie thought happily, he had indeed crowned the prince.

★ EPILOGUE ★

ROBERT LANSING, PRESIDENT OF THE UNITED STATES, looked over the latest report from California. It had been two months since the surrender of the German Army at the small port of Monterey, on the Pacific coast and south of San Francisco. The Germans had been besieged for three months. They had been left stranded when Admiral von Trotha, replacing the seriously wounded Hipper, decided to withdraw the remains of his fleet to Cam Ranh Bay for refit and repair. This had become necessary when the German Navy realized that Los Angeles facilities had all been damaged and were in danger of falling to fast-moving American columns under General Pershing. A spearhead under Lejeune had moved quickly and taken up position in the hills overlooking Los Angeles.

Trotha had been more than a little spooked by the presence of the British fleet, which trailed him and threatened his few ships with annihilation. The threat was never spoken, but it was understood nonetheless.

San Diego had fallen earlier to Lejeune's mounted columns. Pershing might have been in overall command of the southern wing, but the American public was cheering the exploits of John Lejeune, pride of the United States Marine Corps. Liggett and Sims were also national heroes.

Mrs. Tuttle knocked and opened the door to the president's office. She was radiant. She had just found out that her young cousin, Luke Martel, had not only survived the fighting but had been promoted and decorated. He was resigning his commission as an officer and would go into civilian life as a hero. He'd received his second Medal of Honor for capturing von Hutier, and Douglas MacArthur had also been given the same medal for leading the insane charge that had broken the German attack. Luke had gotten married and would soon be a father. Lansing was curious about the timing of all that, but he was far too much of a gentleman to comment. The happy couple would stay in southern California, apparently making babies, growing grapes, and making wine. Mrs. Tuttle was already planning a visit.

"Sir, the British are here and it's that silly Mr. Churchill."

"Thank you, Mrs. Tuttle," Lansing said, fervently hoping that the silly Mr. Churchill hadn't heard the comment. Apparently he had. He glared at her as she departed.

Lansing sighed. He didn't much like Churchill either. Just a tad overbearing, even for a Brit.

"I have excellent news, Mr. Lansing. It appears that the kaiser will abdicate in favor of his second son and will declare for a constitutional monarchy. The defeat in California was too much for the German public to stomach."

With Crown Prince Wilhelm dead from a sniper's bullet, the next in line was Prince Eitel Friedrich, age thirty-seven. He was an unknown quantity save for rumors of corruption. Apparently the kaiser-to-be was susceptible to bribes. Lansing wondered if the rumors of a British sniper killing the younger Wilhelm were true. The Brits solemnly denied it.

Kaiser Wilhelm II had been devastated by the loss of his oldest son. Lansing found it hard to find sympathy for the man who had ordered the invasion of the United States and who had participated in the destruction of Belgium and France in 1914.

Churchill continued. "The overall German military position has been seriously compromised. She lost nearly half her main battle fleet at San Francisco, and I understand that your people are taking great advantage of that."

Lansing smiled. "Indeed." It was no secret. The *Bayern* and *Arizona* had been refloated and were being repaired. The *Bayern* would be added to the American Navy, as would at least two other fairly modern but badly damaged German capital ships. Sadly, the *Nevada* had sunk in deep water and would remain there.

"Kaiser Wilhelm wants his army back," Churchill said with a grin.

Lansing smiled tolerantly. "And he shall have it once he agrees to pay indemnity for all the damage Germany caused. Constitutional monarchy or not, the new German government cannot hold themselves blameless for their kaiser's actions. The military and the aristocracy, along with the average German, indulged in Wilhelm the Second's insane desires for a German empire."

Lansing continued. "In the meantime, the prisoners will work on repairing what they have destroyed. We are paying them and they are, allegedly at least, volunteers, so the terms of the Geneva Convention are not being violated. Besides, the victors write the terms, not the losers. Same too with war criminals. We've already hanged the man who ran the prison camp near the town of Raleigh, and others will follow."

Churchill shrugged. The winners always wrote the rules. "Would you care for a cigar? It's Cuban."

Lansing accepted and, after the appropriate cutting and sniffing ritual, lit up. "Ecstasy," he said. Perhaps this Churchill fellow wasn't such a bad chap after all.

"The Germans are in bad shape in Russia," Churchill added. "Or perhaps I should call it the Soviet Union. Trotsky's armies are pushing the German and Austrian armies back by sheer weight of numbers. It's an incredible bloodbath. Epic proportions, they say. It is rumored that the Germans will sign a treaty with the French, which will enable them to evacuate both the Channel ports and Belgium in return for a nonaggression pact. That would permit them to move troops against Trotsky."

Lansing offered brandy which Churchill accepted. England would be delighted to have Belgium and the Channel ports out of Germany's control. It would mean no feasible threat of a cross-channel German invasion.

"And your brief war has turned military thinking on its head," Churchill added with a knowing smile. After all, the landships, now universally called tanks, had been his idea. Or at least Churchill was taking full credit for it. "Now everyone will want tanks, and everyone also realizes that airplanes are the weapon of the future of naval warfare, and not battleships. I have it on good authority that no warship will go within flying distance of enemy land until this new weapon is figured out."

"Which won't take long," Lansing said. "As you are doubtless aware, my own people are planning both antitank weapons and antiplane weapons along with bigger and stronger tanks and additional capital ships. It appears that war is a series of cycles, and damned expensive ones at that."

America and Britain were quietly building ships that could launch and recover planes. Carriers, they were called. In the months since the German Army's surrender, the American Army had been reduced in size from the more than a million it had reached. But Congress had already approved an increase in the standing army to two hundred thousand men and authorized increases in the various states' National Guard units. Hopefully, there would never be a need for untrained volunteers to defend the United States. Additional budget increases had come to strengthen the Navy and the infant Air Corps.

"Where will it ever end?" Lansing sighed.

Churchill shrugged. "It won't."

The train pulled into the station in Seattle and a young woman got off carrying a threadbare cloth carry-bag. She was young and thin and an observer would logically conclude that the cloth bag contained all her worldly positions.

Trains coming from the east and heading in that

direction were no longer a novelty. All of the bridges had either been repaired or temporary replacements had been built, and the same with the other rail lines. California was no longer isolated and transcontinental commerce was beginning anew.

Other passengers swirled around the woman, who scanned the crowd. She was nervous and tired. She'd spent almost a week sitting on a bench since she couldn't afford Pullman accommodations. She hoped to God the trip had been worth it and that she hadn't been stranded at a train station. Regardless, she'd needed to escape the emotional hell that her home back east had become.

Tim Randall watched cautiously. She hadn't spotted him yet. It had taken all his nerve to invite Kathy Fenton to join him. He'd been discharged and had no plans to go back to Camden. There were too many memories and still too much guilt being laid on him by his family.

He'd been shocked and delighted when she'd responded to his telegram and agreed to come.

He walked up behind her. "Kathy?"

Startled, she wheeled and turned. She recognized him and her smile became radiant.

They embraced discreetly, timidly. She pulled apart. "Did you find us a place?"

Tim grinned. "I did and it overlooks Puget Sound."

Kathy picked up her bag and handed it to him. "Then let's go see it."

"What do you think?" Marcus Tovey asked. The end of the fighting had brought an end to the need for volunteer units like his and he too had been discharged.

He had no plans to go back to being a Texas Ranger. He'd had enough of guns to last a lifetime.

"I don't think I've ever seen anything flatter," Martina said with a hint of a smile. The land north of San Antonio seemed to go on forever with only slight undulations to the ground. It was certainly nothing like the mountains of her home that formed the spine of Mexico.

"How much of it do you own?" she asked.

"Several thousand acres with options to buy more. And I'll raise cattle on them. Beef cattle for the people out east and for the growing population of California. I've heard from an engineer that there might also be oil underneath the land, but I'll deal with that when the time comes. Right now, California supplies all the oil we need."

"That will change, Marcus. Just think of all the automobiles that are being built."

Tovey grunted and concurred. He decided to make sure he owned the mineral rights to his property.

Martina urged her horse forward. "Do you call that a house?"

The one-story building looked dilapidated, but at least it was built of stone. "I'll admit it needs work."

"A lot of work if you expect me to live there, Marcus Tovey. And I will require something more than an outhouse."

"Of course. But is it a place where you can learn to forget the past?"

She reached over and took his hand. "No. It's a place to begin a future."

Postscript

WHILE SOME OF THE NAMES OF THE PARTICIPANTS in *1920* are very familiar to those with knowledge of twentieth-century history, some are not. In order to satisfy the curious, here is a summary of the real people and what they actually did in real history during and after the period covered by the novel.

Of the Germans, von Trotha, Scheer, the Crown Prince, Mackensen, and Hutier were real and were major players in World War I. The diplomats, Bernsdorff and Eckhardt were also real. After the defeat of Germany in 1918, they largely disappeared from the public eye. The crown prince followed his father into exile and was no longer a factor in Germany. Von Seekt gained some notoriety by helping rebuild the German Army through a secret accord with the Soviet Union. To my knowledge and with the exception of Rommel, he is the only one who had any significant Nazi connections.

The genially corrupt Italian diplomat, Golitti, continued in Italian politics until he and his cronies were pushed out by the rise of the even more corrupt Benito Mussolini.

The governors of Texas and California, as well as the mayor of San Francisco were also real people, although I used my imagination regarding their behavior, etc.

Some of the American military: Sims, Pershing, Liggett, Nolan, Connor, and Harbord, played major roles in our World War I and after.

Robert Lansing resigned as Secretary of State in 1919 and went into private law practice.

Charles Evans Hughes was named Secretary of State in 1921 and later served as Chief Justice of the Supreme Court.

Carranza was overthrown by his numerous enemies and murdered in 1920.

A number of American military personnel are recognized as major players in World War II, including Patton, Nimitz, MacArthur, and Marshall. Herbert Hoover and Eisenhower both served as presidents of the United States, with Hoover unfairly getting much of the blame for the Great Depression. John Lejeune became the Commandant of the Marine Corps and Dr. Grayson was Woodrow Wilson's personal physician.

D.W. Griffith continued to make movies, but none were as successful, or as controversial, as *Birth of a Nation*.

Amelia Earhart disappeared in 1937 while flying over the Pacific.

Most of the other characters: Luke Martel, Kirsten Biel, Elise Thompson, Josh Cornell, Marcus Tovey,

Mrs. Tuttle, the Dubbins boys, Steiner and Olson, and others were all figments of my imagination.

If I've missed anyone and you're still curious, do what I did and look it up.

Robert Conroy

The following is an excerpt from:

1882

◇◇◇◇◇◇◇◇◇◇◇◇◇◇◇◇◇◇◇◇◇◇◇◇◇◇◇◇◇◇◇◇

CUSTER IN CHAINS

ROBERT CONROY

Available from Baen Books
May 2015
hardcover

CHAPTER 1

The spent bullet slammed into Custer's shoulder, spinning him and dropping him face down on the ground where he tasted dirt and blood through split lips. He staggered to his knees. Blood streamed from a cut in his scalp, which, he thought ruefully, might not be his for very much longer. At least the red-skinned savages would have a difficult time lifting it. He'd cut his hair short in anticipation of the fight, although not his death. His long golden locks, now graying slightly, had been thrown away and were blowing around the Dakotas. The Indians would never get them.

Custer snapped an order and Sergeant Haney helped him to his feet. If he had to die, Custer thought, he would do so standing up. "What the devil are they waiting for, Haney?" The blood from the cut was dripping into his eyes and he couldn't see very clearly. Being blind, however, was the least of his problems.

"Fucked if I know, general dearest," the short, stocky sergeant who'd been with him since the Civil War muttered. Custer usually yelled at him when Haney referred to him as general dearest, but it didn't seem to matter this sunny day of June 25, 1876. And the hell with him if it did, Haney thought. He'd been wounded several times this day and the next could finish him. Custer, the stupid bastard who commanded the Seventh Cavalry had just gone and gotten all of them killed. Why the hell hadn't Custer waited for General Terry and the rest of the army to come up before attacking? Because he wanted the glory of victory and he was afraid that the Indians would flee before he could be reinforced.

Custer's vision cleared a little. The Sioux were riding their ponies in swirling clusters, whooping and shooting wildly at the small number of men still alive on the grassy knob. He looked around and counted only a dozen of his men still standing with him. A number of others lay prone on the ground along with an almost equal number of Indians. He had taken five companies of his 7th Cavalry to attack the main Sioux camp while other units hit them from the other side of the river. He'd figured that two hundred and ten soldiers were more than enough for this part of the attack. The savages wouldn't stand up to an assault on their homes. In previous battles, they'd broken up in attempts to save their families and had fled. Custer had laughed when planning the assault. Only fools would take their women and children along on a war. His own wife, Libbie, along with a number of others, was safely ensconced on a steamer in the Missouri.

Only he hadn't counted on there being so damned many of the Indians. There must be at least a thousand warriors, not the few hundred he expected to find on this side of the Little Big Horn. He'd also anticipated that Reno, with the rest of the regiment, would support him by attacking from the other side of the river. Caught in a vise, the Indians would break. But where the hell was Reno? And where was Benteen. Reno was just across the river, so why didn't he come and help. Benteen was farther away, but he too should be arriving soon. Benteen was junior to Reno, so maybe he was coming with Reno. But where the hell were they? If they didn't arrive in the next few minutes it would all be over.

Custer swore and called Reno a son of a bitch. Reno hated Custer but he always obeyed orders. Custer rarely swore, even to himself, but this day was an exception. Of course, he laughed ruefully, being surrounded by a thousand angry Indians will do that to a man.

Custer checked his pistol. He had two bullets left. Should he save one for himself? Yes. If taken prisoner, they'd cut him into little pieces and then roast what remained of his still living carcass over a small, slow fire. Or maybe they'd parade him naked all throughout the Great Plains and defer cutting him into those little living pieces for agonizing, humiliating weeks. No, he'd rather be dead this day.

"Haney, if I fail, kill me."

Haney snorted and checked his Springfield. It was loaded and wasn't jammed.

Bullets fired from a long distance rained down on the knob, kicking up dust and only occasionally hitting someone. Only the fact that many of the Indians were unused to rifles and, therefore, poor shots, had kept them alive for this long. Haney had one of Mr. Colt's big revolvers stuck in his waistband and a bullet was intended for himself and Custer could go to hell. After all, hadn't the arrogant son of a bitch gotten them into this mess? Let him solve his own damned problems.

"Look, general, they're gathering a lot of them together. They're going to ride right over us and there isn't a damn thing we can do."

"We can die well," Custer announced. Haney looked away and almost fell over. He'd taken three arrows and one bullet already. Fortunately the arrows had barely penetrated flesh and the bullet had gone through the meat of this thigh without hitting an artery, but fatigue and loss of blood were weakening him. He didn't want to pass out and be scalped alive. Or worse, be taken by the savages for their sadistic entertainment.

Nor did Sergeant Haney particularly wish to die well. If given a choice, he'd choose to live poorly rather than die well. It was all well and good for an Irish Catholic to believe in the after-life, but did it have to begin today? Besides he hadn't been to Confession in several months of Sundays.

"They're coming," a trooper said a bit redundantly. The Indians were moving slowly towards them. Haney estimated maybe two hundred horsemen in the bunch, including some leaders. It would be more than enough to trample them into the dirt beside the Little Big Horn River.

The Indians were howling and picking up speed. They were only a few hundred yards away. Haney shook his rifle at them. "Come on, you fuckers! Mike Haney ain't gonna die all that easily. Some of you are going to die as well."

Custer laughed, his voice a cackle. He was about to say something when a harsh screeching sound erupted. Suddenly, the Sioux horde seemed to shudder as if it'd been punched. Warriors and horses tumbled and fell. Screams of fear and dismay, mingled with pain, came from Indian throats. Horses screamed in agony and there was chaos.

More bodies fell and formed ghastly piles. Some Indians tried to get up and were trampled by their panic-stricken horses.

"Bloody fucking hell, general dearest, would you mind telling me just what is happening?"

Custer turned to his left and began to cackle even more loudly. At first he couldn't see because of the gunsmoke, but then it cleared. "Gatlings.

Somebody disobeyed my orders and brought the Gatling battery along. It must be Lieutenant Low."

Despite his wounds, Haney's eyesight was much better than Custer's. "No sir, it ain't Low. It looks like that young pup, Lieutenant Ryder."

The two hand cranked machine guns were several hundred yards away and each was firing at three hundred and fifty rounds a minute, spraying the close-packed Indians like watering a lawn with a hose and dropping the Sioux warriors into piles of bodies.

It was enough. The Sioux began to pull back, slowly at first and then at a gallop as the Gatlings' bullets followed them.

Custer sagged to his knees. "We're going to live."

"Indeed we are. At least for a while, general dearest.

Custer swung his good arm and hit Haney on the thigh. "Then quit calling me 'general dearest' you bow-legged shanty Irish bastard."

Second Lieutenant William Ryder, Seventh U.S. Cavalry, walked among the dead and was appalled. So many of them were men he'd known and now they were mere lumps of meat. A number had already been scalped or mutilated by the Indians before the rain of death from his guns had chased them away. The Indians liked to disembowel their victims as well as slicing the muscles of their arms and legs. He'd heard that it was supposed to hamper them in the afterlife. Whatever the reason, the wounds were hideous. General Terry had arrived with the rest of the column and men were just beginning to gather up the dead. They had bloated in the sun and already stank to high heaven.

Among the dead, Ryder had recognized Custer's two brothers and he'd been informed that all of Custer's officers had been killed. The death total was one hundred and eighty seven out of the two hundred and ten men who'd accompanied Custer, and it was likely to go higher since some of the survivors were severely wounded. There were additional casualties from the two detachments commanded by Benteen and Reno that had fought desperately on the other side of the Little Big Horn. They too had almost been overrun by larger than expected numbers of Indians.

"If I'd arrived an hour earlier, how many others would still be alive?" Ryder wondered out loud.

"The survivors are lucky you arrived at all."

Ryder wheeled. He hadn't noticed the man in civilian clothes who was slowly walking up to him.

"Who the devil are you?"

"James Kendrick," the other man said with a warm smile, "and I'm a freelance reporter who's been following the campaign. I'm attached to

General Terry's headquarters. I'm surprised you didn't notice me."

"My mind was elsewhere, Mr. Kendrick. I was thinking of so many dead friends. I've never seen anything like this in my life."

Kendrick shook his head sadly. "I'm a decade older than you and I haven't either, and the reporter in me says I have to find out what happened. For instance, why the devil did Custer divide his forces when confronted by a vastly superior enemy? For that matter, why did he attack in the first place? Then why didn't Benteen and Reno come to his assistance sooner instead of waiting until you arrived with your guns?"

"Have you talked to Custer?"

"He's still recovering and dictating a report to his aide. He'll recover from his physical wounds, but I fear the loss of his brothers will be harder for him. I also feel that the official report will show General George Armstrong Custer in a most favorable light. I want the truth, lieutenant. For instance, is it true that your guns were left behind because only miserable nags were assigned to pull them?"

"Cavalry always gets first crack at the good mounts. Cavalry is supposed to ride ahead of the army; thus dragging artillery, and Gatlings are defined as artillery, would definitely slow them down. I did convince Lieutenant Low and General Terry that, with better horses, I would be able to keep up with Custer. Terry agreed after Custer left and he gave me good mounts, some remounts, and a total of fifty men. Low didn't want to do it. He felt that he had to obey Custer's orders and leave them behind. Riding hard and alternating horses, I was able to make up the lost time. I only wish I had gotten here sooner."

"As do the almost two hundred men of the Seventh Cavalry who are now dead. The savages aren't stupid, lieutenant. They retreated because it was obvious they were going to suffer heavy casualties if they didn't, and that's something they don't want to do. The Indians realize that there are far more white men than red and they don't want a stand-up fight if they can possibly avoid it. Every dead white man can and will be replaced but that's not true for a dead red man. By the way, it looks like your guns managed to kill Crazy Horse which further demoralized them."

"Another good reason for them to pull back," said Ryder.

"I'm going to do you a favor and give you some information for free. Custer's first draft of his report indicted you for dereliction of duty. It said that the reason you were late was because you were responsible for the poor horses and then took your own sweet time getting to the battle. You're not alone. He also condemned Benteen and Reno."

Ryder was stunned. "You can't be serious. He was the one who insisted on the poor horses. It was a joke around the regiment that he hated the idea of machine guns taking the glory away from his cavalry."

"He felt you should be court-martialed."

"Son of a bitch!"

Kendrick laughed. "Don't worry, it won't happen. That report will never leave the camp. Terry knows the truth, as do a number of others. A sergeant named Haney told them what was happening and they put a halt to that nonsense. The only one in trouble is Reno and that's because there are rumors that he was drunk. In the new and latest official version, you will be commended for recognizing the problem with the horses, replacing them, and riding like a bat out of hell to rescue Custer and what remained of his men. Along with a commendation, you will likely be promoted."

"So why are you telling me all this?"

"I'm a reporter and I like to report the truth, and the truth is that Custer's responsible for all the dead and wounded currently rotting on this hill. I'm going to write articles and perhaps even a book on this battle, only with my version showing the world just what a headstrong bastard Custer is. And I wouldn't mind making a lot of money and a name for myself with it. On the other hand, I'm going to have to move quickly. Some very important people want him to run for president. If he becomes too powerful politically, his friends will protect him and the truth will never come out."

"Thank you I guess, but any early promotion will be resented by others."

"Christ, Ryder, they're not making you a general, just a first lieutenant. Even Sergeant Haney thinks you deserve it for saving his Irish ass. He's recovering nicely and sends his regards."

Ryder laughed. The last he'd seen of Haney was on the knob where Custer was making his final stand. He'd had arrows sticking out of him and looked like a human pincushion. Haney was highly regarded and it was good to have the older NCO's concurrence with his actions.

"Assuming I actually am promoted, what will happen to me then?"

"If the political part of this gets as messy as I think it will, the army is going to circle the wagons to protect one of their own, Custer, and you will be sent far, far away so nobody can ask you difficult questions. My guess would be Oregon or even Alaska, at least until things settle down."

Oregon? Alaska? Ryder's mind whirled. They were at the end of the world. What the hell had he done to deserve this? Why not just send him to Siberia? So much for being rewarded for doing the right thing, he mused. What the hell, at least he'd be promoted.

CHAPTER 2

Libbie Custer stretched her bare legs under the silk cover and listened to her husband snore. It was comforting but also worrisome. He'd returned to the White House late after a meeting at the Willard Hotel with some political allies. As usual since it was a political meeting where women weren't welcome, she hadn't been with him and she didn't like that. She worried about what he might have agreed to. He was still so naïve when it came to politics and she didn't want his presidency to become a national disgrace like Ulysses Grant's had become. She accepted that she was by far the smarter of the two very ambitious people and that George needed her to control him as well as lead him. She and George were a team and a team should not make decisions without both members being present. She was not yet forty and some said she was even lovelier than she had been when she was twenty.

She and George were also still passionately in love and there were many times when they laughingly thought their White House lovemaking would wake the servants.

It could have been paradise, but it wasn't. She

acknowledged that George was in well over his head. If power corrupts, then he was also being corrupted. He'd begun drinking heavily and he seemed distracted by events he didn't quite understand. She didn't think he had a woman on the side, or, she laughed softly, on her back. However, if he did, she would exact the only form of revenge a woman could. She would betray and humiliate him as well, and he understood that.

Until and if that unlikely event occurred, she had two goals – protecting him and advancing his presidency.

Beside her, Custer stirred and yawned. "Libbie, I'm bored."

"That sir is a terrible thing to say to a woman you just had your way with. Did my ripe and lovely naked body not please you?"

Only an hour before, she'd been awakened by the familiar feel of his hands roaming her body. He'd gotten her nightgown up to her shoulders and had discarded the silk pajamas from India that she'd given him for his birthday. She'd responded eagerly and matched him stroke for stroke after he'd entered her. When they were finished and he seemed to be dozing, she wondered why so many of her married friends felt uncomfortable with sex. Why did they feel that it was a chore to be endured instead of a pleasure to be savored? For all his faults, she immensely enjoyed having sex with him.

Still, she wondered at his comment.

"How can the President of the United States and master of all he surveys be bored?"

"Because it's a boring damn job, that's why. Nothing has happened since I was elected and nothing will. I also had that damn dream again. Once again I was lying on the ground with a bunch of Sioux standing there and laughing at me. Then one of them reaches down and starts scalping me."

She stroked his head. "And that's when you awake because it is only a dream."

His notoriety as the man who had subdued the Sioux, as a reporter named Kendrick had put it, had carried him all the way to the White House. He had been nominated as the Republican candidate for President, defeating the other Republican nominee, James Garfield in the primaries. And later he had narrowly defeated former Civil War General and Democratic candidate, Winfield Scott Hancock, in the general election of 1880.

Yet George, or Autie as his family had sometimes called him before his brothers were killed, was correct. He was serving at a time when not much was occurring in the United States. The Indians had been reduced to a minimal menace and there was peace in the land. Europe might be in turmoil with the Prussians trying to gobble it up, but those wars were far away. The Reconstruction Era of the south was over and those former Confederate states were now free to do whatever they wished. That this meant suffocating the desires of the newly freed Negroes was of no concern to him, or most other people for that matter.

"Libbie, I am terribly afraid that my four, or, God forbid, eight years as president, will be as little more than a night watchman. I'll become a footnote in history like some other presidents such as Fillmore or Pierce or my own predecessor, Rutherford B. Hayes. I need something exciting to fulfill me. I need to accomplish something important. I need to start a war."

Libbie sat up. Her nightgown was still above her waist and he grinned at the sight of her exposed body. "You can't be ready again," she chided him playfully as she saw his eyes widen. If he was indeed ready she would be as well. "Now, let's talk about a war. Who would you want to fight? Clearly, it can't be the Indians again."

She got up and walked barefoot across the bedroom. "Nor can it be the Mexicans. They've done nothing to provoke us and Congress will not let you just up and invade them. We did that once already. Somebody has to start the war and it can't be the United States. The nation is still recovering from horrors of the Civil War."

Custer yawned. "And that also leaves out the nations of Central and South America. They're all too helpless and too far away and besides, they'd never start anything against us."

"Agreed, George. Therefore, it must be a European power. However, we must choose carefully. Great Britain is out. Not only she too powerful, but our economic ties with her are too close. War with Great Britain would be a total disaster. France is too powerful as well, although we very nearly did fight them at the end of the Civil War. They do hate us, so let's keep them in mind for the future. But right now, they are too powerful. Their navy is second only to Britain's."

George smiled at the memory. The French had backed a puppet emperor in Mexico; a pliant fool named Maximilian, and sent troops to support him in violation of America's Monroe Doctrine. With the Civil War raging, Lincoln did nothing. After the war, an Army under General Phil Sheridan was sent to the Rio Grande with the clear message that the French Army in Mexico had to leave. They did and poor Maximilian wound up in front of a firing squad while his mentally ill wife fled to Europe. Neither George nor Libbie would mind rubbing France's nose in the dirt, but, again, would the French oblige by starting a conflict that the U.S. could win? Probably not, they concluded. The French had their own internal conflicts tormenting them. Their Third Republic had begun with a massive bloodbath.

Germany was a newly created nation dominated by the always belligerent Prussians. She was still trying to get organized, although she might be a possible combatant in the future. But Germany too was doubtless already too strong for American to fight after she'd defeated both

France and Austria. Also understood was the fact that Germany and the United States were almost half a world away and couldn't reach each other.

Italy, an equally new nation, was immersed in internal problems and was also far, far away.

They decided that the Ottomans would make marvelous enemies and not just because they were Moslems who'd abused Americans decades earlier. But they too were far away and doubtless cared nothing about starting a war with the United States. Ottoman ships in the Mediterranean had captured American merchantmen and held their crews as hostages, but that was in the past.

The lands of Asia were already being carved up by the Great Powers. Perhaps the US could slice off a piece of China or Japan, but for what purpose? No, Asia was out.

"Russia?" he asked. "Maybe we could get them to attack us because they want Alaska back."

"I don't think so, George. And besides, they are almost our allies."

He laughed. "You're right, and who would ever want Alaska returned to them?"

Libbie smiled like a cat. "That leaves Spain."

"Yes," he said thoughtfully, "Spain. Her remaining possessions in the Caribbean are close by and always on the verge of exploding. The Spanish are corrupt and keep slaves, even though they've begun to abolish slavery. We can provoke something and a war can easily follow. The Spanish are nothing militarily and we'll have an easy victory."

She pulled the nightgown over her head and watched him revel in the sight of her naked body. Even though it was mid-morning, the servants knew enough not to enter without being invited. She saw that he was aroused again and it pleased her. Controlling him with her sex was so easy. It was even better because she truly loved him and wanted him to be a great man.

She ran her hand down his chest and belly and began to stroke him. "First, George, you will finish what you are obviously about to start and then we'll go about provoking Spain. When we're done with Spain you will have become one of America's great presidents."

Custer laughed and pulled her body to him. What a hell of a woman, he thought. I am the luckiest man in the world.

The *Eldorado* was a decrepit wooden steamship of about fifteen hundred tons and she was stuffed with military supplies for the insurgents fighting Spanish oppression in Cuba. At least that's what journalist James Kendrick had written in his notebook. Unfortunately, he hadn't gotten much farther in his writing because he didn't quite believe it. The peasant revolution in Cuba was in a quiet phase, so why the rush to arm a population that wasn't doing anything? There had been a long revolutionary war in Cuba that was now quiet, with both sides suffering from severe exhaustion.

Along with the guns and ammunition, about a hundred men, mostly Americans, were coming along as volunteers. To do what, Kendrick wondered. At the moment, that question was a minor concern. A Spanish gunboat was approaching them and gaining quickly. The *Eldorado's* captain had his ship fleeing as fast as it could, but it was a sick turtle racing against a rabbit. Kendrick thought that was clever and wrote it down.

Worse, the crew and passengers had nothing but rifles and side arms to protect them and these they'd taken from the ship's hold. They'd been disgusted and dismayed to find that the weapons being shipped to Cuba were rusty and most didn't work. Some even dated to well before the Civil War. It was clear that someone had unloaded a large quantity of junk for a huge profit. Some of the young American warriors now looked frightened. It occurred to Kendrick that he should feel that way too.

When the Spanish gunboat was less than a hundred yards away, she pulled alongside and ordered the *Eldorado* to heave to. Faced with a pair of cannon and a host of armed men lining the rails, the *Eldorado's* captain was about to surrender when shots rang out. Some of the undisciplined American volunteers had begun shooting and others followed suit. Kendrick watched in horror as several Spanish soldiers were hit and fell, with one dropping into the water and disappearing.

The Spaniards returned fire almost immediately. Their cannon were loaded with grape and their shells swept the deck of the Eldorado with flying metal, while the Spanish soldiers fired into what was now a confused mob of Americans. As shells struck the ship, Kendrick threw himself on the deck and tried to make himself invisible. Shells ripped the wooden hull and deck, sending knife-like splinters through the air. He screamed as one imbedded itself in his cheek. He pulled it out and blood began to pour down his face and chest.

Only a few moments later, armed Spaniards climbed over the gunwale and killed those foolish enough to still carry weapons. The others, including Kendrick were gathered in a bunch by the bow. The reporter in him estimated maybe thirty survivors and the *Eldorado's* captain was not one of them.

An officer approached the group. "Which one of you is the journalist named Kendrick?"

Kendrick was surprised. He stepped forward and tried to look as unconcerned as he could. "I am James Kendrick, sir, and you are?"

"My name is Gilberto Salazar and I am a major in the Spanish army, and I am delighted that you were not harmed," he said with thinly veiled sarcasm. "We have been following the course of this wreck since it left Charleston several days ago. You Americans think we are stupid and ignorant of the ship's intentions, but we are not. Our spies have been well informed about this stinking ship and its cargo, both human and otherwise. You have come to start another civil war and to free the slaves who are already being freed." He waved his arm at the other prisoners. "These men will be executed for their efforts."

Kendrick's mind worked quickly. "You are not counting me among the invaders?"

Salazar laughed. "I would like to, but men more important than I want you to witness the justice we will be handing out."

"A small point, major, but aren't we in international waters? Should you have stopped an American flagged ship in international waters, or any other ship for that matter?"

Salazar looked about dramatically. There was no sign of land on the horizon. "You are that good at judging distances? I assure you that we are well within Spanish territorial waters. I suggest that you accept that declaration as a fact and not annoy me."

Kendrick decided that it was an excellent idea. Just as important, he wondered how Salazar knew his name along with all the information about the ship. Obviously, the Spanish had spies in the group that had chartered the *Eldorado.*

"What will happen to these men, and me, for that matter?"

"Watch," Salazar said.

He gave a signal and his soldiers pushed the men, now screaming in terror, into the ocean.

Kendrick watched in horror as their heads bobbed in the waves. Soldiers lined the ship's railing and began shooting at them. In a few seconds there were no more heads bobbing in the water, just an occasional red stain that was being swallowed and erased by the sea.

Kendrick was so stunned that he nearly fell to his knees. Laughing soldiers held him upright. Finally, he regained some of his composure. Salazar stood in front of him and slashed him across the face with the flat of a short sword, splitting his cheek and adding to the blood from the splinter.

"I was ordered to bring you back alive. Nothing was said about keeping you unhurt. You are far from innocent, Kendrick, and while I would like to throw you overboard as well, Spain has uses for you. We will scuttle the *Eldorado* after first taking anything of value, of course. Then we will steam to Florida and drop you off at St. Augustine. I urge you to write a full and accurate report of what you have seen this day. Let your foolish and arrogant people understand that Spain is a great power and we will not be insulted by your sending miserable abolitionist revolutionaries into Cuba."

—end excerpt—